D1710553

Ms. Infinity: Earth's Greatest Hero

© 2015, 2022 Andrew Kirschner

Second Edition, January 2022

Published by Andrew Kirschner
www.andrewkirschner.net

ISBN: 978—1521594803

Edited by Audrey Seddon
Cover Design by Jill Brock

Table of Contents

Prologue: Alien Arrival

Thirteen years ago, Earth's greatest hero was a frightened teenage refugee from a distant world.

She arrived secretly on Earth late one winter night, in the culmination of a vast, two-year flight, confined in a small metallic spaceship, alone with her mother. Though that ship could never be called home, at least it was safe. Safety was not something she was used to.

She now faced a whole new world with a new name: Bonnie Boring. There was the promise of a better home, and a future wide open with possibility, but also the daunting prospect of starting over in a strange and unfamiliar world where she could never truly belong.

At least outwardly, Bonnie seemed human. From their studies, the pair had adopted human language and culture to near perfection; they could very well pass for New Yorkers. Both Bonnie and her mother, now called Betty Boring, were petite and slender, with dark brown eyes and olive-colored skin. They were dressed casually in t-shirts and jeans, their dark hair pulled back in ponytails. Bonnie was thirteen in Earth years while Betty was thirty-two.

They now sat together in the ship's small kitchen, sharing their last meal before landing. Betty talked excitedly of their future. Bonnie did little but smile and nod politely. As they began to clear the table, Bonnie finally spoke.

"Mom," said Bonnie, "I'm still finding this name strange. 'Bonnie Boring'? I don't know."

"It is your name, dear," answered Betty, "As close as we can get in human language."

"Yeah, I know. This whole human language is weird

and gross. Who speaks with the same thing you eat with?"

"We do. From now on, this is how we communicate. We are going to live as they do."

"I know."

"There's really nothing to argue about. Look honey, the time has finally come. Tonight we are going to our new world."

And so late that winter night, in an isolated section of Rockaway Beach, Queens, New York, aliens landed.

The ship was invisible and undetectable. It appeared in the utter darkness of an abandoned beach, unseen by human eyes. As the wind blew mercilessly across the barren white sand, the vessel slowly descended in the last seconds of its journey, then came to a stop a few feet from the ground.

Aboard the ship, the companions were about to disembark. Betty got up from the bridge and approached her daughter in the kitchen. With a warm smile, she put her hand on her daughter's shoulder.

"This is it! We're here! It's time!"

Betty motioned at her daughter to begin their exit, but Bonnie did not move. She stood still, with a blank look on her face.

"Bonnie," said Betty, "this is what we have been waiting for. We are now entering our new world."

Bonnie was still silent, looking down, glued to the floor.

"Honey, we can't stay here forever. We need to move on with our lives."

Bonnie stayed defiant in her stillness and silence.

Finally, Betty reverted to the ways of their old world

one last time. In a communication that could not be heard or perceived by human senses, she assured her daughter, *I will protect you.*

Bonnie looked at her mother and was comforted. At last, she moved toward her. Betty put her arm gently around her daughter's back, and they made for the exit.

A crevice opened in the air. Two figures climbed out, and into the dark February cold. As they exited, they both took a deep breath and embraced, tears in their eyes.

"This is it!" shouted Bonnie. "Wow! We've really made it, Mommy! It feels amazing to be on solid ground again!"

"It really does," said Betty. "I thought we'd never make it. Bonnie dear, look around. We're safe! This is our new world."

It might not have been much to look at: the beach in the wee hours of the morning in the dead of winter. But after what had seemed like an eternity in a cold, sealed, lifeless spaceship, any living, natural landscape looked like a paradise. With childlike wonder, they looked upon ivory sand dunes, blowing stark against the black sky and the ocean, equally dark save for the white foam that periodically bubbled and faded. An occasional weeping plant interrupted the blankness of the ground, each seeming desperate to hang on in a cruel environment. The voices of Bonnie and Betty were all but overwhelmed by the white noise, with the powerful whistling wind prevailing over the gentle caresses of the tides. In the distance was the faint glint of the Manhattan skyline.

Bonnie looked around, marveling at the sights in each direction. "Wow! It doesn't seem real. We finally have a home. You know something? I even like the talk. I'm still convinced that burping has to be part of the language. I'm going to have to try it out sometime."

"The important thing," said Betty, "is that we have found a world where we can be safe."

"Right," said Bonnie, "and where I'm not persecuted for my abilities."

Betty took a deep breath. "I know."

"I picked this planet because it is so far away," said Bonnie. "I don't think they can reach us here. But one thing worries me. Human abilities are way below our kind. I'm only going to stand out way more here. They are nowhere near as strong as us. They think in only three dimensions. They can't even fly. Even their space program is pathetic. They've never gone anywhere but their own moon. Look at that! I can leap to that thing without trying!"

Betty looked at her daughter with concern. "Listen honey. Somehow we are going to have to fit in here. I'm not liking the idea of you doing things like that around them."

"But then what was the point of leaving? I want to be myself and not have to worry about what people think."

"You know, I understand that. You are special, and it's your right to be special. What you have to understand is that we want to be part of this culture, dear."

"Maybe if I sneak up to the moon…," said Bonnie.

Betty became increasingly concerned. It was now clear to her that she had a potentially dangerous situation on her hands. There were many things that she had always wanted to teach her daughter, yet these could not be learned in either the hostile environment of their old world or the sealed-in existence of the spaceship. It was going to take time for her to learn. There were going to have to be some hard decisions made in the meantime.

"Bonnie honey," Betty began, "there is another thing I wanted to discuss. We aren't going to just be part of this world. We want to be helpful and responsible members of it. You know that we escaped an oppressive and dangerous place. Others are not so lucky. It still hurts me inside to think we left behind everyone we knew."

"I really hope I can make friends here," said Bonnie.

"Well honey, you are a delightful girl. I'm sure..."

"You know what?" interrupted Bonnie, "Do I have to look like this? As long as I'm starting over..."

Bonnie started to transform. She became taller, and her hair became lighter. She might have continued, but Betty interrupted her.

"No Bonnie!" she demanded, "stop that right this minute!"

"Mom?"

"Change back right now!"

Bonnie looked at her mother defiantly, but Betty conveyed an authority far greater. After a moment, Bonnie reversed her transformation and became herself again. The look on her face showed she was not only angry but frightened as well. It was clearer than ever to Betty that she would have to watch her daughter very carefully.

"Bonnie dear," said Betty gently, "you will be yourself here. There is no reason to change this beautiful and perfect face and body. Forget what you learned from the old world. They can't hurt you anymore. You are beautiful, and you have so much to offer. Don't run away from yourself. This is where you will shine. I know it."

"Even if I'm a freak?"

"So that's also what this is about?" said Betty. "My baby, you are wonderful! The things that are different about you are what make you most special. Honey, you are going to be part of this world, and you are going to matter. This is certainly a better place, but it's far from perfect. This world still has plenty of suffering and injustice, and many dangers as well. In the long run, it will be our place to help those who need us."

Bonnie smiled once again. "Well, shouldn't be too hard for us. Next to these humans, we're as powerful as anything. Kind of like giants, except that we're not particularly big. Actually, I was hoping we would be tall here, but no. Humans are no smaller, and we're short here just like before. But never mind that! Compared to them, we have superpowers! We could probably fix all the problems here in half a day if we wanted to."

"Bonnie, no!" cried Betty, "that's the last thing I want you to think! That's the thinking that ruined life in our old world."

"Well, that's a new one on me. I thought it was the jerks that called themselves leaders. Look, with my superpowers…"

"Bonnie dear!" interrupted Betty, "What you call 'superpowers'… bless you honey, but don't you see the danger here?"

Bonnie stared at her mother suspiciously. "Mom, what are you trying to say?"

"My sweetheart, you are coming here with only the best of intentions. But do you understand? Even oppressors often begin with good intentions. Whatever we do, we should never, ever become the oppressor. That is a tragedy that happens again and again, and I don't want to be one to repeat it."

"Mom, you're confusing to talk to, especially when you get into one of your preachy speechies. But I really don't like this one. Where are you going with this?"

Betty closed her eyes, and taking a deep breath, put her hand gently on her daughter's shoulder. "Bonnie, my love, you have been hurt. I cannot pretend to understand all that you have been through, and I have been there with you for nearly all of it. I love you dearly, and nothing destroys me more than seeing you go through pain. But you're going to have to trust me. What I'm about to say will no doubt be the last thing you want to hear. It might hurt. But you have to know I would never say it if I didn't love you with everything I have. Bonnie, my baby, you're going to have to hide your powers."

"What?" cried Bonnie.

"Shhh," whispered Betty, gently patting her daughter's hand. "I'm sorry dear. But this isn't like before. This isn't about people who will hurt you. This is about people who are much, much weaker than you. We have to learn how to live among them. I want you to be part of this world and enjoy all it has to offer. I want you to have friends and go to school like everyone else, and then have a job and a career. Maybe one day have a relationship, and maybe get married and have a family of your own."

"And nobody will ever know who I really am?"

"Now listen. I didn't say never. You will grow up, and you will find your place in this world. One day, you will figure out how and where you can use your powers to the benefit of the people of this world. But we're going to have to begin by hiding our powers. This is just a necessity."

"And now I can't do anything that humans can't do? Do you know how hard that will be for me?"

"Well," said Betty, "I understand you have gifts you want to use. You may do things in private."

"Thank you!" shouted Bonnie, "At least that's something. If I'm going to have to go native, at least I want one corner to use my powers to infinity."

Betty laughed, "Well, I hope you don't mean that literally. I'll need to see you sooner or later."

"Not infinite time. You know, infinite power."

"Now I really hope you're not being literal. You don't seriously believe your abilities are infinite, do you?"

"Well, I never have found the outer limit of my strength. And if I never do…"

"It's not infinite! I assure you of that much. Everyone has limits. I don't care who you are. We are mortal living creatures my dear, and infinity is a big number."

"It's also an eight lying on its side."

"Right," laughed Betty. "This language can be funny with its iconography."

"The ship!" shouted Bonnie.

"What about it?" asked Betty.

"Well, it sucks. I mean, not to be ungrateful. It got us here, but it looks like a fridge inside. There's where I'm going to use my powers to infinity, or if you say so, not infinity. I'm going to soup that baby up!"

"I don't know," said Betty, "I really want you to live your new life here on Earth, not crawl back into the spaceship we inhabited all that time."

"Just in my spare time. You can't tell me it's not private enough. It's invisible from the outside! Please, Mom! I'll keep it on the Dark Side of the Moon and go there from time to time."

"I guess it's alright," said Betty. "Just don't forget your priorities."

"Awesome!" shouted Bonnie. "You'll see. This thing is

gonna rock! I have lots of ideas for it. This is my infinity powers project!"

"Alright 'Ms. Infinity,'" laughed Betty, "so that's our decision. And so, we begin our new lives. One thing we can say: we certainly picked an excellent city for starting over. Nobody stands out too much in New York."

"Maybe I have a bright future here."

So Betty and Bonnie Boring began their new lives by moving into Woodside, a multicultural section of Queens. Like many who start over in an unfamiliar environment, they would take some time to adapt. For while they had studied and adopted Earth ways at a truly superhuman rate, inevitably there were some flaws in their learning. Noticeably, the mother's adaptation of their names to Earth speech showed an imperfect understanding of the use and meaning of surnames in Western civilization. This mistake would hardly prove fatal, but both mother and daughter would always have to endure occasional jokes about their last name.

This day of their arrival on Earth would turn out to be momentous for another, similar reason. With her innocent quip — "Alright 'Ms. Infinity'!" — Betty Boring had effectively renamed her daughter a second time. Strange that such a small moment would be remembered so well so many years later, but then this was a sensitive time. It was a monumental day for both of them, and Bonnie would remember their conversation vividly.

And so, years later, when Bonnie Boring was ready, the world was introduced to its greatest hero...

1. Threat From Above

Where was Bonnie? Lisa Lin's patience was running out. Once again, Bonnie had walked off casually without a word, leaving her to deal with the line. She might have been her best friend, but she was frustrating to work with.

"Sorry for the delay, everyone," called Lisa, "I'm handling this line by myself. My coworker will be back momentarily."

It was Friday evening at The Big Box, and it felt like half of Queens was there. Aggressive shoppers dominated the landscape almost completely; only a few strange loiterers were hanging around the clothing aisles, speaking quietly, just out of sight of the registers. Every department was swarmed, from the electronics to the clothing to the toys to the groceries. Even the adjoining garage was full, causing a traffic backup on Northern Boulevard.

In the harsh flood lighting of the store, the staff did their best to keep up with the demand. Salespeople were running back and forth, scrambling to answer constant pages from the loudspeaker. Porters were struggling to keep up with New York customers' typical regard for cleanliness. Many forgotten shopping carts were strewn about near the registers, all of which were backed up with long lines. Lisa's line at the customer service desk was particularly overwhelmed with returns and exchanges, as well as complaints that the sale prices were not matching those advertised in the circular. She stood alone at an oversized counter, doing the work of two or more. Towards the back of the line, the customers were getting impatient.

"Where's the manager?" called a man waiting a few places down the line.

"I called for him a while ago," explained Lisa, "I can try again if you want." Denny, the manager of the front end, was also frequently unavailable. He spent a considerable amount of time in security, watching the cameras. The front end would often receive a call from him when the camera caught someone disengaged. It seemed however that there was little recourse when he was disengaged.

"You know what?" shouted a man towards the middle of the line. "If your supervisor isn't around, then I'm complaining to the store manager! Which way to him?"

"Her name is Yvonne," said Lisa, "I don't know if you could get her attention, but she's in the back, past the bicycles."

He stormed off shouting, "Who's with me?" Nobody went with him, but he continued. For a moment, Lisa was slightly relieved that she would not have to use the paging system again to call Denny. She hated hearing her voice on that thing. Then it occurred to her that she had likely just gotten herself in trouble. A complaint over her supervisor's head would almost certainly boomerang on her. Denny was known by one and all to be a vengeful and unforgiving manager. Her eyes were closed in an expression of dread.

"Your friend is some worker!" said another customer. "You should really tell her off!"

"Thank you," replied Lisa, "but I assure you, Bonnie's actually an extremely responsible person. She can work like anything…"

"So where is she?" shouted another man.

"You know what?" said Lisa, "Never mind!"

Lisa didn't look like someone tough enough to handle an endless line of irate New Yorkers. She was short and thin, with Asian features that some took for "delicate," and an expression that often seemed to convey contrition. Yet her slight exterior contained a young woman with a tremendous will and endless endurance. Even with a flood of angry customers, she could be counted on to stay assertive, and keep her cool at the same time.

"Why don't you take me first?" called another customer. "I'm only returning a jacket and paying off my store card."

"I'm sorry," answered Lisa, "nobody cuts. Store rule."

The man mumbled something rude under his breath. Meanwhile the woman she was serving was babbling incoherently. She was a frequent customer, and a very frustrating one. It was very unclear whether she was just returning her clothes, or meant to exchange some of them, or if she was complaining about a price, or all of the above. It didn't help that she was obviously drunk. Lisa handled her with her usual patience, but frustration was mounting.

"Isn't there any way someone can just take care of her somewhere else?" shouted another woman.

"I'm sorry," said Lisa, "this is the only customer service desk. I promise I will get to you as soon as possible."

Lisa felt tension in her back and shoulders and a persistent headache, but as always continued stoically. "Look, I'm sorry about everything. I'm sure my friend will be back any second, and this line will pick up."

From some distance down the line, someone shouted out, "Where did your friend go? The moon?"

Lisa shouted back, "We will get to you as soon as possible. I promise."

Although, she thought to herself, *I'm wondering that myself...*

Bonnie was not on the moon. She was several million miles past it. And maybe her customers might have forgiven her if they knew why. Only minutes ago, her super senses had picked up something ominous coming from space. She then transformed into her alter ego and flew in its direction.

As the Earth and Moon receded into the distance behind her, the awesome Ms. Infinity flew on with vigor. Tall and powerful, her dark hair flowed perfectly behind her, even in space. Like a burning sun, she glowed mightily against the darkness. All else forgotten, she looked with determination upon her mission.

Well, she wondered to herself, *let's have a little look at my challenge for the day. Anything fun?*

Ms. Infinity stared upon the vast expanse of space. She scrutinized the view in front of her, scanning in every direction, comparing it with her exhaustive knowledge of the galaxy and beyond. After a few moments, she was sure. Something was very wrong.

There, still a great distance away, was the threat. To an untrained human eye, it would have looked like a star, and no different from any other. Yet if one watched it for some time, it would gradually become apparent that it was growing. At first it might have been subtle, but after a time, it became obvious even to the most casual observer. Soon it did not look at all like a distant star. More and more it began to look like a second moon.

But this was neither star, nor moon, nor indeed a planet. No. This was no celestial body holding its natural place in space. This was an asteroid, and a tremendous one at that. And this asteroid was traveling at a breakneck speed, on a collision course with Earth, only minutes away from its target.

Now Ms. Infinity could see its advance clearly. Its flight

against the vastness of space was like a baseball's rush across the field, yet it seemed to hold its momentum indefinitely, as if perpetually freshly slammed by a powerful bat. It was immense, growing ominously in size as it drew near.

And now Ms. Infinity was the only thing standing between it and Earth.

She began to feel a rush of nerves. Thoughts raced through her head. This thing was enormous. It was nothing like anything she had ever seen. Was this threat beyond her?

She summoned her courage and held forth, standing resolutely between the asteroid and its target. She remembered the faith her mother had in her. Then she gathered all of her strength and vigor and flew. She shot forward like a rocket, much faster than a rocket. In her super speed, she disappeared into an unseen but immeasurable force.

Like a wasp flying into a truck she might have seemed. Indeed, the difference in size was vastly greater than that. Anyone watching might have been forgiven for betting on the asteroid. Yet the sight must have been strange to behold. For it was with the force of one tremendously powerful collision with this so-called wasp that suddenly the asteroid bounced back, stopped in its tracks like a giant truck crashing against the side of a mountain.

Look at that! she thought to herself, *I'm an even bigger freak than I thought. Even from my own kind, nobody could dream of pulling a stunt like that. It's as crazy at it looks! But I did it and it didn't even hurt. It barely even tickled.*

She marveled for a moment. Indeed, as hard as she had hit, it seemed as if the force of her impact was double her effort, if not more. That was a phenomenon she wondered about. Sometimes in great emergencies, her strength was much greater than her effort. Often her powers were mysterious even to herself. But then another, more ominous thought occurred to her.

This is strange, though. How did nobody know about this? Earth's scientists are on constant watch for these things. I mean, they don't have my powers, but…

She looked at the stars in front of her and realized the direction she was facing. She immediately felt a sense of apprehension. She had been this way once before.

She collected her thoughts, and then turned her gaze deeper into space. With her super senses, she could see small objects many millions of miles away when she chose to. And so, she scanned with her telescopic sight. Farther and farther out to space she looked, scanning through an increasingly vast distance. Finally at a great length, she caught what she was looking for. Then she gasped.

Misery!

Ms. Infinity shuddered from her revelation. There in a remote corner of the solar system, only a few million miles away, was a face from a distant memory. Misery was a loathed and dreaded name from another lifetime, a malevolent figure belonging to a world that she had never dreamed of knowing again. The thought that she might be threatening now was strange, and extremely disquieting. What this could mean, she could not be sure. But for now, she would take a quick, retaliatory action.

"Alright!" she said to herself. "No more self-conscious Suzy. Time to go full freak!"

Smiling wryly to herself, she wondered: *Does she like snowball fights? Not when I'm done with her!*

Gathering her inner strength, she blew on the asteroid with a great force from her vast respiratory reserve. A great, frigid whirlwind she blew, colder and more powerful than

Earth had ever known. The great rock was soon covered in ice, a layer that would become so thick it increased the body's size by nearly one and a half times.

Calling once again on her super breath, she blew a great wind. She followed up by twirling herself around at an unimaginable speed. Within seconds, she had created a huge cyclone, a unique and bizarre sight in outer space.

She focused her storm just so, that it hit the asteroid with maximum impact. So great was the force that the asteroid became an immense and unstoppable object, shooting across the great void at a rate that light could not even approach. Were the solar system a ballpark, then the asteroid's flight was now not like a baseball but a bullet.

She watched as the great frozen asteroid overtook her foe. Misery had not a second to react before she was overwhelmed by the massive object, swept into its momentum and shot away, in a trajectory leading past the end of the solar system.

Wicked!!! thought Ms. Infinity. *That should take care of her for a while. Still…*

A feeling of dread began to come upon her. Misery had come a vast distance, and she had obviously intended to do great harm. She would not let a setback like this stop her for long.

This would certainly have to be kept secret. It would be wrong to bring panic to her adopted planet. As with so many parts of her life, it would stay between herself and Mom.

And now it was coming to her that Bonnie Boring had left her job waiting. So now it was time to return and face another unpleasant reality.

Responsibility was one of the first truly difficult lessons that

Betty had to teach Bonnie. Bonnie had never had the structure of a normal life; she had always been forced to live on the outside. And then after all, the world they came from could only teach very flawed lessons. The society had collapsed into a severe dictatorship very early into her life.

Betty thus had compelling reasons why she held Bonnie's abilities back. Without the proper lessons, Bonnie could prove very dangerous to the people around her. Betty also felt a need to watch her daughter carefully, a habit that would prove very hard to break.

At any rate, Betty had her work cut out for her. Even the very basic concept of following rules took some learning. Bonnie was reluctant about such simple things as crossing with the traffic light. Fortunately, this being New York City, "jaywalking" was not a behavior that exactly stood out.

Even harder to her was the idea of following a daily schedule for sleep, meals, and school. Bonnie was not averse to the idea so much as she was confused by it. It also took her a long time to get used to being responsible for daily assignments. Yet when it came to issues with education, this was but the tip of the iceberg.

Bonnie would ultimately embrace her responsibility very strongly. Her sense of duty would become central to her life, the core meaning of her existence.

But then the lessons of responsibility are not always simple and concrete. One complex lesson is that sometimes we have more than one commitment, and that commitments can conflict.

2. Hero Behind the Counter

After a quick descent and a quiet transformation, Bonnie
Boring slipped in through the back of The Big Box. She looked
much the same as the teenage girl who had landed on the
beach more than a decade earlier, now grown into a young
adult. She was petite and slender, with her dark hair in a
ponytail. Her face was pleasant, with large brown eyes and an
expression that generally wanted to smile. She wore dark
rimmed glasses and khaki pants together with her blue and
yellow Big Box shirt.

She filtered through the crowd, doing her best to be
inconspicuous. As she approached the front, she failed to take
notice of the loiterers scurrying out of her view as she passed.
Noticing Lisa, she waved. There behind a somewhat quieter
customer service counter was her friend, eyes rolling, barely
containing her frustration.

"Lis, baby," called Bonnie.

"Bonnie," answered Lisa, "still working here, I see."

"Yeah. Kinda got into something there…"

"Uh yeah, Bonnie. There's something I wanted to say.
Can we talk a moment?"

"Sure, Lisa. It isn't my deodorant, is it? Oh no! It is! I
knew it! I'm stinking up the whole store with my B.O.! Good
thing I have a friend like you who tells me the truth."

"Cute. No. Bonnie, please. Can you please listen a
moment?"

Lisa took Bonnie by the hand and brought her closer.

"Bonnie, I love you. You know I do. It's been great having you here. You're cool and funny, and I like working with you a lot–"

"Oh. Thank you," interrupted Bonnie. "You're all that and more, but..."

"The thing is, I'd really like to be working with you a lot more..."

"So, what you're trying to say..."

"I'm sick of you disappearing on me in the middle of the shift!"

"Oh."

"Bonnie, I just had to handle a huge rush all by myself. My head is still reeling from all the complaints I was getting. All the creeps were out too. I had the smelly guy who holds up the line, the guy who's always trying to con us by talking non-stop, and the drunk chick who's always yelling. She was bad today too. I think she must have started drinking early. I really could have used you. I'm exhausted and I have a ton of homework tonight for nursing school. Please! Please! I need help here."

Bonnie smiled, but inside she felt a regret growing. Times like these were especially hard, having to apologize while knowing she could not be certain of mending her wrongs. Nonetheless, she spoke with a stoic humor. "I'm sorry, Lisa," she replied, "I'll make it up to you."

Lisa looked at the tension in her friend's eyes. Then she paused for a moment, shook her head, and giggled apologetically.

"Alright. I'm sorry too. Look at me. I feel like the slowest worker at The Big Box."

"Nah," smiled Bonnie, "you're fine."

"I have another problem. I think I got myself in trouble with Denny. A customer complained and asked for the manager. When he didn't come, he went to Yvonne."

"Oh yeah," said Bonnie, "if he gets in trouble, he might take it out on you... Oh Lisa, I'm sorry!"

"It's alright."

"I really am sorry. You know, Lisa, anything I can do, please just ask!"

"I know. It's not your fault."

"Really. Anything at all!"

"By the way, Bonnie: you do have B.O."

"Yeah, you're just smelling your own farts!"

"No way! This stink has you all over it!"

As customers began to appear again, Bonnie saw an opportunity to make things up to Lisa. "Got this!" she said. A moment later, she was behind the counter, attending to the line. She was instantly efficient, seeming to handle each return, exchange, and complaint better and faster than just about anyone.

"Thank you!" said Bonnie to a man after he signed a return receipt. By the time he was done signing his name, Bonnie was already well into the next transaction, adjusting a price for a coupon that a customer had forgotten to use. She was sometimes dizzying to watch. She also was quick to acknowledge each customer in line as they waited. Sometimes she would even give them preliminary advice to help them move their transactions along when they came up. Whatever she did, the line moved very well when she was there. It was clear that she loved to work.

From the registers came a voice, "I need a bill check!" It was Hal Holstein, "Handsome Hal," as Bonnie called him privately. He was of medium height and build, with brown hair, fair skin, and green eyes. He seemed to smile even when he was shouting.

"Alright!" shouted Bonnie, "I'm on it!"

As Bonnie ran away, Lisa shook her head. "That doesn't really prove anything," she mumbled to herself. "She would be on him if she wasn't on the clock."

Bonnie rushed over to Hal's register. He greeted her with his usual open, friendly manner. "Hi Bonnie."

Bonnie pretended to ignore him. She looked at the bill against the light and declared in her most businesslike voice, "It's good." Hal finished the sale.

Just then, Bonnie noticed the TVs in the adjacent electronics department were playing one of her least favorite interview clips with Ms. Infinity. Hal looked up from his register and watched with his eyes nearly glued, as he usually did. "A goddess," he mumbled under his breath. For a moment it was if Bonnie wasn't there.

Today we caught up with Ms. Infinity, the lovely lady who adorns our skies. Our own correspondent, Mila Merk, interviewed her.

"So, Ms. Infinity: How do you find a man who can protect you when no man is your equal or greater?"

"Well, I don't why that should be necessary. I'm not in a hurry to settle down, but when I do, he does not need to be stronger than me…."

"What do you think, ladies? Afraid of love, or trying too hard to prove herself? You decide on our poll…."

Bonnie hated that interview more every time she heard it, but Hal didn't seem to care much about the content as long as his crush was onscreen.

When Hal's attention was back, Bonnie spoke in an annoyed tone, "Hal, you have to pay attention when you're standing here. Make sure you address every customer as they approach."

"Oh," he said, "sorry Bonnie."

"And make sure you count the money every time. Remember, three times in, three times out."

"Yes, I remember."

"You need a pen?" asked Bonnie. "I saved one for you."

"Oh! Yeah, I did forget it."
"How did you go this long without a pen?"

"Lucky?"

"Yeah, lucky to have me around. You are one spacey cashier!"

Bonnie moved away from Hal, taking a few steps backwards. Failing to notice the next register behind her as she turned, she bumped into it hard and nearly fell. She tried to keep her composure as she rebounded.

"You okay?" asked Hal.

"Just… fine!" she snapped. Her face was red as an apple, feeling the others staring as she walked away.

Hal's neighboring cashiers began to whisper. A new cashier named Isha wondered, "So, Nadine, is she the boss?"

"Nah!" said Nadine. "The customer service people are allowed to the do the bill checks and such, but she's not the boss."

"I'm in charge of this area," said Maria, walking by with a clipboard. "I'm the runner."

"So, wait," said Isha, "is she training him?

Nadine laughed. "No, Isha. Hal's been here a year or so. He's just Bonnie's hobby. That's all."

The phone rang at the customer service desk, and Lisa picked it up. "Hello, Big Box customer service. Oh! Hi Mrs. B.! Bonnie's right here!"

A middle–aged woman was waiting to exchange a pair of pants. "What was with that 'Mrs. B.'?" she asked Lisa. "Are you trying to be Fonzie or something?"

"What's a Fonzie?"

"Oh, never mind. You kids will never get it."

"So, Mom," said Bonnie into the phone, "Why didn't you just call me on my cell? Much simpler. I know, I know, I know. But everyone uses their cellphones here. No, I am not texting on the job!" She put her cellphone away nervously.

"Look, Mom, it was fine. No. I took care of it. Really! I did! No problem. I know what I'm doing. No big deal. Can we talk about it later? …Me? I'm fine. I promise. No. All right, we'll talk about this later. No, later! I do not have a fever. I promise! Really. Look, Mom, I have a customer. I gotta go! Bye, Mom! Bye!!"

"Mom on you again?" asked Lisa.

"What else is new!" said Bonnie, "She's convinced I'm sick for some reason. It's not enough that I live with her. She has to check up on me here too. She really knows how to helicopter. But I'm not a kid anymore. It's not cute now that I'm in my mid-twenties."

"Your mom's cool! I love her!"

"Well of course she seems cool to you. That's because she's not your mom. She doesn't watch you nonstop."

"Nah, I have my own parents for that."

"Well, we're a fine pair of adults, aren't we? When do we get to move out?"

"When we can afford New York City rent."

"Yeah," said Bonnie, "that might happen when we're fifty."

"Well," said Lisa gingerly, "if you go back to school like I am…"

"Yeah, I know, Lisa," said Bonnie, her voice taking on a nervous annoyance.

"You don't have to be on this treadmill forever."

"I hated school! Hated it with everything I had."

"I know, Bonnie. It was hard watching you. But if the alternative is this…"

Bonnie sighed. "You know, I do think about it. I just don't know what I want to do with myself anymore. I can't even imagine where I fit in."

"Ah, Bonnie. C'mon! I know you can do anything!"

"Anything?" said Bonnie. "I don't know about that."

Looking at Bonnie, Lisa noticed a nervous look in her eyes. She sighed, shook her head and corrected herself, "You know what I mean. You're smart. I'm sure you'll think of something."

A man stormed up to the counter and shouted, "Maybe you could explain to me what the hell is wrong with the service here! These shirts are on sale, but the cashiers don't know it! Twenty percent off! It's right there on the sign!"

Bonnie walked with him to the edge of the men's department. It sat across a wide aisle from hardware. After looking at the area, Bonnie saw the mistake—if it could be called that. The sign was on the hardware side, at least five feet from the men's department. It would have to have taken some imagination to think it applied to anything in the men's department, and perhaps some suspension of disbelief.

"Sorry sir," said Bonnie, "the sign is on the other side of the aisle from the shirts. That sale is for hardware."

"Well, you should have made that more clear!" shouted the man. He then slammed his hand on the hardware display. A few items fell and he stormed off.

Bonnie began picking up after him. She had a small mini wrench in her hand when she heard a voice behind her. "Hey Bonnie!"

Bonnie stood up and turned and saw a familiar face from some years back, an acquaintance from high school. "Oh. Hi Kate," she said.

"Fancy meeting you here!" chirped Kate. "I'm just here with Lila and Yasmin picking up a few things before we go out. You know how it is, long week at the office. Gotta blow off some steam! So, what brings you here?" Apparently, she had not noticed the uniform.

"Well, the thing is–"

"Eight years since graduation! Can you believe it? Time flies so fast, and all of us have come so far! Oh! I just got promoted to Vice President of Creative at Splash & Jiggle Advertising…"

Bonnie felt a wound opening inside, and salt beginning to rub. This was not a conversation she felt like having.

"Oh! And Lila is now Assistant Director of Sales at Puppy Crush Publishing. She's engaged. You know, her and Habib. They were always so cute together, right? He might go for his doctorate, but he's making so much money at his law firm. You know how that is, right?"

Bonnie increasingly felt a knife twisting. At any rate,

she was glad she didn't have to say much.

"Yasmin!" called Kate, "you ready yet?" Turning to Bonnie she continued, "Yasmin's now a producer at Action Minute News. Her husband is running for Congress."

Yasmin came up and talked to Kate. "Sorry, I can't find a decent purse to go with this dress. Oh! Hi Connie."

"That's Bonnie..."

"You remember Bonnie," said Kate. "Why don't you try and get someone here to help you?"

"They're idiots here," complained Yasmin. "It's like they barely know how to talk. Lila was trying to get some help before, and they were just making her wait, like she has time on her hands. I mean, do we look like people who want to spend Friday night in a big pathetic store?"

"Yeah, I know," said Kate, "I feel sorry for the people who work here!"

"I know, right!" laughed Yasmin, as the two left without saying goodbye.

"Lila!" called Kate as she departed, "where are you?"

Bonnie's eyes were closed, teeth clenched, her hand in a tight fist, a look of complete and utter pain on her face. When she opened her eyes, she noticed that her fist was the hand holding the mini wrench. She opened it and noticed that she had just ground it into a fine metallic powder. She quietly dumped it into a garbage can and headed back to the customer service desk.

With the store somewhat calmer, the loiterers struggled harder to blend in. Meanwhile, Hal found himself in a spot with a customer with an expired coupon.

"I'm sorry, Miss," said Hal. "The system won't take the

coupon. It's expired."

"You mean *you* won't take it!" snapped the woman, "They can do this for me. I know the guy who was here yesterday did it. Why can't you?"

"I'm sorry. I can't. The register rejects it. And the rules are against it."

"So what? It only expired yesterday. You can do it, so why don't you? Why can't you take it? You don't know how to do your job!"

"I'm sorry Miss. I can't–"

"No! You're lazy!"

"Look, I'm sorry…"

The woman looked Hal closely in his face and screamed, "I'm going to tell the manager about you. You have no idea how to work with people! You shouldn't even be working this kind of job at all! You should be in the back with the rest of the losers!"

Bonnie was already standing next to Hal. "Excuse me, Miss," she said, "I'm in charge here. That coupon is expired. We will not take it, and that is final."

"What's the matter with you?" she whined. "You can't do a simple thing for me?"

Bonnie stood up straight and spoke clearly and forcefully, "This has nothing to do with you. We don't take expired coupons. We never do. Not for you, not for anyone. Thank you."

The woman left in a huff. Bonnie gave Hal a knowing look. The other cashiers stared once again.

Ahmed, the cashier next to Hal, remarked, "She never does that for me."

"Right," answered Maria, "I'm supposed to do that for all of you."

Lisa whispered to Bonnie as she returned, "You know, you're not really in charge here."

"Shhhh!" snapped Bonnie.

"Take your break," said Maria to Hal. She had just noticed that Hal had little to do but sit on his knees and play with a baby in a stroller.

"Thanks Maria!" called Hal, "And what do you think, baby? Fifteen minutes of break time. Should I eat something or talk to the girl I like?"

The baby kicked his legs.

"You're right! It is worth a try. Thanks, you little smarty!"

Lisa and Bonnie were so deep in discussion, they scarcely noticed Hal approaching the customer service desk.

"Look," snickered Bonnie, "can you blame me for smelling bad? I spend all my time with you, Fart Girl!"

"Don't pick on my hobbies, Stinkita!" said Lisa. "Oh! Hi, Hal."

Hal shot Bonnie a smile. "How are things over here?"

"Fine," said Bonnie.

"So, what do you girls do on the weekend?"

"Weekend?" laughed Bonnie, "Same as you. We're here. What did you think?"

Lisa gave Bonnie a strange look.

"Oh, yeah right." said Hal.

"Hal," said Bonnie, "I hope you don't feel too bad about getting yelled at by that customer. You were obviously in the right. You could have done the same thing I did. Just a little more confidence, alright?"

"Oh!" said Hal. "Thanks."

"You're a good guy. Just remember that when someone picks on you like that."

"Thank you."

"Later Hal."

For Lisa, it was a strange but frequent confusion she felt when she was around her friend. She wasn't sure whether Bonnie had just messed up an opportunity or actually seized one in a unique way.

From early on, Bonnie loved to work. That was a consistent thing about her.

It might have taken Betty time to teach her daughter the larger lessons of responsibility. However, there was one caveat in that Bonnie already valued work. She also strived to improve herself in the process. If anything, she was frustrated that she could not do more, with all the abilities she was holding back. Nonetheless, there was no kind of work that was beneath her. If there was anything Bonnie could do that helped someone else, she was happy to oblige.

Indeed, if there was one pill that was hard for Bonnie to swallow, it was when she was doing too much. She had a habit of stepping on other people's feet. At this job, she sometimes had to fight the feeling that she could do any and all of the jobs better than anyone else there.

However, she had mostly learned how to do her own job within the appropriate parameters. After all, Betty had spent many years reminding her of the importance of teamwork. And with this job, Bonnie had learned to enjoy being part of a larger unit. While retail jobs could be taxing (and low paying), nonetheless they did have the advantage of team building. There was something about the garish uniform that reminded each worker that they were all in the same boat. When the hours were long and tiring, and the customers abusive, reminders like this were a great comfort.

There was also a flipside to Bonnie's occasional overstepping: she knew how to lead. She was always alert in discovering and filling voids when they occurred, and would step in to help just about anywhere it was necessary. She would also encourage others to do so too, unofficially delegating authority in the process. Her coworkers frequently stepped right up with her. Such was her charisma, and the power of her example. And so, despite her occasional disappearances, Bonnie Boring was one of The Big Box's best workers.

As the calm persisted, the loiterers spoke quietly.

"Now?" asked the tallest of the three.

"What do you think, Mike?" said another.

"You know Joe, it looks like the perfect opportunity," said Mike. "I was sure by now someone would catch us on the camera and pull us out of here. It looks like nobody's watching. So it's a go."

"Okay Derrick," said Mike. "Wait for us to get outside. We'll be waiting in the car."

"I'm counting on you. You're gonna be there when it's over, right?"

"Of course, Derrick," said Mike, high fiving him. "You know we're cool. You're our pal..."

"Yeah," said Joe. "We love you."

They started to move, but then they noticed a tall man approaching in a suit. They scurried back to the clothing aisle.

It was Denny. He was on his cellphone, talking loudly. "Yeah, so what? You think they know what the hell they're doing here? Yeah right!!! These girls don't know crap about working a real job! You should see what I'm putting up with here!"

In the quiet, Denny called a meeting of the cashiers and customer service. "Everyone over here right now! Maria! You can take care of the checkouts in customer service."

Bonnie, Lisa, and the cashiers gathered around. There was whispering among them. Hal and Ahmed were the last to arrive, being physically the farthest away, and also because they had remaining customers. Denny did not notice this detail, or just didn't care. He shot them a look of contempt and snapped, "Hey! When I call, I expect you to come! No exceptions!"

"Sorry," said Hal. Ahmed just rolled his eyes.

"Listen," Denny announced, "We have a problem. Something is not matching up. The profits are not what they should be according to the sales. I don't know which one of you cashiers is the problem, but someone's been either stealing from the registers or defrauding them.

"We're going to be watching you extra carefully. This is your warning. You are on camera the whole time you work here. We will know if you try anything, or even if you are goofing off."

Both Bonnie and Lisa tried to keep their faces from showing their dread. Neither one of them had ever done anything to deserve that tone of accusation.

Denny continued, "Also everyone on the front end is on cash control. And your transactions will be spot checked using the cameras. You are dismissed."

Everyone returned to their respective posts, showing various signs of anger and disbelief. Denny pulled Bonnie and Lisa aside.

"Right now, I have a job for you girls. We got a shipment of handbags delivered up here by mistake. You two honeys can go bring it downstairs to the storeroom and put them away. I'll take over customer service."

As he walked away, he called, "I expect this done immediately…"

"Ugh," said Bonnie, "I dread him more every day."

"Something is weird here," said Lisa. "That's not our job at all. I don't even think we're allowed to be there. Besides, does he really need both of us to do a simple job like that?"

"You're right," said Bonnie, "I don't even know where the storeroom is. What do you think that's about?"

"Well," said Lisa, "he could be mad at me like I said. Anyway, I don't know. Him on customer service? I don't trust him."

"What do you think he's trying to do?"

"I don't know, but a few good workers have been fired lately without explanation. I bet he has something to do with it. I could swear it."

"Tell you what," said Bonnie, "I'll do it myself."

"I don't know, Bonnie. I really don't want to get in trouble."

"But you can't trust him over here. I sure don't!"

"Be very careful!"

Bonnie pushed the wagon into the elevator. As she left, one of the stock boys came up to Denny. "Hey, why did I just bring those up if you're sending them–"

"Shut up!" whispered Denny furiously. He immediately ran down the stairs after Bonnie. Meanwhile, Hal returned to his register. Two of the loiterers quietly slipped out of the front door. Derrick got on Hal's line.

When Bonnie reached the basement, she pushed the wagon off the elevator. She started toward a swinging door behind a downward ramp that she assumed led to the storeroom. She was surprised when Denny ran over from the stairs.

"I wanted both of you to do this job!"

"Does it matter?" said Bonnie. "It's getting done either way."

"Get over here!"

Bonnie left the wagon leaning against the door and started to run away, down the corridor to the left. She didn't notice the wagon rolling through the door, nor did she know that it would continue down the ramp, across the loading dock, over the edge and into the parking lot. Neither did Denny, for the time being.

"Where did she go?" sneered Denny, running after Bonnie.

The corridor ahead was narrow and winding, meant for small cargo taken by hand trucks. It seemed odd that she'd disappeared through there so fast. He could not have possibly known that an invisible young woman was watching from the ceiling. Using her telekinetic powers, she made carpet rise slightly in front of him, causing him to trip and fall.

Bonnie was about to fly back to the elevator and reappear, but then a strange thing happened. Bobbi, another customer service associate, ran up. She wasn't even supposed to be working that day.

"There you are!" she called.

"Forget it," said Denny as he picked himself up. Then both of them left.

Bonnie floated away as fast as she could. They'd taken the stairs, so she decided to slip invisibly onto the elevator. But then the elevator did not immediately come when she pressed the button, so she looked frantically for another exit. She slipped through the swinging door and became visible just as she exited the basement into the garage. There was little thought about the revelation of where the door actually led.

Bonnie might well have thought to go upstairs, for it was at that very moment that Derrick came up to Hal and pulled a gun.

3. Rescue From the Roof

Hal tried his best to be calm, but with a gun pointed at him, he could only just hold back panic. "What do you want?" he asked.

"Don't worry, handsome," whispered Derrick, "just open that register. Give me the money nice and quick, and everything will be alright."

"I can't open it without a sale. Want me to ask for a key?"

Derrick took a pack of gum out from the racks. "Just scan that," he said.

Hal scanned the gum. Then he closed the sale and opened the register. Not noticing what was going on, Ahmed called, "Hal, you didn't say, 'From the world to your block at The Big Box'."

"Just ignore him," muttered Derrick.

Hal began to empty the register. He hoped for calm, but Ahmed kept calling, "You're gonna get in trouble. Don't forget next time."

Hal was cringing, sweat pouring from his brow, hoping this ordeal would end soon. Then suddenly Jorge the security guard noticed what was going on and began running over. "Hey! Put the gun down!"

Derrick responded by putting the gun against Hal's head. "You don't want this pretty face damaged, do you? Everyone just calm down and let me leave. It'll be OK."

"Please, sir," said Jorge, "This will be over soon if you just give me the gun…"

Still pointing the gun at Hal, Derrick leapt over the island and grabbed him by the collar. "This is my friend here. He's just going to finish emptying that register. Nice and easy..."

Just then he looked out the window and saw his group's car driving away. Now panicking, Derrick took Hal by the collar. "Alright, pretty boy," he shouted, "you're coming with me."

Derrick led Hal, gun to his head, out through the side door to the parking garage, then up the steps to the roof. After they left, Jorge hit his panic button. Lisa quietly sent a text.

Meanwhile, Bonnie had just entered the lower level of the parking lot. She heard the commotion with her super hearing. Peering through the walls and floors, she saw Hal being led with a gun.

She ducked behind a car where she could not be seen, and said the words to herself, "Infinite Power!" In a quick puff of smoke, Bonnie Boring transformed herself into the mighty Ms. Infinity! She failed to notice the handbags, now a mess occupying several parking spots, blowing about in a powerful breeze.

Hal stood against the edge of the roof. Before him was Queens in the April sunset: rooftops of factories, restaurants, and car dealerships, with the Manhattan skyline beyond. Some four stories down was Northern Boulevard, in its usual evening rush, and a crowd on the sidewalk gathering to see the spectacle. Police cars were beginning to pull up.

"Don't worry man," said Derrick, "you're my ticket out of here. Once they let me go, you'll be free."

"What if they don't let you go?"

"Then you're out of luck."

Hal was beginning to wonder if bluffing might be his best bet. "Listen, man," he said, "you don't know what you're dealing with here. I know Ms. Infinity."

Derrick laughed. "Ms. Infinity? That's funny. She's coming here just for you?"

"I know it," insisted Hal. "She'll be here any–"

Suddenly there was a flash of lightning, and there was Ms. Infinity.

"–second," finished Hal, eyes wide open in surprise and relief.

There she stood, a figure of myth, larger than life. She looked like she did on TV, but somehow even greater. She was tall, with dark, flowing hair. Her full-bodied costume was a deep dark blue with the infinity symbol both on her belt and her tiara, both in gold, and a cape of gold that flowed behind her. She stood tall with arms akimbo and spoke with a powerful voice: "Sir, I believe it is time that you kindly release this man."

"Gladly!" shouted Derrick. Suddenly Hal was being flung over the safety bar, into the air. But an instant later he was in the arms of Ms. Infinity.

"You're safe now," said Ms. Infinity, looking into his eyes. Hal stared back as if enchanted.

Indeed, Hal was so excited that he could barely speak. He almost forgot to breathe. It was as if time had frozen in this one, perfect moment. Ms. Infinity seemed even more powerful, more beautiful, altogether more awesome in person than he had ever dreamed. She seemed to glow as he looked at her. "Wow," he beamed, "It's you! It's really you!"

"So I've been led to believe," she replied with a smile.

As Ms. Infinity descended with Hal, she smiled at him warmly. She landed with him, and gently put him down on the sidewalk in front of the store. Putting her hand on his shoulder, she spoke.

"You have handled a frightening situation with dignity and grace. I sense a man with kindness and decency, and much to admire. Never forget the power you have inside you."

Hal's heart was beating so fast, he almost forgot how to talk. "Thank you so much," he said.

"If you understand now, I have a criminal to deal with."

As Ms. Infinity flew away, Hal watched in complete awe. He stood there watching her disappear, as a police officer approached. "Sir? Can we ask you a few questions?"

Hal did not answer; it seemed hard to rouse him from his near trance-like state. "Sir?" asked the officer a second time.

"Oh!" he shouted, "I'm sorry, officer."

Down in the basement, Denny tried to open the door to the parking lot, but it was held closed by a powerful wind. He waited until it stopped, then pushed the door open. He immediately noticed the handbags scattered out on the pavement.

"I knew it!" he shouted. "That little dippy just ran off to play on her phone. I'll show her." He went back inside, teeth clenched, thinking of revenge.

Ms. Infinity flew after the assailant as he ran away.

"Nice!" she shouted. "A minute ago you looked like

someone a person might be scared of. You know, not me, but some people. Anyway, here you are running away like a little insect."

As Ms. Infinity approached, Derrick shot at her three times, only to see the bullets bounce off her. He then dropped the gun suddenly, as if something had struck him on the hand.

She shook her head. "If you humans don't stop playing with the dangerous toys, you're going to hurt yourselves. The police are on their way. I just need to wrap up my little gift for them." She flew around him at super speed. When she was done, he was tied up. The cops were then arriving on the roof.

Looking at Derrick in the eye, she asked urgently, "There were others, right? Who were they and where did they go?"

Derrick did not speak, but Ms. Infinity continued to probe him. She possessed the power to read minds, human minds anyway; this could not be done nearly so easily to one of her native world, who possessed powers nearly equal to her own. In fact, she almost never used her telepathy, believing that reading another person's mind was invasive and dangerous. But this time she felt there was an emergency. After she probed his mind for a few seconds, she stood up, as if in shock. "Wow!" she cried.

Turning to one of the officers, she said, "Please be gentle. The bonds should break with a simple knife or scissors. He is not the mastermind behind this crime. Please, I ask you to be merciful."

"Miss, this is a crime scene. We have other things to worry about."

"I know. Just please don't harm him."

She looked at Derrick with compassion. "You are

certain to be arrested now. I will catch the two men who betrayed you. But then the justice system will have to make the decisions beyond this, and I do not know how well this will go. You have made some wrong choices, indeed very foolish and reckless ones, but then you have had far fewer choices than most others. I wish that I could help you more. But do not think that your life is always fated to be cruel and hopeless. I hope one day you will have the full opportunity to embrace freedom and see a more hopeful future. I fear it will never be fair, but it need not always be as bleak as this."

Derrick looked back at her, quite surprised. "Thank you."

"Good luck," she replied, "If you'll excuse me, I have two more criminals to catch. Never forget the power you have inside you."

Ms. Infinity took off like lightning. Over the urban landscape she flew, flashing past parking lots, train tracks, and apartment buildings. She carefully scoured every street to find the car she was looking for. It was on the speeding mass of the Brooklyn-Queens Expressway that she found it, skidding into the shoulder just before she approached it from the back. She grabbed it with her left hand and forced it to a stop. Looking inside, she recognized the other two loiterers from the store. She tore the car in two pieces, from the back to the front, easily as paper. Before them she stood as they fell onto the roadway, an omnipotent figure passing judgment.

"Well, you certainly have an unusual definition of love and friendship, using a vulnerable boy to stand in the way of danger for you. If he has to pay a debt to society, then so do you."

Both men turned and attempted to run, but they had nowhere to go but the highway. Before they could go far, both had been scooped up by Ms. Infinity. With one under each arm, she disappeared from the highway in a blur, returning to the scene of the crime as quickly as walking across a room. She placed them down in front a line of police officers.

"These men were the real masterminds of the operation, though that word might be putting it a little too kindly."

Ms. Infinity flew up into the air. From on high, she looked back down at the store. Her friends were gathered just inside the store, watching the commotion, with Lisa looking on particularly intently. Ms. Infinity flew behind a wall, where she changed into Bonnie Boring and quietly reemerged. She snuck into the store, and quietly took her place beside Lisa.

"Wow," said Lisa, "that was amazing."

"Of course," said Bonnie, "I saw it. We all did. So, you know, so did I, 'cause you know, I was here."

Lisa rolled her eyes and shook her head. She looked directly at Bonnie. "Well, I sure can't wait to see what Hal has to say. He got to meet Ms. Infinity. That was like his dream come true. You know he's totally in love with her."

Bonnie tried to keep from blushing. She didn't have time to notice the penetrating glance on Lisa's face, for only a second later, Denny came up behind her.

"Hey Bonnie," he said, "I have a question for you."

"What?"

"A few minutes ago, you were down in the basement with that shipment of handbags. So, what happened to the handbags? I just saw an entire cart full of them in the parking garage."

She tried to think, but she was truly at a loss. All that

emerged from her mouth was a pathetic "Ummm…"

"Yeah, 'ummm…' is right. Too bad for you. You can't laugh off this one. Stupid-ass girls think you're working. Yeah right! I know you don't care, like all girls. You can just go to the mall with Daddy's credit card, and you just think this whole job is a joke. Well, guess what? You screwed up, and you have to face the consequences. You're punching out now and going home. Consider this your first write-up. You get three of these before you get suspended. If things don't get better after that, you're fired. Are you clear on that?"

"Uh…yes."

He then turned to Lisa and shot her a look of contempt. "And you, Lisa," he sneered, "You're in just as much trouble. You were both supposed to be down there. You disobeyed a direct order, so you're also written up."

"You gotta be kidding me!"

"Don't take that tone with me or there will be more trouble. Both of you can now punch out and go home."

Bonnie was now visibly crying. "Come on, Bonnie," said Lisa, "I'll walk home with you."

As they left, Hal was returning from being interviewed by the police, and also the press. He seemed to be the hero of the minute. Everyone around him was asking him questions.

"Guys," he called, "take it easy! I was with her for maybe a minute."

"Yeah Hal," laughed Teddy from the electronics department. "That was the best sixty seconds of your life, if you know what I mean!"

"Mind out of the gutter!" replied Hal.

"What did she say to you?" asked Ahmed

"Very little. Now I'm trying to remember…"

"Oh, I know," said Nadine, "you're trying to keep it a secret. She told you some nice sweet nothings and you just don't want to share it."

"I wish," said Hal. "Wow! That would be something. To have some real time with her, what must that be like? I mean, imagine what it would be like to be with her for a while. Not just… you know, not just that, but to get to know her. Go on one of her adventures. That must be something! I wish I could."

"Ah," laughed Nadine, "Hal wants to get close to Ms. Infinity!"

"Yeah, I really do. I mean, where is she now? What amazing things must she be doing? What awesome, cosmic thoughts must she be having?"

4. Friends and Mothers

"Denny's a doodyhead!" shouted Bonnie at the top of her lungs.

"Maybe not so loud," said Lisa, "Or I don't know. Maybe they can't quite hear you in The Bronx."

The two friends were walking together on Roosevelt Avenue, headed home. The elevated "7" subway line was above them, the squeaks and roars of the frequent trains periodically dominating the soundtrack of Woodside. The activity of the street provided the rest of the cacophony. All around were shops and eateries of every culture. Crowds of people circulated the sidewalks; passersby seemed to be abutting them every second, some nearly bumping into them as they exited the local businesses. Even as Bonnie shouted, she was scarcely noticed amidst the bustle.

"I know I'm loud!" shouted Bonnie. "Sorry, but I'm mad. I really hate that guy."

"I know," said Lisa, "vent it out if you must. I'm no great fan of his either."

"Whatever. It's not as much fun if you can't argue."

"Well okay. Sorry to be too agreeable."

They turned off Roosevelt Avenue and onto their street. Before them was a mix of apartment buildings and attached houses. The street was busy with many pedestrians winding their way around each other and crossing amidst the double-parked cars. As they reached Bonnie's home, a brick townhouse, Lisa looked at her friend. "Bonnie, can we talk a second?"

"Oh no. This never ends well. Now it's my butt, right?

Look, I know my personal hygiene isn't up to your standards but–"

"Bonnie, stop!" said Lisa, now urgent in her tone.

"Sorry."

"Can I please ask you something? What exactly happened when you went down to the basement?"

"Lisa, I'd really rather not…"

"Listen, Bonnie, can't you at least tell me what Denny did down there?"

"He yelled at me because you didn't come down. Then I ran away. I guess I didn't notice the bags falling down the ramp."

"There! Was that so hard?"

Bonnie was looking down, clearly very upset. Lisa could not be sure, but had a pretty good idea why Bonnie was so hurt by Denny's abuse. Yet there was nothing she could say about it directly. She was treading on sensitive ground, and she knew it.

"Bonnie, I hope you're not too bothered over what Denny said to you. He's a jerk. He knows nothing about you, and what he says means nothing. Don't let him get to you."

"I guess," said Bonnie tentatively.

"Bonnie, I meant it when I said that I like working with you. I love working with you. When you're around, we're great together. Just being with you makes the day go by that much faster. If I have to work evenings and weekends, well then, I want them to be with you. So please, please. Let's be in this together."

"You're right, Lisa," said Bonnie as they embraced.

"In fact," said Lisa, "I think you're capable of much

more than anyone realizes."

"Oh, I don't know about that..." demurred Bonnie.

"Alright," said Lisa, "One thing is for sure. We can't let this go on. I can't work under these conditions. I don't know what to do about it, but somehow, we have to take action. We should have just said no to Denny in the first place. I feel like he was pushing us into something. Maybe he just wanted me in trouble, or both of us, and then he got just what he wanted. I don't know. Seems like a lot of trouble for a vendetta. Maybe there is more to this. Either way..."

"You're right, Lisa," snapped Bonnie. "Okay? I'm just overwhelmed right now."

Just then Betty Boring emerged from Bonnie's house. She wore a green peasant top and jeans with her dark hair pulled back.

"Hey girls!" she called.

"Oh hi, Mrs. B.," said Lisa.

"Hey Lisa. Do you want to stay for dinner?"

"Oh, I'd love to, but my grandmother's over from China. She's been bothering me to play my cello for her."

"Well, isn't she lucky. You are a natural. I'd love to hear you again some time."

"Hopefully not too soon," said Lisa, blushing, "but I'd love to stay for dinner soon."

"Next time. Okay honey?"

"Definitely next time," said Bonnie.

"Of course," said Lisa to Bonnie. "I love your mother's cooking. It's otherworldly."

The Boring house was like many others in the outer boroughs

of New York City. It was narrow, with its primary length vertical, and (to a lesser degree) front-to-back. Stairs seemed to dominate the place, with the flight leading upstairs walling a side of the living room. The rest of the living room was small but homey: carpeted and decorated with balsa wood, family pictures of mother and daughter, and class pictures of Bonnie. There were many typical homey touches, from vases to candlesticks and throw pillows. A short hallway connected it to a small kitchen, where Betty and Bonnie now sat. The steps to the basement interrupted a side of the kitchen, just inside from the hallway. The dining room formed a narrower back end of the living room, connecting to the kitchen.

"Do you feel okay?" Betty asked, feeling Bonnie's forehead. "I was right before. You are sick. I worry about you out there. It's not healthy being in outer space without a jacket."

"A jacket?" sneered Bonnie, "Forget it. That would ruin the costume. Talk about a mother's fashion sense."

Betty reached into the air and pulled out what looked vaguely like a thermometer. She placed it into Bonnie's hair.

"When are they gonna design these things so they don't take forev…" complained Bonnie, but by the time she finished it had beeped. Betty took it out of Bonnie's hair, flicked it with her finger, and waved her hands until a message appeared in front of her

"Oh, okay," said Betty, "It's just another viral tiff. You will be better by last week, or by the least ironic page of a star's orbital range. You have to remember to keep the flights within an inadhesive objective, and the colors of your coin bounces should remain warm or within an eighth of a galaxy's ink stain. For tonight, you should also keep the carpets unliquidized…"

"Mom, I'm not a little kid! You don't have to break it

down for me like someone who doesn't understand basic multidimensional logic."

"And you don't have to give me super-powered attitude."

"No, I guess I don't technically *have* to."

"You should get a good rest, too. You know as well as I do that Misery isn't staying away for long. You can argue all you want, but what you did really doesn't pass for taking care of the problem. You're going to be fighting her again before you know it. In fact, I'd be thinking about that soon."

"Maybe not," said Bonnie. "Yeah, I know. She will be back."

"So, can you stay off those social networks for maybe one night. I see you in there lurking on that boy's page. That Hal."

"Mom!"

"Look, if you like him, fine. I like his taste in television. I see he's also up on current events, and that's a positive in my book."

"Yeah?" said Bonnie, "What does he..."

"I know," laughed Betty, "You just look at the pictures of him. That's my girl. Looking through the photo albums to find a shot of him without a shirt."

Bonnie didn't speak. She only glared at her mother in shock and anger.

"Sorry, dear. I'm your mother."

"Yes, but none of my friends' mothers have X-ray vision."

"And none of my friends' daughters are superheroes."

"And that's an excuse to invade my privacy?"

"It's a reason to be concerned about you," said Betty. "In fact, before I forget, you had a scary incident at work."

"Yes," said Bonnie. "Only in my life are an armed robbery and a hostage situation the back page story."

"Think what that's like for me, baby. You know it's not easy watching you. A mother can only stand by so much. Anyway, you must have enjoyed that opportunity to get close to your crush."

"Mom…"

"I think we should talk about that, don't you?"

Bonnie rolled her eyes. "Alright mom."

Betty pulled closer to Bonnie. "So, I saw that you got close to your Hal, but one little catch there. It wasn't exactly you. It was her: Ms. Infinity, your alter-ego."

"Hal's pretty crazy about her," said Bonnie. "I don't really know how he feels about me, but he can't take his eyes off her. I see his eyes glued to every TV appearance, every magazine shot. And then there was today."

"And you're jealous of yourself. This would be a good time to note that this whole thing was your idea. Now I think it's wonderful, using your powers to help others, and obviously the earth needs protecting…"

"Mom, do we need to do this again?"

"Well, look at your approach. You turned yourself into a vision of perfection, an omnipotent superhero who looks like a supermodel. That's an image that nobody can truly live up to, yourself included. So can you really be surprised if you have trouble competing with it?"

These discussions were always frustrating to Bonnie. The right to use her powers openly with her mother's approval had been hard earned, but even now, the right to do so without criticism was still clearly a long way off.

"Look, I don't want to always be using my powers in secret. That weighs on me after a while. That might be good enough for you, but I want to be able to do things in public. So I do it this way. I use my shape shifting and change into someone else when I do it."

"That transformation makes me uneasy," said Betty, "you know that, right? You are more beautiful than that manufactured image. At least I hope you know that. I mean, I get it. If you're going to disguise yourself, and you have that power, well obviously you would. But I just wish you weren't so… I don't know. Do you have to look like a runway model? I don't like the statement. Besides, there was no reason you had to make yourself taller, was there? C'mon. Be a proud petite! I wear my five feet with pride!"

"Mom! I'm an adult. I get it, really. But you do have to lay off my personal choices here."

"Alright," said Betty. "As long as you know how I feel about it. I do have a question though. Why the explosion, and the magic words? 'Infinite Power'? Besides the fact that your powers are not infinite, you don't need magic words to change, or the pyrotechnics. What gives?"

"It's all mindset," explained Bonnie. "It helps me get in the mood. I kind of wish I could get some music going too, but that might be giving myself away."

Betty smiled and shook her head. "Why stop there? Why not wake up every morning with a title sequence?"

"You know I do in my head," said Bonnie. "Look, I get it. I'm flashy. You're under the radar. Can we just agree to disagree?"

"I really do. But you know why I do things my way. A good act can be enhanced when it is anonymous. It is not about getting the accolades. It's about doing what is necessary, whether anyone knows it or not. You might not fully appreciate the importance of one who works behind the scenes. There are many hands that are invisible, and are taken for granted, in many lives, yours not least.

"But I understand. It is very hard on you, always hiding who you really are. I see the point to the dual identity, and I don't judge. Still, whatever your choices, you have to live with the consequences."

"And so, it's me versus myself..."

Betty put her hand lovingly on her daughter's shoulder. "But you're still you. Why don't you ask him out? You know, you. Bonnie Boring. Go up to him as yourself and ask him out. Is that so hard? He might like you more than you think. Ms. Infinity is just an abstraction to him. You're a real person. Just approach him as an equal. Go out to a movie. Have dinner together. Ask him his interests. Tell him yours. You might be surprised how well it goes. If not, then on to the next."

"But what if he finds out my secret? Or if we get permanent, do I tell him?"

"You know what? If you trust him, then yes. We don't have to be an island here forever. We have our reasons for staying hidden, but it doesn't have to mean hidden from everyone. If he is someone who can be trusted, then by all means trust him. These humans are not to be underestimated, dear. Living among them is an improvement, don't you think?"

"Hal forgot a pen again today. I saved him one."

"Nice of you. You know, I suspect there's more to him than forgetting things. And good looks."

"Yeah," said Bonnie. "He likes kids. He's sweet."

Getting up from the table, Betty began to walk to the living room, but then turned back to her daughter. "Bonnie," she said gingerly, "I think this is as good a time as any to discuss going back to school. I mean, your associate's degree is never going to cut it in this economy. You need to have a permanent job. I can't keep supporting you forever."

"Please, Mom," whined Bonnie, "I'm in no mood."

"Look, Bonnie. It's not like I'm not proud of what you do. But fighting crime is reactive. You should also be working proactively toward the common good. Remember how lucky we are. Nobody else has it quite like us. It is our responsibility to give back. I thought you had a wonderful idea. You'd be a great social worker."

"Alright Mom, I promise I'll give it serious consideration."

"Thank you, dear. You know what? It's getting late. You really should be getting to bed."

"Okay fine," said Bonnie. Then in a stream of stars her clothes transformed into her pajamas.

"You know Bonnie," chirped Betty, "it wouldn't kill you to put your clothes on one leg at a time."

"Never!" shouted Bonnie as she flew up to her room.

Betty sighed. "My girl's going to get a rude awakening one day."

Bonnie lay awake in her bed that night. Her mind was a rush of anger and confusion. She wasn't sure what upset her more: the deliberate meanness of her supervisor, or the oblivious brush-off by high school acquaintances. Either way, she was disappointed in life. Sure, it was much, much safer here than in her old world. Yet even here it seemed like she didn't belong.

She read for a while, and eventually fell asleep to the TV. Soon her anger and disappointment were overcome by anxiety and bad dreams, just like most nights.

Bonnie and Betty kept many secrets, their very identity not least. While some of these were unusual, unique even, the need for secrecy was not. And while some secrets might be dangerous, theirs were not. Betty had taken great pains to assure that what their neighbors didn't know would never hurt them. They simply kept their personal details quiet, much like anyone. Their privacy was the space they needed to live as a family, however small. Such was true of families of all sizes and shapes.

Their native culture was also a society that valued privacy. Propriety was also important, and an aspect of propriety meant respecting boundaries. These things were not really as "alien" as all that. Many human cultures had similar values. Indeed, this value was part of life in New York City, where it was common to have very different cultures living quite literally on top of one another. Respect for boundaries was central to the peace of a neighborhood.

Lisa understood this as well as anyone. As Bonnie's best friend, she knew how essential it was to respect her space. It went hand in hand with trust, and trust was something that was very important to her. Bonnie's trust was very hard earned, especially the amount that Lisa received. Yet it could be very frustrating at times. No matter how deep their friendship was, Bonnie could only give so much of herself.

For her part, Lisa always provided her a safe ear when she did choose to speak. Yet Bonnie rarely did open up, and Lisa had to be content with the inevitable distance between them. If Lisa had known it, this was just as frustrating for Bonnie. She also needed Lisa's friendship, and deep inside she wanted to trust her more, even if it was difficult for her to do so.

Yet there was always more to that picture than met the eye. And Lisa also understood another essential piece of context that made this situation less bitter. Bonnie and Betty were not much more open with each other. Deep though the love was between mother and daughter, there was also an eerily deep silence. So many things were simply never discussed, many of them important details of their past. And then the two also kept not a few secrets from each other, Betty more effectively than her daughter. But then if privacy was essential to a family's living space, so too was a measure of space necessary to the individuals in a family. That respect was one of many things a family needed to survive as a unit.

Whatever the difficulties, this family unit was carrying on quite well on its terms. It was not every family that held together this well. Some didn't hold together at all.

5. Competition With Herself

In a small, spartan apartment in Jackson Heights, Jerry Holstein finished getting breakfast ready. "Hal," he called, "come to breakfast. You have work soon."

"Hey, Dad," said Hal as he came in. "I finally got a good night's sleep for achange. Well, next to my apartment, everything seems quiet."

"Yeah, that roommate of yours. I know. Listen, I spoke to your mother."

"You spoke to Mom? And it didn't wake me up?"

"Listen, after yesterday, of course we were going to talk. You're more important than any argument. We're both just relieved that you're safe. Anyway, your mother wants to see you tonight. Please, please talk to her at least. She misses you. See what you can arrange. Maybe you can stay there tonight and have two quiet nights in a row."

"That's pushing my luck. Quiet in either of your places is a miracle. Why do you think I moved out? Besides, Stacy is staying over at my apartment for pretty much the same reason."

"She's done that a few times, right? You are a great brother, Hal. I don't know how many guys your age would put up with a nine-year old girl staying over. But is it safe with that drunk roommate?"

"She takes the bedroom and I sleep on the couch. I can manage."

Jerry was beginning to cry. "This is not how family is

supposed to be! Divorce is hard on everyone, but at least you should both feel like you have a home." He then wiped his tears and shook his head. "Listen, Hal. Stacy lives with Mom over the week, and me for the weekend. That's the arrangement for now. You're an adult, so it's different. And it's wonderful that you want to help, but you actually complicate it this way."

"Oh yeah. It's just, neither one of us wants to be there…"

Jerry's tone became more derisive. "Yeah. It's… him. Right? Your mother's new squeeze."

"Please dad," begged Hal, "let's not bring him up. We've been getting along so well up until now."

"Damn that woman!" snapped Jerry. "Doesn't even wait till I'm packed to invite her new boyfriend in!"

"Dad! Stop! This is why I had to move out!"

Jerry took a deep breath. After a moment, he collected himself and spoke again. "Okay. I'm sorry. Soon we'll have this divorce worked out, and this will stop. It has to. But you, you're twenty-four. A boy your age should be living his life, not working twenty-four hours a day just to afford a horrible upstairs conversion with a miserable roommate. At the very least, you should never forget that you have a home here, and at your mother's."

"I know, Dad. I promise."

"Hal, there's another thing that concerns me. "Are you dating anyone?"

"Not at this moment. No."

"Here's the thing. We all heard how excited you were to meet that Ms. Infinity. And of course you were. Who wouldn't be? I just hope you're not thinking of that as a relationship."

"Way to burst my bubble, Dad."

"I had my crushes too, Hal. And she would be lucky as anyone to have you, but be realistic. You'll probably never see her again. Look, this is the thing with fantasy crushes like this: all you know is the image. Even if you did somehow get close to her, what would you being getting yourself into? You don't know what she's really like. It makes much more sense to date someone you actually know."

"I was kidding. I just wish I got her autograph."

"So, is there someone else you're seeing? You know, a woman who you really know, presumably one who can't fly, but still nice to talk to?"

"Well, there is one girl I think about at work, but I don't know…"

"Here's my other concern. I don't want you to lose hope because of what happened to your parents. Lots of couples stay married for life. Please don't let this discourage you."

"I know, Dad. I really want to be hopeful. It's hard…"

"Hal, it's important that you believe in something. There is more to life than an endless treadmill. If you have someone you can dedicate your life to, then that is what gives life meaning, that and some meaningful work. I also hope you are giving your future a hard look."

"That's another frustrating thing, Dad. I don't know when my career is taking off."

"Well, aspiring to TV reporting wasn't exactly thinking practically, was it? The possibility exists that you might have to rethink things somewhere down the line. But I still believe you will figure this all out. You have a future, a bright one. Got it?"

"Got it, Dad. By the way, I do have time to stop at my

apartment before work, so…"

Jerry laughed, "I know, Hal, go to the pantry and do your shopping. I figured you'd be coming, so I bought double."

"Bonnie," said Betty the same morning, "I do hope you've been working on some kind of plan. You're going to be fighting Misery again at any time."

"I know, Mom," said Bonnie, "but I can beat her."

Betty was sitting on a chair in Bonnie's room while Bonnie worked at getting herself out of bed. The room was like many bedrooms of young adults living at home. There were vestiges of teenage life here and there, such as the bright colors of the linen. Her desk had a few pictures of herself and friends, particularly Lisa. The wall had several superhero posters, with an especially large picture of Wonder Woman.

"You see, Bonnie," said Betty, "this is what I'm concerned about. I wouldn't be too sure. This is not the time for overconfidence. It's not like beating some street criminal. This is someone who might just be up to fighting you."

"You didn't see our battle yesterday. I bowled her over!"

Betty was barely holding her tongue. There were many things that were unsaid. She could not be sure whether it was time to bring them up. For now, all she could do was argue.

"Look Bonnie, you are beginning to get a little too used to winning, and it's dangerous. Do not take it for granted that you're always going to be the strongest person around. You never know if you're going to meet someone tougher. You might not think much about what it's like to be competing with her, someone who is similar to you in strength. It has been a while. But it is high time you remembered."

Bonnie sighed and spoke with token interest. "So, what kind of plan are you thinking of?"

"That's just it, Bonnie. We have to think of one. We should begin by looking at her method of attack, and then considering where her weaknesses might be. I would also want to at least begin to guess her motives. It's all speculation now, but it's better than nothing at all."

"Really? All this for someone who just sent a giant bowling ball across space? Look, I don't remember her being the sharpest tool in the shed, and this doesn't exactly change the equation."

"Bonnie, listen! What she did was tremendously dangerous, and she came a great distance for that effort. I wouldn't be too quick to underestimate her. There is definitely something more going on than just a reckless sport. You have to realize that too."

"I was joking. I do know that. You know what? I'll think about it. Okay?"

"By the way," said Betty, "How is that spaceship? I haven't been on it in some time now. Is it ready if you have to go any distance?"

"You know it, Mom! Starship Infinity is better than ever."

"You had to call it that?"

"And what would you call it? The Boring Family Rocket?"

"Never mind. Starship Infinity it is."

"You'd never recognize it, Mom. It's awesome now. I have made this thing like no other ship anywhere. It's first class in every possible way. So don't tell me I'm not ready."

Betty looked at Bonnie dubiously. "I'll tell you what. I'll

be on the ready. I have personal time if I need to take it. I'll even go with you if you need me to."

"You really think that's necessary?"

"Bonnie, my love," said Betty, "I am your mother. I am here for you. You don't always have to work alone. I want to say, 'Don't be afraid to ask', but that's not enough. There are times when things are too big. Yes, Bonnie, too big even for you. And when that happens, you had better come to me. This is something that is big enough by far. Bonnie, when the time comes, I want to know that you will ask me."

"Mom..."

"Bonnie, I want you to promise me."

"What am I promising you?"

"Bonnie, you will promise me that when Misery does strike, you will let me know immediately. I don't care what time of day it is. When it happens, you will not be concerned about interrupting anything, or asking too much, and most of all, you will not be embarrassed about asking your mother for help. I will be there immediately without question. Is that understood?"

"I understand."

"Do you promise?"

"I do."

Bonnie considered her mother's words, but took little action. She had other matters on her mind. After the incident on the roof, she had been concerned about Derrick. She had begun to feel sympathy for him since reading his mind.

Derrick's parents had never been around, and he was raised primarily by his elderly grandmother. With little family around to look out for him, he had fallen in with some dangerous crowds. This gang had found him in a fairly desperate state. They had given him a sense of security. He hadn't seemed to understand that he was deliberately being used.

Bonnie realized that he had done wrong, nearly killing Hal. Yet she also believed that he was a case of a kid who had made a mistake rather than a hardened criminal. She felt that he should at least be given a fair chance at rehabilitation.

She visited the precinct house as Ms. Infinity and asked what was happening in the case. She was very alarmed to hear that both of the accomplices had been let go. There was no evidence against them apart from her own word (based on the dubiously admissible grounds of a psychic reading). Derrick had confessed, but would not say a word against them, probably because of fear of retaliation. There was a chance that he might be talked into testifying for a plea deal. Yet even under the best circumstances, he was almost certain to serve prison time.

She felt sad about the whole thing. There were many worse criminals who got away with much less punishment, or indeed, none at all. She began to wonder what part she could play as a superhero that could change the world.

"I'm afraid your powers are not much use here," said Betty. "As hard as it sounds, be glad there is a law here, flawed though it is. And I will certainly not hear of breaking it."

"Of course I know that," said Bonnie, "but do you understand why it upsets me?"

Betty looked at her warmly. "I know that you empathize, and it makes you special. But here you must always think about working within the law. Now do you understand why I want you to think about a career in the public interest? There are many people who do wonderful work with much lesser abilities than you. What they have in common with you is empathy. I am sure the personal stories of many such people would surprise you. You are not necessarily as unique as you might think."

"That's a comforting thought," said Bonnie.

The next time Bonnie went to work, she nearly ran into a huge cardboard cutout of her alter ego just inside the entrance. Clearly the store was trying to capitalize on the heroine's recent appearance, and the attention it had received; but in her eyes, it was pretty unsettling.

The media coverage she had seen so far was none too encouraging. The reports seemed to focus heavily on her looks, with minimal concern for the feats she had performed, and the fact that she had saved a life.

Security at The Big Box had been stepped up considerably. Unfortunately, the effort was anything but even-handed. The guards were showing extra suspicion with African American customers, and even employees. Nadine was particularly upset when she had to prove to a new security guard that she worked there. It was an indignity that her coworkers did not have to face. Ironically, all three of the perpetrators had been white.

Betty shopped there that day and spent a little time with Nadine during her break. The two discussed parenting, especially Nadine's son, who was in kindergarten.

"I am very sorry to hear that," said Betty. "At only five years old, nobody should be facing racism. It's bad enough that it hits adults."

"Richard is a very sweet boy," said Nadine, "but he's a kid and he acts like one. So, he snatched a crayon from another kid, and suddenly the dean's telling me to stop raising a gangster."

"I can't imagine a child who doesn't act selfishly. Doesn't exactly make you a mugger if you get rude."

"So, Betty, what do I say to him exactly? Not to anger the white kids? Is that it?"

"That's the thing. The same action is often taken different ways, depending on who does it. Girls learn the same lesson in a different way. What's 'strong' for boys is called 'bossy' for girls, and worse. It's a hard lesson. Still, that doesn't mean we have to accept it, does it?"

"What do you do about it?"

"Well, short of leaving the whole world behind, I think you have to speak up."

"Easier said than done."

Racism was not a thing on Bonnie and Betty's native world. By no means was their world any utopia. It was certainly no stranger to many forms of inequality, extreme sexism not least. While the people there had the same range of skin tones as human beings, they didn't have the perceptions that came with these differences on Earth. It was just that the history that produced "race" as was known on Earth had no equivalent there. People there simply didn't think of skin color as something significant.

This caused a culture shock when the Borings arrived on Earth. While Bonnie and Betty greatly enjoyed the relatively liberal attitude toward gender, nonetheless they were not prepared for the disadvantage their dark skin tone suddenly gave them. They were quite surprised that simply being "brown" skinned caused many people around them to make many different assumptions about them, and sometimes view them with suspicion.

Despite Bonnie's fear of being discovered, it was also her secret wish when it came to Hal. She had played out the drama in her mind many times: They were alone. She told him who she really was. He doubted her, but then she transformed in front of him. He was then amazed and awed, and nearly fell over telling her how much he idolized her. Then she took him on a trip around the world. At the end of the day, he told her he loved her. Finally, they did what came naturally. How could he resist?

One day, maybe she could make it happen. But reality was not looking much like her fantasy. To Bonnie's chagrin, Hal was being recognized by people left and right for the events on the roof with Ms. Infinity. Customers and coworkers alike were asking him about the incident, and he was enjoying the attention.

Nonetheless, Hal had clearly not forgotten Bonnie. When a man she knew from high school came in and talked with her, Hal seemed unable to take his eyes off them. After it was over, she whispered to her friend Julia, who was with her at the customer service counter, "Look! Somebody's a little 'peanut butter and jealous'."

Julia looked back at her wide eyed and laughed, "Not that you noticed!"

At the end of her shift, Bonnie finally asked Hal out. It was an awkward moment. She was about to leave, and he was working a line. But he graciously accepted. "Bonnie," he answered, "I would love to go out with you."

Bonnie and Hal settled on a day date, since both of them had to work throughout the next few evenings. They visited a nearby carnival. It was a small venue, situated in the parking lot of a church, boxed in by buildings and traffic. They ate ice cream and talked on the Ferris wheel. From their vantage above the small fairground, they could see much of Queens, and beyond it the city's bridges, the Manhattan skyline, and more. It was quiet, apart from one teenage boy, climbing around in another car in an attempt to show off to his girlfriend.

"I never cared for my name," said Hal, "it sounds like an old man's. And well, it is. I'm named after my great grandfather, who died in the Holocaust. It's a Jewish tradition, naming after a dead relative, although usually that's confined to the Hebrew name. I got that also. My Hebrew name is Chaim. That means 'Life.' But lucky me, I got the English name too."

"I think it's a nice name," said Bonnie, "I also think it's a lovely tradition. I wonder if there's more meaning, considering the tragedy in this case. I mean, it's after someone you never knew, so I can understand why you wouldn't feel too much attachment. Still, I guess your grandparents must have appreciated it. One of them lost him under horrible circumstances."

"He was my grandmother's father, on my dad's side. My grandparents did talk about him from time to time," said Hal.

"…And it's also good that you knew them."

"Good point. You know what? Bonnie's a really nice name. Any story there?"

"My mom liked it?"

"I guess that's as good a reason as any."

"So how is your family life?" asked Bonnie.

"My parents are divorced," said Hal, sounding uneasy, "Well, divorcing. It's the reason I moved out. It's hard to be around either of them without hearing about their arguments.

My mom also has a boyfriend now, and I never go to her house anymore. It's been a long time since I've even talked to her. Ugh! It's enough. Too depressing."

"That really is a shame. It's hard hearing about families falling apart."

"So, what's your family like?" asked Hal.

"I live with my mother," said Bonnie.

"Do you get along?"

"Well, she does helicopter a lot, and I give her a lot of attitude, but it could be worse."

"That's cool."

For the most part, Hal asked little besides what Bonnie volunteered. In a way she was relieved. There were many questions she did not want to answer. Yet she could not be sure whether this was due to good manners or a lack of interest. But then the inevitable question of family background came up.

"So Bonnie," asked Hal, "where does your family come from?"

"Oh," said Bonnie, "A lot of places…"

"I was going to guess you might be Indian, or maybe Hispanic. But then with the last name Boring, there must be some English in there."

"Yeah. I'm kind of dark. Umm. This is really not my favorite topic."

"Oh. Well listen. I hope you're not afraid or something. I know there's a lot of prejudice out there. You know, being Jewish, sometimes I've been afraid of saying so myself. The worst thing I could do is judge someone else…"

"Oh Hal. It's nothing like that. I just have some issues

of my own. Could we just drop it?"

Suddenly, the teenage boy from the neighboring car began to slip and fall. Bonnie could ignore the situation no longer. Seeing that Hal was distracted by the spectacle, Bonnie nervously turned into Ms. Infinity. She had to think the words "Infinite Power" instead of saying them, and skip the smoke cloud.

She then flew to the scene so fast that she seemed to appear out of thin air. Happily, his foot had momentarily gotten stuck in the railing for just long enough. She caught the boy as he fell. He gasped at his rescuer, surprised and relieved.

"You have to be careful!" she said. "You don't get another chance."

"Ms. Infinity!" cried the boy.

Hal was clearly amazed and captivated by the sight of the heroine suddenly in his sight. His eyes were glued, so much so that he did not notice that his date had disappeared.

Ms. Infinity flew the boy safely onto the ground, to a predictable round of applause. "Thank you," she said, trying not to look tense. She flew away, again fast enough to seem to disappear.

"Wow!" cried Hal, "that was magic!" He didn't notice the other 'magic' right behind him, Ms. Infinity quietly transforming into Bonnie Boring.

"I know, Hal," admonished Bonnie, "but please remember that I'm right here. It's not especially good manners to talk about another woman when you're on a date."

After the Ferris wheel, they happened upon the high striker. "Wanna try your strength and impress the lady?" called the barker.

"Not really my thing," said Hal, "I'm not especially strong. But I suppose…"

He picked up the hammer and hit the target. The lights went up to the "Big Kid" level. He laughed nervously. "Don't say I didn't warn you!"

"That's okay," answered Bonnie, smiling.

"Why don't you try?" asked Hal.

"Oh… I don't think so…" demurred Bonnie.

"It's no extra charge, Miss," said the barker. "Two for the price of one. His and hers."

Bonnie hated things like this. It was very hard for her not to reveal her superpowers, no matter how small an effort she put in. Yet she didn't want to make a scene. "Alright, sir," she said.

"Here's the lady hammer."

"Nah. I'll take the same one my date used."

"Your choice, Miss."

She struck the target with what she thought was a very slight effort. Yet the lights went decisively to the top, the area reading "Super Strong," with bells ringing.

"That must be an accident," said Bonnie sheepishly.

"Bonnie," said Hal, "that was awesome! Don't you go calling that an accident."

Bonnie looked at Hal in surprise.

"Look," said Hal, "never mind me. If you can do something like that, the last thing you should ever have to do is apologize for it. I think that's great if you're strong. More power to you."

"Wow, Hal. I'm glad you feel that way."

"Of course I do. I can tell you're a pretty special girl. I love that you just did that."

"I knew I liked you!"

"I think I like him too!" said Betty, sitting with Bonnie in the kitchen once again. "In fact, I was pretty sure I liked him before."

"Well, I mean, it's great that he likes that I'm strong, but Ms. Infinity has superpowers…"

Betty shook her head, rolling her eyes, mouth open in a gesture of bemused disbelief. "Uh, yeah. I happen to know a little trivia about Bonnie Boring too…"

"Not the point, Mom. He doesn't know that."

"And honestly, how much sympathy do you really want? It's like you have both winning horses in the same race. Talk to someone with real problems."

"So, another date, you think?"

"Well, what do you think?" asked Betty.

"I'll do it."

"I'm glad."

"So, Mom, how do I answer that family background question? I don't want to tell a lie, but it's not like I can go ahead and tell him I'm from another planet."

"Now Bonnie, you aren't ashamed of our culture, are you?"

"Mom, stop the guilt! Obviously that's not what this is about. Do you go around telling people you're a space alien?"

"No. I don't. And I do understand your dilemma. For now, I guess I'd avoid the question. But sometimes I feel like you wish you weren't who you are. You know, you really

should be proud. There is more to our culture than you seem
to think."

"Yeah, whatever Mom."

"Okay Bonnie. Now, you are planning for that attack,
right? Misery could be hitting any day now…"

"Always."

Apart from her powers, Bonnie felt strongly that her native
planet had nothing to offer her. She had abandoned
everything from her life there: her name, her history, and her
culture. She even tried to ignore her memories, as best as she
could.

Betty's attitude was very different. While both of their
lives there had been very difficult, their flight had meant
leaving her past behind forever, and for Betty that had been a
very bitter pill to swallow. While Betty had also adapted
enthusiastically to Earth, she still privately maintained
vestiges of her old culture.

Food was easy enough. The many and varied shops in
their Queens neighborhood offered every possibility when it
came to finding ingredients. Often all the shopping could be
done on one block of Roosevelt Avenue. And really, the food
of their heritage wasn't so 'otherworldly'; it was just food. The
vegetation and animals of Earth might have been different
from those of their native planet, but they certainly came close
enough for comfort. The meats turned out to be surprisingly
similar in both nutritional content and palate; 'tastes like
chicken' turned out to be surprisingly true even on the
interplanetary level.

The dishes were similar to items found in many Earth
cultures. Some were hardly even exotic to the average native-
born American. The dessert Betty came to cheekily call the
'blastoff' was essentially just a devil's food cake with hints of

various citrus fruits baked in for flavor. Bonnie still wouldn't touch it, but Lisa loved it, and was quick to tell "Mrs. B." so.

Betty even still observed some holidays. Since they occurred on a faraway planet with a different sun, observance would involve a fairly exhaustive process of consulting star charts to find the right 'day'. Whenever she did observe, Bonnie would want to be as far away as possible.

"Dad," said Hal excitedly. "She called me! We're going on another date!"

Hal was on his break at work, sitting near the door with his cellphone. Bonnie had just called him, and he was elated.

"So that's who now?" asked Jerry.

"Bonnie, the girl from work."

"And she asked you out?"

"Yes!"

"Well, it's a new era. So, you like her?"

"You know what? A lot. She's very sweet. Strong too. Beat me at the high striker. I don't know. I just really like being with her."

"Well, that's great. Please keep me posted. And please remember, you always have a home here. I worry about you."

Hal hung up and smiled, Bonnie still on his mind. After a moment, it suddenly occurred to him that he'd forgotten all about the appearance of Ms. Infinity.

6. A Hero's Secrets

On their second date, Bonnie and Hal went to the Queens Zoo. Again, it was daytime. They held hands and talked as they walked the past the various animals' habitats. They took a special interest in the aviary, with its winding metal path, which led up and down around the attraction. As they stopped on a high point watching birds go by, the topic of careers came up.

"I don't really know right now," said Bonnie, "I have an associate's degree from LaGuardia Community College, here in Queens. I think about going back to school. I don't really know what I'll go for though."

"What is your interest in?" asked Hal.

"I have given some thought to social work. Well, my mom has talked about that more than I have, but I see the point to it. It's great that she thinks about the greater good. So do I. Why wouldn't I?"

Hal smiled, looking truly interested. "That's nice to hear. Not enough people think that way."

"I just wish she weren't driving my decisions so much, you know?"

"Well, yeah. You are an adult."

"I'm sure you wouldn't like it if your parents were doing that to you."

"Sure. That's not really my issue though. I have a bachelor's–"

"I mean," interrupted Bonnie, "I can see why she would say that. I do care a lot about the public interest. I just don't know. Where exactly are my talents best applied?"

"I know what you mean, but it can be hard to find work. You see, I have a degree–"

"And anyway, there are so many different professions that are about the public good. Teaching, medicine, law. Where do I fit in?"

"Bonnie?"

"Yes, Hal?"

"You are fascinating. I really like you."

"Well, thank you."

"So he seems like a good listener," said Lisa. "That's not too surprising or anything, but it's good."

Bonnie and Julia were sitting in Lisa's room. It was much neater than Bonnie's, and showing somewhat more maturity, with paintings hanging rather than posters. A picture of herself with Bonnie sat prominently on her desk.

"He is that," said Bonnie, "and I appreciate it."

"Yeah. You appreciate his looks," quipped Julia.

"Hey," said Lisa, "you know what? Appreciate that you're dating. Lately I haven't–"

"He told me about his family," interrupted Bonnie, "Not too chatty, but sweet."

"Sweet to look at," said Julia. "I bet you were behind him the whole time."

"Oh, you stop it!" said Bonnie. "You are so bad. I don't mind listening to him though. He was interested when I talked about my career stuff."

"Sure," said Lisa, "I see that. But look, for me I'm not even–"

"–And that's all good," interrupted Bonnie again, "but you know, he doesn't ask a whole lot of questions. I sometimes wish he did. It makes me wonder if he's not interested. But at least he doesn't interrupt a whole lot either."

Lisa thought that was an odd comment. Knowing Bonnie, a man who didn't ask too many questions should be right up her alley. Of course, interrupting was often her department.

"Big question," said Julia. "Good kisser?"

"Oh, do I have to?" laughed Bonnie.

"Hey! We want to know," said Julia. "I mean, you have to be picky, right? Bad kisser, and I'm out. You know what I'm saying. Right, Lisa?"

"Honestly, Julia, right now I don't even have–"

"I'm happy," interrupted Bonnie once again. "Does that answer your question?"

"So, do you want to keep going with him?" asked Lisa.

"I think I do," answered Bonnie.

"Lisa has to study now!" called a voice from the other room. A small woman came in.

"Hi, Mrs. L.," said Bonnie.

"Don't any of you girls you recognize an entire last name?"

"Umm, sorry about that. Hi Mrs. Lin."

"I was kidding. You can call me 'Mrs. L.,' or Tracy even. You are adults. Tell your mother I said hi."

"Yeah, adults," said Lisa to Julia under her breath. "Good to hear it said, anyway."

"See you at work tomorrow," said Bonnie.

"Yeah. See you at work tomorrow, Bonnie," said Lisa. "Don't forget the deodorant, Stinky!"

Upon Lisa's arrival at work the next day, she was called over by Denny.

"I have a receipt from yesterday," he said. "You checked out a customer from someone's line during a rush. You missed some of the items in his order. When the security guard checked the receipt, there was a major discrepancy."

"Really?" said Lisa. "Nothing remotely like this has ever happened to me in three years on the job."

"Now listen, sweetie, this might be hard on you, but it is your responsibility to make sure to scan every item on every order. Now the customer might have been trying to shoplift, but you need to be on the ball. There were seven items you never scanned."

Lisa looked at the receipt. It was not remotely familiar. However, it did bear her name. "I don't recognize this," she insisted.

"You were signed in. You are being written up for this. Consider this your second warning."

"Bonnie," said Lisa as she returned to the customer service desk, "I don't know what to do any more."

"Stop your whining," shouted Bobbi, who was now being relieved by Lisa.

"Nice to see you Bobbi," said Lisa sarcastically. Bonnie looked away in disgust, eyes rolling.

"You two don't understand men," Bobbi said. "Instead of being afraid of him, you have to use your charms on him. That's how it has worked since the beginning of time. It's never going to change."

"Let me understand then," interjected Bonnie, "you're saying she should flirt with him?"

"He's a man. They all think with their little heads. That's all they understand. You just have to figure out how to work it."

"You know what?" said Bonnie, "I'd rather just work my job. What do you think, Lisa?"

"Exactly," said Lisa.

"Yeah," said Bobbi with a huff. "Modern women. You try to impress people, saying you're all liberated and stuff. You know nothing. Sooner or later, you'll learn."

Bobbi left. Bonnie gave a look of relief, like she was just released from a long and arduous lecture.

"About that receipt," said Bonnie, "can I see it?"

Lisa handed Bonnie the receipt. Bonnie looked it over, then showed it to Lisa. "I have a question. Do you recognize the time on here?"

Lisa glanced at the time stamp, then gasped. "I was on break!"

"I guessed it was that. Now, did you remember to sign out?"

"I always do. I'm extremely cautious about that."

"Alright. I believe you. So how else would someone know your login and PIN? Not even the supervisor gets that."

Lisa and Bonnie thought for a minute. Then they looked at each other with a sudden cognizance. "The cameras!" shouted Lisa.

"So, it has to have something to so with security," said Bonnie.

"But why would it? Security has nothing to do directly with this department. And they watch everybody, don't they? I mean, even Denny's only supposed to get a casual look at the cameras to catch us slacking off."

"Don't be so sure. Who is to say someone isn't abusing the system? Surveillance is the kind of power that is very easily abused."

Lisa gave Bonnie a knowing look. "Do you know something?"

Bonnie demurred, "I wish I could say."

Something in Bonnie's eyes told Lisa that there was more to the story. She was also finding her earlier reaction to Bobbi interesting. She looked her friend squarely in the eye. "Bonnie," she asked in a simple, straightforward tone, "do you think Bobbi could be part of this?"

Bonnie looked at Lisa and said simply, "Yes I do."

Lisa paused a second, then looked her again in the eye, "You're pretty sure about that, right?"

Bonnie looked back and once again said simply, "Yes."

"Nothing we can prove though, is it?"

"No."

"Thank you," said Lisa.

"The important thing is that someone is abusing the system," said Bonnie. "That receipt is evidence."

"And you know what? I think I've seen the last straw. Are you with me? I want to finally take care of this problem today. If this was an accident of some kind, then fine. We should simply straighten it out. But then if Denny did something on purpose, then it may come down to confronting him. What do you say, Bonnie?"

"Do you know exactly how you plan to do it?"

"I'm not sure. To tell you the truth, I don't really know where to start. You know what? You can help me plan it. So, are you with me?"

"Sure!"

"Alright!" said Lisa, "This is our project."

Bonnie noticed that Hal had left his register to talk to a small child. He was on his knees, talking to the girl at her eye level.

"What are you doing?" asked Bonnie.

"Hi, Bonnie," replied Hal. "This big girl is showing me what she has in her purse." He handed her back the toy mirror she had just given to him.

"Hal," said Bonnie, "please don't leave the register unless someone relieves you."

"Oh," replied Hal contritely, "Sorry."

Just then, an attractive woman walked by, tall and dark with glasses. As soon as Hal saw her, he began to stare. Bonnie rolled her eyes in annoyance.

"Hey Bonnie," whispered Hal, "you don't think…"

"Of course I think," said Bonnie. "I always think. I'm not always sure about you, though."

"No. No. That woman. Doesn't she look like Ms. Infinity? You know, in a different outfit. Do you think that might be her in her secret identity?"

"Hal, you really have to get over this already. I'm tired of hearing about this obsession of yours."

Lisa marveled at the scene in front of her. It was a strange situation, the kind only Bonnie could get into. After Bonnie stormed away from Hal, she decided it was time to step in.

"Hal," she said, "can we talk a minute?"

"Sure," answered Hal.

"The thing is, I really think Bonnie doesn't want to hear about your crush."

"Oh! I guess it is bad manners. You're right. That was pretty bad of me. I should apologize to her."

"You know what?" said Maria as she walked up, "You have split shifts today, right? Why don't you leave for now? We're covered here, and it's almost time for you to go."

"Yeah. Thanks," said Hal. "I did want to talk to Bonnie about a number of things."

At that moment Bonnie's super senses picked up something strange from a great distance in outer space. It wasn't another asteroid, but it was something amiss. She quietly snuck up to the roof of the garage to take a look. Not understanding what she was doing, Hal followed a little bit behind.

"Damn!" said Bonnie to herself as she scanned the sky. She saw a giant meteor shower, and large waves of antimatter, clearly originating from an unnatural source. There was little doubt about who had sent them. It was also clear that there would be more. "Misery is sending this from a long way," she said to herself. "I'm not exactly ready, but…"

She sighed. "Alright. No choice. I have to deal with this."

First, she tried to call her mother. There was no answer. It was almost three o'clock, and her office hours would begin soon. Under the circumstances, she decided not to leave a voice mail. Instead, she texted her a code message they had agreed on: "missyou."

"Well, no use waiting for Mom," said Bonnie to herself, "I have to change and deal with Misery, once and for all."

Hal reached the roof of the garage just in time to hear Bonnie finish talking to herself. She was clearly distracted, looking up in the air for some reason. He was about to say hello, but then something extraordinary happened. She began to transform.

It only took two or three seconds, but in the freeze-frame unreality of the moment, it seemed like more. Bonnie said the cryptic words, "Infinite Power." Then there was a small explosion, and right before his eyes, her entire being changed. When the smoke cleared, she had grown by nearly a foot. Her face and body had reshaped. Her clothes had morphed into the famous costume of the superheroine. Hal gasped at what he had just witnessed. It couldn't be, but it was. He had just discovered that the woman he was dating was really a figure of legend, the superhero of his dreams. Bonnie Boring had just changed into Ms. Infinity!

Ms. Infinity gasped as she looked at the stunned Hal in front of her. "Hal!" she shouted.

"Oh my god!" shouted Hal, "It's you! She's you! You're her! Bonnie! You're..."

"Oh no," said Ms. Infinity, her blood pressure reaching a sudden crescendo, "Hal! No! I...Hal! You can't ever tell anybody what you just saw!"

"Wow! I won't! I promise Bon...uh, Ms. Infinity? I...don't know what to say! I mean, I'm sorry! I had no idea!"

Ms. Infinity's nerves died down as she watched Hal,

clearly as innocent, and well-meaning as ever. "Listen Hal," she said, "I have an emergency to deal with. I know this was an accident, but we have to handle this situation."

"Umm…wow! I…I just can't believe this. Wow! Bonnie? I had no idea it was you. Did you know how much I idolize you?"

"Thank you, Hal. Wow. But Hal, I mean it! You really can't tell anyone! And I don't know about you walking around like that. You really have to calm down. Maybe I can take you home. Can you make an excuse and punch out?"

"I did just punch out. I'm on split shifts. Is it possible…?"

"Pardon?"

"Do you think I could come with you?"

"You know what?" said Ms. Infinity, "Let me take you out of here first, then we can discuss it. This could be a big one."

With that, Ms. Infinity scooped Hal up in her arms and flew away.

Back at customer service, Lisa waited for Bonnie to return. As she watched the door to the parking garage, it soon became clear that her friend would not. She sighed and shook her head, resigning herself to another one of those inevitable frustrating days.

"Alright Bonnie," she said under her breath, "I get it. This is just how it must be. Fine, but I'm not waiting. This thing is my project alone."

7. Starship Infinity

Hal looked back at the roof as it rapidly disappeared from view. He was enthralled, if a bit frightened, to be flying with Ms. Infinity. After a minute, he turned to her and spoke.

"May I ask a question?"

"You just did," said Ms. Infinity.

"What? Oh…"

"What is it, Hal?"

"Where are we going?"

"Well, for you, nothing is decided yet. But at least for myself, there's a villain who has been dogging me. Her name is Misery. I have to handle several of her threats. I've also decided to deal with her in person."

"So that's where?"

"In space."

"Space?"

"Yes."

"Um…Okay," said Hal. "Another question…"

"Yes Hal," said Ms. Infinity.

"Since you're going into space, and you might take me with you…"

"Yes?"

"Were you planning to take a spaceship?"

"Oh."

"I'm pretty sure you can fly to distant planets just as is, but you know, I'm human. I need to breathe and stuff."

"It's okay, Hal. I'm bringing a spaceship. It's a long trip and I want to be comfortable."

Ms. Infinity then landed with Hal on a high rooftop in Midtown. As Hal looked out around the city and beyond, the superhero produced her cellphone, apparently from her cape. "I just have to try something," she said. She made another attempt to call her mother on her cellphone, but there was no answer.

"So, Ms. Infinity," said Hal, "I'm sorry about before. I just assumed you put glasses on or something."

"Oh, Hal," said Ms. Infinity warmly, "never mind that. That is not your fault. I can transform myself, and if I'm going to do that, then obviously I don't want to be recognized. Clearly I should not be upset with you if you did not recognize me."

Hal was even more awed with his crush than before. Yet he was having a hard time assimilating the new information he'd been confronted with. He was especially confused and disturbed about the woman he had increasingly strong feelings for, and thought he knew. So, was Bonnie simply a disguise? Was the woman he was dating just a form that Ms. Infinity changed into to fit in? Was he falling for a made-up person? Who was she really?

"Listen Hal," said Ms. Infinity, "this may not be the mission you want to go on. It could be dangerous. I don't think Misery is too much for me to handle, but one never knows. Yes, there is a spaceship, and I have worked to make it a comfortable one, but I'm not certain exactly how long this might take. Do you still want to go?"

Hal might have been overwhelmed by the day's events. Or perhaps he saw an opportunity to live a dream. Either way, he did not seem to think much of the warnings given to him by Ms. Infinity at that moment. All he said was, "Of course I do."

"Very well then," said Ms. Infinity. "Off we go!"

She picked him up and flew into the clouds, extremely fast. Hal might have expected the experience to be very frightening. Yet somehow in her arms, he felt not only safe, but even comfortable.

In fact, it was a wondrous thing, experiencing Ms. Infinity's flight. She held him in her arms in front of her, and as he looked out to see ahead, he saw and felt things he had never imagined. He felt his heart racing as they passed through the clouds. A moment later they were high above them, and beyond was only the deep blue sky. He felt the wind of the stratosphere, strangely gentle as he was caressed in her arms. That should have been a mighty blast. In fact, as he looked out and listened, he could discern that it was every bit as powerful as he'd imagined. Yet he seemed somehow sheltered. The clouds seemed to race beneath them, and the wind roared like a hurricane that was somehow outside of them in every direction. It was like a dream, yet even more fantastic. It was perhaps even better than he could ever have imagined. Put simply, it was magic.

The flight lasted only a minute or two, until they came to a remote place in the mountains. She placed him down on a cliff.

Hal looked around for a minute, shivering, then turned to Ms. Infinity and asked, "We were flying really fast. I didn't see where we were going. Where are we? The Catskills? The Berkshires?"

"The Himalayas."

"Oh."

"You see," said Ms. Infinity, "we have to be somewhere very remote. I need a lot of room. I'm about to call my ship, and it's a big one."

It was time to call Starship Infinity, which was hovering at the ready at the dark side of the Moon. This was technically the ship that she and her mother had arrived in years ago, but now it was vastly improved. It was now many, many times bigger, and indeed changed in countless other ways; altogether it was a very different vessel from the ship that had once landed on Rockaway Beach. This being her "Infinity Powers Project," she had given it an overhaul that was truly superhuman in scale. It was a tremendous creation in every way, a heroic expression of her many powers, as well as the product of many hours of time and sweat.

Many of the additions on the ship had made use of what she called her "power of creation." Technically it was transformation. She could not make something out of nothing. This power could also not be used to create life where there was no life, nor even organic materials such as food.

This might have seemed like effortless magic to an onlooker, but it was far more complex than that. It was a skill that she had to develop and perfect with endless practice. Indeed, with this as with all of her powers, she was always stretching herself beyond her limits. So it is with anyone who possesses a tremendous natural talent. Becoming truly skilled still requires dedication and devotion. And this was an extremely difficult craft. Even creating a seemingly simple object required tremendous concentration and discipline, as well as endless attention to detail. Far from making a wish and snapping her fingers, she had to make thousands, even millions of miniscule decisions in the space of a split second.

"How do you like my spaceship?" asked Ms. Infinity.

Hal looked, but could not figure out what she was talking about. There did not seem to be anything in front of him except the same great expanse of air that was there before. After a few seconds, he looked back and said, "Where?"

"Ah, sorry," she said, "let me open it up."

With a wave of her hand, a narrow, dark crevice opened up in the air directly in front of him. At least, it seemed dark at first. But as he peered inside, he could faintly see through a long, narrow hallway that there was a room inside.

"Go on," said Ms. Infinity, "let's go inside."

Hal had been amazed before, but nothing could have prepared him for what he saw when he stepped aboard Starship Infinity. It looked nothing like a spaceship. It came closer to a futuristic mansion. He entered into a great hall, essentially a tremendous atrium. The room was brightly lit, and nearly big enough to be a parking lot. It was beautifully furnished, with large leather couches, swiveling chairs, and coffee tables. The ceiling toward the end of the room was extremely high. In fact, he could not be sure just how high it was. There were doorways in every direction. He could only guess where they might lead. One of them seemed to be a kitchen. Another, if he could see properly, and if his eyes didn't deceive him, might have contained a hot tub.

"Here it is," said Ms. Infinity, "Starship Infinity! So please make yourself comfortable. Explore a little bit, but don't get lost. I'll be back in a few minutes."

"Where are you going?"

"I have to stock the fridge."

She flew away, and Hal again felt bewildered. He began to explore, though he stayed close to the main hall for fear of getting lost. There was indeed a large, full kitchen, several luxuriant bathrooms, and at least one bedroom. There was also a den with a large entertainment center. Many other hallways yet remained unexplored.

After a few minutes, Ms. Infinity returned with many canvas bags full of groceries. It was a surprisingly awkward sight. Though she clearly was not struggling with the weight, the bulkiness made it a little hard to maneuver. She actually looked a bit comical carrying the load.

"Listen Hal," she said, "I'm having second thoughts about this. I don't want to make you a prisoner. Are you absolutely sure you want to come? I can still take you home. I do trust you to keep my secret."

"This place is amazing!" shouted Hal. "So this thing is yours?"

"Yes. I'm glad you like it."

"Please! Please take me with you! This is a once in a lifetime opportunity that may never come again. Please! I promise I won't get in the way."

"Alright. It will be fun to have you along."

"Oh! I have to call work."

"Oh, don't worry. I took care of that."

"Really?"

"Yes. I promise. It's fine."

"This thing is amazing. I mean, this is a spaceship with how many rooms, and a full kitchen and bathrooms. I'm relieved that there are bathrooms."

"Well of course. Powers or no, I'm still a living creature. I need to breathe, eat, sleep, pee and poop just like you. What did you think?"

Hal blushed. "I… guess I didn't know."

"It's time to take off. I'm going to the bridge. Speaking of eating, it's already the afternoon, and I have barely eaten all day. Why don't you go to the kitchen and make us something? I bought a pretty good supply of groceries."

"Oh!"

As Hal grabbed the grocery bags and took them into the kitchen, he noticed the ship lifting off. He was amazed at how smooth the ride was. They were going extremely fast, how fast he dared not imagine. Within a few seconds the Earth was in full view from the kitchen window. Soon it was disappearing into the distance. The movement looked rather like an old science fiction movie, or maybe even a cartoon. Yet it barely felt like they were moving at all.

He began to go through the groceries, looking for perishables to put away and trying to figure out what to make. He noticed that she had done her shopping back at The Big Box; several of the canned goods bore the store brand. He marveled once again at how quickly she had flown halfway around the world and back.

Unfortunately, the selection did not offer much. It was mainly microwave meals, with a number of canned vegetables mixed in. There were also a couple of cartons of eggs and some jugs of spring water, some coffee, tea, and milk. Not much to work with.

The kitchen was certainly nice enough. It had all stainless steel appliances, including a tremendous refrigerator with a built-in water filter and ice maker, a beautiful electric stove, a large sink, and an espresso machine. It seemed a shame there wasn't more food to work with.

The inevitable thought came to him about what the guys would think if they saw him now. There would certainly be insinuations of emasculation, and he might never live it down. Or maybe that would not be the case, considering the woman he was cooking for.

But Hal liked cooking. It was something he took pride

in, one of his small, daily pleasures. He relished the thought of cooking for a woman he admired, or indeed for anyone besides an alcoholic roommate who left the table looking like a war zone. He wished he could do some real cooking, rather than putting together a kid's lunch.

Hal tried to think of what to make. What did she eat, anyway? At first it seemed a crazy thought: What to cook for Ms. Infinity, Earth's Greatest Hero? But it suddenly occurred to him that he did know Bonnie Boring, and he had indeed seen her eat lunch. That could not have been an effort at disguise.

At any rate, Bonnie's lunch was almost always the same thing: Two hard boiled eggs, with canned asparagus thrown in, uncut. She would usually squeeze a couple of ketchup and mayonnaise packets in, and call it a meal. It seemed like a half-hearted effort. Could that really be all the world's most powerful woman could do?

There wasn't really much to cook anyway, so he made Bonnie's usual lunch. He varied it by cutting the asparagus and eggs and mixing the dressings beforehand. It looked somewhat more civilized. For himself, he scrambled a couple of eggs and opened a can of carrots. Then he called, "Mealtime!" Suddenly there she was beside him.

"So!" said Ms. Infinity, "what have we got?"

"I made this for you," said Hal. "More or less the same lunch I always see you with, but I thought I'd give it a little more attention, if that's alright. There aren't a lot of choices here…"

"That's so sweet! Thank you! My goodness. What a man! Thank you, Hal."

"You're welcome," said Hal, surprised that such a powerful woman would be impressed by such a small deed.

"This is very thoughtful of you," she said warmly.

"There isn't a lot to work with. If you'd brought a few rolls, I might have reworked this and made you a hero."

"Pardon me?" she said, "*You* would make *me* a hero?"

Hal was momentarily confused at the answer. Then he realized the misunderstanding. "I mean a hero sandwich. You know, what some people call grinders, or wedges, or subs, like submarine sandwiches."

"I know. We're New Yorkers. That's our local dialect. I was just playing with you." She began to hum something, though Hal could not identify it.

"What is that?" asked Hal.

"You know," giggled Ms. Infinity, "'Yellow Submarine.'"

"We have a song by that name by The Beatles, but…"

"I know. That's the song." She then began to sing the refrain, though "sing" might be a generous description of what she did. She got the words right, but she accomplished only a passing resemblance to the melody. The result was not much more tuneful than a school bell.

"Wow," said Hal, looking with a curious amazement.

"What is it?"

"There *is* something you can't do!"

"You don't like my singing?" said Ms. Infinity.

Hal looked at Ms. Infinity, and saw the wounded look on her face. To his surprise and alarm, he saw that he had hurt her feelings.

"Oh! Listen," he said, "I admire you. I revere you. The last thing I ever want to do is hurt you or bring you down…"

"…Because I can't sing."

"I'm sorry," said Hal, "It doesn't bother me. You know I think the world of you."

"You're right," said Ms. Infinity, her head in her arms in a sulking position, "I'm a lousy singer."

"And so what? So you're not perfect. Big deal. Singing isn't required for a superhero anyway. You're expected to do things like fly, and lift huge boulders, and save people. You can do all that and much more. Look. I was only surprised because it always seemed to me that that you can do just about anything. I mean, it's right there in your name."

"You think I can do anything?" said Ms. Infinity. "That's sweet. Wrong, but sweet."

"I can't think of anything else you can't do."

"I can't accept an expired coupon."

"Well, right. I suppose that's something we have in common."

"Alright Hal," said Ms. Infinity, "I'm sorry I got so upset, but I want you to think about something else now. Maybe I overreacted. Okay, I definitely overreacted. But you should never forget your own part here. Are you so surprised that you can say something that affects me? What you say matters. What you do matters. You are part of my world, and I'm part of your world."

"I am sorry," he said.

"Not the point," answered Ms. Infinity, pointing at him in a whimsical tone, "Just remember that you have power too. Use it wisely."

"Well, thank you," said Hal, blushing.

"You know what? Never mind singing. Let's dance!"

Then with a clap of her hands, music started playing. She grabbed his hand and flew him nearly to the ceiling and began to dance with him.

"I've never believed men should always lead in dancing. What about you, Hal?"

"Well, sure. I agree," shouted Hal, "But can you understand something?"

"What?"

"This is a little hard for me up here. Remember, I can't fly."

"What?"

"I can't fly!"

"Oh! Right. Gravity off!"

As the song played the pair danced in various creative, impossible choreographies. They did backflips, front flips, and slide flips. They kicked sideways in opposite directions. They held on to each other while turning dizzily in every possible direction. Clearly Ms. Infinity had the advantage, since she could dive down and back up again with little effort. Hal still had to push off of the wall or ceiling to move, and when he did, he moved awkwardly. He was glad she was leading.

Either way, it was a thrill. Between the energy of the music, the freedom of being in the air, and most of all, the joy of being together, away from outside interference, both companions were having the time of their lives. Hal was still confused as to who this woman really was. For now, though, he could put that concern aside and enjoy the ride.

When the song ended, the gravity switched back on, and Ms. Infinity flew Hal back down to the floor. Both of them were laughing.

"What a rush!" shouted Ms. Infinity.

"I don't dance much," said Hal, "But I've definitely never danced like that before!"

"You can cross that off your bucket list! I'd love to continue talking, but I've got to watch the bridge."

"I'll follow you in a moment," said Hal. He hoped to clean up, since the table looked like a war zone.

"You do that. Why don't you make some coffee? I'll have an iced latte, decaf, with skim milk. In a moment, I'm going to have to handle the first of those threats. After that, I'll explain what's going on. And maybe we can continue getting acquainted."

"Not a bad idea. I thought I was getting to know you pretty well, but right now, it's looking like I barely know anything."

8. A Hero's Tale

"I shouldn't be more than a few minutes," said Ms. Infinity to Hal, "You can come and watch me from the bridge."

"So, you don't want your latte yet?" asked Hal.

"Oh. Thanks. Just leave that here in the atrium, on the coffee table. I will now be handling the first of Misery's threats. The thing is, I don't think she really gets me if she thought that I couldn't stop this."

"Doesn't get you? I don't really have a clear idea of your power levels myself. I mean, for all I know, you might be able to turn the entire universe inside out. So is she vaporizing the entire galaxy and challenging you to reshape the whole thing with your powers, or is she just throwing some foam balls around and trying to pass it off as the apocalypse?"

"Neither. This is just a meteor shower. It ordinarily would not be much cause for concern. Most meteors burn up upon hitting the atmosphere. But there are so many in this cluster, and they are going at an extreme velocity. I can also see that many of them are tremendously dense…"

"You can see that?"

"Sure. I'm looking at some of them right now."

"How?" asked Hal in wide-eyed amazement, "You're not even looking out the window!"

"Well, no. I can see through things."

"Wow! That's awesome. So, I take it these walls are not made of lead?"

"I'm sorry. Why should that matter?"

"I…I don't know. Never mind."

"Anyway, this shouldn't be much for me. I just need to work up an opposing force that's big enough to knock it off course, and send it away from Earth's neighborhood."

Hal listened in awe. *Just a meteor shower indeed*, he thought. He loved the way she made it sound like something she simply knocked off, like an email.

"So," she continued, "you can watch if you want. The window over at the bridge should be the best view."

Ms. Infinity flew up to the heights of the atrium, seeming to disappear through an unknown exit. Hal wondered exactly how that worked; it was almost as if she faded into the ceiling. He ran to the bridge, then looked outward to see the heroine's super feats. Sure enough, there she was outside. She was flying around in outer space without a spacesuit, just in her usual costume, as easily as swimming underwater at a city pool.

Then she blew a great wind. Now he was blindsided. He could only imagine how she could pull off such a feat! Then she flew in circles, quickly reaching a speed so intense that she was rendered invisible. All Hal saw was a giant cyclone, a very strange sight for outer space.

Then he noticed the meteor shower. It was a majestic, if frightening sight. There were many, many rocks moving in a huge cluster at a tremendous speed. There was something eerie about the sight of so many objects moving together in isolation. They reminded him of a stampede of horses running in the darkness, but they were silent in the void of space, and much, much faster.

The meteors had been a considerable distance away; how far he could not measure. Hundreds of thousands of miles, he guessed. Maybe millions? Yet Ms. Infinity seemed undaunted by the scope of the thing. He wondered to himself: how fast could she fly? How great a distance could she cover in a short time? She had taken him halfway across the Earth in a minute or two without breaking a sweat. Could she reach speeds even greater than that? Could she fly to distant planets in minutes...or seconds?

Suddenly the meteor shower was sucked up into the vortex of the great cyclone, piece by piece. It was a strange and tremendous sight. It almost looked like the storm was devouring the great rocks. Then the cyclone turned, seeming to jerk around like a power cord when it was tripped on. All at once, the cyclone disappeared, and the meteors flew in the opposite direction.

"So, what do you think?" asked a sudden voice behind him. It was Ms. Infinity, already back and seeming to live up to her title.

"I think," stuttered Hal, "I think I have never seen anything like that in my life! I mean, how? That looked impossible! I would have thought that was against the all the laws of physics!"

"Oh yeah, laws of physics. I like to think of those as guidelines."

"Wow! You really are amazing!"

Ms. Infinity smiled. "Nah. Just a little thing."

Their eyes met. She looked at him invitingly, as if looking for a kiss.

"Wow," said Hal, "I've never met anyone like you before."

"Yeah," she answered. "You try that, Mr. High Striker."

Hal was stopped in his tracks. His face showed shock and disappointment. He looked away.

Collecting her thoughts, Ms. Infinity tried her best to save face. "So, I'll just take care of a few things now..."

Soon the companions were sitting together in the atrium, in swiveling chairs by a coffee table. Ms. Infinity was sipping her iced latte, while Hal had an iced tea.

"So Hal," said Ms. Infinity, "I wanted to tell you my story."

"I would be honored to hear it," said Hal.

"First there is something I want to clear up. I have heard various people elevate me to the level of a goddess. In fact, I even once heard you use that word. Let me state right now: No. I am not a god, goddess, anything of the sort.

"Where I come from, they have a state religion. They enforce it on the entire planet. In theory, it's about awe for a higher being, the creator of all things. However, the reality is that it's about worshiping the political leaders. It's not said in so many words. In fact, I didn't appreciate it until after I left. It took distance and time until I could look back and really appreciate that situation for what it was. And now that I understand that, it is something that disturbs me in a big way. It's very dangerous when people are worshipped like that.

"And you know, when I came to Earth, I was actually surprised at the human conceptions of the Creator. I mean, the fact that there are so many of them, the concept that there could be more than one answer. I didn't get it at first, but when it did hit me, I nearly crashed into an asteroid!"

"Really?"

"Joking. Joking. I was at home. But the whole concept really astounded and fascinated me. This is actually something I admire about humanity, that there is this question asked about the Creator. I think it's great that there are so many different religions. So many different possible answers, and that makes the discussion that much richer. It's a shame that these differences so often have to lead to war. It's also sad that religion is so often used as a pretext for oppressive politics in other ways. Religion can and should be a beautiful thing."

Hal smiled. Her naiveté was disarming, and her viewpoint no less wise for it.

"You know," she continued, "it's something I particularly love about our country too. In America there is no state religion. Each of us worships as we please, and it's none of the government's business.

"It's part of the pluralism that the country is founded on. Being American can mean coming from any culture. Whoever you are, if you're American, you're American, no culture more than any other. I mean, think of it. I'm American, and I'm not even from Earth.

"Anyway, don't ever mistake me for more than I am. Just because I have a bunch of fancy powers, that does not make me a god, or any closer to the Creator than you are. Let's be clear on this: I am a living creature. That is to say, someone like you, who has been created; not the Creator. So please, don't bow to me. You might spill my latte."

"Got it," answered Hal. "I'll stop using the 'goddess' tag."

"Thank you. So now the big story, that being me. By now you must have gathered that I'm from another planet. Now its name I cannot say, because its language is something that simply cannot work with human ears. It doesn't even use sound. It involves the transfer of energy along a dimensional plane that humans cannot perceive. But its name translates to Center, as in 'Center of the Universe'."

"Wow! So, you're from the center of the universe?"

"Well, that's the thing. No. No it's not. Not remotely.

How could it be? It's a planet. It's not even the center of its own solar system. But the propaganda machine has everyone convinced that it is. And maybe the political leaders believe it too. I don't know."

"So then, what do I refer to you as, you know, besides generically 'alien'? You know, what would you call someone who comes from your planet?"

"Good question. I never know what to call myself. Since I had to give it a simple English name, there isn't the fancy science fiction-y name that other planets might have in a similar situation. So what am I? 'Centerian'? Or else I could be 'Beaconian'. The other name of the planet is that of the country that has now taken over the whole world. It translates to 'Beacon of Freedom'."

"Beacon of Freedom?" said Hal, eyes narrowed incredulously.

"Yes."

"Let me guess. Dictatorship?"

Ms. Infinity looked at Hal with a mixture of annoyance and amusement. "And have you been there?"

"Uh…no."

"Actually, you're right," she said with a smile, "Total dictatorship.

"But before I start trashing the place, I should add that there are many good people there. I'll go as far as to say that most people there are decent, and in fact there were some whom I may not have survived without. However, I seriously doubt any such people are in charge.

"These are people with great powers, relative to humans, as well as – if you will understand – a certain type of intelligence that humans don't possess. And their primary use of it is to conquer and subjugate people who are weaker. They have colonized many planets and exploited many other life forms.

"Look. 'Beacon of Freedom' does have meaning. Growing up there, I heard the many tales of our War of Independence. Our people once lived under an oppressive foreign leader. He was overthrown, and the nation started anew, becoming a powerful new light of liberty and justice. And so, we spread our message to every other country on the planet, and every other planet within flying distance.

"My mom remembers when it wasn't so bad. She knew a time when there were still working institutions with purposes other than spying on the public or, more to the point, keeping the current president in power. She talks about times when there was still some belief in its ideology, its purpose.

"But there was a junta not long after I was born. Apparently, the military was on the forefront of a reform movement, or so it seemed. It promised to fix some problems that were going on, some injustices. My mom knows the details of that. She used to tell a number of stories from that period. Anyway, the whole thing became nothing but a military government very fast, and all I remember is a life of oppression.

"If you ask me, this is a society that values power over everything else. Pretty much every leader will tell you that he is the champion of freedom, a man of the little people. Of course he does. It's always what the public wants to hear. But it is just hollow talk. In practice, there is nothing but contempt for things like equality, and more so for individual rights. I would say that the primary value is for blind loyalty, but that would not account for the sheer number of times the presidency has changed hands, always by assassination."

"That's sad to hear," Hal said. "I always wondered how they get away with saying they're about freedom when they're obviously the opposite."

Ms. Infinity laughed grimly. "Well Hal, it's done on Earth too. You can have a whole system of laws, and even a constitution that on paper seems to be about fairness and liberty. But there are many ways of getting around it.

"Besides fixed elections, well, you can even use laws. For instance, there are many laws that are ridiculously strict, but they'll only enforce them selectively. You know there's a grudge at work when suddenly laws pop up out of nowhere that you didn't even know existed. It's a kind of persecution, often used when someone is saying the wrong things against the wrong person. The real goal is hiding something embarrassing to someone in power."

"Oh," said Hal, beginning to feel a little overwhelmed.

"Then we have the cultural element of this society. You see, this world is also an extreme patriarchy. Females are treated like property, and not given the most basic rights. It's so extreme that some girls' names show absolute misogyny. Sure, many human female names convey weakness, but at least there is usually some beauty to go with it. There are some female names on Center that convey nothing but contempt. 'Misery' — that is as the name translates — is not named that because she's a supervillain. It's actually a fairly common name there for females."

"What name were you born with?"

Ms. Infinity sighed. "The name I was born with was better than many, I think because my mother intervened. It translated to 'Bland Beauty'. Considering the culture, it was actually almost a compliment."

"Wait a minute! Your name, Bon…"

"Yes. You're right. Bonnie Boring. My Earth name means essentially the same thing. That was my mother's doing. She wanted us to continue being ourselves on Earth, and keep our real names, though they had to be adapted to human language. My mom's name translated to 'Bland Homemaker', so she became Betty Boring. Betty is a variation of Elizabeth, or it could also be Beth, which comes from the Hebrew for 'house'."

"So, you really are Bonnie. I mean, you didn't just make her up…"

"Oh Hal, of course not! Did you think I was just pretending to be Bonnie Boring? No. Bonnie is who I really am. The girl you've been dating is for real, I promise."

"That's a relief. As exciting as this identity is…"

"Aw, thanks. But yes. This – Ms. Infinity – is what is made up. I'm really Bonnie."

A name such as Bland Beauty was more powerful than Hal might have realized. It was the sum of all the expectations for a person from birth onwards. One expected it to have a tremendous amount of influence on a person's character. Yet Bland Beauty proved to be the rare Centerian who seemed all-but immune to the consequences of her name. A rebellious spirit was in her from the start. This was one thing about her that was truly remarkable, and it portended more surprises.

"Anyway," she continued, "living in this society was not a whole lot of fun for me, because as it turned out, I'm a prodigy. Not to toot my horn, but my abilities turned out to be exceptional. As time went on, it became clear that I was the strongest, fastest, altogether most powerful person around. And there that was a problem, since I was a girl."

She paused. There was an uncomfortable look on her face, as if an unpleasant topic had come up. After a moment, she continued, now more tentatively.

"So, after a while, I had to leave. I had to find

somewhere else to go. I escaped with my mother to a distant planet, meaning Earth."

Hal thought a moment. "I'm thinking of our first date," he said, "I remember you mentioned you live with your mother. So, she's an alien like you?"

"Yes. Another 'Centerian', or 'Beaconian', or whatever we are. I never said much about her on our two dates. She's a physics professor at City College. You know, Lisa calls her 'Mrs. B.,' which is not technically correct since–"

"Wait! What about Lisa?"

"Well, no. She's not an alien. She's not a superhero either. Not unless you mean Captain Obvious."

"But does she know?"

Ms. Infinity gave Hal a sly look. "No, Hal. As of now, you are the only human who knows my secret identity. Otherwise, I keep it between me and Mom."

"Hmmm," said Hal, trying to hold back a self-satisfied look.

Ms. Infinity hesitated a moment, then went on. "Alright. So, we make it to Earth. And since then, my mom has always been quick to remind me how fortunate we are. She always talks about our responsibility to those less fortunate. And the reality is that nearly everyone is that. So..."

"That made you decide to become a superhero?"

"Well, my mom does things differently. She has not created any separate identity. She does things quietly behind the scenes. She can be so subtle that nobody will even know that this invisible hand was at work. She privately likes to call herself the 'Guerilla Public Servant'. That's actually a thing. A guerrilla public servant is someone who fixes local problems secretly, but my mom is that with superpowers. You might know some of her work. Remember how they used to call

Queens Boulevard the 'Boulevard of Death'? You know, *used to*."

"Wow! Really? So does she float over it all day or what?"

"I'm kidding. Well, partly kidding. She used to do it that way sometimes. But she's also civically involved. She goes to a lot of community board meetings and is active in local affairs. So she was involved in the effort to make safety improvements, the way any citizen might be. But then, the city gets some credit there too, as do a number of citizens. She has stopped her share of accidents though.

"Anyway, for me…" she smiled and looked wryly at Hal, "I read a few comic books, and I thought to myself, 'Yeah. I could do that!'"

"Really? Just like that?"

She was enjoying the discussion more and more, and her energy built up as she continued. "The name, 'Ms. Infinity'… I suppose you were right when you said that something in the name suggests omnipotence, and maybe it's a little bit of hubris. Like I said, I'm far from omnipotent, although I understand why it might seem that way. My mom is constantly reminding me not to think of my powers as infinite, but then I had to go and name myself that anyway. I'm funny like that. But you know something? It often seems that many of these heroes in the comics make much the same claim and fall much shorter."

Hal wasn't quite sure whether to react with amazement or laughter. After looking at her for a moment with raised eyebrows, he finally replied, "Oh really?"

Ms. Infinity laughed. "Okay. That was a little over the top. I admit it. Actually, if anything, I don't know what to think with some of them. You know, sometimes the creators seem to be guilty of a little hyperbole. But then, if I were writing this stuff, I'm not sure I'd do better."

"How do you mean?" asked Hal.

"Well look at it this way. They'll have a character who might have a defined set of powers, but then how often does it seem like the writers are suddenly making up powers just for the convenience of the story?"

"Like when?"

"Just a second. Is your chair a little wobbly?"

"Oh. Yeah. I guess just a little."

"Yeah, mine too. Give me a second."

Ms. Infinity closed her eyes for a few seconds, as if concentrating. Then she opened them and said, "There! Is that better?"

"Uh, yeah, actually," said Hal. "What did you just do?"

"Nothing much. I just rearranged the universe slightly. Now, what were we talking about?"

"I don't remember…"

In fact, Bonnie Boring didn't read a few comic books. She read hundreds of them, maybe thousands. She collected them voraciously, with stacks in her room, and many more in the attic. Betty seemed annoyed by the clutter, but then many a time, Bonnie caught her mother reading some herself.

It was only natural that Bonnie would love the superhero genre. After all, this was the literature about people like her, near as could be anyway. True, they sometimes showed many false perceptions, but this she could find forgivable. She was much more frustrated at the scarcity of female superheroes, and even more angered at the way the few females were portrayed. Yet she was a staunch supporter of the few published titles she really loved.

For a time, she tried to find a community on the internet, first on the chat rooms, then on the social networks. Yet she was always frustrated by the "trolls," and more generally by misogynistic sentiments that often dominated the discussions. By no means did they represent everyone, but there were enough to make it an unpleasant experience. It didn't take long before she decided she'd had enough.

Before becoming a costumed superhero herself, she tested the waters by visiting the New York Comic Con wearing a costume. She went as an obscure superheroine that had long since been discontinued, but amazingly there were many people who recognized the character. She found herself mildly annoyed by the leering, but she could not deny that the overall attention was something that she really enjoyed. Between posing for pictures with fans, high fiving with young girls, and pretending to perform super feats, she had the time of her life. She had not felt that alive in a long time. The whole day, she fought the temptation to use her powers.

When it was over, she finally slipped away, and flew far into the clouds. She felt euphoric. Never before had she been more herself than in that moment. Suddenly she knew in her heart that this was who she was, and that in that discovery lay something tremendous and important that she needed to do. Why settle for "cosplay" when you can do the real thing!

For some time, Ms. Infinity worked the bridge controls while Hal attended to the kitchen. After a while, she returned. "So Hal, if you don't mind hearing more, we never really talked about Misery."

"I wouldn't mind hearing about her," said Hal.

"I didn't know her growing up. I started to see her around shortly before I left. When she did appear, things went from bad to worse on my end. I haven't exactly been up on the politics of Center since I left, but this much I know: she is a shill for people in power, but at heart she is a bully. She's ruthless when it serves her. It seems to me that the leaders are comfortable with a strong female, as long as they think they can control her. Anyway, I'm not sure exactly what her game is. She probably is after me."

"Oh," said Hal, looking very apprehensive. Something in this story seemed off. It seemed to him that there was more to this than she was telling.

"Now don't worry," said Ms. Infinity, moving in closer, "I can handle her."

Seeming not to notice her tone or intention, Hal asked, "Do you need help? I mean, you seemed to run into this very fast. Do you want to talk about this? Maybe I can help you plan."

"Oh Hal, dear, don't worry yourself about this. This is my mission. You just sit back and watch, and enjoy yourself."

"Something occurred to me. Just how far are we going? I mean, are we going to your native planet? How far is that?"

"Oh, no! Of course not. Center is many billions of light years from Earth. I'd never get home in time to watch Stephen Colbert. No, I scoped it out. Misery is operating from a space station in relative proximity, right here in our own galaxy. Just sixty thousand light years."

Hal's face nearly turned white. "What? Sixty thousand light years? I don't even have one light year to spare! I didn't know I'd be dying in space!"

"Calm down. This isn't one of your NASA rockets. If we operated the way human technology did, then yes. It would take more time than human civilization has existed. But I have other ways. Trust me when I tell you that you will not be away from home long at all."

She touched his shoulder amorously. "Now you know who I am. I can take care of you. Don't worry about a thing. You're in my power here."

Their eyes met. She was clearly making another advance on him, but Hal demurred once again. He nervously looked away.

She struggled to compose herself. Then stepping back, she spoke again. "I'm glad you brought it up though. There are some more things to take care of. First, I have to handle the waves of antimatter. Then there's the next stage of the journey. You see, now that we've cleared the solar system, we're ready to go express. This will take some manipulations that you will definitely not be used to. So be warned. This ride is about to get bumpy."

9. Store Rules

In the deepest regions of The Big Box, Lisa had just been called to the office of Yvonne, the store manager. She waited outside in the hall for a few minutes, wondering what could possibly have prompted the call. The crowd noises of the store were slightly distant, the many complaints and conversations all coalescing into one mass; the soundtrack in this region of the store was dominated by the Muzak. Standing on a hard white floor, she leaned against a marble wall, next to a picture of the founder of the Big Box chain. From there, she looked outward at the back of the sales floor, watching guys from a distance, occasionally finding a good looking one to ogle, but it was hard to keep her mind off her troubles.

It was unusual to be called to the store manager. Was she in that much trouble for the earlier incident, or was there something else? Lisa was nervous but determined to move forward with her own concerns. Maybe this could be an opportunity.

The door opened. A tall woman was behind it. "Hello Lisa," she said. "Come on in, and please close the door."

Lisa entered. The office was fairly large, even a bit luxuriant. It was carpeted, with a large desk of finished wood toward the back. Behind it a wide window looked out toward the urban landscape, largely dominated by train tracks. There was also a bookshelf on the side, with several hardcover books on the subject of management.

Yvonne gestured to Lisa. "Sit down, please."

"I'm glad you called me in," said Lisa, "I had something to speak to you about too."

"Do you know why you're here?"

"I don't know exactly."

"Well, we had a bad quarter, and we cannot continue like we have been. I have made the decision to crack down on things that we might have let go before. Often, it's many small things that are the cause of larger problems. So do you know what this is about?"

"Umm, I might. Is it alright if I ask you what it is?"

"Alright, but in the future, I hope you are more on the ball. Now a few minutes ago, Denny was watching you on the camera, and he noticed that you were checking out Bonnie's order. Now I happen to know that the two of you are best friends. When she was hired, you agreed that she would be treated as though she were family, so you would not check her out. Remember that this is a conflict of interest."

This was a rule that some stores had, that cashiers could not check out family members. It could also extend to close friends. The fear was that the employee might be tempted to help steal or discount items. Nonetheless it was a fairly minor rule, and not usually something a store manager would be likely to get directly involved in.

"Oh! I am sorry about that! Bonnie did kind of pressure me."

"I see. I might have to talk to her too."

"You know what? Blame it on me."

"That's beside the point. You both really should have known better. What was your excuse?"

Lisa clearly realized she had said the wrong thing. She hadn't meant to get Bonnie in trouble too. She had tried to tell her not to use the customer service desk, but at that moment, it had been the only place without a long line. Bonnie had obviously needed to hurry out for some unspoken reason. She'd tried to be nonchalant about it, but her eyes had suggested that the world depended on it. Or maybe she had a guy waiting. Or…considering the circumstances, Lisa wondered if maybe it was both. Be that as it may, Lisa was typically "on the ball" in case the matter did come up.

"Anyway," Lisa said, "I thought it might be that. I actually have a copy of the receipt."

"You do? Why didn't you say so before?"

"I'm sorry. I couldn't be sure."

"Alright Lisa, let me see the receipt."

She handed Yvonne the receipt. "I assure you there are no irregularities."

Yvonne read through the paper for a moment and laughed grimly. "Well, that depends on what you mean. Maybe she hasn't stolen anything, but she sure seems to eat like a high school kid."

"Yeah, I know," laughed Lisa, "I've stayed over. If Mrs. B. isn't around, I insist on ordering in."

"Mrs. B.?"

"Mrs. Boring, Bonnie's mother."

"Whatever. By the way, Denny also caught you texting right after that. You're far from the only offender, but let me remind you, no texting on the job."

"I really don't. There was kind of an emergency…"

"So they all say. Okay. I'll make another copy of the receipt. I'll just talk to Bonnie about it next time she's in. Is that tomorrow?"

"Yes. Tomorrow morning. So, listen. There is something else I wanted to discuss…"

"It will have to wait."

"It is important. It's a problem…"

"Mention it to your supervisor. I'm very busy here. Have you seen Hal? I need to speak to him as well."

"He left. He's on split shifts."

"Fine. I'll talk to him later too. I'm expecting him back on time. That's another thing I hope all of you remember. No more latecomers. I expect Hal on time. No excuses. Nothing short of an alien abduction should keep him from arriving back here on time."

Lisa reacted with a silent, wide-eyed look of worry. Misinterpreting it, Yvonne shot at her, "Yes, Lisa. That means you too."

"Believe me," said Lisa in an injured tone, "I do know that. I'm nothing if not punctual. Four years here should have shown you that." She began to leave, frustrated and worried. But then she turned back one more time.

"You know, I think you may really want to hear–"

"Your supervisor!" said Yvonne abruptly.

Lisa returned to the customer service desk, frustrated and angry. Maria looked at her compassionately. "So," she asked, "what was that about?"

"Denny caught me on the camera," said Lisa. "I wasn't supposed to check out Bonnie before. There's that conflict-of-interest thing."

Maria's face showed a look of dread. "Wow. He had to really dig deep. Hey. It means you're a good worker. Take heart."

"Thanks. But why does Yvonne care so much?"

"Oh, she's on a kick about catching small things. I think Denny promised to crack down. That's his whole thing. He's 'Mister Discipline'. He got me too. For me it was wasting plastic bags, and not smiling enough."

"What is all this about? Why do they feel a need to nitpick on the people on the lowest rung of the ladder?"

"That's how it's done, babe. They pick on you because they can."

Denny was clearly picking and choosing whom to "nitpick," based on his own biases. Yet while his vendetta against Lisa was recent, the problems between Denny and Maria ran much deeper. There were several reasons for this, but one had to do with his promotion. Both had been up for the position of Front End Manager at the same time. Maria had the advantage of being already in the department while Denny had worked in Electronics.

More importantly, during the period when the powers-that-be had made their selection, the two candidates worked in very different methods. Maria was ever efficient, faithful, dutiful, and above all, a team player. She would also go out of her way to bow to the needs of management. By contrast, Denny was a bully even then. He did everything he could to sabotage Maria, from interrupting her at meetings, to purposely ruining her work, to starting cruel rumors about her.

Yvonne could not have been entirely oblivious to his actions, but she found his style appealing. His aggressive nature seemed to support his promise to bring discipline. Even now, months after he had prevailed over Maria, he still resented her even more than she resented him. Perhaps he was afraid that she knew his true nature. Lisa knew the story as well as anyone. With Bonnie gone, and Yvonne refusing to listen, Lisa now hoped that Maria would be a useful ally.

"So what do we do about it?" asked Lisa. "It's awful. They should pick on the people who really screw up. I'm getting really sick of working here."

"Oh honey, welcome to the real world. You can't let these kinds of things bother you so much. It's just work."

"And how do you handle it?"

"Well, these people may be more powerful than you, but they're still just people. They might be able to make your life difficult. The worst ones can really put you through the wringer. But just remember that they're just as human as you."

"But I still don't see why you would stand for this treatment. C'mon Maria. We have to do something."

"My dear Lisa, I appreciate what you're trying to say, but it's not as simple as you think. Believe me, I have my own notions too of what should be done here, but I also have kids to support. They know that. Again, that's why they are able to mess with me. Honey, welcome to the work world."

"I guess I understand. But why do they do this to us anyway?"

"Honey, this is how they show power. Most of them aren't as mean as Denny. I've had good managers too. Yvonne isn't so bad. I think she's just a little out of touch. She has her reasons for leaning on Denny right now. Didn't she mention to you that the store had a bad quarter?"

"Yeah. She did say that."

"Well, the way it's explained to me, she believes this is addressing the central problem at the source."

"And what problem is that?" asked Lisa.

Maria raised her eyebrows. "Poor employee morale," she said.

"Well," said Lisa, "if nothing else, she has found the problem."

"Oh! She's right on the money."

10. Hyperspace

Ms. Infinity stood at the bridge once again with Hal, now preparing for her next action.

"So in a moment," she said, "I'm going to fly out into the antimatter. Watch if you like, but it might not be easy for you to follow."

"Oh," replied Hal. "So I take it you have a plan."

"The thing is, this isn't simple like stopping a meteor shower. Sending gigantic waves of antimatter to Earth is actually a very destructive action. It may be hard for you to visualize this. I mean, these are the actions of superhumans. But think of it as the equivalent of detonating a few nuclear bombs. You see how it might keep me slightly on my toes. Anyway, I have to put a little more effort into this intervention."

"Oh…"

"I've figured it out now. This is the thing though. I don't think I can quite explain it to you. It means working in many different dimensions."

"How do you mean?"

"Hal, humans think in three dimensions, at least thinking spatially. If you count time, then I guess there's a fourth. How do I put this? There are a lot more than that. People from my planet are able to work with twenty or so, depending on how you count."

"Depending on how you count?"

"Well, there are some arguments as to what qualifies as a dimension, especially when you get into the high teens, but there's no way I'm getting that argument through to you."

"Okay, just get this down enough so I can get some idea of what's going on."

"Look," said Ms. Infinity. "Antimatter in quantities this great is dangerous. I have to get rid of it. And the goal is to get it to the nearest black hole."

"Okay," said Hal, "sounds peachy so far, but as far as I know there aren't any in the solar system. Or at least I hope there aren't."

"Well, no. Not nearby the way you understand. Not spatially."

"Not spatially? What other way is there?"

"There's no way to explain this to you."

"No way?"

"No way."

"All I'm getting is that you have some other cosmic route."

Ms. Infinity laughed grimly. "I guess if it helps you to think of it that way. The thing is, I have to do some fancy footwork to make this happen. I just have to find a few strategically placed black holes, nothing too big."

"Oh no? So, what is a black hole to you anyway?"

"Don't be silly. That's not how I meant it. Look, I have my limits, and a black hole would be the end of me too. I'm talking relatively here. I'm not going into black holes. I'm just sending most of the antimatter into them. What little is left will actually be useful for the next stage of our journey. Now the trick to moving it, that's the hardest part. Basically, I have to use my body to attract it, then fly out of the way at the crucial moment."

Hal did his best to follow. "I see. Now maybe I'm misunderstanding, but I don't get how you could bullfight this stuff away. I remember vaguely hearing what Einstein said about antimatter and relativity. I mean, I did alright in science, and I do remember that antimatter was predicted from the theory of relativity. Right? There was the negative square root..."

Ms. Infinity looked at Hal endearingly. "Look Hal, I give your Albert Einstein credit. He did pretty well for a human when it came to grasping the basics of these dynamics. But he was only human, and he had the same limitations you do. You can only understand what your brain allows you to understand. Look, try to get your dog to play a video game and you'll get the idea."

"I don't have a dog."

"Well, right. Even harder."

"Oh," said Hal, now feeling utterly overwhelmed. He was also not much liking the comparison to a dog.

"So, I'd better do this now. You can watch, but it might get confusing. It won't even be exactly like super speed. This time, well with a human mind, I'd expect that your very definitions of time and space could get mixed up. The object from the future might be the past of the anti-object, and that's just getting started. I'm not even sure your eyes could follow it."

"Like whack-a-mole?"

"Sure. I can put one of those into the rec room later if you want. Just remind me."

"No, I mean...Oh never mind. I'll...I'll try to watch."

Ms. Infinity disappeared out through the atrium ceiling once again. Looking outside, Hal saw the target. It was a strangely beautiful sight, a tremendous splatter of violet and other colors. He first saw her flying through space towards it. But then she was flying away from it. Then she seemed to disappear.

The splashes of color flickered in all manners. They seemed to suddenly get bigger and smaller without warning. She reappeared, but only for a split second. Then it seemed there were two of her, or more. His eyes were too confused by the constant flicker to tell. She might have been all over the place.

The images continued to become more unpredictable. Hal wondered if he should look away for his own sanity, but he couldn't. He was so fascinated, that he found himself glued. Increasingly the images of Ms. Infinity seemed to distort, intermittently becoming like a kaleidoscope of patterns that competed with the antimatter.

As Hal watched the weirdness unfold, he started wondering just who she really was. Yes, her name was Bonnie Boring, but just what sort of alien was she? She seemed increasingly remote now as he watched her. Indeed, judging by this odd game of space chicken, she must be a powerful being indeed. And if she could change her form, then what did she truly look like?

The vision reached a disturbing crescendo, the various splatters and splashes intensifying suddenly into a great flash that encompassed all he saw. And then all seemed to freeze. He was terrified. Did time stop? But then Ms. Infinity was behind him.

"Alright," she said.

"So," said Hal, "It worked?"

"Yes."

"So then, the antimatter is on its way?"

"No. This isn't spatial. It doesn't work that way."

"What way?"

"There is no way."

"No way?"

"Enough. You're just not going to get this, Hal. I'm sorry."

"Fine," said Hal, "But you owe me a whack-a-mole."

It was now time for the next stage of the journey. Hal was feeling some apprehension, since it was clear that this was going to be uncomfortable, and much would happen that he would not be able to understand.

As he looked on, the heroine quietly rambled off a checklist. Though she was ostensibly running through routine maintenance issues, some of the items sounded bizarre. At some points, she was looking at various gauges and indicators, but at other times she seemed to be talking into the air.

"Velocity is picking up, nearing 500 million miles per second. Time set to remain in the range of twenty minutes. Not reaching infinity yet but will add one when we do." She looked at Hal and smiled, "That's a joke."

"Oh," he said, trying to be amused.

"No undue galactic ink stain or discolored coin bounce. Carpets remain unliquidated…"

Hal listened, but soon was utterly lost. After a while he broke in, "So should I be doing something right now?"

"Not this second. Actually, have you used the bathroom? Now is the time."

"Alright, but…"

"Soon you're not going to be able to go anywhere, so I would go now."

"How about you, do you need…?"

"I'm fine."

As Hal washed up, he felt increasingly nervous. Just what was he in for now? Maybe Ms. Infinity had been right when she warned him that this might be too much for him.

When he returned, the superhero instructed him to sit down.

"So, Hal," she began, "This is where we have to get into more complex maneuvers. If we're ever going to make it in enough time, I have to work once again in many different dimensions. Now please bear with me. I don't mean to be condescending when I say this. But again, humans like yourself work within three, or in a way, four dimensions if you count time.

My people are like you in that we go forward in time in the same way. I can't time travel, although I am experimenting with a time manipulation of a different kind. Anyway, we do work with a good number more than three dimensions. I have to move us through dimensional planes that you won't understand; it's just not within human range of understanding."

"So, like, is this a wormhole?

"Uh… no. It's not a wormhole. If you need a semi-familiar word, I guess you could get away with calling it hyperspace. I've seen that word in science fiction, and I guess this more or less applies. We'll call it 'hyperspace'. But this is not exactly like anything that exists in human science. I've heard some vague conceptualizations, but…you know what? There's no time for talk. I have to get us moving."

She touched a few controls, and then seemed to move her arms aimlessly in the air. Suddenly the ship jerked upward. Or at least it seemed to be upward, relative to the floor. But then, there didn't seem to be a floor. Then Hal saw something truly disturbing: himself.

It was him from a few seconds earlier, asking the same questions that he had been. He was not reacting to the current him. Then that vision was gone, and he fell. Or was that falling? He didn't seem to be going anywhere. But there was some unexplained sensation of movement. Then he saw two selves: the one he saw before and the one looking at the one from before, but they were down below him – no, next to – no, inside? He gasped. It seemed he could not even define directions or dimensions.

More strange sensations followed. Again he seemed to be moving, but he could not explain where or how. He saw a growing number of his selves increasingly looking like a chain of undefined mass. He tried to close his eyes, but he still saw everything. There was no escape. They were everywhere. Or he was everywhere.

He tried desperately to understand what he saw and heard and felt. Had time stopped? Was he in a loop? But try as he might, he could not make sense of it. And the rationalizations were useless, since nothing could stop the bizarre sights, sounds, or feelings. So much was happening to him, in him, of him. Even simply understanding himself was impossible.

The sensations continued for what seemed like an eternity. Or was it no time at all? He had no idea. Time was now something outside him. Everything seemed to move impossibly fast yet also be frozen all at once. But it was more than that. Even he was everywhere and nowhere at once, or not at once—all times, and no times. It was exhausting to try to understand it, but he could not turn it off. He felt sick, violently sick.

Then he felt something or someone tugging on his arm, and he heard a voice. He saw a face, perfectly defined, right in front of him. It was Ms. Infinity. "It's okay Hal," she said gently. "I've got you."

"I'm sick!" cried Hal.

"Hold on a moment, I'll take care of it."

A second later he felt better. "Thanks," he said.

"Listen," said Ms. Infinity, "Try to keep your head… I can't keep holding on to you the whole time."

She let go, and he began to feel even more odd sensations. Suddenly he lost control of his movements. He seemed to jerk forward violently. It was if he was pulled out into another reality. Not that he could define it at all. His first thought was to wonder what was different from before, but that question proved useless. In fact, he didn't know where he was. There was nothing anywhere that he could identify. It was worse than that. He couldn't even figure out what was where, or up from down, or in any way make sense of the information in front of him.

Then without warning, it was over, and he felt as if he was being dragged backwards into darkness. Worse than darkness: a complete void. There was no light, no sound. Now he wondered if his eyes were closed. But now he was trapped even more profoundly than the reality that had made him ill. He could not even feel his eyes, ears, his body at all. Was he dead?

He was in a deep and penetrating panic. Where was he? Could Ms. Infinity hear him? Hear what? He couldn't even speak! There was nothing, no him at all. Or was there? He was thinking, right? So, he must still be, somehow. After a torturously long time wondering if he was alive or dead, he suddenly felt a huge stir; his body was there again. Then it seemed as if a light had been turned on. He tried to scream but could not make a sound.

He found himself back on the ship. Was he awake? He seemed to be falling repeatedly from the ceiling to the floor, like an endlessly looped video. Then it stopped, and for a split second, he was face to face with…something. He couldn't say what. He wasn't sure if he exactly saw anything, but he was certain something was there in front of him, and it was terrifying. He wanted to cry out, but again, no sound came. Then he felt as if he was pulled backwards, with the falling vision reversed.

The vision faded, or in fact it turned into something even stranger. It became less and less of a vision, and more and more a complex reality, with sight now intermingled with sound, and sound intermingled with touch, and all senses intermingled with something much more complex. Was it time? Was it space? He was not even sure if those distinctions mattered now.

The reality became increasingly complex, encompassing more and more aspects. Then it seemed to take him over. It seemed like he was not merely in the situation, but of it. He was intermingled, by body and mind.

Increasingly he lost understanding, not only of the outside but even himself. Was he even there? He felt undefined, stretched out over many, many directions he could not name. He hardly seemed to have any significance at all. Was there even a him? Did he mean anything? It seemed like he was nothing but a nameless and faceless stretch of material, just an amorphous part of an endless continuum. It took a great strength of will just to remember that he existed at all.

It might have been like that forever, it might have been not at all, but at some point, it finally came to a head. There was an abrupt and intense feeling of awakening, an explosion of being. Then he felt a tremendous sensation of falling, but he suddenly realized he was back in his seat, hyperventilating and sweating hard.

After a minute, he caught his breath. He was still flustered, but he could just summon up enough presence of mind to turn to Ms. Infinity and to ask her, "Is it over?"

"Yes" she replied, "until the trip back. I think you need a rest."

Ms. Infinity gently picked Hal up from his seat and flew him into a bedroom. Like the rest of the ship, it was luxuriant. It contained a king-sized bed, track lighting, and a flat screen TV. She descended, then put him down on the bed and said, "You rest now."

Hal was barely coherent. "Am I back? Am I alive? Who am I?"

"You're Hal, Hal Holstein, just like before. You're here with me, Ms. Infinity…" After a moment, she shook her head and smiled, then said gently, "You know, it's me, Bonnie."

"I…mean…I know, but…I… it doesn't make sense anymore. I can barely even feel myself. Will I ever be the same?"

"Yes honey, I promise. You're already getting better. I can see it. You'll be back to yourself in no time. Just rest."

"I don't know. Something's not right. Something in my senses…Everything looks okay…"

"Don't worry Hal," she said tentatively. "There's nothing much…"

"No! Something is off. I can feel it in the air. No strange sounds…."

"It's nothing…"

"Something…I don't know…You know what? I think it's something I smell, but…"

"I farted! All right? I'm sorry."

"Oh." Hal was silent for a moment. "You know something? Lisa was right about you."

"No, Hal. She's the one with the stinky farts. I have the B.O."

"You might want to rethink that."

"Oh no!" said Ms. Infinity, "I just thought of something."

"Is something wrong?" asked Hal.

"Not here, but back when I did my grocery shopping at The Big Box, I made a horrible mistake. Oh no. I shouldn't have used customer service to check out. You know…"

"Right. Right. With Lisa, there's that…"

"It's the one line with no candy! Now I'm light years away from home and I already need a chocolate fix."

"Oh."

"You don't have any candy, do you?"

"Sorry. I didn't plan for this…"

"It's alright. Not your fault. I think it's time you rested. Good night."

"Good night."

Ms. Infinity turned out the light and left. Yet as exhausted as Hal was, he was having trouble sleeping. The experience he had just had was disturbing, and brought up uncomfortable, existential questions. He struggled to think of simple, comforting things.

Throughout her teen years, school had frustrated Bonnie Boring endlessly. For someone with superhuman intelligence, she achieved amazingly low grades. Like so many "gifted" youths, she was bored by the structure and lack of challenges that her classes provided. She was often rude to her teachers, and frequently failed to show up to class. Lisa's influence helped to keep her grounded slightly. She might not have inspired her to love school, but at least her friend convinced her not to drop out.

Her mother was called in many times by the school for unpleasant discussions with teachers and administration. And indeed, Betty was not one to take her daughter's behaviors lightly. She herself was working her way through school at the same time, eventually achieving a PhD so she could become a physics professor. There were many volatile nights and loud arguments between mother and daughter. Betty was determined to get through to Bonnie, if not by example, then by sheer force of will. But somehow, she could not convince her daughter of the need for academic achievement.

Nothing embodied Bonnie's frustration more than science. After all, many of the principles taught by Earth's teachers were things that she knew or believed to be false. She herself could easily defy many of the supposed laws of physics, so acquiescing to them in classwork seemed very disingenuous. Betty would tell her that this should not bother her. If these theories were true for humans, then they were relevant to their lives on Earth. If anything, these were truths that she needed to understand: truths that were eye opening and mind broadening. However, this line of thinking moved her little.

History and English were more interesting to her. She truly wanted to learn the stories of the world she now belonged to. Yet in her experience, she had also learned a deep cynicism for the narratives given by historians. And anyway, she could finish her work very quickly. Here as well as everywhere, the dearth of challenges was fatal to her success.

Nonetheless, she did ultimately agree to attend college, after much arm-twisting from her mother. She attended nearby LaGuardia Community College, the only certain option available to her after her dismal performance in high school. Here she did at least learn the skill of doing enough to suffice, if not distinguish herself. She achieved her associate's degree after two years. She then went on to do virtually nothing of importance, at least in the conventional world of academia and careers.

And so, a young woman of tremendous ability became an underachiever. It is sometimes so with people of high intelligence. They slip through the cracks. They never discover the challenges and opportunities that suit them, and so their talents are wasted. That frustration was with her all the time. If she seemed arrogant at times, she was also expressing a hidden anger. Behind her smugness was the deep disappointment of someone who simply could not fit in.

11. Behind Every Great Hero...

On the campus of City College, a young man stood outside the office of Professor Boring, waiting for her office hours to begin. He wasn't sure when it was appropriate to knock. "2:59" read his watch. *I'll wait one minute*, he thought. But then about thirty seconds later, doubt struck again. *Should I knock?* he wondered. Before he could make up his mind, the professor arrived behind him.

"Hi Scott," said Betty warmly. "Could you please wait a moment?"

"Oh, sure," said Scott, befuddled.

Betty went into her office and closed the door. After a minute or so, the door opened. "Come on inside, dear."

In the intersection immediately outside, a driver wiped the sweat off his brow. Somehow, he had just barely missed being hit by a truck as he turned. Remarkably, the truck had stopped in the nick of time.

"I'm sorry, Scott," explained Betty as they sat down, "I had to fix a few quick things around the office. I just came from a long and noisy faculty meeting. It seemed like you could hear it from space." The thought that it could also distract superhuman senses from disturbances in space did not occur to her. She failed to notice her cellphone in her bag, carrying a missed call from her daughter, and a text message reading, "missyou."

"That's okay, Professor Boring," said Scott.

"I know my name has become a joke all over this

school. 'Whatever you do, don't end up with Professor Boring'."

"Then they don't know what they're missing."

"Aw, thanks," said Betty. "So, what can I help you with?"

"I really just don't get anything from this book," said Scott. "Physics scares the hell out of me. I'm no Einstein."

Betty looked at her student endearingly. "Well Scott, I give our Albert Einstein credit. We wouldn't be where we are now without him, for better or for worse. But here's a little secret: genius though he was, so is every one of us. Each of us has wonderful and unique talents. And besides, you can learn anything if you put your mind to it."

Scott looked at Betty and smiled bashfully. "Do you really think so?"

"Of course! Besides, this is mostly high school physics done over. This is a thing with our freshmen. We're finding out that many of our students haven't learned all they need to know to be prepared for college."

"Yeah. I never learned any of this stuff."

"Well, that's quite alright. Don't be intimidated by all this. At this point we're just using basic formulas. We're still neglecting friction."

"That doesn't sound very nice to friction."

"That's cute. Listen, why don't you open the book and we'll go over it."

Scott looked in his bag, and then looked up. "Oh, wait. I left it just outside your office. I was reading it to try and get ready for this meeting. Give me a second."

Scott stepped outside and reached for his book. Meanwhile, in a building down the block, a painter narrowly avoided falling off the window ledge when, by coincidence, his foot got caught in the window. Betty missed a second call from Bonnie.

"Okay," said Scott, "got it. These things are expensive. A hundred and ninety bucks!"

"I know," said Betty. "It's very unfair to low-income students. Listen, if you need assistance..."

"Ah, that's alright. Thanks, professor."

"Any time. You know what? Why don't you tell me about yourself first? What do you do when you're not in school?"

"Well, I have to work. I have a job at a factory."

"That's great. What do you do there?"

"Shipping. I have to pack and send pencils. Sometimes there's paintbrushes in there too."

"So, it sounds like you have to do a lot of lifting."

"Yeah. Sometimes it gets pretty heavy."

Betty looked at Scott and smiled. "It's hard work. I don't doubt it. And a long day of it, right?"

"Very."

"I wish more people appreciated it. Have you ever heard of an 'invisible hand'?"

"No, I haven't," said Scott.

"The thing is," said Betty, "usually when you hear it, they are talking about economics: the 'Invisible Hand of the Market'. The logic being that everything takes care of itself if we leave things alone. It's almost as if to say that the money does the work for us. But I disagree. Do you feel like money does the work for you?"

Scott was finding the professor confusing to talk to, but

he felt he could answer this question. "Well, no," he said, "I work for money."

"Right," said Betty, "you're doing the work. People do the work. The real invisible hands belong to people like you who work hard and get no appreciation for it. Without you, there is no money for the people you work for. There are many invisible hands which make things possible. You know that without the privilege of wealthy parents and powerful connections, it's hard to climb that ladder. Those are also invisible hands, the things that are about privilege, behind the scenes matters that can be the difference between making it and not making it."

"Oh, yeah. I don't know what I've got there."

"Yeah. It's not fair," said Betty sadly. For a moment, she stared into space. "Sad, but some things cannot be amended. There are many hard truths that are out of reach forever. The past, can't change the past…"

"You okay, professor?"

"Oh!" said Betty, snapping back to attention. "Okay, maybe you cannot help where you come from. That's not to say there isn't hope for you, though. Knowledge is power, and that is why we are here."

"Well, I like to think so."

"So, here's where you remember the science. Physics is another kind of invisible hand. It's with you whether you realize it or not. In a way, each of these concepts, like momentum and energy, are all here around us. They are always here. That's why we never really notice them. Sort of like the air you breathe. But each of them is also changeable. If you change one part of them, the whole thing changes."

"Okay. So how does that help with the subject?"

"Every time you move, you transfer energy. That also

applies when you move an object such as a box. So, you could think of that as 'work'. When you pick up a box, we measure it by the force you put to it, times the distance it travels. Does that make sense? Each of them, we measure, just like measuring someone at the doctor, right? You're pretty tall, right?"

"Six feet."

"Wow! You have a whole foot on me. But you can measure things like force too, and distance. If either one of those numbers changes, then work changes. And you measure the whole thing by multiplying."

"So, it's math?"

"Yes, dear. Once you get each concept, it's all about following the formulas. It's just plugging in the numbers. You replace the letters with the numbers given…"

After a few minutes, Scott began to catch up with the concepts. But suddenly, Betty heard a strange and ominous sound. "Tell you what," she said, "why don't you practice for a few minutes. There are some practice problems at the end of the chapter. I'll be back in a few minutes."

There was a major derailment on the Sixth Avenue subway line, some ninety blocks downtown. On an intersecting rail, the signal had failed, and the operator of the train had accidentally passed, and was now on a collision course with the derailed train. Betty could hear the panic in the train operator's voice. If the Guerilla Public Servant did not intervene immediately, lives would be at stake. Betty slipped into the ladies' room. Then she became invisible and flew downtown at super speed.

She flew invisibly into the subway at the Rockefeller Center station at such a speed that commuters assumed they were being treated to a breeze. Then she flew down through the mezzanine, across the platform area, and along the tracks.

There before her was a stopped "F" train. Just a few yards away was an "M" train, about to collide. Invisibly holding her feet to the track floor, she held her arms against the oncoming train. With immense, super powered exertion, she brought it to a stop, an example of "work" that might have been instructional, had it not been both invisible and secret. It was also a noisy job, enough to drown out even to superhuman senses the distant perturbation of a meteor shower clearing.

Exiting the ladies' room, Professor Boring returned to her office and saw Scott beginning to pack up.

"Thank you so much, professor," he said. "You were a big help."

"Any time," she replied.

"By the way, your cellphone rang a few times."

Betty looked and saw a few missed calls from Bonnie. Then she saw a couple of texts, particularly the code message from Bonnie. It was almost half an hour old. She tried to keep her face from turning white.

"Listen, Scott," she said. "I'm not feeling too well right now. Can you tell any of your classmates you happen to meet that I had to go home?"

"Sure professor. Feel better."

"Thanks, Scott."

Betty slipped quietly into the stairway and turned herself invisible once again. She flew out through the door onto the roof, and across Manhattan, the East River, and into Queens. Finally, outside The Big Box, she peered inside. Lisa was there, among others, but Bonnie was gone. She must have taken off on her mission by herself.

Into space Betty flew, faster than human imagination.

There, just outside Earth's orbit, she saw the vapor trail. Bonnie must have taken their ship and flown into space. Betty flew on, following the trail, determined to catch her daughter.

Did Bonnie really know what she was up against? She was certainly sure of herself the other day. But now she was going into a battle, far from her help. There were so many things that she did not know, things that should have been said. Maybe it wasn't too late!

Some distance past Jupiter, she saw the remains of the meteor shower. Past the end of the solar system, there were signs of leftover antimatter. Then the vapor trail ended. This could mean one thing. She had gone into very deep space, and needed to use many different dimensional planes. She could not follow her any farther.

Her daughter was now alone, facing a dangerous enemy. Indeed, it was even worse than it sounded. Bonnie was her first love, and she would do anything to protect her. Yet if she were to fail now — the thought was unthinkable — but if she were, Betty's protection might well have been the cause of her downfall.

From the day she was born, Betty Boring was one who shunned attention. She loved to do for others. Yet she never took credit, nor wanted it. It wasn't just unselfishness. Attention made her uncomfortable. Her own life was a closed topic that she never wanted to discuss. It was just in her makeup.

It was part of what made her so effective; she was a superb listener. She was always more interested in talking about the person she was talking to than herself. Just as she was now, so she always had been. She might make an inconsequential joke about her name or her height, but that was virtually all. Betty was always approachable, kind, warm, and completely silent about herself.

Maybe it was something in her birth name. "Bland Homemaker," as it translated, was a safe appellation if there ever was one. This was a necessity in a time and place when female names had to be safe; in that culture it was actually a compliment. A boldly named female was certain to be shunned. Like most people of her culture, she understood the consequences of her name; it was the expression of the expectations that would always be upon her. And she had little choice but to follow the script that was given to her. She led the life that a woman was expected to lead, that of a homemaker, a mother, and also a wife. If she was uncomfortable with any one of those roles, indeed if there was something in her that was profoundly dissonant with a role that she played, then the more reason to be silent.

Yet Betty shared something with her daughter, and for that matter, also her mother. She was, by nature, tremendously powerful. Like them, she possessed strength, speed, and many other powers that were far greater than anyone else. It was something in her bloodline, the origin of which was the subject of many private legends.

Yet unlike her mother and her daughter, she kept her powers secret. She used one of their unique powers, invisibility, as her cloak. This was but one way that she kept her actions quiet. She would develop many subtleties, many ways of operating that none could detect. And so, she was content to be unknown, her actions taken as happenstance when they were noticed at all.

Friends and acquaintances on Earth might not have known the secret of Betty's powers, or her true origin. Still, many guessed other things about her, even things she never told. They would respectfully give her space, figuring that private details were hers to disclose if she chose to. Yet there were also certain unusual things that stood out. For one thing, one might surmise that she was a woman of many deep, unspoken regrets. It was there in her bearing, her manner. There was something too in her speech. If one listened, there was a fascination with tyranny, with abuses of power. If one listened very carefully for an extended time, she might reveal something more specific. There was also a deep-seated determination to right an unspoken wrong, though in some way it seemed that it was eternally out of reach.

But never would she tell the specifics. There were things she simply never discussed, even with her daughter. There were memories that she would not share, mistakes from her youth that could not be recalled. Once upon a time, decisions in her life could rest upon her romantic notions of progress and reform, and on trust in someone who promised to deliver. But she would never forget how her hopes turned to disaster, how she was suddenly left in isolation. Her parents, her siblings, all other family from her youth now gone, she alone had the task of protecting her daughter from powerful interests who despised her.

And so, her ways were hardened. Now she was her daughter's protector, the invisible hand that kept her safe against all odds. She operated frequently out of sight. Many years she managed so, through different phases and many terrifying events. Her daughter's survival depended on many maneuvers; strange, complex, and often hidden. Even her daughter knew little about her mother's part in her own story.

And then one day they escaped. Her part in that chapter was also unknown. Here too there were deep regrets, and memories too dark to discuss. She and her daughter would have a chance to start again. But for the rest of her life, she would be severed from her past, the family she had lost, and everyone she had once known. And she would carry this with her, no matter how many years would pass. Her daughter alone remained from her old life.

Living in New York City was a welcome change. She relished her newfound ability to live openly and safely within a community. Yet Betty still hid much of herself, even where it was unnecessary, even where it was now safe to be open. The habit of silence proved hard to break.

It also saddened her to see that Bonnie saw their native culture through such a dark lens, a result of growing up under cruel circumstances, and under a despotic regime. Betty knew another side to their heritage. Their people had made wonderful achievements in the worlds of art, literature, and science. In her own childhood, she had learned an appreciation for beauty, and for keeping an open mind.

There was also much more to their religion than what Bonnie had known; she had only experienced a cruel distortion of their faith by a deeply corrupt government. At its heart, the religion was indeed about awe for the higher being, and much more. The most important values were kindness and decency, and respect for others. There was a special requirement to respect those with less power and privilege than one's self; that value was considered a prerequisite in the struggle to work for justice for all people.

Their new world presented new challenges and dangers, which she met in the manner she was accustomed to. At first, she worked to keep Bonnie in check; the girl might not know her own strength, or the full consequences of her actions. So Betty alone had the task of preventing her from harming others, or from overreaching, or becoming tyrannical.

And throughout these long years on Earth, she again acted as her child's sole protector. These years were far less dark to be sure. Yet she still felt a great burden as the sole bearer of a great responsibility. She was the one parent of a daughter who both possessed great powers—and could potentially pose great dangers to those around her—and who eventually would also put herself in great danger.

Even now, Betty still protected her daughter. A mother could only stand by so much. She was still there in many ways unknown to Bonnie. She might even be present, completely unseen and unnoticed, in the midst of Ms. Infinity's heroic pursuits. She would contribute quietly in many ways, even by doubling Bonnie's strength in emergencies, for instance her force of impact on an asteroid. Truth be told, she more than doubled it. Betty's strength wasn't equal to her daughter's, but greater.

And Bonnie took the credit, when anyone did. Or Ms. Infinity took the credit. So, if that was how her daughter wanted it, then that was fine with her. Nothing gave her more pleasure than seeing her daughter's success, her pride. Such is a parent's heart. She had found much of the same love in teaching. With Scott and with many others, the student's success was all the thanks she needed.

But now it seemed her protective nature had proven her undoing. She had made a fatal mistake. In letting her daughter believe she was alone responsible for her success, she let her face danger without crucial knowledge. Betty had only herself to blame.

Betty flew back to Earth. As she landed, she became visible once again, and stepped out onto Northern Boulevard. She took out her phone, containing her long and detailed plan for fighting Misery. Bonnie had never asked her for help or expressed any interest in planning for the attack. Now the plan was unlikely to be useful. Yet it occurred to her that she might have to do some more planning; she might now be the only person around who could fight back an oncoming invasion. She did her best to take it with the calm and quiet that had always been her demeanor, no matter what the cost to herself. She was now Earth's sole inhabitant bearing the knowledge of its deadly peril, and of the dubiously prepared hero whose fate it now rested on.

12. Superhuman Confrontation

Resting in her quarters as best she could, was Ms. Infinity. Or so she still seemed. Outwardly she wore the form of the great superheroine. But inwardly, alone with her private thoughts, she was Bonnie again, missing her home and her mother. Long missions like this made her appreciate her simple daily comforts, the kinds of things that others took for granted. Being a great distance from home didn't get any easier, no matter how many times she did it.

She had hoped that having a guest with her might make the journey more palatable, and in a way it was. Yet there was also an unexpected downside. Throughout the trip there had been many reminders of Hal's human vulnerabilities and limitations. Try as she might, she simply could not forget the things that separated her from everyone else.

Maybe it was her fault too. She had been very consciously showing off, making each action look as big and magical and heroic as possible. Hal was certain to be awed. The odd thing was, she was actually exerting herself far more than usual. She was not sure why.

Still, Ms. Infinity greatly enjoyed her missions, for all their difficulties. She wore her superhero guise with pride. Even as she longed for home and its comforts, she was also getting impatient; she was craving some action. They were not yet at their destination, but they were getting close. The nearer she came, the more excited she got for battle. There was an instinct inside her that was waking up. She had an itching to protect her home and all the people of Earth. It would soon be time to unleash her power and release her wrath on Misery.

After a while, she gave up on resting, and began her preliminary preparations for battle. That enemy was all she could think of.

Her name, such as humans could understand it, was Misery. Perhaps in her world, the name she bore was common enough to sap its meaning, great though the language's power might be in conferring expectations. Yet she lived its meaning to the extreme. She was ruthless, and without mercy or conscience. She was grimly determined to amass power to herself by any means available to her.

In the years since the departure of her rival, Misery had grown in stature. She had risen through the ranks of her people through flattery and fraud, her success built on a foundation stained with the suffering of many others. And yet, she could not be satisfied. Even as she improved her status, she faced forbidding limitations. A female in her world could only rise so high; even at her apex, she was still a servant. Her masters treated her harshly, tormenting her with acts of simple cruelty, ever flaunting the authority that was forever out of her reach.

But she would not accept this fate, not forever. On the surface, she did as her circumstances demanded. She accepted her inferior role, playing it to perfection. Yet beneath her servile actions, she quietly maintained a will ever bent on her ultimate attainment. And resolved she had always been, without ambivalence, without misgivings, that when the time came, she would stop at nothing. No expense would she spare. No laws would she hesitate to break. No moral code, no conscience, no concern for anyone else would get in her way. And no number of deaths or ruined lives was too many. Her superiors never perceived the danger they faced, right under their noses.

Yet as much as she hated the cruel men she served, she had an even greater hatred for the woman she knew as Bland Beauty, for power was something she possessed naturally. A number of times they had fought, and her enemy had prevailed every time, only to release her in the end. She resented Bland Beauty the more for her mercy, for Misery would surely have killed her enemy had she prevailed. And now she was within her reach. She would not let this opportunity pass. But there was more to this venture than revenge.

Misery sat outside her space station, all lights unlit, alone, in complete and utter darkness. She awaited her sworn enemy with a grim and endless patience. Much was ahead of her, but very soon she would have her revenge.

Hal awoke after a short and uneasy slumber. If nothing else, he was more or less recovered from the frightening experiences from earlier. Still, he was beginning to feel a deepening unease about the distance travelled, and the isolation now upon him. Just where were they? All he knew was that they were about sixty thousand lightyears from Earth. He wished he had paid more attention in science. He had no concept of what that even meant, at least in any meaningful way. How far was that, relatively speaking?

He took out his cell phone and selected the calculator. Remembering that light traveled at approximately six trillion miles per year, he multiplied that by sixty thousand. He got a thirty-six followed by many zeroes. When he counted them, he figured out that he was approximately three hundred sixty quadrillion miles from home. Inside him was a deep, nervous shiver.

Next, he hit the home button, expecting to look at the time. The reading was blank. When he thought a minute, he realized that this was obvious. There was no service in space.

So, he reached for his Big Box uniform and took out his watch from the pocket. To his surprise, it had stopped too. That was strange. It was new and worked on a battery.

He stepped outside his room into the main hall and walked to the nearest window. He hoped to see a moon, a planet, or at least some stars. To his disappointment, there was little but blackness. The void seemed to reach inside him, where he felt a deep and growing sense of foreboding.

Suddenly he heard the voice of Ms. Infinity from above. "I'm glad you're up," she said, as she floated down from the ceiling where she had been doing some exercises. "We have a couple of things to talk about. I have a job for you. Come with me to the TV studio."

"There's a TV studio?"

They crossed the main hall into a room that Hal had not previously noticed. Inside there were cameras, computers, and a control board.

"So," said Hal, "this too, you keep on a spaceship? Just how big is this place?"

"I'm going into battle. I like to film my battles when I can. It's useful for me to study my performance, see at what I've done well, and consider where I can improve. I usually have to let it just go on automatic, but if I have you working it, that would be better. Do you think you can work the camera?"

"Actually yes. I have a degr–"

"Alright. So here is the switcher. There are many cameras outside. You can switch among them with this console. This decides what will be recorded."

"I actually know about this stuff, you see–"

"Play around a minute and see how you do."

Hal worked a few switches, showing her his familiarity

with the equipment. "It's really no problem. This is up my alley. The thing is–"

"Alright. Good to have that out of the way. Come with me to the atrium. I'm about to leave to do battle, and there is more to discuss."

"Actually, I'm wondering about something."

"Yes?"

"Well, it's about Misery. If she's after you, did she need to go through all this trouble to get you? Couldn't she have just kidnapped you or something? Or is this really all about you? Is she targeting the planet for something else?"

"Hal! I told you this is none of your concern. You can just sit back and let me handle this."

Ms. Infinity led Hal out to the atrium. She stopped in front of a large window looking out into space.

"So, Hal," she said, "Don't get overly concerned about what you see out there. I know some of my battles do get ugly, but it is okay."

"How do you mean?"

"Well for one thing, Misery is pretty mean. I know that from experience. I'm sure it won't be nearly as easy for me to defeat her as it is with the usual enemies. You saw me fighting a few common criminals, humans with guns. Misery is from the same planet as me, and I can tell you she's no wimp. But I've always beaten her before."

"So…are you going to be alright?"

"Never lost a battle."

"Okay…"

"The other thing is that I will likely get very nasty and harsh with her too. She has ways of getting under my skin.

Don't let that get to you. You don't have to worry about me. Misery, now she has to worry about what I might do. You don't. I promise."

"Oh."

"I'm off!" declared Ms. Infinity. She flew off once again, apparently through the ceiling.

Hal paused for a moment. Ms. Infinity's warnings had put Hal at unease. For some reason, the second one was even more disturbing than the first. Just how nasty did she get?

Suddenly, Hal was treated to another strange surprise from his back pocket. His cellphone was ringing. He took it out and saw a picture of Ms. Infinity in the caller identification. He didn't remember adding her to his contacts, except as Bonnie Boring. He answered, and indeed it was she at the other end, speaking almost matter-of-factly.

"Hal," she said, "you need to start that video now. Also, can you please have dinner ready?"

"Oh!" said Hal, trying desperately to take it in stride. "Sure. Of course I will."

"See you later," she said. Then she hung up.

Hal put his phone back. Then he took a deep breath and continued into the TV studio.

Into the void of space flew Ms. Infinity. She was filled with energy, "pumped up," and eager to fight. With her whole world at stake, she came upon her enemy as a tremendous, unforgiving force of nature.

As she approached Misery, she communicated in their Centerian manner that it was she, Bland Beauty, transformed as she was, now come to defend the Earth. She gave her a warning: *This is your chance to leave. You will not win this battle.*

I will not attack you if you return home and leave the Earth alone.

Misery did not answer. She showed nothing but complete defiance. Whatever her plan, she was determined to go forward with it.

Ms. Infinity warned her once again: *I will not be merciful this time. There is a whole world at stake. You must end your attacks immediately, or it will be your end. Will you cease your attacks?*

Misery maintained her defiant posture. It was clear that the battle was on.

Ms. Infinity prepared to attack. But in her single-minded focus, she could not see the danger that was about to confront her. Misery had prepared a lethally improved weapon. Hidden in the darkness at her space station, a tremendous catapult was set. In its oversized bucket lay a chunk of the asteroid, still frozen over from their earlier encounter. Misery had taken great pains to increase its deadly force by coating it with thousands of spikes, each of them coated in a dangerous poison. As her enemy approached, she relayed a message back to her space station. The enormous cable was cut, and the lethal payload was sent flying at a breakneck speed.

Blissfully ignorant of her danger, Ms. Infinity looked at Misery with a hard, cold eye, thinking to land a hard blow on her. She was about to unleash her powers to their fullest, landing a catastrophic, unforgiving strike upon her at last. But suddenly the enormous asteroid came into view.

Before she had time to react, she was hit; the projectile rammed into her as suddenly as a truck that comes around a corner. Now she was flailing from the force of impact, too shocked and confused to think or act. She was helpless on the giant meteoroid, trapped in its gravity, imprisoned to its motion. In an instant, she was gone, vanished into a vast distance.

"So, as I was saying, I have a Communications degree from the State University of New York at New Paltz, with a concentration in Video News Production. It's now been almost two years since I graduated. Anyway, I am going to be a TV reporter. Any day now, a big-name network is bound to snap me up, and The Big Box will have to do without me. So of course, I'll work the cameras."

Hal was speaking into the air. He had a dim hope that Ms. Infinity could pick it up with her super senses. But if he was just talking to himself, that was fine too. At least he would be able to finish a whole sentence.

He was thinking that he might use this video for his demo reel. Or better yet, he could sell it to a network. This was certainly a hot item, a real live superhero battle in space. He figured he would bring the matter up to her when she returned. He practiced switching a few times, then finally went live as the hero approached her enemy.

He got his first look at Misery. She looked human, a blonde, though wearing a very strange outfit. It looked something like a robe covering her entire body, nearly all in white with some light blue trim. There was a hood that hung behind her neck, apparently a head covering that was not engaged. He wondered about her story, and also what pieces might be missing from the story he had heard.

As impressed as Hal was with the studio, it was more advanced than he even knew, more so than any human technology. Though he could not hear or perceive it, the cameras picked up Ms. Infinity's Centerian communication with Misery. He did notice that there was no light on the subjects, and he wondered how the cameras could capture them. He also marveled that he could zoom in from a great distance, with surprisingly good picture quality. Altogether, he was like a kid in a candy shop. He had never had such an opportunity before; he had complete control of an entire news production.

He was glad there were as many cameras as there were. One would certainly never have captured the action. It was clear that this was going to be a kinetic battle. He also decided that making dinner would have to wait a while. He really should not take his eyes off the job he was doing. Maybe he would just stick in a couple of microwave dinners afterward.

Then he saw Ms. Infinity hit by the chunk from the asteroid. He was instantly shocked. At first, he took it for granted that she would be back in an instant. But then she did not return. It slowly came to him that this was more than a media event. This was a real battle between two powerful and dangerous people who hated each other completely, and would not hesitate to kill each other.

Anxiety crept in as he pondered his predicament. He thought for the first time about what would happen if Ms. Infinity was taken out, and he was left alone on the ship many light years from home. Just how dangerous a spot might he be in?

He kept the live camera trained on Misery, looking at every other camera for a sign of Ms. Infinity. Again and again, he switched the preview monitor, hoping to see her, but to no avail. A long time passed with no action. He was in deep suspense, biting his fingernails, and feeling a horrible sensation at the pit of his stomach. However, he noticed that Misery was still waiting impatiently. That seemed to tip him off that the battle was not over after all.

For a few seconds, Ms. Infinity was in a panic. She was not sure where she was. The pain was sharp, and she felt dizzy and disoriented. It took her a moment to put together what had just happened. She had taken a powerful blow, and the spikes had hurt her. Yet she was lucid, perfectly together.

She picked herself up, carefully positioning herself so not to touch any of the spikes. It was not easy. They were nearly everywhere. She found herself poised awkwardly. She only needed a moment to get her bearings. She was cut and bruised in many spots, but that was all. She felt the discomfort from the poisons, but her body was easily fighting them off. Misery had underestimated her. Now she would fight back even harder. Her eyes glowed with anger as she prepared for a cruel counterattack.

After the blow that Ms. Infinity had taken, it could easily have seemed to the untrained eye that she was finished. Many fighters might have assumed victory at that moment, yet Misery was clearly not fooled. She stayed, floating at attention, awaiting Ms. Infinity's reprisal.

This was how Ms. Infinity expected to find her enemy. So before approaching, she turned herself invisible. Then she came up quietly. She watched as Misery waited and waited. After some time, Misery lost her patience. First, she began to grit her teeth, and shake her head. Soon after, she began to float back and forth in an aimless, impatient pacing motion. Before long, she was in a flying rage.

That was exactly what Ms. Infinity was waiting for. As Misery cursed at her opponent, she failed to notice her approaching quietly from behind. Suddenly she was on the receiving end of a powerful blow.

Now she was the one in a tailspin. She went flying at a breakneck speed; the force of Ms. Infinity's impact was a mighty thing indeed. For a moment she was flailing helplessly, and in seconds she covered a great distance. Yet she was also prepared. From her pack, she grabbed a device, and aimed it carefully. She sent a powerful series of waves to her space station. The blowback from the energy was enough to stop her trajectory. She then flew back.

Misery took an indirect route and attempted to surprise Ms. Infinity from behind. Before Misery struck, Ms. Infinity turned and saw her, but it was too late. Misery managed to get one hard kick, which sent her reeling. But Ms. Infinity quickly rebounded. Faster than Misery could react, Ms. Infinity snared her enemy in her arms.

With one arm holding her arms and one around her neck, Misery was trapped. Ms. Infinity's grip was tremendously powerful, and she was nearly helpless against it. She struggled. She squirmed, trying to get free. She was close to panic. Then in her desperation, she tried a cruel move. She began to transform. As Ms. Infinity squeezed tighter, it seemed she would strangle her. Then suddenly, the arm holding Misery's arm was struck by several sharp spikes from within. She gasped as her grip was lost in a bloody mess.

At the sudden reappearance of Ms. Infinity, Hal let out a sigh of relief. He filmed the continuing struggle, watching it turn this way and that. He was also thrilled to see that it was indeed shaping up to be an exciting spectacle. This video had action, suspense, and fireworks. His career might have the boost it needed.

As he watched this stage of the battle, he thought for sure that Ms. Infinity was about to win. She had just grabbed Misery, and it seemed as if the villain was at her mercy. Then he noticed his hero suddenly loosen her grip on her enemy, almost as if she had just been bitten. He noticed Ms. Infinity looked like she was flinching. Which way was the battle going?

Then he saw something that shocked him. Ms. Infinity started to change!

As Ms. Infinity jerked back from the wound that Misery had inflicted, she shrieked in pain. Were they not in space, it would have been a mighty sound. Before she had time to retaliate, she saw her enemy upon her, now more menacing than ever before. She felt a fear such as she had not felt in many years. But a moment later, fear turned to anger. And in her anger, she began to change.

At first, her transformation was like those in the classic horror movies — red eyes, claws appearing out of her hands, her teeth turning into fangs. But then as her body began to shift, she began changing into something much bigger, more powerful, and far more frightening than a werewolf. She grew immensely. Tentacles grew out of everywhere, each one branching out, with spikes — or teeth — appearing along the edges. Her head changed into something resembling that of a dragon, but shrouded in darkness, and now with many eyes. After another minute, she was ten times human size, if not more.

Meanwhile, Misery's face became a fierce, fanged mask of vengeance. Claws shot out from her bloody hands. Her eyes glazed with fire, a small but powerful beast determined to put an end to the goliath before her.

The transformed Ms. Infinity attacked Misery. First, she pounced at her with her tremendous bulk. Then she grabbed her in her gigantic, sharp claws. Finally, she poked and pierced her with each of her many sharp tentacles. The villain looked like an insect trapped insect in a giant Venus flytrap. A moment later, her enormous head came into view, a mammoth, demonic visage with dozens of cruel eyes, and a huge mouth adorned with many, many razor-sharp teeth. There could be no mistaking the picture. She was about to devour her prey. There seemed no possible escape.

But Misery had not spent one second of the attack in

idleness. She had quietly drawn out a sword, a small, elegant, and deeply sophisticated weapon used by Center's military. It was light to hold, and very easy to conceal, being very slight in width and depth and retractable at its bearer's will. Yet it was extraordinarily sharp at the tip. Furthermore, if used by someone with the intelligence of fighters from Center, it could strike in many dimensions at once.

By the time the creature's head reached her, Misery had pierced her numerous times, matching the strikes of her tentacles ten to one. Her enemy was hurt and weakened, yet unaware of the wounds in remote places. Now, Misery was ready for her crucial attack. As the mouth approached her, she flew suddenly under her chin and pierced her deeply. The beast froze in shock, then quivered, her many tentacles now finally feeling the pain from Misery's strikes. When Misery pulled the weapon out, her enemy was bleeding hard all over.

A moment later, the beast rebounded, but she did not dare risk another attempt at devouring her prey. She used a tentacle to knock Misery into a tailspin, and the woman went flying much farther and faster than before. Yet once again she used the device from her pack and rebounded. And powerful though that move was, there was no mistaking the meaning. Ms. Infinity was now on the defensive.

Misery flew at the transformed Ms. Infinity at a tremendous speed. She drew her weapon again, now making sure it was plainly visible, and as frightening as possible. She was also certain to show her own claws, and the fangs in her mouth. Then she took out one more cruel weapon: a small but heavy mace. She threw it at her adversary with awesome precision, hitting hard against several of her eyes. The monster was thrown back in pain. Misery approached, looking very much like she was about to prevail.

Shape shifting was a power that was rather central to Bonnie's arsenal. Indeed, it was essential to her whole secret identity. It was also another thing that her bloodline did much better than the rest of the people of Center. While other people could shift, in most cases, it was little more than enough to distort their faces and bodies. This was a look that the military class employed sometimes to look "threatening." Misery was much better at it than most, though she knew better than to be open about her superior skills among so many men.

For her part, Bonnie could transform herself completely into an altogether different being. In her youth, she used it often to hide from her enemies. She also refused to hold back her skills, even when people around her objected. Like the rest of Bonnie's superior abilities, it was a double-edged sword, both the apparent cause of her pain and the means to her survival.

She continued to develop the skill once on Earth. A desire to change might have become habit by now, perhaps a leftover "fight or flight" response. But then she also thought it was cool. She almost seemed to make a hobby out of it. Forms of all kinds fascinated her, including many she had seen in comic books and movies. She liked to try any and all of them out when she had time alone. Bonnie would change into anything from werewolves to panthers to original monstrous creations of her own. She also liked changing into humanoid "aliens" of the movies, relishing the irony as one who was an alien who naturally looked human. She liked to think herself edgy, but in time she came to admit there was something terribly geeky about it.

By contrast, Betty almost never seemed to use this power at all, at least around Bonnie. But then if there was one thing Bonnie knew about her mother, it was that there were always more secrets that she feared delving into. Betty did joke that the power might come in handy for Halloween, but that would certainly have been out of character. Betty Boring's

Halloween "transformation," such as it was, consisted of putting on a pair of plastic mouse ears and drawing a few whiskers on her face with an eyeliner pencil. After all, she only wanted to fawn over the children in their cute costumes when they came trick-or-treating. Of course, she also secretly protected them from danger.

At any rate, using shape shifting as a disguise or a hobby was one thing. Using a strange body in battle was proving to be quite another. She had to get used to a newly formed body, with a great deal of extra weight and bulk. This creature was a behemoth that was proving very hard to control. And much as she hated to admit it, Misery had found her weak point, defeating what was much the purpose of the strategy.

Ms. Infinity flinched as Misery drew nearer, desperately trying to find a hidden strength in herself. But then she noticed her enemy's eyes, lighting up as if on fire. She remembered a power she had not yet thought of using. It was tricky in space; she had to create a small atmosphere to light it on fire. But it could work.

Misery pounced and dug her claws straight into her neck. The pain was almost unbearable. Yet Ms. Infinity held firm and concentrated. She had another surprise of her own in return. Quietly blowing air out, she struggled to create an atmosphere around the two of them. Her size in this form was now an advantage. It would take time to create the field, but it would certainly not be hard to envelop her enemy.

She tried desperately to ignore the pain, and the blood that was beginning to pour out from the deepening wounds. In a few seconds, the deed was done. Noting an adequate air mass, she blew a dragon's burst of fire into Misery's face.

Misery jerked back from shock. The fire did not last

long, but her grip was instantly broken, and the local air mass was mostly intact.

Ms. Infinity blew again, this time harder, crueler. For a moment she seemed to char her rival like a great blowtorch. This would surely be the end of the battle. A few more seconds and victory would be hers, and Misery would be no more. She roasted her harder, crueler and hotter with every passing instant. And then it burned out.

To her great dismay, Misery was not dead. She was horribly burned. But her eyes were madder than ever. And now the air mass was spent. There was only one thing left to do. Ms. Infinity turned and flew away, apparently out of fear.

This fight was proving even harder than Misery had expected. She had hoped that her sheer cruelty and determination were enough against her enemy's powers. There were signs that it might be working, but she was also exhausted.

As much as she hated to admit it, she was out of her element. Open battles like this had never been her strong suit. She was much better at ruining people through their reputations. She was extremely clever at manipulating people into believing what she wanted about an enemy. A favorite trick of hers was bullying a person on the pretext of helping someone else. If you seemed to be "sticking up" for someone who others could feel sympathy for, you could turn opinions against anyone you wanted. On some level, she now found herself instinctively trying a variation of that gambit; effectively she had tricked her opponent into becoming an unpleasant character, making herself seem like the underdog. But of course, this game was worthless in this theater. Here she was alone with her enemy, with nobody to perform for. Bland Beauty already hated her. There was nothing to do but fight openly and take the hits when they came.

But now, after taking hit after hit, at last her enemy was flying away. Could this be a sign that victory was near? Or was she going somewhere to rearm? Either way, she was not going to let her get away.

She flew after Bland Beauty with brutal determination. She knew she was not her match in speed, but she also knew that her enemy could not run forever. If this battle was proving anything, it was that even Bland Beauty had her limits. It seemed that her brutal persistence was finally paying off.

Several times it seemed that she was losing her, but then she began to catch up. She was working on the assumption that her enemy was slowing down out of weariness. She did not give sufficient consideration to a second possibility, that catching up was exactly what her enemy wanted her to do. For just as Bland Beauty was almost within her grasp, she suddenly vanished into what seemed like an invisible pocket. She had only the last instant to consider the possibility of a trap. Yet by the time she could act, she was already inside Starship Infinity, with the door slamming shut.

Hal had wondered exactly what Ms. Infinity had meant when she said she might "get nasty." He figured she might fight mercilessly, but he had not imagined anything like this. He also knew she could change her form, but somehow, he had not considered the full consequences. He had to admit that this was pretty cool, thrilling even, but it was also disturbing. He didn't know what to call this creature. It wasn't quite a dragon, nor was it a kraken. It wasn't a hydra either. Whatever it was, it was terrifying. At least she was on his side. But then a very unsettling thought occurred to him. Was this her true form? Was he dating a monster?

Watching her blow fire at Misery was one truly

amazing spectacle. Whatever she was, she certainly was a truly powerful being. Hal was quite sure the battle was nearing its end, and that very soon Ms. Infinity would win. But then she didn't. He watched her turn back and fly away, and suddenly he was more dismayed than ever. Yet then he saw something that frightened him far more. Both of them were heading right for the ship.

All of a sudden, he heard a crashing sound. Neither woman was within view. Were they now aboard? He had his answer a split second later. Suddenly he nearly fell out of his seat when he was startled by a loud noise outside the door.

Now back in her usual form, Ms. Infinity looked at her trapped prey. She was about to circle her and bind her.

But Misery was not giving up. If she could not escape, she would at least not be captured. In a flash, she flew into the corridors of the ship. Ms. Infinity followed her. Both disappeared in a rush of super speed.

Hal had peered outside the door just long enough to see it. Misery was on board, with Ms. Infinity chasing her. He saw them for a split second before both of them flew away.

He tried not to be terrified of the new development. He knew very little about Misery, but he did know that she was an alien like Ms. Infinity, and that she was evil. That was enough. He only hoped Ms. Infinity knew what she was doing.

He closed the door and listened outside. He mostly heard nothing, but periodically he heard the sound of both women flying by very fast, rather like cars speeding by. He tried to think of what he could do to help. No idea came, other than to wait it out.

Misery had spent most of this time flying frantically away from Bland Beauty. But then out of the corner of her eye, she noticed something else going on. She only had a quick glance, but with her superhuman senses, it was enough. The battle was being filmed.

She tried to fly into the TV studio to put a stop to it, but Ms. Infinity stopped her with a powerful blow. By the time Misery rebounded, she was blocking the door. So Misery began ramming into the walls.

After several times, Ms. Infinity gave her swift kick, and she fell far across the main hall into a dark hallway. Now, Misery was exactly where she wanted her.

There were no two ways about it. Hal was scared. This seemed like a new definition of "in over his head": he was the sole human on an alien spaceship, many light years from Earth, in the middle of a superhuman battle. He tried to tell himself that somehow this would be alright. After all, he was with Earth's Greatest Hero. She would never lead him wrong. He had already been through things he could not understand, and she had steered him through it just fine. This would be okay too, even if he could not understand how.

Suddenly the floor began to shake. Judging from the sounds outside, it seemed like the battle was now right outside the door. A moment later, he was sure of it; the walls had begun to quake from impact. Then it dawned on him that he was in the company of heavy equipment that could be very dangerous if it came loose.

Unfortunately for him, this revelation came too late. Suddenly the floor began to shake, and several items collapsed. A second later he was face to face with the approach of an unknown piece of equipment. He felt a powerful blow to the head, and then nothing.

In the depths of Starship Infinity, Misery found herself trapped. All around her were nothing but walls, except in one far corner where unbreakable bars now slammed shut. Behind them was Ms. Infinity. In their native language, the heroine communicated that she was now her prisoner, forever if necessary. Completely forgotten upstairs in the TV studio was Hal Holstein, sprawled out unconscious amidst the wreckage.

13. Management Style

As Misery was locked in Ms. Infinity's prison, and Hal lay unconscious elsewhere on Starship Infinity, many light years away, things were continuing on as always at The Big Box. Lisa Lin was carrying on her routine at the customer service counter. Julia was supposed to accompany her, but she was late. Once again, Lisa endured a long period handling the crowd alone.

For now, there was relative calm, and Lisa hoped for a few minutes of peace. But this hope was dashed when Denny showed up. He seemed quieter than usual, ominously quiet. He moved aggressively into the customer service area and crept up very close to Lisa.

"Lisa, honey," he said, "why don't you take a break? I got this."

Lisa looked up at Denny suspiciously. "Little early, isn't it?"

"Go!" he said abruptly.

Lisa rolled her eyes and shook her head. She started toward the register to sign out, but Denny was posturing aggressively, blocking her way.

"Excuse me," she said, "I haven't signed out."

"Don't worry about that, little girl. Just go!"

"Hold on," said Maria. "This is really not a good time for her break. It's going to get busy here any minute. Besides, Julia's not–"

"She has to go!" snapped Denny.

"Oh, does she?" retorted Maria, "because last I heard,

I'm still the runner, and her immediate supervisor."

Denny looked like he was about to scream at her, but he stopped. It might have had to do with the approach of a couple of men in suits, likely visitors from the company. He walked away, but he was visibly angry.

Business soon began to pick up again. As the line grew, frustration among customers grew with it. Being served by only one person did not help. One woman came to her with an uneven exchange. Unfortunately, the sweater she wanted had no price tag.

"Miss," said Lisa calmly, "do you think you can do me a favor, and find another one with a tag?"

"What?!" snapped the customer.

"This doesn't have a tag. So, could you please find me one that does? I need the line to keep moving."

"You can't find the price tag, and you want me to go back there for you?"

"I don't mean to cause a problem."

"This place is pathetic. You know what? I'm starting to hate shopping here. Everything about this store is incompetent. So, what are you trying to make me do now? I just want this to be done quick. Now you want me to run back for you?"

"I'm sorry to cause a problem, but I can't find out the price without a tag. All I need is another one with a price tag. When you come back, I'll take you first. It doesn't even have to be the same size or color."

"You're the customer service. You can find it."

Technically the customer was right. It was her job to find the garment with the tag. She had little choice but to search for the item. It was some distance to the women's department and back. By the time she got back, the customers behind the woman were irate.

"Why did I have to wait for that?" complained a woman a few places down the line. "You don't know what you're doing."

"I'm sorry," said Lisa patiently, "this is what I have to–"

"This isn't fair to her," said Denny, who had now returned, and was standing beside the customer. "You should apologize to her right now."

"Thank you for standing up for me," said the woman.

"My pleasure," said Denny, smirking.

"It's disgusting how incompetent this girl is," shouted the man behind her. "I'm sorry, but in my day, someone this lazy and incompetent would be out of a job. Where's the manager? It's time someone stood up for the people here."

"I'm the manager," said Denny with a satisfied look on his face.

"Hi. So, if you don't mind my saying so, you should fire this girl. She doesn't know what the hell she's doing."

Denny looked at her coldly. "Yeah, you're right," he said, "but I'm stuck with her."

"You can't get rid of her?"

"If you only knew the lazy kids I'm dealing with. She's the worst one."

"Is this job too hard for you?" called a woman with cruel sarcasm. "Maybe you can go home and get a foot rub."

"She didn't understand that," shouted the man who had called for the manager. "The little geisha girl doesn't understand English."

"Geisha!?" snapped Lisa, "What the hell? I'm not even Japanese!" Then she stopped and shook her head. The customer probably didn't even know the difference.

"Oh!" mocked the man, "did I offend your politically correct sensibilities? Are your little feelings hurt? Well, that's too bad. Do me a favor. The next time one of your people takes an American job, make sure you know how the hell to do it. Otherwise, get the hell out of my country."

Lisa finally lost her composure and began to cry. Maria came up and intervened. "Listen, why don't you take your break. I'll handle this for a while."

When Lisa walked away, several people began to cheer cruelly. Denny smirked at her. The customer continued to shout racist cracks. It didn't even die down when she tripped and fell and cut herself on her forehead. She ran to the ladies' room, feeling mortified.

Isha entered as Lisa was washing her face, attempting to stop the bleeding, and doing her best to clear up her tears. Lisa did not feel much like talking, but she could not disguise her agitation, and Isha looked at her with concern. "Are you alright, Lisa?" she asked.

"Oh, it's nothing to do with you," said Lisa. "I'm just really starting to hate this job."

"I know. Just remember, it's not forever."

"Yeah. I know."

Isha looked at Lisa kindly. "Look at it this way. Just surviving every day as a victory. I know this might not make sense to you, but just being here is like a rebellion to me. My parents don't even want me to work. They would have me married to someone of their choosing. I'm defying them just being here."

"I sympathize. Thank you."

Lisa might have said more, but she was in no mood. She certainly understood. Those kinds of pressures were on her too, though happily not from her parents. During her grandmother's visit from China, she had made numerous intrusive comments. She would not stop asking why she wasn't married, and why she was pursuing a career.

Her parents took her side on that matter. The frustrations she had with her parents were not about that basic issue. They might have had trouble treating her as an adult, but at least they agreed with her career goals.

They also agreed that relationships and marriage should come in their own time, and at her discretion. Her mother had told her to be careful in selecting a husband. "You want to know the man very well first," she would say. "That feeling of love ends, and sooner or later you will find yourself stuck with him. You'd better know what you're getting into."

Bonnie agreed whole-heartedly, and at that, also had her mother's blessing. The worst thing to her was a man who was too "dominating." She had recently had a date with a wealthy young man who had told her that he would never allow his woman to work. He actually saw that as a selling point. To Bonnie that was a deal breaker. The date was ended almost immediately.

Bonnie had said many times that she did not want to be tied down. The idea actually scared her. Her anxieties about it were strangely vivid. She spoke of men who might promise to take care of her, but would ultimately imprison her. She told of gilded cages; sad stories often emerged about being locked in lovely places with beautiful gardens, but with no choices and no escape. That future seemed strangely specific. Lisa was quite sure it really spoke to something else. Like many cryptic things Bonnie and Betty spoke of, it was a hint of their past, a window into darker times that they would never discuss overtly.

"Why was Lisa alone here?" whispered Denny.

"You know what?" snapped Maria. "You might have asked that question before you humiliated her. She's one of your best workers, and you might know that if you spent any time here."

"Mind your own goddamn business!" shouted Denny. Then he grabbed her on her buttocks.

"Stop that! Just stop!"

"What are you going to do about it?"

"I don't have to take this."

"It's your word against mine. Besides, they're going to start wondering why there's nobody here on customer service. You can't manage this place, can you?"

"You have some goddamn nerve."

Denny looked around. "Where is the other customer service girl?"

"Julia is a little late," answered Maria.

"You see? This is what I've been talking about. These girls are all like that. You can't seriously think this Lisa's any different. They're all just here for a couple of months, or maybe a year or two. So what? And where's the one who was here before?"

"Bonnie had to leave a few minutes early. She didn't say why."

"Yeah. See what I mean? Just like that. And when did Bonnie leave?"

"I don't know," said Maria. "She left little while after Hal. Fifteen, maybe twenty minutes ago."

14. To the Next Level

Ms. Infinity approached Misery's prison somewhat more ostentatiously than she had before: she appeared in a flash of lightning. She then used her powers to enhance her appearance. As she stood before Misery, her gloating was unmistakable. "Bland Beauty" she was no more. Now she was more like "Invincible Beauty." Tall and powerful beyond measure, she was utterly flawless, and indescribably beautiful.

This was the cruelest gesture possible, and she knew it. She hoped by conveying superiority, she might persuade Misery to disseminate some information. Truth be told, it was as much about her own frustration as anything. This was the third time she had questioned Misery since capturing her. So far, she had gotten nowhere. If there was one thing Misery knew, it was how to answer in ways that upset her old enemy.

For Ms. Infinity, it didn't help that she had to use her old communication. Once upon a time, a newly renamed Bonnie Boring had been casually repulsed by human language. In the many years since, Bonnie had come to insist on using English exclusively. She now hated her old language, perhaps more than anything. And here she was being forced to use it by someone she despised.

In this alien communication, Misery wondered: *What is that image for? It certainly was not invented for me alone. Was it contrived for the animals of Earth? Are you now to be counted as one of them?*

This is none of your concern, answered Ms. Infinity. *Why are you attacking Earth?*

You must be afraid. This is not the first time you have been on the run, is it?

You will answer my questions, said Ms. Infinity sharply. *Why are you so far from home?*

And I might ask the same question from you, said Misery. *You have been away from Center for much longer.*

Who are you working with? Who is secreted at your space station?

Misery would not answer. She simply looked back in defiance. Ms. Infinity found this interesting.

What is going on? demanded Ms. Infinity. *I am certain that there is more to this than is apparent. You have to be fighting me for a reason.*

Is everything about you now? said Misery. *So it seems it always was with you. It is not to be wondered that you are despised. You stepped on the great, courageous men of Center. You are naught but a harlot.*

So then, is this the reason why you are here? Are you attacking a whole inhabited world just to avenge one person whom you feel has dishonored your people?

So indeed, we are not your people anymore. Or were we ever, really? For your treason, you deserve everything ever done to you and more, and everything coming to you too.

You must answer my questions! You are the prisoner here.

Misery looked at Ms. Infinity coldly. *Yes, I am a prisoner, being without invisible hands to rescue me. But at least I am not imprisoned by my own.*

Ms. Infinity was suddenly furious at her captive. She threatened her. Misery taunted her back. After a moment, Ms. Infinity smashed the wall so hard that the whole room shook and made a deafening sound.

Hal marveled that he was even still alive. His head throbbing, he struggled to sit up. It seemed he had aches in every part of his body.

He looked around at the wreckage. At first glance, the entire room seemed ruined. But he soon saw that it was mostly the chairs strewn about, with a couple of broken monitors on the floor as well. He counted himself lucky that he had not been hit by one of those. As heavy as they were, they might well have finished him off.

Out of sheer curiosity, he tested the video equipment to see if it still worked. Surprisingly it still did. Not only that, but the recording he had made was completely intact.

"Come to think of it," he wondered, "Where is she?"

In fact, he had never seen the end of the battle. What if it hadn't gone her way? Would he now be at Misery's mercy? The thought of that possibility brought a terror so great that he could only block it from his mind for now. There was, of course, nothing to do but face the new reality. Hal got up and started to look for Ms. Infinity.

The main hall was empty. So was the kitchen. He checked the bedroom he had slept in. He knocked on another door, which he presumed to be Ms. Infinity's bedroom. No answer. When he carefully opened it, he saw it to be empty too. There was nobody on the bridge either. Then he looked toward the farther corners, toward hallways he had so far not dared to explore. Was it time to explore them now?

He looked around the atrium at the various hallways. He had not realized before just how many there were. He walked by a few of them until he thought he heard a sound. Then he stopped and listened. Then he heard something else, a faint rumbling. When he looked into that corridor, all he saw was darkness.

Hal closed his eyes and sighed deeply. There was a decision to be made. He could wait for Ms. Infinity to come back. Most likely she would. But how long would he wait until that happened? And what if she didn't?

So then, what was he getting into now by exploring? If she had won, then there was little to worry about; the worst was possibly disturbing her sleep. If she had lost, then he would face Misery. He would have to confront that reality sooner or later. But then, there was the possibility that a vestige of the battle was still going on.

He decided that he could not wait forever. He tentatively started down the hallway. As he moved, he looked back to make sure he remembered how to retrace his footsteps. Sure enough, this hallway was a dark one, and it got darker as it continued. After some distance, it led down a winding staircase.

This was making him nervous. He was not sure where he was going. It was strange enough being on this magic spaceship in the first place. How did he know that this would not take him somewhere he could not return from? Still, he pressed on.

After some distance, the stairway came to an end. The landing was narrow, and somewhat lighter than before. Ahead the passageway turned sharply. Hal was about to continue, but then he was stopped in his tracks by a deafening crash. The floor shook with enough force to knock him right off his feet.

Hal might not have been capable of super speed. However, there was little doubt that it was at this exact moment that he came the closest he would ever come to achieving it. He ran for dear life back around the narrow corridor, up the stairs, through the hallway, and back to the atrium. As he arrived, he heard the whishing sound of someone coming after him. His heart raced as the sound came closer, then over his head. A second later he was face to face with Ms. Infinity.

"Oh!" cried Hal with relief, "It's you."

"You didn't make dinner!" said Ms. Infinity.

"Excuse me?"

"I asked you to have dinner ready. What happened?"

Hal looked at Ms. Infinity in absolute shock. He wanted to tell her what had just happened, but the words did not come.

"What were you doing up there?" she continued. "Do you know what I'm dealing with? I nearly got myself killed out there! And now I have a prisoner to work with. I'm sorry, but unless you were knocked out cold, there is no excuse. I just asked for one simple thing."

Hal could find no words. He stared at her in shock for a few moments more before he began to cry.

"Now what's that about?" shouted Ms. Infinity, "What did I say? Alright, fine! I'll make dinner. Damnit! One simple thing I asked from you!"

"Excuse me," said Hal through his tears, "I was trying to make your video. Remember? You know, that wasn't easy either. Did you notice that this place wasn't exactly safe? I almost got…What? Wait! Back up! What was that about a prisoner?"

"Misery is my prisoner now. Yeah. Do you understand what this is like for me?"

"You took Misery prisoner?"

"So, what? Now you're going to criticize my work? I don't see you trying to do this. If you can't do it better yourself, then I don't want to hear it."

"So that was what was going on down there? I just think I have a right to know if we're suddenly in the dungeon business. Let the record show that I never signed anything."

"It's a prison cell. There's nothing going on here like that. She's here because she's a criminal and I have to deal with her. Don't make this sound like a cheap exploitation novel."

"Forgive me if I'm a little scared after all that I saw. You know, I have to wonder, just how many different guises do you have? I mean, what is your true form anyway?"

"What kind of question is that?"

"Alright. I'm sorry. You try watching someone you've been dating turn into something ten times your size."

"You know what? I told you not to be scared. Like I said, that was for Misery. You had nothing to fear from me. She did. And she's now my prisoner, so yes. That is what is going on. I'll try to remember to keep you posted from now on."

"Can you forgive me for wanting to know? I have to live with this kind of decision. I mean…we have a prisoner now? I didn't even know you did that. Can you understand my discomfort? And then I can only guess at the complications. You're the one who told me we wouldn't be up here long. Now what? Remember something. I have a family. Two parents. A little sister. They might start to wonder where I am after a week or two. I also need to continue paying rent, or I lose my apartment. And then too you know, I might want to hold on to that job. Money is pretty important to us humans, even if to you we're like dogs trying to play video games."

"Hal, you can calm down now! I'm sorry if this isn't turning out like you dreamed it would. But I have no choice but to see it through. I promise you will see your mommy again soon enough and…wait a minute…"

She took a closer look at Hal. After a moment, her expression turned to surprise, then sympathy. "Oh my god,

Hal! You did get knocked out!"

Hal's tone became grave. "Yes, I did."

"Why didn't you say something before?"

"You didn't exactly make it easy."

"Wow," said Ms. Infinity as she moved in closer. "Hal, I'm sorry. Here, I can heal myself with my powers, but I cannot do the same for you. I'm not a doctor. It would be dangerous for me to poke around your body. But I can give you this."

She blew into the air for a moment. Then out of nowhere she pulled out an ice pack.

"Here, Hal. Just for you. This wasn't really all that magical. I just blew on the moisture in the air with my freeze breath."

"Oh. Okay, Ms. Infinity. I'll be sure to try that trick myself sometime."

"The plastic casing took some more manipulation, and right. You don't have freeze breath. I can also do this for you." She leaned in and gently kissed the bump. "There. Good as Mom?"

"Actually, that seemed magical."

"Aw. Thanks."

"I don't know what I'm supposed to do with myself now."

Ms. Infinity looked at Hal with sympathy. "I know you're trapped here, and I'm sorry. I feel terrible looking at you and seeing the disappointment in your eyes. I know you had this beautiful image of me, and I feel like I just killed it. But I'm sorry if I simply can't live up to the vision of perfection that you had in your mind. Did you think I would sweep you off your feet and make your dreams come true?

I'm not a genie. You have to understand, I can't worry about such things. There are things I have to do, no matter what.

"I have a tremendous responsibility. It doesn't matter what I want, or what anybody else thinks. I have to perform, or there are serious consequences. Nobody else will do this work if I fail. I cannot fail. This is all up to me."

"Alright. I'm sorry too. Look, is there any way I can help? Obviously, I'm on this mission too. If there's anything..."

"No Hal. This is my mission. I agreed to let you come along, but the fact remains that there is nobody who can do this except for me. I appreciate the offer though.

"I could use a chocolate fix, but no such luck up here. I'll tell you what, though. Let's go and make dinner. Then I'll go on to my next move. You can go and use the pool for a while–"

"Wait! There's a pool?"

"Right past the rec room. I never did give you a proper tour."

"I don't know. That would be nice and all. But I didn't bring my suit..."

"Are you sure? What's that behind your ear?" She reached behind his ear and pulled out a bathing suit.

"I should have seen that coming," murmured Hal as she smiled. "Come to think of it, I didn't bring much money either. Fifty grand or so wouldn't be bad..."

"Like I told you, I'm not a genie."

"How did you...?"

"I have drawers full of clothes on this ship. That was telekinesis just now. I can create objects, as long as I have some kind of matter to work with, like I just did with the ice pack. A simple thing like that I could just make with a little air. A bathing suit would be tough if I just had the air to work with. And even if I could create money, that would be counterfeiting. I don't break laws."

"Pretty cool. One of these days, you're going to have to give me a nice little magic show."

"Magic show? I'm not a genie, and I'm not a magician either. And before you ask, no I'm not a witch either. Get this straight: Superhero! I save people, protect the Earth, and so forth. I don't grant wishes. I don't put on shows, and while we're at it, I don't need any lousy broomstick when I want to fly."

"Thanks for clearing that up. I guess I never really did appreciate the distinctions until now. I should write it down..."

"Yeah, you would, but I bet you forgot to bring a pen."

"Well, that's outa left field!"

"It's alright. That's why you have me. C'mon, you space cadet. Let's have dinner. Frozen chicken nuggets on me. Or do you prefer the fish fillet?"

As the companions finished their dinner, Ms. Infinity looked at Hal longingly. "So, Hal, it's great to be with you. The thing is, I'm afraid I've got to go right back out again. I've had to carefully consider my next move. I started questioning Misery. But here's the thing. She is now neutralized. I can get back to her later. I have to think of other priorities. You see, there was no way she could have been acting alone."

Hal listened intently as the superhero spoke. He was feeling overwhelmed by the scene unfolding around him, but he was doing his best to keep up. Whatever decision Ms. Infinity made would affect him as well. He had a swelling and a throbbing headache to remind him of that reality. "Okay," he said, "so that means…"

"I'm going to search Misery's space station."

"So, can I ask you something?"

"You just did."

"I know. I know," said Hal, "but you know, I wouldn't mind knowing what's going on here. What brought you to this decision?"

"Hal, you're starting to pry here. Remember whose mission this is."

"Yeah, I know, and I accept it, but please understand, I have to live with this decision."

Ms. Infinity shook her head and sighed. "Alright. It came from questioning Misery. She was not very forthcoming about anything, but when I brought up the space station, she simply wouldn't answer. That was pretty telling. Clearly it's a loose end that needs to be tied up."

"Thank you," said Hal, "But can I ask you something else? What are the plans for Misery? Is this indefinite? Are you going to release her? Kill her?"

"Now you really are prying."

"Well, don't you think maybe I have a stake in this?"

"Hal, I'm sorry, but I simply can't discuss this now. I'm afraid a lot of this is over your head."

"I beg your pardon?"

"Okay," said Ms. Infinity, "Maybe that wasn't the most diplomatic way to put it. But there is a world of things here that you don't understand, and I'm afraid I can't explain them to you. And Hal, when I say there's a loose end out there, I mean it's potentially urgent. This is something I must attend to right away. Why don't you come see me off?"

As Ms. Infinity led Hal to the atrium, he was visibly nervous. "Can you please listen to one thing?" he said. "How do you know she isn't deliberately misleading you? What if this is an ambush?"

Ms. Infinity stopped looked back at Hal in annoyance. "Now Hal, I'm afraid you are going to have to remember who the superhero is here. I take risks every day. You are going to have to trust me. You know I can take care of myself."

"Misery wasn't easy for you to beat, was she? What if there are more like her?"

"Hal, like I just said, I can take care of myself."

"Please, Bonnie. Please be careful out there."

"'Bonnie'? Okay. Call me that if you want. Just not among folks when I'm in this form. You know I have a secret to keep."

"Not the point. I'm worried about you."

"You are? You know what? Thank you." She kissed him on the cheek.

"Thank you. Now are you sure about this?"

"Listen, Hal. This is something I have to do. Do you understand that Misery has put the entire Earth in tremendous danger? Before this mission, she sent a gigantic asteroid flying towards us. I had to stop it, or else who knows what might have happened. The threats you saw me deal with were also extremely dangerous. This mission is not for fun. There is an existential crisis here for our entire world. You get that, right?"

"Yeah," said Hal, his expression showing a deepening understanding and fear.

"It may be an ambush, but if it is, then it's only more

important that I face it. Whatever or whoever is involved, I have to fight and neutralize the threat. This might be extremely dangerous. But Hal, that's my life. Do you understand? Comes with the powers."

"Isn't there another way to do this? Can't we, like, shoot at them or something?"

"Hal, honey," said Ms. Infinity, "This ship isn't like that. It's not equipped for a space battle, such as you might have in mind. Anyway, you don't need to understand Centerian level science to see that it really doesn't work the way it does in the movies. I know what you're thinking of. I've seen where the bad guy hits a button, and like there's a laser or something aimed at a target, maybe even a whole planet, and the whole thing blows up. Right? Like that? So, you see, that wouldn't work. Of course, Misery didn't try that. She went for humongous projectiles and the like…Hal? Are you okay?"

"Well sure," said Hal. "I mean, I get it. It's just a little disconcerting to hear you tell me that something like that is too fanciful."

"I'm sorry. Why should that be?"

"You know what? Never mind."

"Anyway, please also understand that I don't believe in shooting first. What if there are innocent people there?"

"Yeah. I understand."

"So listen. It is a few hundred thousand miles away, so I will not need you to shoot any video. I am not bringing the ship any closer. That is a risk that should not be taken. Watch the ship, will you?"

"Well, obviously. I mean, where else am I going?"

"Good point. But there's something else to remember. Whatever you do, do not go near the prison cell. Misery is clever, and she might find ways of tricking you. You don't have to worry about her well-being. Her prison cell has all the amenities she needs, and she already has provisions to last her a very long period of time. Anyway, at all costs, never do anything to free her."

"That's for sure! That's one thing you need not worry about."

"I have to go. Thank you, Hal."

"Be careful, Bonnie."

Their eyes locked. There was so much more they wanted to say to each other, yet somehow, they did not say it. After a few seconds, Ms. Infinity said, "So long, Hal. I expect to see you later. Don't worry too much."

Hal watched as Ms. Infinity disappeared once again through the ceiling. As he watched, he felt a growing sense of unease and apprehension.

15 Into the Unknown

Hal did not have to be told twice not to go near Misery. Being alone on a vessel with a powerful sociopath bent on Earth's destruction was terrifying enough, and one warning was enough warning for him.

Ms. Infinity had told him before that her prison was strong enough for any of her kind, and he was pretty sure he believed her. But he had his reservations. He was even more concerned about his companion's venture onto the space station. He did not doubt her powers, or her intelligence, or her overall capability, but he was starting to feel concern at her capacity for hubris.

As Bonnie Boring, she had always been one of the strongest workers at The Big Box. However, he had also seen her get in trouble a number of times for the most foolish of reasons. She had frequently taken over registers without signing the previous occupant out to sign herself in, a huge and unnecessary infraction that saved her only seconds. When the company ran a promotion for "The Box Card, "she invariably declined to do her part, potentially risking her job in the process. All anyone had to do was simply ask once in each transaction if the customer was interested in the store's credit card. These weren't issues of laziness, just arrogance. She just couldn't be bothered with following orders.

When he thought about it now, this mission was showing much of that same headstrong tendency. She had told him that she could handle Misery. There had never been a word about taking her prisoner. It was clear to him that she had never expected this to happen; it was simply an unplanned detour. He was also pretty sure he knew why she wouldn't tell him her plans for Misery. It was because she didn't have any.

He was now getting over the feeling of disappointment in the superhero he had known in the media and in a few brief encounters. It was coming home to him that this was really someone he had already known for nearly two years, and that if anything, her behavior was completely consistent with everything he knew about her.

It was easy to lose sight of this, even long after he had discovered it. Remembering who she really was demanded the disbelief of one's own eyes and ears. Her secret identity was very effectively executed. After all, she was able to transform herself into a completely different being. She also used a superficially different persona, seeming more powerful and authoritative as the awesome Ms. Infinity than she did as the modest Bonnie Boring, customer service girl. Yet over time, he was getting to see the same habits coming out. The longer he spent with her, the more he came to see the same overall personality. She was even addressing him the same way.

He recognized her completely now. This was the same Bonnie: Highly intelligent, and headstrong. Friendly and warm, but at turns brash and dismissive. Arrogant but also extremely giving, caring in her heart, and altogether wonderful where it mattered.

He thought about the time since he first met her. She was the first person he had known at The Big Box. He had met her there before he had worked there, when he was just a customer. They would chat for some time after each transaction, and clearly, they had enjoyed each other's company.

After he started working there, she became unpredictable. Sometimes she would be unexpectedly rude to him, often putting him down in front of their friends. Yet she would also frequently go out of her way to include him if he was being left out of a conversation.

After some months, she was promoted to customer service. Yet she would still frequently step in as needed around the registers. She helped a lot of people out, but it was obvious to him and everyone else who most of her attention went to. He thought himself lucky. He considered her attention to be a precious gift. She loved to rescue him from tough customers, and he had to admit to himself that he just loved that. And if she criticized his work, then that too was a gift. She knew her stuff. Most of the time she was right. She helped to make him a better worker.

Let others call her bossy or controlling. As far as he was concerned, she was a natural leader. He admired her. She wasn't perfect, but she was good and strong, and honest as well. He appreciated her attention. She was showing that she really cared for him. If he never acknowledged it outright, he knew it, and he really cared for her.

Did she know it?

When he thought about it, he wasn't sure if she knew. It was obvious to one and all that he was crushing on Ms. Infinity. But then that wasn't the same thing, was it? No. That was an illusion. He had now learned that lesson. But did Bonnie know that he cared for Bonnie? If he was perfectly honest, he didn't think she did.

Would he ever be able to tell her? He had blown a chance before she left, and it might now be too late. The danger she was in was far beyond his help.

For now, there was nothing to do but wait.

Ms. Infinity flew out again into the void of space. She had not wanted to leave things the way she did. There were so many things she wanted to say. But somehow, she couldn't be sure how to put them into words. She hoped she would have the opportunity later to tell Hal how she felt.

She was feeling increasingly nervous about the possibility of facing more people from her native world. Her battle with Misery had presented her with a sobering reality: she was not always guaranteed to win. True, she had always beaten Misery before. But then those battles were many years ago, in her youth when she was on the run.

On at least one occasion, she remembered Misery blaming her loss on the wind somehow being against her. But then she also remembered a far more disturbing event. Misery was actually close to defeating her when a strange and feral beast came out of nowhere and attacked. Luckily for her, it was only interested in Misery, and it chased her out of range. She never did find out how that encounter ended, let alone make sense of the incident. There were a number of disturbing moments like that from her childhood that she could never explain. It only made her that much more uneasy about revisiting a figure from her old world.

As she approached the space station, it became clear that it was much larger than it had appeared from her ship, or even during her battle with Misery. She had assumed that it was maybe double or triple the size of the average spaceship. It was more like a small colony. What had looked like a façade of one or two stories was in fact a wall of great height. It had been hard to detect this; there were no windows, or other features to break up the vertical aspect. When she landed on the outside platform, she felt dwarfed by the structure.

Were the outside wall a building on a city block, it would have been a skyscraper. Yet it was a vast, metallic wall, continuing far in both directions. The top was hard to make out. In the darkness, it seemed to fade into the void of space. There were openings at intervals of perhaps a thousand feet. The platform outside was quite large, clearly intended for landing spaceships, or for stationing ships for battle. The surface was like a dark pavement, hard and rough with a good traction. She was surprised to see she could take a breath. The object was big enough to have an atmosphere.

Nervously she began to probe through the walls, seeking for signs of life. At first, she saw little but makeshift huts and towers. But after a minute, she saw strange looking men running towards an entrance. But she noticed too late. By this time, similar men were arriving from every angle, armed to the teeth, weapons aimed at her.

With nothing else to do, Hal began to explore Starship Infinity. First, he used the pool, and indeed it was nicer than any hotel's pool he had ever seen. In fact, it was Olympic sized, fully heated, with lounge chairs, and a full supply of towels. There was a hot tub, complete with jets, as well as saunas and showers. There was also an exercise room adjoining it. As he explored farther, he was only moderately surprised to find a tennis court.

The place was beginning to remind him of the stories his grandparents had told him of the Catskills Resorts of years ago. They were great once, but they were now run down. This might well have had them beat, except that the food was bad.

But obviously, there was one other thing missing, and that was the rest of humanity. He was here alone, completely alone now since his superhero companion was absent.

Now that he thought about it, this had a more disquieting resemblance. It was starting to make him think of the large, clean, and mostly empty capital cities built by dictators as monuments to their greatness. This had different visuals, to be sure. There were no towers or obelisks. Things here were more rounded, with narrow, ornate entrances leading to long hallways. But they were still oversized and heroic in scale. The overarching feel was an eerily quiet testament to its creator's power.

He remembered that the society she came from was a dictatorship. Was there an irony here? Had she made an unintentional recreation of the spirit of her birthplace?

If nothing else, the place was certainly comfortable. Hal found that the entertainment center had many movies, and almost any video game he could think of. The library was also well stocked, with classics and many recent titles, and a particularly large section devoted to comic books and graphic novels.

There was also plenty to explore. It seemed that he might never run out of places to see. The ship contained many beautiful rooms with elaborate furniture. It had spaces made to look like outdoor patios, complete with fake plants. There were also play areas of all types. Yet he found himself getting restless and uneasy. The bigger and more luxuriant the place came to seem, the lonelier he felt inside.

Before long, he gave up on his explorations to stare out a window into space. After a few minutes, he found himself crying. No matter how beautiful a place this was, the fact remained that he was stuck. There were no two ways about it. He was trapped in a beautiful and tremendous gilded cage.

This army was not from Center. That much was clear. Ms. Infinity had no idea who they were, or where they were from. At one time or another in her youth, she had seen representatives of each of her native planet's many colonial subjects. These men bore no resemblance to any group she had met. They seemed roughly human in appearance, but their mode of dress was not like Earth or Center. They were mostly light skinned. Their hair was long and unkempt, with long beards. Their uniforms were a dull grey, tight fitting but only minimally adorned. Their weapons consisted of both complex projectiles and bayonets. It was a strange sight. They looked both primitive and futuristic at the same time.

A man began to gesture in a bizarre manner. By his slightly differentiated dress, she presumed that he was the ranking officer, and she guessed by his manner that he was ordering her to surrender. Everywhere she looked, there were soldiers, all focused on her. Were they as strong as her native species? Stronger? Weaker? She could not say. But she could certainly not find out by waiting around.

She paused for a brief moment, then suddenly dove at the officer. Instantly she was caught in a hail of rockets and lasers. The soldiers gasped at the sight before them. All of their ammunition had bounced off her! Yet Ms. Infinity faced a surprise of her own in that the officer was unexpectedly hard to prevail over. Clearly the soldiers were also strong. If their ammunition did not destroy her, then their strength and numbers might well suffice.

Ms. Infinity attacked the officer. She was able to grab his right arm, which was holding the weapon, but the fight was much harder than she expected. She struggled. He resisted and tried to stab at her with the bayonet. By the time his arm was engaged enough to maneuver, he was faced with a sudden, hard kick from her left leg, knocking the weapon out of his hand. The officer reached her leg and began to tackle her, but this proved a useless maneuver on someone who could fly. She floated off the ground and kicked him once again in the stomach. Returning swiftly to the ground, she flipped him by the arm. She caught him in her arms, just long enough to bang him hard on his head, knocking him unconscious. She held him down by her foot. The officer was defeated.

For a split second, she considered whether she should

kill the officer. But she had no time to act on any such decision. Now there was an army in front of her.

These men were not her equals, but they were far stronger than humans. More to the point, they were strong enough that any one of them would require a significant effort to beat. Even if her strength did double, and this gift had not come to her recently, the math was not on her side. She could certainly beat one. Two or three would be harder, but easily within her power. Maybe, just maybe, with a great effort, she could beat up to a hundred. But there were thousands before her. Still, whatever the numbers, this army was clearly a threat to Earth. There was no choice but to fight.

She worked at super speed. Taking the weapons from the ground, she tore them apart and crushed them in her hands. She then slid under the next, nearest soldier, aiming for his legs. But the soldier was fast too. Guessing the strategy, he responded with a hard kick to the head. The impact was hard, but she was unwavering. Grabbing the other foot, she flew into an abrupt upswing. Now holding the soldier by the leg some eight feet off the ground, she swung him suddenly at a cluster of a dozen or more soldiers. All were knocked over, instantly.

She quickly grabbed all the weapons she could and crushed them, but there were many more soldiers. Within seconds there were hands gripping her from behind. A soldier was now holding her by the waist, hoping to prevent her from flying away. She responded with a hard backwards kick, but he was ready for this too. He grabbed her foot with his other hand and held it tight. A number of other soldiers joined in the effort as well, with another grabbing her other foot, and two others diving for her arms.

This might have proved fatal had she not still been significantly stronger than all of them. She wriggled her body, legs, arms, and torso. This simple action alone made her very hard to constrain. The soldiers struggled to hold on, but their grip loosened with every second. Reinforcements ran in from every direction, but they were too late. Ms. Infinity swung in a flip, up into the air, free again.

She dove at the largest contingent of soldiers she could see, flying super-fast into the crowd. Many of them were knocked over, but she was immediately surrounded. She used a combination of moves. She elbowed a soldier coming at her from behind, knocking him over instantly. She then flipped herself over backwards at super speed, catching him before he reached the ground. She then threw him like a Frisbee into a crowd of men. Most of them fell, but many others were still running at her.

She now tried to use her super speed against them. She twirled herself around so fast that she became like a small tornado. She shot in every direction, sending men flying into the air.

At first the remaining soldiers were afraid, each flinching from the challenge. But soon the officer roused from his prone position. He "announced" something by gesturing in a broad, demonstrative manner. Grabbing a sharp weapon from a soldier, he held it firmly in front of himself as an example. The other soldiers followed suit, some daring to move closer and closer to the fast-moving target. Soon she was surrounded again. Guessing her trajectory, a line of soldiers held their weapons together and waited. All at once, she was stopped, bouncing back. Then there was Ms. Infinity, now in a kneeling position, bleeding from her left side.

As they charged at her, she struggled to keep her head. The conclusion that followed was hard and frightening. The army she now faced was beyond her skill. She thought of the powers she had not yet used. Shape shifting had not worked well with Misery. Using tricks like super breath might well bring a temporary victory. But this army was huge and well organized and would likely regroup. And if anything, using too many powers now was poor strategy, rather like showing her cards. She needed something that was much better planned.

Ms. Infinity leaped once again into the air. She then made another dive into the crowd, but this time she aimed near the edge of the space station. She hit only a few soldiers in her impact, but she hit the ground much harder. This made the soldiers uneasy. She took a mental note.

She did all she could to stay near the edge. At all costs she could not be captured. The first few men she defeated, once again with hard kicks, but she rolled consistently toward the edge of the station. By this time, she was bleeding and beginning to look desperate. Then several dozen men charged at her. She stepped farther and farther back, until she was barely an inch from the edge. Then with a powerful blow from a soldier, she slipped and fell off, and so she fell into the abyss.

The front line watched their enemy fall, hard and cold. Some might have expected her to fly and were prepared to fight an enemy in the air. No doubt some were quite surprised to see her simply topple over from their blow and fall like a dead thing. They watched her fall farther and farther, a helpless body, now trapped in an endless momentum, waiting for death if indeed it had not already come. They continued their watch as she grew smaller and smaller, then disappeared from their sight.

16. Human Potential

One thing Ms. Infinity had not told Hal was how long she might be gone. Hal was growing increasingly concerned about her. But he was also becoming more and more disoriented. He had no idea how long he had been in space, or even how much time had passed since his companion had left; he could not even say whether it had been a long time. In his confusion, he was near despair.

It had now dawned on him that he had made an incredibly dangerous and careless decision: going on a dangerous mission, lightyears from home, involving people and deeds far above his abilities. But it was worse than that. He had also allowed himself to be sealed up alone in deep space for an unknown period of time, with a powerful woman whom he did not know as well as he thought. He could thank his lucky stars that she was decent and was not someone who would hurt or kill him, or indeed, violate him.

It was amazing to him now that he had never thought of this before. Women thought about these things all the time. Lisa never traveled alone at night. She usually had Bonnie, or Julia, or someone else going with her. She had even asked him to walk with her once. Bonnie did walk alone, but now he understood the unique context behind that. But he was now beginning to think that men might have to worry about such things too. He was not invincible either.

At any rate, he had every reason to be terrified of Misery. If she were to get out, there was no telling what she might do to him.

As worried as he was about Bonnie, there were other concerns he had to address. Increasingly he felt that it was upon him to take responsibility for the mission, at least to the extent that he could. Ms. Infinity had left him alone on Starship Infinity with Misery, and there was the possibility that she might not get back. It was time for him to step up.

Whatever her flaws, it was clear that Ms. Infinity was still a tremendously brave and important hero. Her mistake, as he saw it, was failing to think of a "Plan B." Perhaps her extreme powers had spoiled her; she might not have been used to the possibility of failure. So indeed, he did have a contribution to make. "Plan B" it was then. So then, what was it?

His first thought was what to do if Misery did get free. If Earth's Greatest Hero could barely contain her, what chance did he have? But at least he could be as prepared as possible. Could he arm himself?

He thought about the spaceship. It had everything, including a huge kitchen, many bedrooms, a TV studio, tennis courts, a pool, a prison cell, and much more. Did it have an armory? He didn't even know where to begin looking. Sure, Ms. Infinity didn't need weapons. She was all about her powers, and her powers were all she needed. That was well enough for her, but what about visitors? Did she keep anything for guests? A hammer? A lasso? A radioactive invertebrate? Anything?

A brief exploration of previously unexplored hallways turned up nothing but a racetrack and a roller coaster. He was running out of capacity for surprise. Soon he gave up. All he could think of was using a few pots and pans from the kitchen, a fairly pathetic defense against a powerful foe. So, he would have to think in another direction.

What if Ms. Infinity didn't return? What then? He certainly could not stay adrift in space forever, with Misery as his companion. For one thing, food would eventually run out, and she might easily outlast him. She would probably escape sooner or later, and she would then have the spaceship to do with as she pleased.

He could not go home either. He had no idea how. The maneuvers through multidimensional planes had rendered him temporarily unable to function even when Ms. Infinity controlled the travel. He definitely could not even begin to execute such movements himself. And just travelling without such manipulations would never get him home. He was many, many thousands of lightyears away.

And then even if he could get home, there was no good reason why he should under these circumstances. He was carrying some very dangerous cargo. His prisoner was Earth's would-be destroyer. He had no desire to function as an unwilling Trojan Horse. What could he do? Ask the President to send the military on her? There probably wasn't enough military power in the world to stop her.

"Well, damn!" he said out loud in frustration, "I might as well just steer this whole thing into the nearest sun!"

A deafening silence followed his outburst. He could not believe what his mouth had just said out loud. But it was worse than that. The fact was, he had indeed just delivered himself the very answer he needed, and he could not for the life of him imagine how there could possibly be any other. Try as he might, there was no lie he could tell himself to make that go away. There was the contingency plan. He would die, but Earth would be saved.

Bonnie had told him that she risked her life every day; that was a hero's life. She told him about the responsibility that was upon her. If she were no longer around to fulfill it, then who could? The entire planet would now depend on him, Hal Holstein of Queens. If it meant giving up his life, then that was what he would have to do. There was no other answer.

He began to cry. He could not believe that it had come to this. This was not at all what he had expected when he begged Ms. Infinity to let him go with her. He had never dreamed that he might never see his family again, his home, his friends. Among many other things, the possibility of death also carried a huge disappointment; that video he had shot had given him hope that his career might take off after all. At the same time, he had to admit that he was feeling something else that was unfamiliar. There inside him, he was beginning to know some self-esteem, pride, even courage. This too was the last thing he had expected. Maybe on some level, this was all meant to be.

Hal dried his tears. So, he had a role to fulfill, and there was no choice but to step up. He thought his protocol through for a while. He would not do anything unless he was quite sure that Ms. Infinity was not coming back. It would take a sign, like the approach of enemy ships from the space station. Barring that, there would have to be a very long wait, though that was a much more difficult consideration. What qualified as a very long wait? At this point, he had absolutely no idea what hour or day it was, let alone how long he had been on the ship. But he decided it would simply have to be a very, very long time before he acted.

With that consideration out of the way, the only remaining questions was *how*?

Earth's sun was far out of reach, but he wondered whether there was another within relative vicinity. Were they in a solar system? Running to the bridge, he looked out the window. Then he looked through the equipment. Somewhere there had to be some navigational tools. He soon found that there were. There was actually an electronic map, right next to the pilot's seat, and it was surprisingly user friendly. And after a few moments, he could confirm that he was indeed in a solar system. The star had a name of sorts, an alphanumeric code beginning with "M53." The planets had longer alphanumeric names, and the moons had even longer ones.

After further consulting, he discovered that the star of this system was just over a hundred million miles away. That was a distance this ship could reach. How long would it take? He couldn't say. Again, he didn't even know what that meant anymore. But he was pretty sure that it could be done.

So now it came down to controlling the ship. That was another problem. How did this ship work exactly? He had never really stopped to consider just what Bonnie was doing with the controls. So how did this thing operate?

The controls were far less user-friendly than the map. There was nothing in front of him that he could understand. He saw no "forward" button, no "back." All he saw were numerous controls with bizarre names.

The task ahead of him seemed bewildering. Even considering all the impossible, magical things that Ms. Infinity did, he hadn't really considered the act of piloting the ship to be a "power" But now that he thought of it, this was a spaceship that was far beyond the capabilities of human science. What did he expect?

For a time, he sat there, thinking. There was a way. There had to be. He had come to think of Bonnie's powers as "magic," but he was coming to think that it really wasn't that. "Magic" was simply a catch-all word for anything humans could not do, though admittedly her abilities included a long and impressive list of such things. But then, many people could not operate a video camera. He could. Was that magic? Even Bonnie was not omnipotent. Among other things, she could not carry a tune. And he could, quite well. So, was that magic?

She had talked about the many dimensional planes, and how people from her native planet understood many more than humans did. Maybe the key to understanding her powers was in there somewhere. A little understanding was all he needed. Flight, super strength, shape shifting: these were overwhelming to think of. But maybe, just maybe, with a little imagination, he could grasp a little piece of knowledge that he could use. All he wanted to do was pilot the ship.

So, he knew three dimensions, or four if you counted time. Bonnie had said something about there being other dimensions that were not "spatial." He didn't understand that at all. However, that was perhaps a crucial piece of information.

As he thought some more, he mused that sometimes, doing one thing often required doing something else to make it possible. This was true in many aspects of daily life. Just walking forward meant pushing back on the ground with your feet. Playing an instrument was about making sound, but it required many different manipulations, be it the hammering and plucking of strings on a guitar, the blowing of air and movement of fingers on a wind instrument, or the hammering of keys on a keyboard.

The more he thought about it, the more he realized that almost no effect was possible without a lot of actions and reactions. Some might be much more complex than he ever imagined. Maybe some involved dimensions he did not know of. Perhaps that thinking was the key to operating the ship.

Looking at the controls, there were lots of cryptic names. He dared not even guess what "Galactic Coin Bounce Color Set" meant. Was that a vending machine? He thought he remembered her mentioning something about that in a maintenance check. He also remembered hearing "Unliquidated Carpets," among other non-sequiturs.

He guessed that the meaning was out of his grasp somehow. But then that was the point. These made sense according to the logic of multidimensional thinking. He also remembered that Bonnie's language had not used sound at all. No doubt the use of English to describe this logic was imperfect at best.

He was terrified about what might happen, but he pressed the button labeled "Orbital Irony." The ship didn't move, but the room seemed to blur. He immediately turned it back. Then he tried another one, and another. Some seemed to do nothing. Another had the terrifying effect of stretching everything out before he reversed it. He was almost out of patience. But after many frustrated trials, when he finally turned one of several dials labeled something called "Inferred Collapse of Instance," suddenly the ship moved.

"Ah!" he exclaimed, "It's pushing off of something! Or hanging or grasping! Or bouncing! Or just... something!" He could not pretend to know what was there, let alone believe he understood it. But he did understand the most important thing. Whatever it was, the ship could somehow interface with it. He turned it some more. Strangely, turning the same dial continuously in the same direction did not result in continuous forward motion. It was erratic and unpredictable. So, he tried a few of them in tandem.

He did not want to go far. Bonnie would hopefully return, and he needed to stay close to where she had left him, but he also needed to figure this out. There was much trial and error, and he never could predict exactly what would happen with each knob turn. But after some practice, he could say he had some idea. He made a few tentative movements, this way and that.

He was impressed at how far the ship went in such a short time: tens of thousands of miles barely in a blink. When it came time to return, the frustration grew. He knew where he was going, but for whatever reason, it was incredibly hard to bring the ship back there. After a while, he decided that close enough was good enough, and settled when the ship was within a few hundred miles from the starting point.

So now his contingency plan was complete. Now with nothing else to occupy his mind, he could not forget how frightened he was. He thought of his family, and dearly hoped he would see them again. He hoped he would see Bonnie too, and finally tell her how he felt.

He said a few prayers, both his traditional Jewish prayers and a few personal ones. Whatever might happen now, this had been the adventure of a lifetime. He only hoped that he would live to tell about it.

17. Secrets of the Back Room

Since Lisa was now on her break, she decided to make the most of the time, and visit Human Resources in the back of the store. If nothing else, she did receive a sympathetic ear from Emily, the HR director.

"I'm sorry to hear that you're in trouble," said Emily. "I see that there is a formal write-up here."

"Right," said Lisa, "that's what I'm talking about. The incident happened when I was on my break. Somebody else signed in with my ID."

"I see. That's a pretty serious charge. Can anyone confirm this?"

"Yes. Maria knew I was on break. You can ask her."

"Do you think you know who is responsible?"

"I don't, but I strongly suspect Denny. He has a grudge against me from last week. He got in trouble because he was missing when a customer complained to me. He asked for the manager, and when Denny didn't answer, I sent him to Yvonne."

"Denny. Yes. So that's a grudge. Anyway, you are going to have to write a statement. I would first have to ask: Do you have a solid reason to believe what you are telling me? We would need a lot of evidence before we could go ahead with a complaint."

"I do… Wait. A complaint? What are you…?"

"Without strong evidence, it would mean your word against his."

"Well, can you at least overturn the write-up? Why do you need...?"

"Here's the decision you have to make. Are you only trying to remove your problem, or make a complaint against your supervisor? Now if this is a complaint against your supervisor, then okay. There might be legitimate grievances. If he's giving you problems, there might be other cases. But there would have to be hard evidence for any actions to be taken."

"Why would I...? Are there other cases? Have other employees complained about Denny?"

Emily shook her head. "I can't discuss other employees with you."

Lisa was finding this conversation curious. Emily was strangely interested in getting a complaint against Denny. On the surface, it seemed as if she was warning against it, but Lisa hadn't even suggested it in the first place; Emily was the one who had brought it up. She seemed to be covertly trying to get Lisa to sign on to something.

"So," said Lisa, "what you're asking is: am I saving my job or complaining about my supervisor?"

"Right."

"I'm just curious. What if I only tried to overturn the write-up?"

"I don't know. It's hard to say if you could do one thing without the other."

Lisa thought for a moment. "You know what? I think I will make a complaint."

"Your decision."

"By the way, Emily, do you have a Band-aid for my forehead? It's still bleeding, isn't it?"

"It is a little, yeah. I'm afraid we're out. You know where they keep some? Over by Security."

"Really? Security? Ugh. No. They're really mean over there."

"Well, I know. Nobody ever wants to go there, but that's where First Aid is, and if you are hurt, they are supposed to help you. If they don't, then you should tell me."

Lisa left Human Resources and started over to Security. It was a short walk through the hallway containing the various offices in the back of the store. Security was the farthest back. She was about to enter, but she stopped short when she heard several voices inside, including a familiar booming one.

"You had the cameras off, right?"

"Stop worrying, Den. I told you, we have your back."

Lisa quickly stepped back a few paces, ducking farther into the hallway. She definitely had to hear this conversation.

"I'm going to be there in a few minutes–"

"Stop there!" broke in a third voice. "You should always be aware that we have bosses too. We'll do favors for you when we can. But you have to remember something. We have to explain–"

"Mitch," interrupted Denny, "I'm asking you for one little thing."

"I'm not arguing with you," said Mitch, "but you have to remember that we're the ones who are responsible when things go missing. We're already reeling from last week. That was one of your employees who almost got killed when this place got robbed. It was on us that the camera over the front end was off when that happened!"

"So?"

"So? So, we were doing it for you! It's our heads when there's a security breach. This isn't something we can just do every time you feel like going under the radar. Look, you're a friend, and you have a problem. So, we'll do this one more time. But you'd better not expect us to be doing all these favors for you again and again. It's bad enough letting you watch the cameras, doing God knows what. That could be our heads too."

"Alright," said Denny. "Just this one more time."

"Oh, no!" corrected Mitch. "You're not telling me one more time. I'm telling you that. This is the last time. We can only cover for you so many times. We have a job and we're professionals. So are you. You're going to have to get used to that idea."

"And I'd be careful about mouthing off to me like that," said Denny. "You're right. You're not as safe you think."

"Excuse me?" asked Mitch.

Lisa snuck away, sensing the end of the conversation. She scurried back through the hall and made her way quickly back to Customer Service.

So Bonnie was right. Denny had been using Security, for something. She was pretty sure she knew why he wanted to watch the cameras. No doubt that was how he had gotten her login. It wasn't exactly clear why he wanted to have the camera shut off at a specific time. Obviously, there was something he was doing, or intending to do, that was under the table. No doubt he would not be using his own login—it would likely be hers. One thing was for sure. She was going to have to be there when it happened.

She was not sure what else she could do with this information. So far, she had been taking things as they came. It was now clear that the situation demanded a strategy. Unfortunately, there wasn't much time. It looked like she was headed straight for the shark tank.

18. A Hero's Reach

As Ms. Infinity fell to her apparent doom, the platoon was elated. The officer held up his weapon in a sign of victory. The troops all cheered in response. The roar of the army was very loud indeed, and could be heard throughout the small colony.

Soon the ranking officer arrived from within. When the news was delivered to him, he addressed the crowd. He spoke with a vibrant spirit of a new dawn for their people. Enthusiastically he told his army that victory was at hand, and that soon the next stage of their venture would begin.

Floating still and silently for a great distance was Ms. Infinity. She felt like she was trapped in an endless stretch of inaction. The charade of death was not difficult to keep up, but it was monotonous.

As she floated, she paid close attention. As the celebration picked up, she could finally surmise that she was no longer being watched. *About time*, she thought to herself, *I can't float like this forever*. She turned, and quietly began to fly back to the space station. *Alright*, she thought to herself as she approached, *this time with a plan*.

The celebration was long and spirited. The soldiers were soon joined by women, and by the political leaders of the colony. As they drank and danced, stories of the battle were told. Many of the soldiers told the women of their valor in battle, sometimes with much embellishment. And already the tales were growing of the strangely dressed woman with great powers whom their heroes had defeated.

And behind the scenes, the officers and the political

leaders began to discuss their next move. With the enemy out of the way, they would now rescue their master from her captivity. There were also preliminary discussions for the phase that would follow her rescue.

As the ranking officer discussed his plans, he noticed a strange sight outside his window. One of their own many ships was passing by, then pulling up to the dock. Then another came. Then another. He excused himself and stepped outside. He then shouted at his underlings, since he had not ordered any such movement. But they were every bit as surprised as he was.

And more of their ships pulled up, one behind the other. And strange the sight was, since nobody could recall receiving any orders to move out, and there did not seem to be anyone missing. Yet as they examined the ships, they made an even stranger discovery: There was nobody piloting them.

Then an extraordinary thing happened. The whole colony began to quake. It shook slightly at first, then harder and harder. Soon the inhabitants struggled to stand. They began to panic, running this way and that, clinging to each other and to anything they could find to anchor themselves. But they had not yet seen their strangest sight yet.

For then, they heard a loud roar like thunder. There were flashes of lightning all around, seemingly coming from nowhere. Suddenly they saw a tremendous figure before them, godlike in scale, and they discovered that their entire colony was in her hands. It was indeed Ms. Infinity, the enemy they thought they had just defeated, now grown to a scale far beyond any living creature. Her image filled the sky above, like an omnipotent figure passing judgment, her enormous arms reaching beneath their horizon. And in panic, all began to run for their ships.

And she called, in a voice resonating with tremendous power: "Get out while you still can, you bunch of weenies!"

And the giantess stayed until the entire colony was cleared, periodically threatening the army below her with taunts and slurs. As the last soldiers embarked, they looked back, and saw her tremendous body filling their view, her mammoth hand about to reach for them. And so, they raced inside and began their flight.

And even after the ships evacuated, she flew after in pursuit. Many of the ships began to fly in formation, about to attack their enormous foe in a desperate last attempt at victory. But before they could attack, she changed into another monstrous form. And she was enormous, much larger and far more threatening than the monster that had attacked Misery. She had many giant heads, each of them breathing fire, and countless tentacles, all of them grabbing at the mass of ships. And on each of her heads, her mouths opened, revealing many thousands of tremendous teeth, as sharp as saw blades. From their view, she seemed as big as a planet.

So, an entire military force had the sight of a single unarmed enemy so powerful, so terrible, so threatening, that every single ship turned around in fear. The colony was then abandoned once and for all. When they finally did regroup some distance away, the decision was made to return home, and never to trust in Misery again. And in time the stories would be told among them of the foolish mission commanded by the cruel blonde woman, who would have them attempt an attack on a planet full of people who could transform into gigantic, godlike monsters.

But as the ships flew away, the real Ms. Infinity waited behind the image of the monster, still the same size and shape as usual; indeed, still nursing a wound on her side. After the ships were far away, she put an end to the great illusion.

Brave as the victory was, Ms. Infinity had actually been in tremendous danger. She had actually not faced such a threat in many years.

For this reason, she had fallen back on an old trick from her youth. Avoiding capture at all costs, she would "lose" the fight. She would seem to fall completely, but crucially, she would be outside the field of battle when that happened. She would wait for a period of time. Then she would mount a spectacular and well-staged retaliation, something that would shock and awe her enemy into submission or retreat.

In tandem with her super strength and telekinesis she used another of her powers: casting illusions. She made a giant image of herself appear in front of the army. That with the unusual events of their ships arriving and the colony's "earthquake" was enough to convince them that she was back as an omnipotent rival.

For some reason, employing such an attack in retaliation seemed more effective than leading with it. Perhaps it carried the advantage of confusion. Still, it was risky. It depended on psychology, and results varied depending on the enemy. The same tactic had never fooled Misery, for one.

Bonnie might have dismissed the idea of "magic shows." However, as she knew from her many comics, theatrics were naturally built right into the very idea of a superhero. Everything about the archetype depended on showmanship, from the absurd names to the outlandish costumes, to moves that would make the flashiest magician blush. And indeed the "show" was often important to the superhero known as Ms. Infinity, when she made her appearance.

As recently as her rescue of Hal from the roof of The Big Box, there was a major case of fakery. The flash of lightning that she "appeared" out of was nothing but fireworks; teleportation was one power she did not possess. The effect made for a spectacular entrance. But more importantly, it also protected her secret identity by masking her real entrance, a simple ascent from five stories below.

Even more recently, she'd used the same trick to make an impression on Misery. She also regularly enhanced her transformation into Ms. Infinity with a similar "explosion," essentially for her own motivation.

Then too, it was Bonnie's nature to overstate her abilities, superhuman and otherwise. When she told Hal that she had just "rearranged the universe" just to fix two wobbly chairs, there was more than a little hyperbole. She had simply used her telekinesis to fix the chairs. Hal could have "rearranged the universe" just as substantially by putting a book under a chair leg. This same tendency occasionally extended to her Bonnie Boring persona. Even when she was with Lisa, she might exaggerate about anything, from her work to blowing bubbles and even belching. Fortunately for her, Lisa found it endearing rather than off putting.

As Ms. Infinity landed once again, she saw that many ships still remained. There was one that was much larger than the others and bore all the hallmarks of a ship from Center. Clearly that ship belonged to Misery. She scanned the ships with her super senses to confirm that all were unoccupied.

She then began to survey the space station. She used her x-ray vision, efficiently and patiently. For some time, she found little that surprised her. There were many military facilities, barracks, and training areas. Predictably there were many smaller facilities for the soldiers, and fewer, larger quarters for the officers.

In an isolated area, she found a desolate building with no windows. She gathered that it must be a prison. The walls were very thick and took an effort to peer through. She soon discovered that there were indeed prisoners inside. She flew around to find the door and tore it open.

An ominous thought occurred to her. What would be the consequences of freeing everyone? Were some of these prisoners real criminals? Were all of them or most of them political prisoners? How could she possibly know the difference? She certainly did not have time to question all of them to tell "good" prisoners apart from "bad." What if she was setting dangerous people free?

She soon decided that she had little choice, because she intended to destroy the entire colony soon, and everyone left would perish. She had to trust in mercy, and the only humane choice was to let people go.

She entered and was soon shocked at what she saw. She was no stranger to confinement, or to unpleasant surroundings, but this place was a category in itself. The prison was, in a word, disgusting. It was dark, with dim and inconsistent lighting. The walls were stained with water and possibly blood. The floors were flooded, ceilings dripping with a liquid she dared not identify. There were many competing smells, all strong and unpleasant.

She ran through the prison, conveying in the communication of Center that she was there as a liberator. She tore the enclosures apart, one by one, motioning to the prisoners to go. Many of them were confused at her appearance. Some were apparently not sure whether she was there to rescue them, or if she was in league with Misery, and they feared a trick.

It was clear that her message in her native language was of little help. The prisoners came from many different worlds and spoke many different languages. The process turned out to be complicated and required patience. After a while, she learned to depend on each group to communicate her message to each other, which was at times a tricky thing to accomplish.

With each room she found more unpleasant surprises.

But her greatest shock came in the deepest reaches of the prison.

There in a dark corner, in an especially desolate and cramped cell, was someone she knew from her distant past. It took her a moment until she recognized him, dark and haggard as he looked. He was perhaps seventy years old in Earth years, fair-skinned and bearded, much thinner than he had been in her youth. He was chained to the wall, looking desperate. Realizing that he would not recognize her, she communicated to him who she was. Upon this revelation, he communicated: *That is a surprise.*

It is, she answered. *And it is you, General Imperial. I dare not guess how you might have become the prisoner of Misery.*

This was my colony. She attacked us with her army.

I might wonder then why you were so far away from 'Center of the Universe'.

That is a long story. Since I have last seen you, I was exiled. You should not be surprised. I was lucky it was not worse. Still, I had done well until Misery arrived.

Ms. Infinity found herself in a difficult position. She certainly did not want him to know her present business. Yet she felt that she had a responsibility. As she looked hard at him, she explained, *I have a debt to you, so I will free you.*

She tore apart the man's chains, and he marveled at her strength. *You are even more powerful than before*, he remarked.

She questioned him for some time. He had been banished from Center many years ago. He now had an extensive colonial project in the region. This space station was his main base of operations.

The men who Ms. Infinity had scared away had come with Misery. General Imperial actually did recognize them. They lived on a moon in the outer regions of Center's own solar system. The reason this moon was so obscure was that it had few natural resources, and there was little interest in colonizing it.

He seemed unable to deliver any other valuable answers. Indeed, he seemed as confused by Misery's mission as Ms. Infinity was. It seemed unlikely that they would profit from a colonial mission to a single, isolated inhabited planet so vastly distant from Center. After all, he himself had only come this distance because he had been exiled and knew he would not return. He also didn't understand why Center would be using a female for an attack, or why they would be employing such a ragtag group to go with her.

Ms. Infinity thanked him, but then continued: *You must leave. This now settles my debt. This place will not be here much longer. There are ships for all of the freed prisoners. You must go.*

Ms. Infinity left the prison, then continued to search the colony. After further scanning, she found one building that was significantly larger and more extravagant than the others. She knew what that meant: "Misery's Place."

The rooms were enormous, with an extravagance that seemed to convey power and importance. Many were large halls with high ceilings, yet were nearly empty save for furnishings in the deep center. It said a lot about her relationship to the army she was working with.

Yet nothing she saw had prepared her for the surprise that met her in Misery's sleeping quarters. It had many creature comforts, including media such as people used from Center. But when she looked on a table near the center of the room, she was stunned to see dozens of materials in English. These were all from Earth!

There were books and magazines of all types. There were even some superhero comic books, though none were of her particular taste. Many of the items before her could easily be found in the checkout lines at The Big Box, among many other places. These things were a long way from their point of origin.

She could draw some obvious conclusions. Misery had been to Earth, or at least one of her underlings had. She had also learned English. Clearly, she intended to be a permanent part of Earth, probably as much more than a customer service associate.

Finding a bag, Ms. Infinity collected a few of the items, letting out a sigh of disappointment that there was no candy. Once again, she would have to wait for her chocolate fix.

There was one more thing that interested her. On a desk was a communication device, such as they used on her native world. Yet she could tell from looking at it that it was much more advanced than any that she had ever seen. It reminded her of discussions from the days just before her departure from Center. There was much rumor of the advance of technology. There was said to be a communication device in development that could work across many, many light years. She wondered if this was that very item. She decided she would take it with her as well. Placing it in the bag, she took leave of the building.

Upon leaving, she was alarmed when she saw the man she had freed, General Imperial, wandering around, seemingly without aim.

Why are you still here? she asked. *You are free, and you must leave.*

Where is she?

Where is who? There is only me, but be not deceived. That is enough. I have destroyed the entire army on my own. If you were thinking of attacking, I can certainly defend myself.

But she must be here somewhere. She always has been, whenever you have been free. This is a secret I have known when others have been deceived.

Ms. Infinity was both confused and alarmed. She was also beginning to suspect that General Imperial might know more than he had let on.

She reached in her bag and took out one of the magazines from Misery's quarters, a copy of *Cosmopolitan*. Then she looked at him in the eye and asked in English, "Do you recognize this thing?"

He looked back blankly, giving no reaction at all. It was not clear that he even knew that her speech was an attempt to communicate.

She then asked him in her native language. *Do you recognize this?*

That is not whom I seek, yet she is fair. Is she near?

The woman on the cover is not the concern, explained Ms. Infinity, trying not to be amused. *Have you seen this publication before?*

I have not. I do not know that thing.

I found this in Misery's quarters.

I have languished in captivity. I have no knowledge of things since I was imprisoned.

Have you told Misery anything?

I have told her what I know, though that is not much.

I think it is enough. You will not find whom you seek. You must leave immediately. My debt to you is now paid. You will find a spaceship for yourself. You may go where you will, but you will leave Earth alone at all costs. You shall never even enter its solar system. You will not follow me. You will have nothing to do with me, or any of my family or friends. Be assured that I am greater even than you have seen, and you will not do well if you defy me.

General Imperial looked at Ms. Infinity once more. Instantly, she turned back at him with a threatening look. He finally turned away. She watched intently as he entered a ship, and pulled away into space.

Ms. Infinity decided to take Misery's spaceship back with her. She flew to the ship, and placed in it the materials she had found in Misery's quarters. She then flew it just out of range of the colony.

Exiting the ship, she scanned the colony once more to assure that no living souls remained. She then began her labor of destruction. Over and over, she flew into space, then smashed into the abandoned colony at super speed, crashing it into pieces. She repeated this effort many times. Quickly the buildings were destroyed. Soon after the ground beneath crumbled. Finally, the entire structure came apart. When she was done, there was nothing but many piles of debris, floating around in space.

Ms. Infinity took Misery's spaceship and began the journey back. It felt very much like her own ship before her many alterations, before its transformation into Starship Infinity. In other words, it was like any from the military of Beacon of Freedom: cold and metallic, large and standardized. It was perfectly efficient, but it made her uneasy.

Seeing General Imperial's fall was a profound realization. The tyrannical leaders of Center had always seemed so invincible. It was now clear to her that they were anything but. Like any bullies, they lived to make others miserable; it seemed sometimes that they had nothing better to do than to push people around. But she now understood something about bullies. In truth they were operating out of fear, for behind the façade lay profound weakness. Once you looked past the curtain and saw the inner workings, it was clear that their rule rested on a house of cards.

The many threats and punishments the public faced prevented almost everyone from knowing this reality. Yet the corruption that the despots hid was a secret that was very dangerous to them. There were security personnel who were misused, and who knew many damaging things about the leaders they served. There were many other actors who were bribed or threatened, or both. Anyone could turn on anyone else. The status quo depended on a steady stream of secrets and manipulations. A tyrant often had to live day to day.

Then of course, nothing was more dangerous to a tyrant than a truly informed and empowered subject. That was why speaking out was such a risk. A person who knew the truth, and would speak up, was someone a despot would want to silence at all costs. Sadly, they usually could do just that. Yet, if the people only knew it, the real weakness was with tyranny.

She had to admit that she had some good memories, even back in Center. When she was in hiding, there had been many kind people who had helped her. At different times, she and her mother had been taken in and cared for by many good and decent people. Indeed, they were risking their own lives by protecting them. Most of them were extremely generous, even though some were of modest means. She remembered how kind they were, and how her mother had always reminded her to be kind to them in turn. She wondered what had become of these people.

Looking back now, it was a marvel that she had not become cynical or criminal, considering her past. When she thought of it, her mother deserved a great deal of credit. Betty Boring, as she was now known, had gone to heroic lengths to see that her daughter experienced love and caring, and was taught morality; most importantly to value herself and others. All of this was done under very difficult and hostile circumstances.

Still, even the best of memories contained a bitter taste for her. Her childhood was not a happy one. And yet there was more than a silver lining in that her life today was vastly improved. Not long ago, she had been lying in bed, feeling disappointed in life. Now that she thought about it, a major reason for that feeling was simply that she had the luxury to feel that way. She certainly had never had any such thoughts when she was locked up, or in hiding, or fleeing for her life.

But now she was safe and free, and living in a nice comfortable home with her mother. She had good friends, one "bestie" in particular whom she loved dearly. And this alias of Ms. Infinity was created for her own purposes, not because of a need to escape anyone. How great was that! She was living a dream! Life was good, and it was time to appreciate what she had.

She also seemed to have a relationship blooming. Perhaps it was time to stop neglecting it.

Hal's protocol was to carry out "Plan B" in two scenarios: if Ms. Infinity didn't return in an undefined "long time," or if any number of enemy ships approached. Hal had waited and waited, putting off the decision as long as possible. But now as he looked out the window, he saw something he could not ignore: an enemy ship.

"Oh no!" he said to himself. "No! They must be here to get Misery. Bonnie must have lost. I've been putting this off and putting this off, but this is it. Now I've finally been a coward for too long, and if I don't step up now, RIGHT now, all will be lost!"

Hal sat down for a moment and collected himself. Then after a deep breath, he prepared for the inevitable.

"Alright," he said to himself, "this is it. I wish it hadn't come to this. I love you, Mom, Dad, Stacy. Oh, Bonnie, I'm sorry this has happened."

He ran to the bridge and began to work the controls. He began his erratic path into the nearest star.

"Where's my ship?" shouted Ms. Infinity. "Oh no! If Misery has done anything, she will *die!*"

She looked outside for any sign of Starship Infinity. "Why did I have to make it invisible?" she said. It was only a moment before she discovered a vapor trail. It was brand new. The ship had only just moved.

She flew Misery's ship in pursuit. The path was erratic. "Okay," she said to herself, "the pilot must be someone who doesn't have a lot of experience. So that would mean that Misery is probably not running it. It must be Hal. But why?"

She thought another moment, then it came to her. "Oh no. I know why. It's my own stupid fault. Why didn't I think of this? How long has this been for him? He must think I was gone for... Oh! And now I'm in an enemy ship, so he thinks... No! I have to catch him!"

She flew after the vapor trail as fast as the ship could go. However, try as she might, Misery's ship just could not keep up. Starship Infinity had benefitted from many improvements over the years; Bonnie's genius with space technology was well beyond even the best of Center's scientists. Even flying in a straighter path could not make up for the difference.

She stopped the ship. Then in a fury of action, she opened the hatch, and climbed outside. She tried to use her telepathic control to call the ship, but the distance was too great to be effective. It now became clear that she had but one choice if she was to catch up. And so, she flew.

Way back in the early stages of the mission, Hal had wondered how fast Ms. Infinity could fly. He had experienced her flight halfway around Earth in only a minute or two, and wondered if she could fly to distant planets at a comparable clip.

Truth be told, she herself had not seen the outer limits of her speed. She knew that she could not stay in space forever; she would eventually need to breathe. But she had indeed flown a great distance into space, indeed considerably beyond the limits of Earth's solar system, at speeds far greater than that of light, such that are thought impossible by human science. Yet as she saw Starship Infinity flying into the nearest star, about to be taken into its gravity, she was not sure. For an instant, she wondered if this task was beyond her.

But there was no time to wonder. She simply flew. She disappeared from all visibility as she shot across space, her speed far surpassing that of Misery's ship. But that was just the beginning. With all of her will bent toward her goal, she gained immense velocity with every second. Almost instantly, she was flying many millions of miles per second. No spaceship from any world could have kept up, let alone overtaken her. Still, every ounce of her energy went into increasing her flight.

I know it's ahead, she thought, *I see the vapor trail, getting fresher. I have to keep pushing. Hal, please! Sit tight! I'm coming for you!*

It might have seemed impossible to fly faster than she was already flying. Already she was making short work of the vast distances of a remote solar system. Yet it was not enough for her; the impossible task of reaching her distant target was all that mattered.

And still she burned forward with immense, ever-increasing speed and power. She passed one planet after another, some of them inhabited. The people of these worlds would certainly have been enthralled by the sight of the mysterious object shooting across their skies, had she been large enough to see, and had she not been going so fast she was rendered invisible.

Still, she challenged herself to ever more mind-boggling speeds. So great was the power of her flight that even if a tremendous natural body such as a moon had been in her way, she might have knocked it out of her way, or maybe plowed right through it, as though it were not there.

And then, against all odds, she at last reached her ship, only a few million miles from the star. She could just make it out with her super senses. Yet even as she began to overtake it, she saw that it was speeding up too, trapped in the star's immense gravity.

With one final, tremendous burst of energy, Ms. Infinity sprinted forward one more time. With an immensely powerful force, she leaped forward, using the power of the star's gravity to increase her own flight. And so, she reached her goal at last. She finally flew around and put herself in front of it. Then she stopped. This too, her power to resist the gravity of the sun behind her, required a force greater than the human mind could comprehend. She placed herself in front of the ship and held fast.

"This is it," said Hal. He closed his eyes and waited. He could not imagine what horrific end was ahead of him. He only knew that he was about to be burned or vaporized. The last thing he expected was to be knocked off his seat, the ship crashing into a sudden stop.

"What happened?" he wondered. For some reason the

ship was turning around.

"It's okay, Hal!" called a voice.

He looked behind him, and there she was. "Bonnie!" he shouted heartily.

"Hal!" said Ms. Infinity, as she ran to embrace him.

"You saved me again! So, you are alright."

"I am," said Ms. Infinity as she pulled away, "although you just gave me the scare of my life. But you're okay, and I'm okay. That's all that matters. By the way, you might not realize just how advanced this ship is. Okay, you fell out of your seat, but that's all. Not many spaceships handle this smoothly when they're stopped short after going millions of miles per second."

"Amazing! But how did you…"

"I stopped it."

"From outside?"

"Yes, Hal. From outside."

"You…? Wow! You sure are powerful!"

"And you are a nice-looking man. By the way, you were right. There was an ambush."

"Oh no. Is everything okay?"

"Oh Hal, don't worry your handsome head. I spared every single life. You know I'm a softie at heart. So, I think I have an idea, but what were you doing and why?"

When Hal explained his reasons, Ms. Infinity was amazed and awed. She was beginning to look upon her companion differently. Her mother had indeed been right about him.

"Hal, I'm sorry if I've been keeping you out. You know what? This is your mission too. Seriously, you are a hero!"

"Thank you," he answered, blushing.

She looked at him curiously. For some reason, he seemed to be holding back laughter.

"Okay," said Ms. Infinity, "I know you can't hook me up with a chocolate fix, but can you at least tell me what's so funny?"

"Well, look at this, Bonnie," he laughed, "this is something you never thought I would be able to do. I worked the ship. Think about that now. I figured out how to work in those multidimensional planes. You know, the things you thought I couldn't understand. Nice, huh? Still think we humans are dogs trying to learn video games?"

"Well now, I didn't..."

"Oh! Look at me! I'm a dog playing a video game! What's that? Woof! Woof! This dog just defeated Bowser!"

She looked at him wide-eyed and laughed. "What a smart doggie!"

"That's the best you can say to me?"

"I kid. That's really very amazing. It really is. I have underestimated you. I wish I could say more, but I have to get back to questioning Misery. I have finally had a breakthrough."

Returning to the prison cell once again, Ms. Infinity glared at Misery. Misery looked surprised and dismayed to see her. She tried once to communicate in the language of Center. Ms. Infinity only looked back with contempt.

"Never mind that, Misery!" said Ms. Infinity, in English clear as a bell. "No more games. Now, you are going to tell me, in plain speech, what is really going on?"

19. Confronting the Creep

By the time Lisa returned to her station at the customer service desk, customers were beginning to arrive for the evening rush. A cold sense of dread was upon her. There was a tension in the back of her neck, pain in her sides, and a terrible sense of foreboding. More than ever, she was sure she could not go on as she had before.

Soon Julia finally arrived to accompany her. For a few minutes, they handled the crowd together. There were no more "creeps" than usual. The "Long Winded Guy" attempted to con them, but Julia shut him down with an abrupt demand: "Return something or go!" Both Julia and Lisa agreed that it was a satisfying moment. But soon they saw the approach of another creep, the house creep, Denny. Bobbi was also a short distance away. She seemed to be sneaking around the aisles around the baby section.

"Julia," whispered Lisa urgently, "Look!"

"At what?" said Julia. "I see enough of that jerk."

"I know but wait. It's about to get interesting."

As they watched, Bobbi beckoned to Denny. He tried his best to be inconspicuous as he moved over to her. Remembering what Bonnie had said, Lisa wondered what might be going on.

"Julia," said Lisa, "watch customer service."

"You are daring," said Julia, "but you're leaving me to handle the line…"

"Oh, bitch please!" snapped Lisa as she scurried away.

Lisa snuck into the baby section from the back. She crawled behind a stroller display and listened.

"No! No!" said Bobbi, "Don't! Don't touch me! I said stop!"

"You are a tease," said Denny.

"Don't get too used to this."

"Don't tease me. You want it too."

"Don't take this for granted. Can we get this over with? I can't keep my order hidden forever."

"You really are like the rest of them, just a gold digger."

"Denny!"

"Alright. Alright. Just give me a couple of minutes. I'll get the girls off the register."

Lisa snuck a quick peek, and saw that Denny was indeed groping Bobbi. She was trying to stop him, but he kept persisting. Her expression showed both stress and resignation, as if she knew she was helpless to control the situation.

So now the story was becoming clear. Denny must have been harassing Bobbi, and she must have been extorting him. He must have been letting her steal, or at least get discounted prices, with the register at Customer Service. It was also clear now to Lisa why Denny was using her numbers: that way she would get the blame for the fraudulent sale. No doubt he had the camera turned off at just the right moment so that the sale would not be seen.

Lisa snuck back to the front end. Maria was at Customer Service. "Lisa," she called, "If you needed a bathroom break, you should have said so."

"Come here Maria!" whispered Lisa.

"Now what?"

"I just saw Denny, and he had his hands all over Bobbi. Did you know that this was going on?"

"Know? Lisa dear, I don't just know. Just be glad he's not doing this to you."

"Really?"

"Yeah honey. Denny's a piece of work. Believe me, if I didn't have a family to support, I wouldn't be putting up with this."

"But there's more. Bobbi's trying…"

Lisa then saw Denny approaching Customer Service and ran to her station. "Trying to sneak back?" he sneered.

"I just returned from break," said Lisa. "What's your excuse?"

Denny came up very close to Lisa. Tall as he was, and as short as she was, he was very imposing. "Whatever," he said. "You girls can go to the registers or something. You know what? Help the stock boys downstairs."

Maria was slightly behind Julia. She shook her head quietly, with a look on her face that said she was dying to speak up.

Lisa looked back up at Denny, trying to keep from showing her nerves. "What's the matter? You couldn't pull your operation in the fifteen minutes when I was gone?"

"Do me a favor, girl. Babble somewhere else. I got actual work to do."

"Oh, *you* got work to do. You're well prepared for it too. Security cameras off and everything. You're all ready to steal my ID and use it for your criminal operation."

Denny recoiled in shock. "What the hell you talking about?"

"Oh, you know exactly what I'm talking about. I heard everything."

"This is none of your goddamn business."

"Oh, it's my business!" shouted Lisa. "I'm protecting my job. You're no supervisor. You're a thief! I'm not going anywhere until everyone knows it!"

"I said, mind your own business!"

"I am," said Lisa firmly, "This *is* my business. I know everything, and I won't be quiet anymore. The minute you try to sign on with my name, I'm going to scream."

Denny looked both very nervous and very angry. "Don't you even think of getting involved, you little stink! I'll have you fired so fast you'll be crying to your daddy!"

"Is that your best insult? You're going to get me fired anyway. Why the hell should I even think of listening to you anymore?"

Denny moved in closer. "Don't you talk to me like that, little girl! I can make life very difficult for you. Who do you think they're gonna believe? Go ahead and try and say all you're saying. I dare you. Try it and I'll make you pay!"

Denny was standing over Lisa in as threatening a stance as he could. Yet the more he talked, the more it became clear that he was very nervous. Lisa could see the sweat pouring down his neck. As he raised his voice, she could also detect a note of desperation.

"Oh, I get it!" said Lisa, "you're trying to intimidate me. You're a big bully! That's your whole thing. You're all about being bigger and stronger, too big to screw with. But I understand perfectly now. You're scared. You're scared of all of us. This whole thing is big façade. Well guess what. I'm pretty good at seeing through façades. I've seen through much smarter than yours."

"You know what," said Denny, "punch out and go home. You're being written up for insubordination. Do it now or you're fired!"

Lisa wanted to continue, but she felt doubt kicking in. If she were fired, then she feared that there would be no more she could do. It also occurred to her that if she were punched out, Denny would not be able to use her ID. She took out her wallet from her purse, and found her employee card. Then she punched out, and stormed out the door.

Denny snuck away from the scene as quietly as he could. But even as he stalked away from customer service, he couldn't avoid Bobbi, who came up to him and spoke just over a whisper, "You're not off the hook with me."

Lisa had been at this job for over four years. She had started while she was still at Queens College, when she noticed that it paid better than the campus jobs. She'd expected it to last her through her nursing degree too. It was not much, but it was hers. At twenty-six years old, it was virtually the only part of her life that her parents could not control.

Despite their vastly different origins, Lisa and Bonnie had quite a few things in common. Yet in some ways they were also opposites. For one thing, Lisa was a model student. But then she had little choice. Throughout high school, her parents were on her every second, orchestrating her success. Everything from her homework to her projects to her study time was planned obsessively by her mother, with her father on hand to enforce discipline when necessary. It even extended to her cello, an instrument she had never even wanted to play, but which was the one available for joining the orchestra that the family had insisted she join.

It did not even stop when she entered college. No matter how much Lisa protested, her mother continued to plan her studies, and continued to watch her constantly. It was then that Lisa thought seriously about moving out.

This job seemed to have potential. It promised annual raises and an eventual promotion. There were even benefits for full-time employees. Some of those promises were never fulfilled. The store would never give her enough hours to qualify as "full time," though indeed she could never have worked that many hours anyway with her studies. She did get a few raises, and an eventual promotion to the customer service desk.

It seemed however that no raises could compensate for the realities of New York City real estate. The goal of affording even the smallest apartment was still distant. For his part, Hal could not really afford the illegal upstairs conversion he was sharing with a roommate whom he could hardly stand. Still, he struggled to keep his independence; the impossible seemed a necessity amidst the ugliness surrounding his parents' divorce.

Despite the difficulties, Lisa kept plugging away, eyeing that eventual move out. Then one day, Denny was promoted to Front End Manager from the Electronics department. He was rude and unreliable from the start, and grew crueler as time went on, until the whole environment became hostile. She had thought she would continue, but now things had become very uncertain.

As she left, she felt resentment kicking in. She was kicking herself for not thinking of recording him with her phone. But it was worse than that. After taking the trouble to stand up to Denny, she should never have let him intimidate her into leaving. She wanted to storm back in there and confront him even harder.

Maybe she could only do so much. Maybe even after she spoke up, she might not be heard. She might well find herself still on the sidelines. Yet it was foolish not to try. Still, she had to admit, she was afraid to face him. It killed her inside. Nothing was worse than modest hopes dashed by a bully.

After Lisa stormed out, the cashiers began to chat.

"That was awesome!" said Ahmed.

"Not so great for me," said Julia, "Now I'm alone here."

"It's great that someone finally said something," said Nadine.

"So, wait," said Ahmed. "What got Lisa so mad just now?"

Julia and Nadine looked at Ahmed in utter amazement. "You didn't see that?" asked Julia.

Nadine explained, "Denny's been a horror for as long as he's been the boss here. He's worse to the women. Ask Maria. He's harassed both of us, and others. How did you not know that?"

Julia glanced at Nadine in shock. "Wait. What? I thought he was just trying to steal or something."

Maria shook her head, looking worried, "It's that, it's the other thing. You and Lisa wouldn't know. You don't see the side of him that I do."

"I mean," said Ahmed, "he's a jerk to all of us, and he's never around when we need him, but…"

"So, Nadine," asked Isha, "would you have done what Lisa just did?"

"Hell no! I need this job. I have a son to take care of. I can't risk getting fired. Lisa doesn't know how good she has it, living at home with Mommy and Daddy. Some of us need to work."

Julia looked at Nadine with surprise. "So, why are you just a cashier? You should try and get promoted. At least you should be with us in Customer Service."

"It's not that easy. I have enough responsibility with my other job. Besides, I'm not having an easy time here. You might not have noticed, but I get in a lot of trouble when I get called by my son's school."

Meanwhile, Maria ran the front end quietly. All she could feel was disappointment. She was hoping Lisa would've had the courage of her convictions, but when push came to shove, she had not followed through. It seemed that Denny was right about her after all.

In other parts of the store, the sales people also gossiped about the people they barely knew. Teddy from Electronics was friends with Hal, and knew Bonnie and Lisa. He was talking energetically with presumed authority.

"It's always the quiet ones, right?" he shouted. "I knew Lisa was weird. I bet she has some secrets too."

"Wait," said Josh, his coworker. "Lisa? Which one is that?"

"The Chinese girl from Customer Service," shouted José from the men's department. "You know, the one who was yelling at Denny."

"Oh, right," said Josh, "her. Yeah, she's weird."

"I could tell you. She's got stuff going on," said Teddy. "I bet she's totally into domination. I'd love to see what's in her basement."

The other guys laughed. "I could see her now with Denny!" laughed Josh.

Teddy could barely contain his laughter. "Oh, you KNOW there was something going on with Denny!"

Josh and José started simulating a scene with Denny

begging Lisa, and were soon laughing uncontrollably.

"That's totally Lisa!" shouted Teddy.

They would have gone on longer, but they were interrupted. Rafi, the electronics department manager, came in to break it up, and to remind them to get back to work. As they walked back to their station, Josh asked Teddy, "So what about Bonnie? You think she has some secrets too?"

"Nah," said Teddy, "She's just stuck up."

20. A Villain's Secrets

Misery tried to maintain silence. As if playing dumb, she continued to communicate in the manner of the people of Center. Ms. Infinity ignored it.

"Forget it, Misery," said Ms. Infinity. "I defeated the whole colony. The whole thing is destroyed, and they all went home. Whatever you were planning, it's over. But I found some materials there...

"We call this *Cosmopolitan*, or *Cosmo* for short. My mother, you may remember her as 'Bland Homemaker,' she thinks *Cosmo* is rotting my mind. But I can't stop reading these. I love the sex tips and guy pics. Oh, and the fashion. Love the fashion. So, Misery, do you prefer this or *Glamour*? Honestly, whichever one it is, you desperately need a makeover. That hair flip over the right eye looks horrible. Although with that face, I probably would want to hide as much as–"

"Shut up!" screamed Misery.

"Well, look who joined us!" said Ms. Infinity. "By the way, Misery, that reminds me. These mags also have quizzes. This issue of *Cosmo* has one that I think you should find eye-opening: 'Do You Have a Difficult Personality?' You see, when they say, 'difficult personality', that's code for 'bitch', so I don't know if you took it, but I'm pretty sure that if you did–"

"I SAID SHUT UP!"

Ms. Infinity paused, looked at Misery, and smirked. "Yeah, forget it, Misery. There's no need. I think the question answers itself. Anyway..."

"What is this 'Misery' you keep saying?"

"Why, it's your name, close as this language can get. I don't think it quite does you justice. I would probably call you 'Sludge Butt' if I had the choice…"

"'Uninteresting Pretty' is too nice for you. You should be called 'Dead Slut'!"

"Well, you've perked up. I had that name translated to 'Bland Beauty', but I don't use it anymore. You are to call me 'Ms. Infinity'."

Misery rolled her eyes. "I liked your other aliases better."

Ms. Infinity's tone became graver. "Never mind that! And don't you dare forget who the prisoner is here. Your life is hanging by a thread. You will talk to me now!

"First of all, who sent you? The president? Who is it now? And why would he even care about attacking a planet half a universe away?"

Misery was silent, her face hardening into a look of defiance. There was a long, devastating silence. Ms. Infinity stared at her coldly. Misery tried again to communicate in the language of her planet, this time attempting again to remind her of her past. Ms. Infinity stayed utterly closed to it. She answered with cold speech.

"I am not going to listen to any more of your obfuscations. I'm going to take a little break. But this isn't over between us. Oh, it's never over. Buh-bye."

Ms. Infinity stepped out. To her surprise, Hal was sitting on the stairs, right outside the prison cell. He had apparently been listening to the whole conversation.

"Hal, "said Ms. Infinity, "you really took it to heart when I said it was your mission too. But we might want to have a talk about who gets what."

"Sorry," said Hal, "I couldn't resist."

"Well, I don't blame you. Here! Let's take a walk, or a fly. Do you mind? We really need to get out of shouting distance."

"Oh! I'd love to!"

Ms. Infinity flew Hal to the atrium. She put him down in a chair and sat next to him.

"So, Hal," she said, "I'd just be very careful about getting too close to our prisoner. I really meant it when I said I want to share this with you, but there are still some common-sense issues. I mean, I was joking with her. But remember, she's still extremely dangerous, and if you said the wrong thing where she could hear it…"

"I'm sorry," said Hal, "I won't do it again."

"Well, mostly just keep a very safe distance. Listen around her and don't speak. And don't ever go near her if I'm not around. Remember how much stronger she is. I think you get that."

"Yes. I do."

Ms. Infinity smiled. "It really is nice to see you again."

Hal smiled back. "Thank you. You too, Bonnie."

"And thank you. About that: do not use that name anywhere near Misery either. She isn't privy to my secret identity. Got it?"

"Oh. Of course."

"Hal, can I ask you something? It's a little personal."

"Actually Bonnie, I've been wanting to talk to you, you know… personally."

"Aw, really?"

"You can go first."

"Hal, Will you…"

"Yes?"

"Actually, wait a minute, something my mother said…"

At that moment, Ms. Infinity changed into Bonnie Boring. It was a quiet transformation, just a quick, natural metamorphosis from one guise to another. Hal was quite surprised at the gesture.

"Okay now, Hal," said Bonnie, "Do you want to finally go steady with me?"

"Well, hello, Bonnie Boring!" beamed Hal. "You know something? I have really missed you! Of course I would love to go steady with you. I want to be your boyfriend more than anything. You might want to keep quiet about it though. Ms. Infinity might get jealous. I'm glad it was you who asked me. I'd pick you over her any day."

"You're kidding me!" shouted Bonnie. "Really? Oh my god! Oh my god! Oh my god, Hal!" She leapt into Hal's chair and kissed him. They held the kiss for a good half a minute.

Bonnie whispered, "I have been waiting for this moment for a long time."

"Me too, Bonnie," whispered Hal. "When you were gone, when you flew to the space station, I was worried sick. And well, among other things, I was afraid I might never get to tell you how I felt about you."

"Well, I'm back."

"And I think you're wonderful. I always have. Working with you this past year has been the best thing that ever happened to me, at least up until now. I think I'm falling in love. No. I definitely am."

"Me too, Hal. Let's just say it. I love you, Hal."

"I love you, Bonnie."

They kissed again, but then after a moment they stopped. Bonnie looked around a second.

"I'm sorry, Hal. We really do have to finish this mission. It's just with Misery here…"

"Yeah, I know."

"I'm really getting pissed off at her," said Bonnie as she stood up. "Well, now or never. Infinite Power!"

In a puff of smoke, Bonnie changed into Ms. Infinity. Hal looked on and smiled. "You know, that's like the hottest thing ever!"

Ms. Infinity looked at Hal sidelong and smiled. "Save it! Save it!"

"Well Misery," said Ms. Infinity, "are you ready to talk?"

Misery was looking up at her furiously from the bench in her prison cell. "What is that thing outside?" she snapped. "Your pet? So now you're getting with the humans like a wife?"

"I don't believe that's any of your business. Don't forget who's the prisoner here. You're answering my questions. So, what is going on?"

"You are a typical North Coast elitist!" shouted Misery. "You think you're entitled to everything!"

Ms. Infinity looked at Misery in disbelief. Misery had come from the same area, and was hardly less privileged, though doubtless she hardly cared about being caught in hypocrisy.

"I'll tell you what," continued Ms. Infinity, "I'll start small. Since you're suddenly so interested in my life, I'll ask you a nice simple question about your world. Who is the president now, back in Beacon of Freedom? I've been gone a while. I doubt that good ol' President Death Grip is still in power. I could tell he wasn't in for a long run."

Misery became indignant at the sound of that name, immediately recognizing the translation. "He was a traitor! A rodent! He was a coward and a sellout!"

Ms. Infinity smiled. "He also wasn't all that bright. He never did catch me tying his shoes together. So, I take that to mean that he's now dead. So who is it now?"

Misery held back a smile. There was no reason not to pick on a man who had been shamed and executed. Nonetheless it could not have been easy for her to enjoy the moment. News like this of her enemy's old defiance might have amused her, but it also had to wake feelings of jealousy. "You have left us and sold us out. Why should I tell you anything?"

"Ah, now that's a shame. We were doing so well. We didn't have to take it to that level now. I just wanted news. C'mon. Is it Muscles of Freedom? Power Fist of the People? Lord of Ultimate Power? The Alpha Male of Liberty?"

"None of them are. They were weaklings, phonies! Now they are all dead. We have found our true savior, the great man of freedom, Master of the Masses."

"Oh yeah. I remember him…"

Hal listened outside, some distance up the stairs. It took some effort to make out the conversation. Information came slowly when it came at all. He figured that Ms. Infinity was probably using Misery's emotion to make her talk. It didn't seem that she had much else in the way of strategy.

The whole thing made him uncomfortable. The idea of

having a prisoner in the first place was strange enough, but now hearing Ms. Infinity's threats and taunts made him feel truly shaky. He reminded himself that Misery was, after all, threatening his entire world. He wondered if his companion — indeed, now his girlfriend — felt as much discomfort as he.

The names of the presidents sounded absurd, somewhere between professional wrestlers and porn stars. Nonetheless, Misery obviously took the whole thing very seriously. He supposed that the names must sound better in their native language.

One other thing that interested him was an inference he could make. Clearly Bonnie must have lived in a position close to power, since she obviously had known the president personally. Exactly what her station had been in life, he could not guess.

After a while, he discovered that Misery was not the only one getting aggravated. Ms. Infinity was beginning to shout as well. He noticed that it happened when another name came up. Yet the man they were discussing was not a president at all, but a general, "General Strongman." He guessed there must be some story in that as well.

All in all, listening was a very strange experience. He could only understand a limited amount of what he heard. Without the proper context, he could only wonder about what he did not know.

"What about General Strongman?" said Ms. Infinity.

"Why should you care?" retorted Misery. "You got better than what you deserved. You stepped on the soldiers, the brave men who gave their lives for Beacon of Freedom, and the general."

"Don't you tell me about the general. I knew him long

before you did."

"That was his curse. He had good reason to hate you. You were not worthy of him. Your life was about your own filthy ways, trying to be more man than the men. You were a witch, and now you're even more of a witch!"

"What business is that of yours?"

"I'll tell you what," said Misery indignantly, "the general could have been president if not for you. You destroyed him!"

"So," said Ms. Infinity, "you say I destroyed his chance to be president? What about you now?"

"I tried to save him!"

"You did, then? I do remember you got close to him, right before I returned. Once I was back, I saw you around not a few times."

"What business is that of yours?"

Ms. Infinity laughed grimly. "Well, isn't that the pot calling the kettle black. I don't care much about the nature of your relationship. I mean, I know it, but so what? But maybe I should have cared at the time. I do remember what almost happened to me."

"And you expect me to cry for you?"

"Well, I do wonder what you might have done, and maybe what you might have said to the general."

"What happened was too good for you. He's lucky I was there to protect him. You should have been killed right on the spot."

"So, are you saying you were in on this? Was it all your idea? Was it your plan?"

Misery looked at Ms. Infinity with surprise, as if a

strange revelation was coming to her. After a moment, she laughed harshly. "You wretched little imp! You really do think everyone and everything revolve around you."

"So," said Ms. Infinity, "I seem to have landed on a truth here. I read it in your eyes."

"You read nothing, if that's what you think."

"Answer my question!" snapped Ms. Infinity. "What part did you play? Was it your plan?"

"Oh, Bland Beauty," mocked Misery, "You are even more spoiled than I thought you were. You have some strange and narcissistic ideas. How many people did you think were plotting against you? How important do you really think one brat was to the whole world?"

"Shut up right now! Just answer my question already!"

Misery looked at Ms. Infinity cruelly. "Honestly, did you think the general really needed arm-twisting? He knew what he wanted."

"He knew what?"

"You can blame your sob story on me, but you'd be wrong. The general had his own ideas, and he should have succeeded."

"You can't be…"

"Oh! I'm telling the truth," said Misery, now speaking as clearly as a bell. "Bland Beauty, you have misunderstood everything. You have it backwards. When I fought you, he was the one who sent me. Whatever else happened to you had nothing to do with me. Everything was directly from the general. Yes. Every single thing that made you run away. Him!"

Ms. Infinity looked at her with disgust. After a second, she could only look away. The full weight of the revelation was coming down on her, and with it came a growing shock and persistent pain. She tried to keep calm, but after a moment, she began to lose control. The room began to feel stuffy and constricting, and she felt like she could not stand to remain for one moment longer. She finally stormed out and slammed the door.

Ms. Infinity stopped as soon as she reached Hal. She closed her eyes, teeth gritting, nearly hyperventilating. She held back her tears and took a deep breath, eyes closed. Then she spoke, "I've had enough. C'mon Hal, let's have a meal."

"Oh, okay." he answered. He was about to speak more, but he was afraid of saying too much. He had a strange, ominous feeling as he followed her on the long walk up the stairs and through the main hall into the kitchen. He could only wonder what had gotten her so upset.

"Tell you what, my love," said Hal, "you seem to be in a bad mood. I want to take care of you. There's a couple of eggs left. I'll make you an omelet if you'd like."

"That's alright, Hal. That is very sweet of you. But I'm in no mood. I just want to eat fast. I'm putting in the frozen mac and cheese. There's one more if you want one."

"Sure. Thanks."

They heated their dinners and sat down to eat. Ms. Infinity looked at Hal with compassion.

"Hal," she said, "I want to talk to you. I am sorry for a lot of things. Look. I'm glad we're steady. I really am. I just want it to be on the right terms. I haven't always been great to you, and you have not had much control over this situation. The balance of power here is very uneven, and I've begun to worry about you."

"How do you mean?"

"Hal, this is a captivity, and I'm very sad to put you through it. I know how hard that can be. The worst thing would be if you came back expecting better than you got before, and I made false promises I never intended to keep. That thought makes me terribly sad. It's a cruel situation for anybody."

"I'm not sure I follow," said Hal. Looking at her, he could see that she was just holding back tears.

Ms. Infinity picked up her head. "I'm very sorry that I refused to let you participate in the mission before. Maybe I thought I was protecting you. Or maybe I was just afraid of admitting my own failures. But it was horribly unfair to you. It made you a prisoner."

"Yeah. You did do that. And you're right. But I really do forgive you."

"And I talked to you like you were beneath me. I don't know why I do that. I just have an arrogance about me sometimes. But I had horrible nerve to do that to you. You're not beneath me. I'm very sorry about that."

"I guess you did. Of course I forgive you for that too."

"Now you're stuck here, for the time being. I'm sorry about that. But I promise with everything I have that it is only for a while. The end of this will come, and you will be free. I would love to keep dating you. But I only want it to happen if you want it to happen. And you should always be around other people besides me. It is very important to me that you continue to see your family. Do you know how lucky you are to have your family? I know how your parents' marriage is falling apart, and you must really be hurting from it. But you need them. Believe me. Just having them is a gift that not everyone gets. I count myself lucky just to have my mother. It's more than she has."

Hal did not answer right away. He stared out into the

middle distance for a moment. Then as tears began to well up in his eyes, he said, "I haven't seen my mother in a long time."

"Hal," said Ms. Infinity, "this is what I mean. Look, I can't speak for you, but it sounds like she has disappointed you. The story you tell is disheartening. But you will have to forgive her. She may not live up to the expectations you once had for her. But your mother is human. I have had to learn the same of my mother."

"She has a new boyfriend. It's really hard to accept."

"I don't doubt it. I sympathize. But Hal, has she done anything to you?"

"No. No. She hasn't."

Ms. Infinity spoke gravely. "Believe me, Hal. It could be much, much worse. You are very lucky to have both parents, even if they are not together. And I'm sure she needs you."

"I miss her. When we get home, I will see her. I'm decided on that."

"You know Hal," said Ms. Infinity, "it is nice to see you instead of Birdbrain down there. This interrogation is getting pretty old."

"I can't really tell by listening. How is that going?"

"Well, better anyway. Now that we're speaking in English, it's much less hard on me. It's funny. When my mother and I first arrived on Earth, I found human communication strange. It took a lot of getting used to. The thing is, now it's the only way I ever communicate if I can help it. I prefer it over my old way any day.

"A couple of things about my native language. It is extremely complex, in ways that human language cannot begin to approach. Yet I've come to understand that it can be a weakness. It makes it much, much easier to lie. It's very easy to confuse another person with endless details. With human speech, people certainly lie, but that advantage isn't there. If you scrutinize a liar, you can catch them a lot of the time. It's just not as easy to obscure things.

"Then there's the level of engagement. With my native communication, you are forced to give all of your attention. This also means that things like names really stick. So as odd as a thing like 'Misery' might sound, the thing is, you really do believe them. They are taken as your personality and your measure. But hearing them in English, that attachment just isn't there. A name is just a name. In fact, some of those names sound pretty ridiculous, right? I mean, 'Muscles of Freedom'! Really?

"That's why there's such a difference. When I was questioning Misery before, she was able to upset me just by turning the conversation. She knew this too, and she used it to her full advantage. Now that we're using English, well, it's a whole different ball game. If she gets mean, I just make a joke over it. Most of the time I can, anyway."

"Maybe," said Hal, "but she still got you mad before. Very mad."

"Well, sure," said Ms. Infinity, "she still can… Hal, is there something else you're trying to say?"

He didn't speak, but the nervousness in his face was palpable.

"Hal," she said, "are you afraid? You can say it if you are. Please say it every time you are afraid. I need to know it. I never, ever want you to be afraid to speak up."

"You did make me a little nervous."

"You're afraid because I was harsh with her, right? Do you think I might hurt you?"

"I don't know. I know that you would never want to,

but what if you were angry?"

Ms. Infinity looked sad, but she spoke graciously. "Thank you for saying that. My mother and I have had many discussions about this. Our only choices for dating and marriage on Earth are human. And we have to think about things like this. She has been on me from day one to never, ever let any argument get physical. Not with a friend, not with a lover. Not ever. Even when I'm fighting crime, I have to be extraordinarily careful. I don't hit a human if there's any other way.

"Misery is not human. I could fight her — I had to fight her — because she is a superhuman who threatened Earth. But since she has become a prisoner, I have not laid a hand on her. I think she has picked up on this, and taken full advantage. She does not think twice about being extremely cruel with her words. And to tell you the truth, I'm not cut out for interrogating. I don't really have the stomach for it. But you didn't hear it from me.

"Anyway Hal, I'm glad you brought it up. Once again, remember you are free, and you don't have to be with me. If you do break up with me, you should never, ever fear retribution from me. But please also know that if you are with me, I will never hurt you. I'm sure we will have our arguments. That is what couples do. But I'm confident that we are both civilized enough to keep those arguments verbal. Anyway, always do tell me if you are afraid for any reason. I hope that is good enough."

"I wonder," said Hal, "do you really think you're doing so badly with interrogating Misery?"

"The thing is," said Ms. Infinity, "I'm still no closer to an answer."

"So, what exactly is the question?"

"You have to realize that Earth is a great distance from

Center. It makes no sense that a Centerian would even care about attacking us. The thing too is, now I know that there was a full military contingent. That suggests an attempt to colonize. That seems very unlikely to me. The cost of maintaining a colony like that from such a distance would easily outweigh any benefits."

"So why? Or is there another question?"

"Who sent her? And with a totally unfamiliar army too..."

"Interesting, that," said Hal.

"What is?"

"That means they're not from your planet."

"Right," confirmed Ms. Infinity.

"So, whoever they are..."

"...They aren't going back? Maybe. But then I would assume they have somewhere to go to. Although perhaps they were her colonial subjects too. That's the thing..."

"What?"

Ms. Infinity thought a moment. "I'm wondering. You don't think she might be the mastermind, do you? Could this be her colonial project?"

"It's a thought. She might not intend to go home."

"But why would she even think of Earth in the first place? I doubt she would have gone this far just to get back at me. But then..."

Ms. Infinity paused. When she thought about it, she did know the answer. She got up in a hurry. Wiping her face, she spoke hurriedly, "You might not want to hear this, Hal. Up to you, I guess." Then she flew away in a flash.

"Might not want to?" laughed Hal, "I couldn't catch

you if I tried!"

Within a second, Ms. Infinity was at the prison cell, staring hard at Misery. "Tell me now, Misery. It is the General, isn't it?"

"You are pathetic! You were his shame–"

"I know. I know," said Ms. Infinity, "you made that abundantly clear. And I heard it many times before you ever came around. It was the mantra of my childhood. But there was something else you said before I went out to your space station. It went over my head before, but you said I deserved what was coming to me. So, what was that exactly? From who?"

"You pathetic little wench! You really do think this is about you, don't you!"

Ms. Infinity took out the communicator she had found at the space station. "Oh, I don't think it's all about me. In fact… suppose I contact the general now?"

Misery laughed coldly. "You wouldn't dare! It would be the death of you."

"And you just gave it away. It is him after all. Anyway, he doesn't scare me anymore. What can he do to me now? Nothing. But you had better be terrified. What do you say I contact him right now? You can explain that army of yours. I mean, funny how you talk about treason."

"You know nothing!"

"Oh, I wouldn't be so sure. Do you want me to contact the general right now, and tell him everything? I'll do it right now."

Misery tried to keep her defiance. She stood tall, but there was no mistaking the fear in her eyes.

"Yeah, I thought so," said Ms. Infinity.

"Why do you care?"

"You know what? This whole thing is ridiculous. I don't need any more of this. I have my answers."

21. The Big Reveal

As Ms. Infinity returned to the kitchen, she saw Hal, still cleaning up after their meal. He didn't seem to notice her arrival until she called, "Hey Hal. I have a surprise."

"Oh. Hi," he said. "What's up?"

"I have the mystery all wrapped up. Why don't you come with me and have a powwow with our guest?"

"Really? Are you sure? I mean...really?"

"Yeah Hal. I think it's time for the big Scooby Doo reveal."

"Oh. I'll keep quiet just the same."

"Just follow my lead."

Ms. Infinity led Hal into the prison area. He saw Misery up close for the first time. She looked human, just as she had seemed when he was filming her. She was fair-skinned, tall and thin, her long blonde hair parted to the right, and partly covering her right eye. There was little else he could see; she was covered nearly head to toe, in a white robe with blue trim.

Looking scornfully at Hal, Misery snickered, "So this is your hobby."

Ms. Infinity shook her head. "Ignore her, Hal. We have other things to talk about.

"So, what has been going on? I think it's quite clear now. Not about me, Misery? Oh, I beg to differ.

"Misery was sent by a certain member of the military by the name of 'General Strongman'. My escape some years back was an embarrassment to him. 'Shame' is a word she chose. Now it would seem to me that he has presidential ambitions. And if they are to be met, he has to take care of this little skeleton in his closet."

Hal wondered exactly why his companion was so important. She had said that much of what was going on was "over his head," and now he was beginning to understand what she meant.

She continued, "So there was this job of fetching the embarrassment, me that is, to make a public example, and reclaim the general's honor. But that would mean taking a long journey, and thus an extended leave. He certainly was not going to do it himself. His absence would have had consequences for him. If you want power and influence over people, the least you need to do is be present. I would suppose that's why it has not happened in all these years since I left. When he did finally assign the mission, it was an arduous job for which one would probably get little or no thanks. Now Hal, do you know what that means?"

"I...don't follow."

"Nah. You wouldn't. You're a man. It means women's work."

Hal rolled his eyes, but was silent. Misery watched him intently.

Ms. Infinity continued, "The general also obviously figured the job was to capture a woman, so he might as well send a woman. Misery could do it. No problem. I'm sure he never saw past his sexism. But then there's one other detail.

"Misery had designs of her own. I'm going to take a guess that this is why she chose this moment to agree to this mission. She was in contact with some other interesting characters, people I did not recognize. I don't think most people in the leadership would recognize them either, though I know of one person who did. Whether she was interested in completing the general's orders or not, I don't know. But she was far more interested in her own secret project: colonizing Earth.

"The asteroid, the meteor shower, the waves of antimatter, none would have completely destroyed the Earth, or even the bulk of human civilization. But they would certainly have devastated our cities and our people. It would have been the preparation she needed for her invasion. This is why she took the trouble of learning English.

"Think of it. The general was scheming behind the president's back, preparing for an eventual coup, and she was working for him. But Misery was also scheming behind the general's back, on a much, much grander scale. It almost makes me want to respect her. Almost."

"Excellent!" said Hal, "so then..."

"Then what?"

Hal motioned with his arms. "So..."

"She would have gotten away with it if not for us meddling kids?"

"Of course. So, Ms. Infinity. You have done a wonderful job. This case is blown wide open. So...can we go outside?"

"What?"

"Well, if it is alright, I would like to talk to you some more."

"Oh, alright."

They stepped outside and walked some way up the stairs. Ms. Infinity gave Hal a cold look. "What is it?" she said.

Hal looked at Ms. Infinity pointedly. "So now that the case is solved..."

"Yes…?"

"Now what are we doing about it?"

Ms. Infinity looked at Hal in annoyance. She was silent for a few seconds, seemingly trying to find an appropriate retort. Finally, she snapped, "Oh Hal, I don't know!" Then she walked away up the stairs.

Hal followed Ms. Infinity up the stairs and up into the main hall. She sat down on a couch and looked at him blankly.

"Okay," said Hal, "I guess we don't have to decide this second. But I hadn't exactly planned on spending the rest of my life in a spaceship with a prisoner. Not a reflection on you."

"Just leave it alone right now."

"Well…" he answered, with a pause. Looking back at her, he saw that she was in a poor mood. "Okay, but please, let's come up with something soon. I know you're under pressure. But…"

"No Hal, you don't know pressure. You have never *met* pressure! Do you understand that if I make the wrong move, the consequences could be deadly for everyone? I can't make this decision just like that!"

"Okay, I see that–"

"No! You *don't* see! You want to go home. Great. I get that. But you have to get this. This is what it means to be with me. I'm not a lot of fun sometimes. I'm under tremendous pressure. Are you really prepared to deal with me? Are you, really? Because even after this, it won't be long before I'm dealing with some other huge decision. That is what my life is about. One huge, high-pressure situation after another."

"I see."

"I'm sorry. Maybe we aren't meant to be together. Maybe..."

"Hold on!" said Hal, "Not so fast! You're forgetting something. Not long ago, I nearly made the ultimate sacrifice myself. I nearly ran this thing into the sun."

"Hal," said Ms. Infinity, "that's the point. That's why I can't mess up, ever. Your life is on the line. I have you to worry about, and everyone else."

"Now you're missing the point. I'm not trying to make you feel guilty. Far from it. I'm trying to show you that you're not alone here. I'm willing to share this, you know. I want to share it. C'mon Bonnie. This means a lot to me."

"Well..."

"Look, I might be only human, but I care a great deal about you. Look, I'm sorry. I shouldn't rush you. But please, I would appreciate if you let me in here. I can share your burden, to the extent that my non-superhuman capabilities can help you. You know, nothing much. I'll just dedicate my life to you."

"Are you sure? I mean, really? This whole thing is a humongous burden on me. Are you really ready to take this on?"

"I'll tell you what. I'll handle it like every other difficult thing in life: one day at a time."

"You mean that?"

"I really do."

"You know, this whole thing is way bigger than you even imagine."

"I wonder," said Hal, "it may be big, but is it really over my head, like you would say? Look: these are aliens, to me at least. But let's not forget, I happen to know an alien.

You remember Bonnie Boring, right? And she's not so bad. I'd say she's pretty great. In fact, I dare say that she's not so different from the rest of us. Okay, lots of powers, higher than human intelligence. But you know what? She's still human to me."

"You're trying to cheer me up, right?" said Ms. Infinity.

"Well, hold on. It's more than that. Look. I refuse to believe that it's all an act. Right? I mean, you've said it. Bonnie is not the disguise. This is."

"That is correct."

"So, okay. How different are these people, really? They're of a different world from mine, sure. But then they're people too, right? They have feelings too, and motivation. They can be good or bad.

"So, this Misery. She's a sociopath, like many we have on Earth. But there's more to that picture, I think. I wonder if there isn't some fear here. For one thing, now that she's lost her army, she has nowhere to go but home. And now that she's failed her mission, well, what happens to her there?"

"Well, very simply," said Ms. Infinity, "if her treason is discovered, they'll kill her."

"Right," said Hal. "That's obviously on her mind. Not that I sympathize much with the would-be destroyer of my world, but one must understand her point of view. But besides that, I wonder, if they do kill her, or if you kill her, what happens next?"

Ms. Infinity thought for a moment. "I don't know," she said. "If it were up to the general, he would probably send someone else. There are other variables though…"

"And that's the thing," said Hal. "This really won't be over. How far can we take this? I know you are powerful, but can you really face their whole military?"

"Well, that's not the concern. I really don't think that it would come to that. But then, it's possible that this wouldn't be over. So that is something to consider. It could mean potentially putting the Earth in continued danger."

"Anyway, I believe what I said before still applies. Now I don't know why this general wants to have you killed…"

"That's right," said Ms. Infinity with grim humor, "you really don't."

"Okay," said Hal, "so some of this is over my head. And obviously, it's a demand we will never give in to. But am I wrong to think that there is an element of pride here?"

"Well…"

"You can laugh, but it makes me think of the worst customers back at work, right? You know: the ones who really get into screaming mode when we can't take the coupon, or they're mistaken about the price, or if you won't take the return.

"And you know as well as I do, some of these people are full-on sociopaths. But sometimes when there's no other way, we'll just settle the whole thing by giving them ten percent off of the sale. It's not even much of anything, just a token gesture. But it works, right? It makes them feel better, like they won something. I mean, it's ridiculous, but often it's just a little thing like that and a conflict is resolved."

Ms. Infinity laughed. "Well," she said, "if nothing else, we at least have some of the same reference points. So, what do you recommend we do?"

"Yeah, that's the thing. It doesn't really lead to an answer. It's just a thought. Or maybe it's a guiding principle? At least it's something to consider?"

"Okay Hal. I get it. Look, I promise I will give your

suggestion some thought. I do see that you are serious about helping me. Could you please give me a few minutes?"

Ms. Infinity sat for a considerable time, thinking in silence. She seemed no closer to a decision, but at least her mood had picked up. Something about Hal's determination reminded her why she was in this in the first place. After all, heroism wasn't about powers and costumed identities. At its heart, it was about the willingness to follow one's conscience, to do what was necessary, even when it seemed like too much.

Still, as sincere as Hal's intentions were, he could only help so much. There didn't seem to be much of an answer in his suggestions. It wasn't his fault. While some of his observations were apt, there was still much he didn't know, and he could not help but betray a few mistaken impressions.

Anyway, there didn't seem to be much room for creative solutions. It really boiled down to three simple choices: Release Misery, kill her, or retain her as a prisoner.

The last of those choices was the easiest to eliminate. She obviously could not keep Misery detained forever. Soon enough, there would be many other things to do besides attending to a prisoner, some of them urgent. She was a superhero, not a jailer. There was also nobody else she could hand her over to.

So, should she kill her or release her? This was the most arduous question of all. Misery was undeniably a dangerous person. She had also tried to kill her, and more importantly, had designs on Earth. Still, Misery's attack plan had been thwarted, and she no longer posed a real and present danger. Furthermore, Ms. Infinity knew what her conscience told her. If she could avoid taking a life, she knew that she must.

But which option made sense from a strategic standpoint? There were no guarantees, but it seemed that the best gamble was to send her home. She could not say what Misery would do when she returned, or indeed what Center would do with her. Yet if nothing else, her return was the best shot at restoring normality. This would be the best scenario for avoiding a future attack on Earth.

But how to ensure that Misery returned home? After all, once Misery was out of her prison and on her own ship, she might well go anywhere. She might even somehow rearm, and eventually try to attack Earth again. However, Ms. Infinity had an answer for that. In fact, this was an area in which she had many, many years of experience.

Since Ms. Infinity's return, she had anchored Starship Infinity next to Misery's ship. She now gave it a second visit, this time with a new purpose.

Here she endeavored to make a large number of permanent adjustments. She scoured the ship and made a comprehensive inventory of all of its systems. She overhauled the propulsion and steering, and permanently disabled the navigation. The systems were now confined to an automation that Ms. Infinity had devised with extensive consultations with the star charts. It would now only go to one place.

In her overhaul of the ship, Ms. Infinity made a startling discovery. Behind one of the walls containing the ship's wiring, there was a very strange painting. She did not recognize the face it depicted. It was a woman with what seemed like a cruel face. She was dark skinned, her black hair scattered like tentacles in many directions. She wore an expression of intimidation, her brow furrowed, her teeth baring fangs. A close look revealed that there were several extra eyes on her brow, and more tentacles flailing behind from her body.

This was a figure known primarily in the depths of

Center's most obscure, outlawed subcultures. Her name might be translated as The Harpy, or The She-Devil. If Ms. Infinity had known it, the presence of this painting was a major affront to Center's leadership. Had any of Misery's superiors known of its existence, she would have faced severe consequences; this figure was considered the ultimate evil. It was said that even speaking her name out loud might cause death and destruction. The legends that were whispered told that she was an evil spirit who had murdered her husband and eaten her own children; she now preyed on children who disobeyed their fathers. Her portrait was there precisely because it was so forbidden. For Misery, she was a symbol of her ultimate rebellion.

However, Betty Boring knew her by a very different name, and a radically different nature. In earlier generations, before she was The Harpy, she was known as The Dwelling. She was the symbol of the female aspect of the Higher Being. Even in Betty's day, she was relatively obscure in a culture that was already becoming increasingly patriarchal, yet she was very important to a segment of the population.

In the teachings that Betty had grown up with, The Dwelling was an omnipotent figure who could see, hear, and reach everything and everyone throughout the universe. She could potentially do great damage, but this was not her primary nature. Her first and most important role was empowerment. She would bring aid to the disadvantaged. It was said that anyone who prayed to her with a clear conscience was answered with courage and healing and would be favored in struggles against the arrogant. And so, when the military government took control, they outlawed all use of her name and her image. Open discussion of her was punishable by death. The story that remained was deeply corrupted. This was but one of many beliefs that had been distorted by the leadership.

Looking at the picture, Ms. Infinity felt only fear and apprehension. After she finished her labors, she quickly returned the portrait, and replaced the wall.

Soon after, she returned to her own ship and knocked on Hal's door. "Oh Hal," she called, "this is the moment you've been waiting for!"

"Alright Misery," said Ms. Infinity, "Come and listen. Believe me when I tell you, this is something you want to hear.

"So, Misery, you are never, ever to attack the Earth again. If you do, things will not go well for you. Bearing that in mind, I have good news for you. You are returning home. I have your spaceship just outside."

"And, what?" said Misery.

"And nothing," answered Ms. Infinity. "Your army is gone. I took care of that. Also, I have completely overhauled your ship. It is permanently on autopilot. It can only take you home. I don't know what exactly you can do for yourself, but that is not my concern. What is important is that this battle is over, and that the Earth is safe. That is my responsibility."

With Hal waiting a few steps behind, Ms. Infinity opened the door to the prison cell at last. Misery quietly stepped out. For the first few moments, things seemed quiet. Misery walked next to Ms. Infinity. Hal was a few steps ahead. After starting up the stairs, Misery spoke.

"You do have my communicator, don't you?"

Ms. Infinity was confused. "Yes, I…"

"Are you sure? I think I left it back there."

Ms. Infinity just barely turned her head. "Misery, this had better not be a…"

But by the time Ms. Infinity turned her head back,

Misery was gone.

"Oh no, Misery!" she shouted. "Don't you try anything! Wait here, Hal...Hal?"

She gasped. Hal was gone too.

22. And Scene!

As Lisa started away from The Big Box, she saw Betty Boring approaching. "Hi Mrs. B.," she said. "If you were coming to get Bonnie, she already left."

"Ah, no," answered Betty sardonically, motioning upward with her eyes, "she's already got her ride."

"Uh, yeah," said Lisa. "About that. So maybe an hour ago, I noticed Bonnie running up to the roof. Then Hal went after her. Bonnie soon came back to shop, but Hal never came back. I saw she was trying to call you, but I also knew she was in a mad rush. I'm not sure, but from what Bonnie said, I think she and Hal must have gone together. I don't know if you got my text…"

"Lisa, she was going into space!"

"Oh no, really?"

"And she's fighting someone very dangerous: Misery from our old world. This is definitely not something she should be taking a date to."

"Misery." Lisa had not heard that name before, but from the few weird names she had heard from Bonnie and Betty's native planet, she did know that the contemptuous ones like that were the ones given to females. Could she be the father's mistress? A military connection such as that would likely be necessary, since there were clearly not many opportunities for women there. Lisa was also pretty sure that Bonnie's father had threatened her, and was the reason for their flight to Earth. It would make sense if this attack were by someone tied to him. The tension in Betty's eyes seemed to confirm this, but then she must also have been angry with herself, since Bonnie had obviously slipped away under her nose.

It also seemed like Bonnie had her father on her mind, considering how upset she had gotten at Denny's ignorant comment about "daddy's credit card" the previous week.

"I am really sorry, Mrs. B.!" said Lisa.

"It's not your fault, honey," said Betty. "I can't imagine what possessed her."

"Well, I have a pretty good idea what her intentions were. I mean, not to put too fine a line on it…"

"Lisa dear, I get it. I was young once too. She wants to join the 'Light Year High Club', and if she thinks that she's the first person ever to try this kind of…"

Looking at Lisa's wide-eyed reaction, Betty stopped herself, and cleared her throat. "Well, Lisa," she said, trying to regain her composure, "look at her approach, too. I suggested she treat him as an equal. Doesn't look much like she took that to heart. But most of all, she's putting him in danger. This is not how I taught her…"

Betty stopped once again. There was something in Lisa's eyes.

"My dear Lisa," said Betty, "are you alright?"

"Oh, never mind," said Lisa. "You have bigger things to worry about."

"No, honey. If you have a problem, you can always tell me."

"It's the boss. He accused me of stealing today, or at least making a serious mistake on a transaction somehow. Bonnie and I looked at the receipt, and we could tell by the timestamp that it wasn't me. I was on break. Then he bullied me into leaving customer service. I found out afterwards that he's been hanging around security and watching the cameras.

He got my login that way. He's going to help one of the women steal to bribe her into being quiet. He'll be using my login instead of his own, so I get in trouble instead of him..."

"Honey, you're talking a mile a minute. Quiet about what?"

"I saw him with her. From their conversation, I get that it's sexual harassment. Maria said that he's that way with a lot of the women. Then when he tried to force me off the register again, I refused. I yelled at him and told him I knew everything. He just sent me home with a write-up."

"Bonnie has never said a word about this man. Has he threatened her too?"

"He has before. For one thing, there was an incident last week, over some handbags. That mostly wasn't her fault either."

"Well, Lisa, I don't want you to think I don't care about what has happened to you. But please understand, sexual harassment is a pretty big deal. It's disgusting on so many levels. This is a form of bullying, and nothing makes me angrier."

"I've never really seen it up close before. I mean, I've certainly known many men who were patronizing to me. I've also known a lot who were intimidating. This guy is both of those things. I just didn't see this going on before. Maybe I'm lucky, or just inexperienced. You know what really surprises me, though? The woman whom he's bribing really doesn't act the way I would have expected. Earlier when I was talking about my troubles, she suggested I take advantage of my looks. She thinks I should flirt with him and basically string this guy along. I mean, how Neanderthal is that!"

Betty's face was grave. "Please, don't resent her. What she is suggesting is obviously wrong. It's deeply sexist; it plays into the most harshly patriarchal impulses. But understand that it is a habit that exists in conditions of exploitation, a measure that has been used by those who have few other choices. It's a desperate attempt to take control when there is no control. I urge you not to judge unless you have been in the other person's shoes. Rather, feel sympathy for someone in a difficult position.

"There are extreme cases of this out there. Think, for instance, of those who might have to resort to dehumanizing tactics when there is a life-or-death necessity, such as saving one's child. In this case, I suppose it's simply about this woman's livelihood. Remember, she might also have more riding on this job than you."

Lisa looked at Betty curiously. "I wonder..."

"It's always hard to see another person's point of view, dear. I can't believe Bonnie's never mentioned this."

"I know. She's terrified of him. I don't get it. She can melt him."

"But Lisa dear, that should show you how little that really means. She is still a person with feelings. This kind of thing will hit Bonnie in a very personal way. Make no mistake. She might dazzle with her whole superhero biz, but that's as much showmanship as it is anything. Powers? So what? She's still vulnerable. Believe me, I know!"

"I don't doubt it, but I might stop short at saying 'so what'. If it's either of the two of us facing a mugger or rapist alone..."

Betty smiled warmly. "I'm sorry, Lisa. You're right. This too is the nature of power. One cannot help but take it for granted. Still, I don't want you to think of her as invincible. She needs you as much as you need her. C'mon Lisa. Someone has to keep her from getting a swelled head."

"You're right," said Lisa. "Her B.O. is Beyond Odious."

"That's the stuff! Look, this whole superhero thing is absurd and excessive. Maybe this is a prejudice. Once you've seen enough gratuitous shows of power, and suffered from them, you see things a certain way, fair or not. Look, I am very proud of my daughter. What she does is important. It's just no reason for others to feel like less. Sure, she's useful for sweeping up space rats, and posing for aerial photo ops. But it doesn't mean that she's greater than other heroes, the kind without costumes and powers."

"I don't know. I suppose…"

"You don't know who I'm talking about, do you? I'm talking about you! You just stood up to a bully. That makes you a hero. You can put the word 'super' in front of it if you like, but it won't change the importance of what you have done."

"Wow! Thank you. I never thought of myself that way. I mean, I've always thought of heroes as police, firefighters, military, and such."

"And they are! Absolutely. These are people who risk their lives every day. But there are many kinds of heroes. Think of teachers who sacrifice their time and energy for the good of their students, or doctors and nurses who sacrifice for their patients. And think of your parents, who have given of themselves for many years to see that you have been safe and healthy, and that you grew up to be a strong adult. I must say, they both did a wonderful job. But Lisa, I want you to think about something else. You do have a power that many others haven't. You have economic power."

"I don't follow."

"Honey, you are middle class. You live with your parents. You are working towards becoming a nurse. This job is important to you for now, but it is only a step along the way to a better life with a more lucrative career. Even if you were to lose the job, you still have a home to return to, which you aren't paying for. But there are many here who cannot lose this job. Their lives depend on it. And they can't risk standing up to a boss like this. I would ask you please to understand that before you judge."

"Yeah, it's hard to admit it, but you're right. I can pick on the woman who is extorting the boss. But then, what do I really know? I'm not in her shoes. You know, I really admire Maria now. She puts up with a lot. She's very sweet to me too. It's really sad to see that she has to go to work every day and deal with him."

"Well, sweetheart, it's always sad for me when I see young people like you learning hard realities like this. But you know, it's also very heartening. My dear Lisa! You also proved that there are good people even in the face of cruel realities like this. Look, I know it's hard. You only have so much power in this situation."

"The thing is, speaking of power, what about you and Bonnie? I mean, if you can–"

"Stop right there!" said Betty sharply. "Do not finish that thought. Do not even begin to entertain it. I assure you that you do not want what you think you want. I understand why it might sound great, having the world rearranged the way you think you want it, by powerful people who you assume will always have your best interests at heart. Let me tell you right now that you most certainly do not want that. Trust me when I tell you that it is a disaster. This is the genesis of dictatorship."

Lisa looked at Betty with amazement. This was hardly the first time that she had heard this kind of talk from her; she frequently seemed to veer toward subjects like these sooner or later. Yet there was something ironic about this situation that impressed her. How odd it was that she faced this world with such tremendous abilities, but with nothing but suspicion for power itself. It seemed like anyone else in the world would kill for her powers, and would gladly use them in this and many other situations. But then, Lisa thought about her own power, such as Betty had described. It might just be useful now.

"I'm wondering," said Lisa, "there must be more I can do. I can't leave things like this. I mean, how can I?"

"Lisa, my dear! It is not anyone's duty to solve all the world's problems. You are one person. I believe nobody is absolved from the responsibility of working toward the common good, but I would not place undue burden on you. You have done your part for now."

"But it's not fair! You know, I don't want to lose my job, but right now, that's the least of it. Good people like Maria have to put up with that every day."

"I'm glad you see that. But honey, all this really isn't on you."

"Well, I want to do something. I believe I might just be in a position to help here. Do you think it's wrong if I try?"

"My dear Lisa!" said Betty, "Bonnie made the most wonderful choice for a best friend. You know, when I say I'm proud of her, I hope you are too. When she succeeds, it has everything to do with you. Honey, I want you to know you don't ever have to do anything here. You might be putting yourself in a difficult situation."

"Yeah, I think I am," said Lisa, "but it kills me inside to think I'm just letting that jerk get away with all that he's done. For me it's personal. Besides, what have I really got to lose?"

"You have a point. Honey, this is your decision, of course. Far be it from me to talk you out of courage toward a good cause. I'll tell you what. Maybe that is where I can be of help. I'm here to shop anyway. I'll be around in case of an emergency. You know, I'll be able to hear or see if anything does happen. Here I feel okay about using my powers. You are the one taking action, and I'm sure you will act with integrity. All I will do is look out for your safety."

"Wow! Thank you. But now, you know what? I have no idea what to do about this. I feel like I'm back to square one."

"This is tricky. If you've already gone through the appropriate channels, then I'm not sure of your next step. It would be easier if there were a union, but…"

"No way!" laughed Lisa with ill humor. "Not in this store. Training in The Big Box includes a big anti-union video."

"Right," said Betty, "Shame, but unfortunately this is where they're blocked. But even so, this situation is hurting the store whether the manager realizes it or not. It's a huge blow to productivity when employees don't even feel safe around their supervisor. That causes huge turnover, and poorer work habits among those who stay, and low morale even among the most faithful…"

"…And of course, our wonderful store manager blames the low morale of the employees on the employees."

"Very short sighted. And that's the tip of the iceberg. Companies get sued over these things. They really should be aware of it. Your supervisor is also behaving very unprofessionally, and you know something? He's cheating the store. I'm sure your store manager would find that very interesting, don't you? I mean, that kind of shenanigan would get her in trouble too if it was going on under her nose and she didn't discover it."

"So, what do I do?"

"Well Lisa, whatever you think is best. I trust in your wisdom. But do you want my suggestion? Is there anyone you trust, with at least a little more status?"

"I've been talking to Maria."

"Then maybe you can try conferring with her first. You can even see if she'll go in to talk to the store manager with you. That will at least give the matter a little more weight. Look, try it. The worst you can do is fail."

"Sounds a little overwhelming."

"It won't seem so much so once you do it. You aren't alone. But please, before you do anything, remember that this is your decision. You are under no obligation. Do you want to do this?"

"You know what, Mrs. B.? I do!"

"Then I'm proud of you!" declared Betty. "Remember, this is your mission. And my dear, you are up to it, I promise. You know right from wrong, and you have the conviction to follow your conscience. You are honest and decent, and courageous too. You are a woman, and if that's not good enough, then nothing is."

"Thank you so much, Mrs. B.!"

"Always, my dear."

"I do have a question though. When Hal punched out, he was just taking his break between split shifts, and he was supposed to come back after three hours. When Bonnie punched out, she said to expect him back for his late shift. Now if she's taking him into space, how is she ever getting back with him in time?"

"What?! Three hours? How would she…"

"Is that bad?"

"You know what? Let me worry about that. You now have a mission of your own, and that is what is most important to you right now. In fact, call me later, and we'll debrief about it."

"Okay," said Lisa nervously, "I guess I'm on my way."

"One moment dear," said Betty, "You know, Bonnie does have something she says when she transforms. I thought it was silly and unnecessary..."

"Oh yeah. I remember. You told me."

"Now that I think about it, there is some point to a little motivation. Up to you, dear. Obviously, it won't give you superpowers, but..."

"Why not. Here goes."

Lisa took a deep breath and stood up straight. She said the words out loud, "Infinite Power!"

Nothing happened outwardly. Lisa Lin was still Lisa Lin, a short young woman from Queens in a Big Box shirt and khaki pants. But inwardly, as far as she was concerned, she had just transitioned to hero mode.

"Alright Mrs. B.," she said confidently, "I'm ready."

As Lisa started back inside, an idea came to her. As soon as she thought of it, she stopped short. It scared her. Everything about it made her uncomfortable. For a moment, she was filled with dread.

But then she thought about her fear, and realized why she was afraid. This wasn't about foolish or reckless behavior. It wasn't something that would harm her senselessly. This was the fear of things that carried risk, but which had to be done. This was that fear that courage was made for, the fear that she had to conquer. On the other side of that fear, there was her goal.

Lisa entered nervously, expecting comments on the earlier incident. However, nobody seemed to notice her arrival amidst the growing activity of the evening rush. After a moment, she was approached by Maria.

"Lisa," she said, "I'm glad you're back."

"Uh...yeah," said Lisa, "I'm going to need to talk to you in a couple of minutes."

"So, I know you're in trouble with Denny. But whatever he tries to do, remember he hasn't actually fired you unless you go through the exit interview."

"Actually, I don't know what might happen. In a few minutes, those distinctions might be irrelevant."

Quietly, Lisa sneaked into the electronics section. She saw Teddy straightening up by the video cameras. As she came closer, it became clear that he was mostly just trying to look busy.

"Teddy," said Lisa, "how goes it?"

"Yo, Lis!" said Teddy, "that was awesome what you did to Denny! We were just talking–"

"Shhh! Thank you. But Teddy, can I please ask you to speak quietly? I have a favor to ask."

Lisa buzzed by Customer Service. It didn't take long before she saw Denny.

"I thought I sent you home," he said crossly.

"Oh, you did," said Lisa, "I'm off the clock now. But there's nothing stopping me from talking to Yvonne."

"I can stop you. You do, and you're fired."

"Well, nobody can ever accuse you of being too subtle."

"Did you hear me?" shouted Denny, "I'll do it right now! I have the power to fire anyone. You won't even make it to Yvonne's door."

"Okay," said Lisa. "Actually, that's great. That makes me a customer. I'm going to complain to the store manager about the service here. I hear the head of this department is never around when you need him."

Lisa continued walking towards the back. Denny looked very nervous. Before she got more than a few feet past the registers, he shouted to Lisa, "I need to talk to you!"

"What do you want?" said Lisa.

"I'm sure you want to hear this," said Denny. He motioned to the wall and said, "Just over here, okay?"

"Okay, but I don't know what you can say that can fix this."

As Lisa and Denny stalked over to the wall, Julia watched from behind the customer service desk. There was ominous whispering behind her, in the electronics department.

"Look," said Denny quietly, "I don't think either of us wants this whole thing to get out in the open. I don't want it. You don't want it. Am I right?"

"So…?"

"So, I think we can work out a little something to make this better for you, so we can both forget about the whole thing. Are you listening?"

"I think listening is what I've been doing this whole time, but if you mean–"

"Why don't you pick out a few items, a bunch of nice things. I'll check you out, and you'll get a big discount."

"So, you want to bribe me now?"

"Now listen, this isn't gonna be like that. I just want to do you a favor…"

"But let's be clear. You want to help me steal a lot of things so I'll shut up."

"Well, that's not what I–"

"Forget it! I'm not going to be part of this."

Denny began to get threatening. "You'd better think about this, little girl! I'm tryin' to do you a favor, but you're tryin' to be some kind of bitch. If you're gonna try to mess with me, there's gonna be consequences. You think you can get away with this–"

"You're kidding! You think *I* have to be concerned about what I might have to 'get away with'?"

"Shhh! Now hold on!" said Denny.

"Yeah. You want me to…"

"You better stop right now! You're in bigger trouble than you think."

"Oh no!" said Lisa mockingly, "I'm in trouble with Denny!"

"Don't you talk to me in that tone, you little skank!" snapped Denny.

"Oh! Keep saying that. I think the whole store needs to hear this."

Denny was now shouting, and again getting in her face. "You better shut up right now, or you're in deep trouble!"

"Trouble for what?"

"Oh, don't worry!" said Denny, "I'll find something, even if I have to make something up!"

Lisa looked across customer service to Teddy, who was holding a camera just over the low wall in electronics. "And scene!" she announced.

At the sight of the camera, Denny became furious. He ran to the wall by Teddy and shouted, "Give me that!"

Teddy ran away from the partition, just far enough to be out of reach. Denny shot Lisa a look to kill. Lisa barely acknowledged him. She moved closer to Teddy and shouted, "Did you get that on the monitors?"

"Oh yeah," said Teddy, "every word."

"Are you crazy?" shouted Denny. "You'll get in trouble for that!"

"Oh yeah, Mistah!" said Lisa, "I'm cray cray like you never seen!"

At that, Julia shot Lisa a look of surprise, rather like one who has just seen a parakeet chase a cat. Meanwhile, Rafi came running up from electronics, yelling at Teddy. "Do you realize what you just did? Come over here right now!"

"Okay," said Lisa, "maybe I shouldn't have involved him."

Customers were beginning to gather around to see the spectacle. "You're going to lose your job!" said Denny. "Yvonne will hear about that. She's gonna fire you."

"I wonder," smirked Lisa, "will she? She does seem to miss an awful lot. I mean, I heard what your friend said. Hal was almost killed by that guy last week, the robber who got right past because Security had the cameras off. You know, because you told them to."

Suddenly Yvonne's voice came over the loudspeaker: "Lisa Lin, please come to the store manager's office."

Denny looked at Lisa. He was smirking, though the fear behind his eyes was unmistakable. "Now you're definitely going to lose your job."

"And guess what," said Lisa. "Now I have nothing to lose. I'm telling her everything."

Maria clapped her hands and cheered. "About time someone went ahead with this! I'm going with you."

"That's awesome!" said Lisa. "Let's do this!"

They started back towards Yvonne's office. Lisa half expected Denny to chase her, but he just stormed away, apparently heading for Security. Though he was scarcely being watched, he was intercepted along the way by Bobbi.

Lisa smiled at Maria as they walked, but she felt some nervousness inside. She wondered if she might be in over her head. She thought about how many other secrets she might stumble on now. Was she about to discover some more hard truths?

Nadine was listening intently to the commotion from a few feet away. As Lisa and Maria began to move toward the back, she came to a decision. Seeing Isha returning from the bathroom, she pulled her aside.

"Isha, can you handle my line?"

"Sure, but what are you...?"

"Oh, don't worry, I'll be back."

Isha took over Nadine's line. She watched Nadine as she joined Lisa and Maria, perhaps thinking of joining them herself. But her attention was diverted when she saw Denny approaching the customer service desk.

As she listened to the commotion, Betty felt a certain pride in Lisa. Yet she also felt a great weight upon her.

"That girl of mine!" she said under her breath. "When

I'm done talking to her, she's going to wish she was dealing with Misery."

But when she thought about it, she wasn't really angry. If she was honest with herself, this had everything to do with her too. She had acquiesced to her daughter's headstrong behavior, even quietly aided and abetted it. And now Bonnie was being very reckless, taking a human with her on a dangerous mission, and apparently working a strange time manipulation on top of that. She was beginning to wonder if she had been right to trust her to use her powers publicly at all.

But now it was too late. She only hoped her daughter's actions would not result in dire consequences. Her only consolation was that the whole mission would likely be ending soon, for better or worse.

As she turned a corner, she faced the customer service desk from a distance. She noticed something that looked wrong. As she used her super senses to look closer, she could confirm that there was something very strange indeed.

23. Cruel Revelation

Ms. Infinity took off in a flash. She covered many, many parts of Starship Infinity, the vast majority of which Hal had never seen, but to no avail. She flew to every possible exit, then through all the play areas, then the hallways. It was when her super hearing picked up a shriek that she flew in the right direction at last.

It was a hallway Hal had never tried before. It had been made inaccessible by the height of its entrance, for it led to danger. It connected to a vast, empty area that she had not taken any care in developing yet. At the very end of the hallway, there was nothing. It was darkness, a void only just subject to the ship's atmospheric conditioning. There was no floor, no ceiling, and no walls beyond its entry limits. It was simply darkness.

Misery was floating some distance from the entrance with Hal in a headlock. His legs were kicking in a futile attempt at protest.

"Don't struggle, pet," said Misery. "There is no need. You can't get away from me. It will be over soon enough."

Misery's hands groped him greedily. Hal was so terrified he could not speak.

"Yeah, I see what it's about," she said. "It's fun to be the most powerful person around. She takes whatever she wants. Well, I can do that too."

She started to transform. Her face became a mask of vengeance, her eyes burning like fire, her teeth turning into sharp fangs. But then there was a voice behind them.

"Damn, Misery. I thought I was bad at romance. But you, you're not even doing 'vampire' right."

Misery's face changed back before she spoke. "You forget I had some of those idiot superhero comic books with me. I recognize the banter, and I hate it. Do that again, and I'll kill this animal on the spot."

"Then listen to common sense. This is your chance at freedom, and you're messing it up. Let him go now, and you can still go home, with no consequences. But you can't possibly think that this will get you anywhere. It's the death of you. As soon as you try anything, it will all be over. You know I am far more powerful than you."

Misery's face became twisted with rage. "You disgusting little slut! Do you know how much I hate you? I don't care if I die! It will be worth it to see you suffer, even if it's just for a second. I'd rather…"

Hal noticed a knowing glance given to him by Ms. Infinity. His arm had become free as Misery ranted, and he used it to jab her backwards in the face. It did all but nothing to harm her, but she was startled. Immediately after that, she was hit with a sharp metal object like a boomerang. She instantly dropped Hal, and he went falling into the void. He would have screamed if he could have. But an instant later, he was in the arms of Ms. Infinity once again.

Ms. Infinity laughed as she caught her weapon. "She couldn't have read the comics too carefully, or she'd know the whole point was to distract her. At least, that was how I understood banter."

"Oh, thank goodness!" said Hal. "I can't possibly thank you enough. But I thought you didn't use weapons."

"When did I say that?"

"Fine!" shouted Misery. "But I'm still free to go home."

Ms. Infinity shot Misery a look to kill. Misery flinched, and flew away back through the hallway.

"Now that I think of it," said Ms. Infinity, "She might have been going for 'werewolf'. That she had more or less down, except that she barely has to transform."

"Where did you keep that weapon?" asked Hal.

"The kitchen."

Ms. Infinity flew with Hal back to the main hall. Misery was not there, but it did not take long to guess where she was. There was one door closed, and it was the TV studio.

Holding Hal, she quietly floated to the outside of the studio. She then put him down and stood right outside the door and listened. Here she was particularly dismayed at what she heard, and could otherwise surmise from the action inside.

Misery had her communicator; indeed, she'd had it all along. But that was the least of her treachery. For now, she was playing the video, but only the beginning section, the part where Ms. Infinity had been hit by the chunk of the asteroid. And within that video, Ms. Infinity had communicated in the manner of their people that she was Bland Beauty. And her identity was indeed verified, for each person of Center had a unique signature that could not be mistaken. And so, Misery was communicating to General Strongman that she had defeated Bland Beauty and killed her. And the General's reaction was no doubt as expected, but no less shocking for his cruelty.

Hal could not perceive the communication. He could not know what was being said, or the tone or emotion. And Ms. Infinity stood with her back to him, strongly holding her heroic composure. From his vantage point, she was the invincible heroine who had saved him from the roof of The Big Box. He could not guess the secret that she now held, that by listening to the general's reaction, she was now completely and utterly shattered.

As the general heaped praise on Misery, none could see his daughter's look of shock; her face contorted in agony at the truth she had always known, but never dared to face. As he watched a graphic depiction of his daughter's apparent death, he had no remorse, no regret, no concern whatsoever. He expressed only satisfaction that the pariah that had so long been weighing him down was now once and for all destroyed, and hope that now he might finally see the success that he so richly deserved.

As she stood, desperately holding her composure, she felt the full weight of her youth bearing down on her. It was all there: the shame, the humiliation, the fear and uncertainty, the cruel memories that were with her, no matter how hard she resisted, no matter how much time passed.

"What is going on in there?" asked Hal.

"Well Hal," said Ms. Infinity coldly, "she has just used the video and her communicator to convince the general that she killed me."

"Oh."

"Hal, we can't let her get away with this!"

Hal did not answer. He seemed to be deep in thought.

"Hal! I'm talking to you!"

"I know. I'm just wondering."

"Wondering what?"

"The thing is," he said, "what could we really do here that would be better?"

Ms. Infinity did not answer. She just looked at Hal in shock.

"I know," said Hal, "it's not like this represents any kind of justice. But I see why she just did it. I mean, she basically just saved her own life. Okay, it was at your expense, so don't take it like I sympathize…"

"Hal, you don't know what you're talking about! Do you realize what kind of criminals we're dealing with? I don't even mean Misery now. She's the least of it. I mean, damnit! The whole disgusting leadership! The whole system! It makes me physically ill inside to think of it! They're going to see this and be validated in all their crimes."

"You're right, and I can see that they've done horrors to you that I'm scared to even dream of, but now they can't get to you anymore."

"But what about the rest of the population? What about all the women there who have to live like I did? Like my mother did. The thought that I would acquiesce in that!"

"Yeah. You're right about that too. Now I understand what you meant when you said this was 'over my head'. It really is. Look, it would be awful for me to try to tell you what to do here, or even begin to think I know the 'right' decision. I have never experienced life on Center, and I dare not imagine how horrible life is there, especially for women and girls. I can only suppose that there needs to be a revolution, maybe much more than that. But let me ask you something. Can you give that to them?"

Ms. Infinity was silent.

"Look, you don't own me, and I don't own you either. So, all I would demand here is that you take me home. As long as you do that, the choice would obviously be yours. You could decide to go back."

"No Hal. That I will not do. I belong to Earth now."

"So…"

She thought a moment. And once again, the realization was killing her. True, she had a huge responsibility; as she had said to Hal, it came with the powers. But then, even that had its limits. It certainly did not include the entire universe. Just how powerful was she? And no, she was not responsible for Center. She no longer belonged there. Like she had just said, she belonged to Earth.

Letting go of that still hurt. Misery surely knew her pain and was enjoying every moment of it. The thought that she was now getting away free was a pain that she could hardly bear. Yet as hard as it was, she could not give in to her anger. There was nothing to be gained by revenge, and everything to lose. It was the way of her old world, not the world she now knew, or at least the one she sought to create. And that was just it. That world was on Earth, and had been for many years now. Misery belonged to Center, and Ms. Infinity belonged to Earth.

"If anything," she said, "I think she just decisively ended this, didn't she? Now the general will no longer have any reason to attack. As you might have put it, the crazy customer was just given his ten percent off the sale."

"Right," said Hal. "And if Earth is safe, well, by my understanding, it would seem that the mission has succeeded!"

He then looked at Ms. Infinity with pride and admiration and declared, "Bless you Bonnie, Ms. Infinity! You have saved us all! You really are Earth's Greatest Hero!"

Ms. Infinity could only manage a forced smile. "Thank you," she said grievously.

"I suppose it's a bittersweet victory for you."

"I know! Alright? I know! Can we drop it now? Alright?"

"Sure."

"Just stay with me now. I'm going to carry you while I capture Misery. Not very comfortable, but I will not let her get you again."

Carrying Hal, Ms. Infinity burst through the door of the TV studio. She darted at Misery, but Misery eluded her and flew out the door. Ms. Infinity flew after her, chasing her this way and that through the atrium. They flew unpredictably across, as well as up and down the heights of the room.

It would have been thrilling for Hal if it weren't so terrifying. In their flight, he finally got some idea of the height of the atrium—every bit as tall as a skyscraper, if not even higher.

Ms. Infinity finally caught up to Misery at the far end of the atrium. Misery was about to surprise her with her sword, but Ms. Infinity was ready. She gave her a tremendous kick to the head that sent her reeling. Misery hit the wall like a stray plane crashing into an airport hangar, then plummeted at last to the floor. Ms. Infinity then dove at her with one more kick. Still holding Hal, she then flew around her at super speed. Putting a very dizzy Hal down, she looked at Misery, now tied up.

"Alright Misery, so this is how you're going to leave. I'm sure you'll get out of that sooner or later, but by the time you do, you'll be far away, and you won't be able to bother us anymore. It's a pretty lousy way to leave, but you chose it for yourself.

"Like I said, your ship is on auto pilot. You'll have some maneuverability in case of emergency, but you can't turn around and come back here, or certainly not to Earth. It will never go anywhere else but into Center's orbit. Someone will have to help you when you get there, but you can figure that part out. That's almost two years from now anyway, in Earth time."

"Really?" said Hal.

"Oh yeah. It's a trek. Once was enough for me. Anyway Misery, time for your return trip."

Misery looked at Hal once again. She grunted, then turned to Ms. Infinity one more time. "So then, Bland Beauty, it seems that the Earth is yours to conquer after all. I take it you are moving on with it, right?"

"You've done enough, Misery!"

"Your pet doesn't know this, does he?"

"Misery, I said that's enough!"

Looking again at Hal, she laughed out loud. "You looked so cozy in her arms. You think she's on your planet to protect you, don't you? This woman who can destroy you as fast as look at you? She looks down on you, and the rest of your Earth people. You will never be her equal. Do you know why she came to Earth? Everyone from Center knows why."

Ms. Infinity grimaced at her. "This is not your concern, Misery!"

"Oh, I don't know. Your task was very similar to my mission, wasn't it? You were to destroy human civilization, and begin the new colony. Isn't that right? Have you told this animal that yet? Or are you as big a coward as I thought?"

"Don't listen, Hal! She's deceiving you!"

"Oh no! I'm telling the truth, every single word. Now you know why she was so angry at me. She wasn't trying to protect your pathetic planet. She wanted it for herself. Good luck, you pathetic worm!"

At that moment, Ms. Infinity grabbed Misery. Without looking back, she flew her out of Starship Infinity, and into her ship.

Ms. Infinity entered Misery's ship, and soon put Misery down. "Look," she said, "I hate to send you into space all tied up, but you showed me that I cannot trust you."

But as harsh as the moment was, Ms. Infinity did not want things to end in cruelty. There was no forgetting her many horrid and evil deeds, or the threat that she posed to her world, or indeed, the cruel things she had done just now.

Yet in the time she had spent questioning Misery, she had seen something else. Like herself, Misery was vulnerable, and she had also suffered cruelly. In fact, she now remembered that Misery was, at most, maybe three years older than she. She had never considered this in her youth, but now that she had distance, she realized just how disturbing the consequences of that really were.

Besides, Center was not her world, but it did belong to Misery. Maybe, just maybe...

"Misery," she said, "before you go, there is something else you must hear. This is imperfect in many ways. Of course, I do not believe that you deserve to go free after all that you have done, but so it must be sometimes. Many an adult decision is like this; we have to choose the least bad of many terrible choices. But even so, there is another part to this. You might be surprised to hear it, but I still have hope for you.

"You have done tremendous evil, but I would hate for you to think that you were capable of nothing else. You can do at least as much good if not more so. You have been mistreated by others, but do not think that your own life is ruled by cruelty. If I have also mistreated you out of hand, then I am sorry. Your heart is not bad or dark or cruel by nature, any more than anyone else's. You are capable of love as well, and you can also truly be loved. You can learn to live a decent life, and strive for justice and honesty for yourself and others. It's all there in you too. The choices are yours.

"You can bring change. I know that you are not satisfied with what you have seen, and if you look in your heart, then I think you might see that you want to be a force for a better future. And you of all people have a lot to give. You have power and privilege like very few others. But be careful. Do not mistake this for being more deserving. The universe simply does not work like that, nor has it ever. Power comes with responsibility to those who don't have it. Most of all, you are free. That too is a privilege. You have the rest of your life to do better than you have done, and I hope that you will."

Misery looked confused more than anything else. It was hard to tell what she made of Ms. Infinity's words. At any rate, the superhero then untied her. Before she left the ship, she turned and said, "So long, Misery. Never forget the power you have inside you!"

As she returned to her ship, Ms. Infinity began to feel that she'd had enough heroism for a long time. Without looking left or right, she flew to her bedroom and closed the door.

Misery might have been moved by Ms. Infinity's words. Or maybe she was not. But at least on this one matter, she did act honorably: She did not make any further threats or attacks. She simply waited for Ms. Infinity to leave and return to her ship. She then took off on her long return journey to Center.

But then there was much in Misery's story that Ms.

Infinity still did not understand. For one thing, Misery's youth had been perhaps even harsher than Bland Beauty's. She had indeed lived in a home of wealth and privilege. However, she did not have the love or even the interest of either of her parents. Her name told a story in itself, the tale of disappointment of a father who wished only for a male heir. Once her younger brother was born, Misery's life took a downturn. Her parents' words and actions left her no doubt that he was the only child who mattered. The elder child was treated with apathy and even contempt. When Misery finally ran away from home in her adolescence, her parents did not even pursue her.

And so, she was found by General Strongman, a bitter young girl, easily manipulated to his ends. It was not hard to turn her anger towards his daughter, and thus to direct her to his agenda. Neither he nor any of the men around him would ever consider that she might become uncontrollable, even by them.

Misery had quipped that that her captor thought that everything was about herself. While this might have spoken to her own jealousy, nonetheless the comment was not without truth. Ms. Infinity's perceptions were colored by a self-importance that hindered her understanding of the situation right in front of her.

But then her life and memories on Center had been confined to her childhood, the time of our lives when each of us is the center of our own universe. And so, she might be forgiven for thinking that an entire world was trying to destroy her. What she still failed to see was that her persecution originated almost completely from one man: the general whose career could be destroyed by the culturally unacceptable reality of a daughter more powerful than he.

Ms. Infinity had deduced Misery's intentions shrewdly and correctly, both her orders from the general, and her own intended attack on Earth. However, there was something else that she failed to see, albeit something that might have seemed of little concern to her. There was a third layer to the story that had nothing to do with herself or her adopted planet. There was another reason why Misery was even in Earth's galaxy in the first place, and not long before, that reason had stared her right in the face.

When Ms. Infinity questioned General Imperial, he seemed to wonder why Center had sent a mission so far away, and with a female leader. In fact, he knew exactly what it was about: they had come for him. And it was not at first led by Misery.

General Imperial had been exiled for many years, for reasons going well beyond the daughter of another general. What prompted Center's attack was his emerging colonial empire. It was still small but growing. And while it was far away, Center's president, Master of the Masses, still feared that it might one day present a threat to their empire.

And so, he sent a unit to destroy the colony, using the military from a conquered people with his own officers. It was then that General Strongman saw an opportunity, seeing its relative proximity to Earth. He arranged for Misery to be drafted onto the mission as a servant. He then secretly plotted with her, concocting a side mission to kidnap his daughter so he could have her executed.

General Imperial's colony was attacked and destroyed. However, not long after the attack, Misery turned on her own unit. After a long celebration by the military brass, Misery murdered all of the officers in their sleep. She then took control of the army herself.

She then plotted to invade the Earth. The catastrophes that she sent were all standard attacks that General Imperial had used in advance of his invasions; these had in turn been borrowed from the most aggressive strategies of Center's military. All of them had required advance planning and significant teamwork from the military she had coopted. She intended to kill Bland Beauty, as well as her mother, for both posed an obvious threat to her. However, she had expected to attack both of them as part of her invasion, well after the preemptive attacks. She would then have relayed news of their deaths to General Strongman. But that would have been the end of her loyalty to Center.

While Ms. Infinity underestimated Misery, Misery underestimated her far more. Misery had never imagined that her enemy had the power to single-handedly repel every single one of her catastrophes. She had also never expected to fight her openly. Both that attack and the military's ambush were set up by Misery with some sense of panic. However, she did have the will and intelligence to challenge her. Indeed, she came very close to defeating her once again.

Happily, Ms. Infinity saved the Earth, thwarting all of Misery's plans. But the significance of this was nothing for Center's military. The goals of Center's president were mostly achieved. General Imperial's colony was destroyed, though he himself had escaped.

The president was indeed furious about this failing, as well as at the death of his officers. When the moon's soldiers were contacted, he was not satisfied with their account. In his understanding, their story seemed bizarre and even incoherent. Even stranger than their fanciful monster tales was the claim that the servant girl had attempted a colonial venture, for the very notion of a female conqueror did not exist in his mind.

Shortly after Misery's departure from Starship Infinity, she contacted Center's presidential palace, and had a secret audience with the president. She was clever with her words, both selective with the truth and generous in flattery. And the president found her story satisfactory. For while an ambitious female was beyond his imagination, he could well conceive of the treason of one of his officers. He dealt with the matter immediately, once and for all. In the end, General Strongman's ambition was not realized; indeed, he would not live to scheme again.

Even after being dismissed by Ms. Infinity, Misery could not be free if General Strongman could get to her. It was only upon his execution that she finally achieved freedom. Now she would have the rest of her life. Whether she would indeed do better than she had done remained to be seen.

Upon the execution of General Strongman, rumors began to spread regarding the death of his daughter. The video that Misery had sent began to spread, and the rumor was confirmed. And behind some locked doors, many mourned quietly. Her persecution had been the work of one man, but her protection had been led by her mother, and involved a number of men and women who had helped enthusiastically. In the years since her departure, a legend had grown about Bland Beauty, the powerful girl who had rebelled, she who did not live as her name dictated.

Some whispered to each other that she had lived a remarkable life on another world. It was rumored that she had two separate identities. The tales were told of her life as an ordinary young woman who would transform into a mighty being when her magical powers were needed. Some even believed that she had romances with men whom she could easily overpower.

But the greatest of the legends would emerge from the tales of her death. The rumors surrounding her battle with Misery would be mingled with the accounts of the moon's army, and in time the tales grew into a myth far greater than Ms. Infinity herself. It was said that after Misery slayed Bland Beauty, she disappeared briefly, but then reemerged as an awesome and powerful being. She was omnipotent, and she reached in all directions at once, and she seemed larger than all of space. And so, she was revealed at last in her true form: as the reincarnation of The Dwelling herself.

Center's leadership had tried to destroy all beliefs that they could not control, most of all that of the female aspect of the Higher Being. Yet in the end they had failed; the Dwelling still existed in the hearts of those people who believed in her, and ultimately thrived. And even as Bland Beauty had chosen Earth, she had unwittingly helped to plant the seeds of resistance against the tyranny that had so long plagued her native world.

Hal watched as Ms. Infinity and Misery seemed to disappear into the atrium ceiling. After a few minutes, he could see and hear Misery's spaceship taking off. He figured Ms. Infinity would be back instantly, making one of her sudden reappearances, as was her wont.

"So, she's gone!" he shouted. "Let's celebrate!"

He looked behind him, expecting her to be there with her usual "gotcha" reappearance. She was not.

He called again, "Ms. Infinity?" But she was nowhere to be found.

Hal looked through the atrium, then at the bridge. He checked the kitchen, then the TV studio. He was about to panic. Did Misery kidnap her? What if he was alone again?

He was about to check the prison cell, when he heard crying from a bedroom. He saw the door ajar. "Bonnie?" he called, quietly.

"Yes, Hal."

"Can I come in?"

"You're not scared of me?"

"Can I please come in?"

"Fine. Come in."

Hal had not been in this room before. It looked surprisingly homey, almost like a teenage girl's bedroom, with pink walls and a large mirror. Sitting on the bed was not Ms. Infinity, but Bonnie Boring, dressed in loose fitting sweats. She had obviously been crying. Her eyes and face were red, and she was clasping a teddy bear, and clutching a few tissues in her hand. Her hair was in a poorly contrived bun.

Hal sat down next to her. "Are you alright?" he asked.

"You're not scared of me?"

"Well, if you're talking about what Misery said, one does have to consider the source. Besides, if you are trying to take over the world, you're not in much of a hurry. So far, you've gotten as far as half of the customer service counter at the Woodside location of The Big Box, five to seven hours a day, five days a week. From your reaction though, I'm guessing there is a story in there somewhere."

"My mother is always bothering me about my underachieving, but she just wants me to go back to school and get a decent job, not take over the world. But sure, there's a story, and I'll tell it to you. Uh, but first of all, it's time you finally got something here, Mister Space Cadet. The general? That's my father!"

"Oh," said Hal. Then a second later, he felt the full weight of that revelation. "Oh!"

"Yeah. Let that sink in for a little while. My father wants me dead! Try living with that for your whole life. That's almost the least of what I lived. I would say more, but I really don't want to talk about most of it. I can't. I really can't." Tears again began welling up in her eyes. Hal put his arm around her and began to cry as well.

She took a deep breath and continued, "I was going to be killed. I couldn't go on living there anymore. I had to get away somehow.

"There was this general, General Imperial, a close friend of my father's. He was crazy. Everyone thought so, and if even this bunch thinks that, then you know he had to be nuts. He had a huge book of plans for conquest, and every single planet in the known universe was in there, inhabited and uninhabited. How much of his time he must have spent on that thing, I can't even imagine. But nobody took the thing seriously. Even the hawks of the hawks thought this plan was unmanageable. So, I skipped to the very back of the book, and I found this one extremely distant planet that nobody had heard of, that being Earth. And I found that it was inhabited with people who looked like us, had the same life span, and at least a reasonably similar lifestyle, if lesser abilities. I volunteered for the job of conquering it.

"Mind you, that was an unofficial job. The president did not know about it, and neither did my father. But the military there is like that. It can operate in weird, independent ways. Even some generals operate behind other generals' backs. The president will use one to spy on others. That's often how dictatorship works. But sometimes they lose control of the monsters they create. And this general was able to shield me from my father while I prepared.

"So, I got the mission together. I had a spaceship, a crew, and provisions ready to go. But at the last second, I went and rescued my mother, or 'kidnapped' her, as I'm sure they would think. We snuck in and made a few changes to the ship. I rigged the propulsion to make it faster than anything else on the planet. Then I made it invisible. We left a day early, just the two of us, and were never heard from again.

"Anyway, we had to leave behind everyone we knew, and it was horrible, but that was our survival. There was no looking back. We had to make a new life. We came to Earth and started over.

"And make no mistake now. There is only one planet that I belong to. I could call Center my *native* planet, but it will never again be my *home* planet. Earth is my home, and Ms. Infinity's home, and even the home of the monster I turned into…"

"She didn't seem like something indigenous to Earth…"

"She keeps a low profile. Anyway, after I first caught Misery, you asked what my 'true form' is. That's not a good question for a date, but then I suppose I'm not like other girls. But let's settle this once and for all. My true form is this. I look like me. I look human, and this form, my Bonnie form, is who I really am.

"I am Bonnie Boring of Woodside, Queens, just like you know me. I live with my mother, who helicopters over me and bothers me to go back to school, and I give her endless attitude. I work at the same store you do, where I like to get juvenile with my best friend and fall all over myself around you because I like you. And yes, I'm an alien with a lot of powers. And sometimes I change into a superhero and do a lot of impossible things. And yes, that's me too, letting my freak flag fly."

"I have a question. I've been wondering this since I found out your secret identity. You can shape shift, and so I take it that that's all the disguise you need. You also presumably have better than perfect vision. So do you really need those glasses you wear as Bonnie?"

"Hell yeah! I want to look cool."

"I guess I can't argue with results. Anyway, you should

never have thought I was afraid of you because of something a crazy sociopath said. I trust you. Maybe you have the power to take over our planet, but I'm quite sure that you wouldn't."

"And Hal," said Bonnie, "I want you to think about something too."

"What is that?"

"Well. Hal, you're human, and I have to stop thinking of you as 'only' human. You're not weak. Far from it. Heck, considering your name, how do I know you won't decide all superheroes are unnecessary and scheme to destroy me?"

"What?"

"Never mind," said Bonnie, "It's an old movie. But look at it this way. You're stronger than many other people. Don't take this the wrong way, but physically you are capable of killing."

"I don't follow."

"My point, Hal, is that you wouldn't. Sure, you *could* do bad things, but that is a long way from saying that you *would* do bad things. You are a good person. You're a very good person. Do you remember what I said to you after I rescued you from the roof?"

"It's all a blur now, but I know one thing you said, 'Never forget the power you have inside you'. You always say that."

"Right. That's my tag line. But I also said that I 'sensed' a man with kindness and decency and much to admire. Of course, I more than sensed it. I knew it about you. And Hal, you have power. What you do matters. What you say matters. You have affected me in countless ways over the two years or so that I've known you. And you have helped so much here. I'm not the only player in this mission.

"Look, even a superhero can only do so much. It's

worth nothing if people don't also do for themselves. The worst thing I could do, the worst thing anyone could do, is to ignore someone else's power, their importance, their value. When we come together and recognize our common interests, well then, that's when we are unstoppable. You were part of this too. We did this as a team, and that's why this worked. Never mind superpowers. You are my equal. Don't forget that."

"Wow," said Hal, "When you said that to me back at The Big Box, I just assumed it was something you said to everyone you rescued."

"No," said Bonnie lovingly, "you're forgetting that I really knew you. If anything, I was dying for a chance to say that to you."

"Amazing to think that was for real. That means a lot to me."

"And another thing that is no disguise. I really, really care about you, Hal. I meant it when I said I love you."

"And I really love you."

Bonnie smiled. "She's gone. No more Misery. It's just you and me at last. And if you don't mind a freak flag or two, I'd like to continue where we left off a while back."

"Pardon?"

"Look at me,"

"Yes?"

"Infinite Power!"

Bonnie changed into Ms. Infinity as Hal looked on in awe.

"Oh!" said Hal.

"Hal," she said, "I love you. Come over here already

before I mess things up again."

The two lovers kissed and held it for longer than they ever had before. Ms. Infinity's mission was now over, and she could at last enjoy the love of a man she admired. And in her arms, in her power, Hal felt safer than perhaps he ever had. At the moment, her love was all he needed. He wondered if she could read his mind, and indeed if she could, that would be fine with him.

And so it was...

24. A Creep Exposed

Nadine soon caught up with Lisa and Maria on their way to Yvonne's office. She spoke at just over a whisper. "Look, do you really think you can get Yvonne to listen?"

"Well Nadine," said Lisa, "it's worth a try, right?"

"I'm just worried. What if she doesn't do anything, and then Denny hears…?"

"Well," said Maria, "We are taking a risk, but at this point, I don't know how much worse it can get."

"I'm pretty sure it's worse not to say anything," said Lisa.

"You know what?" said Nadine, "I'm going with you."

As the women approached Yvonne's office, Lisa began to discuss her plan.

"So, listen ladies. I'm pretty sure I know what I want to say. Denny has been messing with the security cameras, and that's bad enough. He's also stealing from the place. That should wake her up. I can hold off on my personal grievances until the end."

"I knew it," said Nadine, "this is all about her."

"Hold on a minute," said Lisa, "what did I do?"

Maria gently held Lisa's wrist. "Listen, you have to remember, we have different reasons why we're here. We're not doing this because you're in trouble, remember?"

Lisa looked at Maria for a moment. Then her eyes went wide. "Oh, right! I'm sorry. You know what? Does either of you want to talk?"

"Honestly," said Nadine, "I think I'm the last one who should talk. I'm in enough trouble with her. But then again, I don't appreciate being searched just for coming to work."

"I got this," said Maria.

None of the women noticed Teddy standing in the doorway of the break room, listening intently to their conversation.

Lisa knocked nervously on Yvonne's door. Within seconds, it jerked open. "Alright Lisa!" shouted Yvonne as she opened the door, but as soon as she saw Maria and Nadine, she fell silent.

"We want to file a complaint," said Maria. "The rights of the workers have been violated by the front-end supervisor, Denny. I can name numerous cases of sexual harassment against myself and several other women. I am willing to sign any affidavits as necessary."

"Sexual harassment?" said Yvonne under her breath. "That would explain a lot."

"Please, Ms. Montez," said Maria, "I believe it is in everyone's best interests if you investigate this matter immediately."

"Very well," said Yvonne. "You should certainly file a complaint, but that is a matter handled by Human Resources. Now I have something to take up with Ms. Lin here–"

"And this has everything to do with that," interrupted Maria. "Do you think she was playing around out there? Denny has made life here miserable for many of us."

"I can vouch for that," said Nadine. "I have other things too–"

"Now look, Ms. Lopez," interrupted Yvonne, looking

squarely at Maria, "I don't want you to think that I don't take you seriously. This is an important matter, and I will have to look into it. It's just that we have a protocol. Let me warn you now. If you were thinking of using this as an impetus for organizing, I'd have to strongly advise against it. The company will not take kindly to it."

Maria shook her head in disbelief. "That really is all that's on your mind, isn't it?"

"Besides," said Lisa, "he's done more than that. Do you want to watch the video? It's all there! He used my ID to cheat the register. He had the cameras turned off for that. When I called him on it, he tried to extort me to keep me quiet. He promised me discounts on high-priced items. I think it started when he was trying to hush up his victims. That would interest you, wouldn't it?"

"Now are you sure about this?" said Yvonne.

"Very. I'd gladly sign a statement about that too. You might want to check the security cameras. I'm sure there are some missing pieces at some particular spots. I can even name them."

"That's just one of our issues," said Maria, "I assure you not the only…"

Maria stopped. It was clear that Yvonne was not listening. She was shuttling through the day's security video. After a moment of searching, she jerked back from shock.

"There are two large sections missing from the last two hours alone!"

"I knew about that," said Lisa. "I also knew that the camera was off the day Hal got held up."

Yvonne was shocked. "How did you know all this?"

"I overheard a conversation between Denny and Security."

"They told me the camera was broken! Who in Security was this?"

"I think his name was Mitch."

There was a knock on the door. "Can you get that?" said Yvonne.

Nadine opened the door. Teddy was behind it. "Hi," he said awkwardly. "So, I saw you're here about Denny. I was wondering…"

"Hi Teddy," said Lisa. "Listen Yvonne, I hope Teddy's not in trouble too. This was my idea."

"Let him speak his piece," said Yvonne. "Please come in. So, what is it that you have to say?"

"You remember that he used to be in Electronics?" said Teddy.

"I do," said Yvonne, "That's where I promoted him from."

"Well, when Denny was training me, he told me I had to use his ID for every sale."

"He did?"

Lisa looked at him curiously. "I didn't even know you had those. You're not cashiers."

"In Electronics they do," said Yvonne. "In this store anyway. They have their own registers. For big ticket items, they get commissions. Customers order things like TV's or computers, then the salesperson takes the order, and has it either taken to the customer's car, or shipped to their home. Anyway, Teddy, you were saying Denny made you use his ID?"

"Yeah, so I later found out that was wrong."

"It certainly is!" said Yvonne. She turned to her

computer and frantically began scanning though her old files. "Interesting. He was promoted partly because of his excellent sales figures. I will have to research this more. But from what I can see here, they spiked significantly several times, all when he had a trainee. It would seem that we have many cases of fraud."

"So, I was also supposed to get commissions for those?" asked Teddy.

"Yes, you were," answered Yvonne. "So were many other trainees."

"Yeah. I remember he used to take on a lot of trainees."

"Alright then," said Yvonne, "I will have to research this further. In the meantime, I'm calling Denny in immediately. You can go. Rest assured; I will take this seriously."

Yvonne dismissed the group from her office. As the companions returned to their stations, they discussed the meeting.

"Do you think she listened?" asked Lisa.

"At least about Denny," said Maria.

"Yeah," said Nadine. "She's all over him at least. We got that much."

Maria sighed as they returned to work. Denny would be removed, and they would not have to worry about him. Yet it seemed like the concerns of hers and Nadine's were last on the list after all. That was a lesson long since learned; even after the promise of equality, some were still less equal than others.

Yvonne was certainly taking the matter very seriously. She may or may not have sympathized with the workers whom

Denny had wronged. She could not have been amused by his reckless frauds, and the charges of sexual harassment. Yet above all, she was looking out for her own survival, and not a moment too soon.

Yvonne activated the loudspeaker and announced, "Dennis Hill, please come to the store manager's office." A few seconds later, her own phone rang.

"This is Security," said the voice. "Denny can't come because he's here."

"Forget it!" shouted Yvonne. "He'd better stop hanging out there immediately! That is a direct order."

"He's not hanging out here. He's being detained."

As Yvonne entered Security, Denny was sitting in a wooden chair looking humiliated. The guards were walking around making calls.

"Alright," said Yvonne. "First, to all here in Security, don't anyone go anywhere. You have a lot to answer for."

"Hi," said one of the guards. "There's something you should know. We didn't know he was stealing. We just thought he was having the cameras turned off so he could do things like generate receipts when he wanted to fire someone."

"What?" said Yvonne. "When did this happen?"

"Uh, I know there was today, with that Chinese girl..."

"This is Queens. That doesn't exactly narrow it down. Wait, today? You mean Lisa?"

"I don't know."

"The one in Customer Service? The short, thin girl?"

"Oh, yeah. Her."

Yvonne shot Denny a look of fury. "So that was fake!" she bellowed. "One of our best associates was given a major reprimand today for something she didn't do? You faked the whole thing?"

"Never mind that," said Denny. "You need me. You know Maria Lopez is going to use this to try to organize. You want to explain that to the company?"

"I'll take my chances with her. It beats having to explain you. Let's get this over with."

She sat down next to Denny, then continued, "Last time I had one of these talks with you was last week, and it was because of a customer complaint that you were missing during a rush. Lisa Lin was on Customer Service then. Interesting, considering what has transpired since then. Well, that's the least of your problems. This latest incident is apparently the tip of the iceberg. I have a long list of things to investigate with you. So, I have good news and bad news for you…"

"I know. The bad news is I'm fired…"

"Well, not exactly. Technically, right now you're suspended without pay, but you're right. There's really no way you're keeping your job. But no, Mister Hill, that is the good news. The bad news for you is that you're going to be prosecuted. What you did includes, at the very least: fraud, theft, and conspiracy, and there might also be charges of reckless endangerment. There might be other things too. We can't let these things go without pressing charges."

"You can't fire me or prosecute me, and you know it! You know I'm looking out for the store. Someone has to whip this place into shape. Nobody else can get discipline like I can."

"Forget it! That's not going to fly anymore. But you listen to this: You had better not try to leave town. That will only get you in much worse trouble. Goodbye, Mister Hill."

Yvonne stood up once again and addressed the rest of the room. "Now, to Security, I will be calling each of you individually into my office. None of you are to go anywhere until I have spoken to you."

She turned and left Security, and began to head towards her office. She looked ahead to a long night and much embarrassment and explanation.

Lisa Lin would never again face Dennis Hill. She could not deliver parting words, as Ms. Infinity had done with Misery. She had not the superhero's privilege of safety in a final meeting, nor the ear of her enemy in words of compassion, nor perhaps even the luxury of ruminating much on the sad fortunes of one who had wronged her. Yet it might be said that Denny's tale was tragic, as surely as his deeds were cruel and corrupt.

The power structure in workplaces such as these often belies larger economic realities. Denny might have ranked above Lisa in the store's pecking order. Yet he lacked the education, the skills, and the personal connections that Lisa, Hal, Betty, or Bonnie had in staking out a career path. And so, it seemed all but certain that a position such as he now held would be the peak he attained for life. Still, many others live so without turning to corruption, and live honest and full lives.

Yet somehow Denny could not or would not trust in the fortunes that he had. His aggression came from a crippling fear that was with him everywhere he went. And he would not trust another soul, not even those who would love him. And in his heart, he could not believe that anyone could act out of true decency. In his mind, every person was acting at all times from vindictive and corrupt motives, and would turn against him sooner rather than later. And in his paranoia, he drove away those who truly cared about him, for he brought pain and damage to anyone who was close to him.

And when he was at last bereft of true friends, he was left with those who truly were his enemies: opportunists who knew all too well how to take advantage of the fear in a person's heart. So it is with the fearful; the prophecy of paranoia brings its own fulfillment.

It is not surprising that Bonnie Boring was so afraid of Denny. In knowing him, she was reminded of something deeply familiar, and endlessly disturbing: the father from whom she had once fled for her life in terror.

25. The Journey Home

Hal woke up in Bonnie's bed alone, feeling like he had been sleeping for a long time. He stretched for a moment, then rose and washed up. Making his way outside, he looked for his love out in the atrium.

"Bonnie!" he called.

"On the bridge!"

When he reached the bridge, he saw her, in the form of Ms. Infinity. They kissed. "Wonderful to see you, my love," he said.

"Wonderful to see you too," said Ms. Infinity, "We are headed home. In fact, I have a surprise. We are already past 'hyperspace', the part with all the multidimensional maneuvers. I did something I should have thought of the first time. I put you to sleep for it. It was my last kiss, you know."

Hal thought a moment, trying to remember. "Oh. Actually, I'm not sure I remember the last kiss. You are a show-off."

"Hey, I didn't hear you complaining!"

"No. You're right. I do not complain. So, it's just the two of us now. Why don't you change into Bonnie? No need to impress me now."

"Well, it's all mindset. I'm working, in a manner of speaking, so it's like work clothes. I prefer to be like this until we get home. "

"I guess that's your call. Listen, I should really shave before we go home. Do you have a razor?"

"Hold on. I'll make you one…" She concentrated for a

few seconds, then produced a pink, plastic razor out of the air.

Hal looked at Ms. Infinity in awe. "You really are amazing! Look at this. You must have every superpower in the book."

"Oh, go on!"

"One little thing, though. This is a woman's razor."

"Oh, sorry. Force of habit." She took it back, turned it blue, and returned it.

"Much better. Thanks. I wanted to ask you something."

"I'll come with you."

Ms. Infinity followed Hal through the atrium towards the bathroom. "So, Bonnie," said Hal, "I wanted to ask you about that video I shot. Is it possible that I could use it?"

"The video?" asked Ms. Infinity. "Why?"

"Yeah, that's something I never got to tell you. It's for my career plans. I have a communications degree, and I'm trying to become a TV reporter. So, if I have a real live superhero battle…"

"Honey, I'm sorry. No."

"What?"

"Hal, I can't let you show that video to anyone. The whole thing is secret, and has to remain that way."

"Well, of course I'm not going to tell anyone who you really are. You see, I figured I'd say that Ms. Infinity gave me a tip after that roof incident–"

"No, honey. It's not just that. The whole mission is secret. I can't let anyone know that Earth was threatened. Think of the panic that would happen. These things are secret for a good reason."

"Oh."

"I'm sorry, honey. I'd hate for you to resent me for this. This is just how I have to operate sometimes. Once again, it's part of being with me. I am sorry."

As Hal listened, he felt his heart sinking. For much of this mission, he had been nursing a hope that he might just save his career. His life for the last two years had been dominated by the frustration and disappointment surrounding his mounting failure, not to mention his consequential nonstop hours at The Big Box. To lose this hope was a bitter pill to swallow, not least because he'd been nearly killed making the video.

Yet in a way, the hardest thing was the inescapable notion that equality was not exactly what it promised in this relationship; this wasn't even the first reminder since he'd woken up. He would always have another hurdle, another hard reality in front of him. Bonnie was Bonnie; Ms. Infinity was not an easy person to be equal to.

He thought about all that his father had said to him. Yet even then, the answers did not come as easily as he hoped. All he had was a collection of loving but conflicting advice. He stood there, a mess of emotions, helpless as ever to manage his own life. But then he looked at her again. For all that was wrong, here was his love, and all that was right. "Yeah. It is much more than worth it."

"Thank you, my love. I will do all I can to make it up to you. But while we're on the topic, you of course have to know the importance of my secret identity. I need my privacy. Without it, I'd have to fly into deep space every single time I have to pee."

"Well Bonnie, I would hope that by now, you know that you can trust me. Of course, I will never breathe a word to anyone."

"Right, I do know it, but I have to emphasize it. I'm

afraid you have to be absolute about it. Not a word about it to anyone, even the people you're closest to. You realize I haven't even told Lisa, and she's my best friend. You have to understand that once a secret is compromised, it can't be recalled."

"Okay. Obviously, it's important. I also see that it is a big trust issue for you. But I wonder, just for curiosity's sake, why haven't you told Lisa? Look, it's not my business. It's between the two of you, and I would never interfere. But I do know that she really cares about you. If there is one person I would trust, it's her."

"I almost want to yell 'none of your business', but I get it. You are speaking out of concern. Just understand that I have my reasons. You wouldn't even know if not for the incident on the roof."

"Oh," said Hal in a wounded tone, "that's a shame you feel that way. Do you regret it?"

"No Hal. I certainly don't."

"That's a relief. I wouldn't trade this for anything."

"Me too, Hal. You do mean the world to me. It was definitely meant to be. But I have another concern. It is great we're steady now. I just hope that things can stay like this when we're not on Starship Infinity. Do you think we can still do this when it's us again back on Earth, working together at The Big Box with everyone else looking on?"

"Well, I know what you mean," said Hal. "All this has a context to it. But it's up to us, isn't it? We have to decide to do the work on our relationship, right? It's time to get serious about dating, go take in some movies, have dinner, talk about our interests, get in some give and take. It's not guaranteed to succeed, but I have a good feeling."

"I hope so..."

"Well Bonnie, I could use some optimism here."

"Yeah. I think you're right."

"You know what? I just named what I miss here. Come back, Bonnie! Just change back into yourself already. Don't be afraid. It's me, and now you know I love you. You don't have to act funny around me anymore."

"Hal, you heard what I just said."

"The mission's over. It's just us. Come on. All of this, the Ms. Infinity image, is great and exciting. But I want Bonnie Boring. She's the woman I'm dating, not the image. C'mon, Ms. Infinity, I'm begging you to release her.

"Bonnie, look. It's safe now. You must realize that. I love you, and I would never do anything to harm you. Please, Bonnie…"

"Alright! Alright!" shouted Ms. Infinity. She looked away for a moment, then looked back at Hal with an expression that seemed to convey either annoyance or fear. But as she looked at him, she became increasingly at ease. She soon smiled warmly. Then at last she metamorphosed into Bonnie Boring.

"There," she said, "I'm Bonnie now. Better?"

"Much," said Hal. "Kiss me already!"

They kissed again. Hal then spoke just above a whisper, "You know something? You are absolutely beautiful."

"Thanks," said Bonnie.

"You know what I mean? I mean you, Bonnie. Not her."

"Well, that's kind of you to say, I guess."

"No, Bonnie, I really mean it. She looks like a

supermodel. So what? A model is just a model. But there is only one Bonnie Boring. Just looking at you now reminds me how much I love you. I want you like this next time."

"Next time, what? Oh!"

"'Next time, what?' That sounds like something I'd say. Now who's the space cadet?"

"I kiss better."

It had at first seemed fitting to Hal that his video news career might rest in the hands of his hero-turned-girlfriend. As with most of humanity, his first encounter with her had come via the media. Yet for him, this had been a profound moment.

Some two years earlier, Hal had returned home after finishing college. Upon his arrival, he discovered his home and family in disarray. In his absence, his parents' marriage had begun to fall apart.

The discovery was a devastating shock for him. His family had always seemed a rock of stability, one that he had long taken for granted. Now that bedrock was crumbling under his feet. Suddenly he could not even be home without constant reminders of the torment.

If one of his parents was home, they would be shouting about the other. If both were home, they were alternately fighting loudly, or sitting in bitter silence, occupying the farthest corners of their apartment. Even when he was home without them, there was his sister in tears, telling him things a seven-year old girl should never be concerned about. And if he was alone, he was alone with his worries and uncertainty.

On one such occasion, he turned on the news, hoping to take his mind off his troubles. Within seconds, he was blindsided by the story that was dominating the local stations. There was this beautiful young woman, apparently with magical powers, singlehandedly saving a school bus from a frightening accident on the Whitestone Bridge. It had somehow tripped the guardrail and was about to fall.

Under normal circumstances, the situation would have been a major tragedy, certainly involving numerous deaths. Yet this magical woman somehow arrived out of nowhere, then pulled it out of danger, and prevented even one death, or even any major injuries. Within a minute or two, the bus was on solid ground, and all children and staff were safe and accounted for. When pressed for information by a reporter, she told very little. She simply identified herself as "Ms. Infinity." Then she quite literally flew away on camera.

This had been Bonnie's first foray in that guise. Betty finally gave Bonnie her blessing after many long years, even though she found the superhero idea frivolous. She made Bonnie promise that she would use her powers responsibly, and that she would always remember to consider the power and importance of the people she was helping.

If one thing had convinced Betty that Bonnie was ready to use her powers in public, it was her recent job at The Big Box. Maybe it wasn't a great job, but it was a job where she demonstrated genuine teamwork, and thus she showed that she could truly show respect for others. Betty had confirmed as much in quiet conversations with Lisa.

The name Ms. Infinity might have sounded like a boast, but it was also for comfort. It was a way of holding a piece of her mother close by when she put herself in danger. Little did she realize that there would often be much more than a piece of Betty Boring nearby.

Bonnie had been actually much more nervous that day than she let on, part of the reason why she flew away so quickly. Of course, Hal was certainly too amazed to notice. He also had no idea that the woman he had just seen actually lived only a few blocks away. In fact, she had gone to the same high school, albeit two years ahead of him.

Nonetheless, the Ms. Infinity he knew from the media was a powerful symbol. She gave him something to hold on to at a time when he desperately needed it. Somewhere there was this omnipotent woman who represented good, an invincible and unstoppable force for those who needed her. That image was a shelter he took to in times of trouble; hope when he had no hope.

The news media had always held a certain fascination for Hal. He had always been aware of current events, and altogether more socially conscious than most others around him. Yet if he was honest, there was also something about the image of a TV reporter that appealed to his young mind. As his father had said, he had not really been thinking practically.

His graduation out of the way, he sent many resumes out. Then many more resumes went out. On a very good week, he got a full written rejection. The rest of the time, he got no answer at all. He tried showing up to TV networks in person, but he could never get past the front desk. Eventually he got a four-month internship at a local cable network, but it led nowhere. He repeatedly called all the contacts he had made, to little avail; he now received no's over the phone instead of by mail. The "demo reel" he had was of little use, basically the few seconds of on-camera time he'd had on the internship (none of which had actually aired) interspersed with his best student work.

This video had seemed like a perfect opportunity to jump-start his career. Yet deep though the disappointment was, he knew that the only acceptable choice was to accede to Ms. Infinity's wishes. Bonnie was clearly acting out of duty. It was on him to do the same. In his heart, it was also important to respect the wishes of his girlfriend, and indeed the woman whom he continued to admire.

Bonnie would try to help her boyfriend. A few weeks

later, Ms. Infinity would grant the budding young reporter an interview on the roof of the Big Box parking garage where she had once rescued him. Yet while she made an honest and valiant effort, it did little to save his career.

The problem was a conflict of interest. He was in no position to "expose" her in any way that the media would find attractive. She did give a few demonstrations of her powers. However, the questions were all decidedly "softball," and the video was carefully edited to prevent any answers that could be taken out of context. So, the product was safe for her, and completely useless for the media market it was aimed at. A short portion did air once or twice on the cable network Hal had interned at. This would prove to be one of the only highlights of his career.

One inevitable side effect of a prolonged job search is frequent unwanted advice. Hal constantly faced people who would give him solutions ranging from the obvious to the absurd and unworkable. There is often a naiveté behind these persuasions. They bespeak an assumption that anyone who hasn't succeeded does not deserve to succeed, as if success is always there for those who pursue it. Had some of these people known who his girlfriend really was, they would certainly have expected her to deliver him the miracle he needed. Yet like she had said, she wasn't a genie. She could no more rescue his career than put his family back together.

The problem wasn't anything Bonnie did or didn't do. Hal had chosen a tremendously difficult career for anyone to break into. It was also a bad fit for him. He didn't really have the killer instinct that it took to make it in that business. He lacked the will to force his way past others, to step on competition, or indeed to distort the truth as the market demanded. The video from this mission would have been unlikely to change that equation anyway. Indeed, had success truly been all he cared about, he might have taken that video without the subject's permission, and perhaps even divulged all the private and secret details he had been trusted with, all for the sake of his own ambition. That was not Hal Holstein. He chose instead to love the woman he loved, completely and honestly. He also chose to live according to his best ideals.

If Bonnie could not rescue Hal's career, she could always inspire him to see a better future. From here on, he would look to his girlfriend's example, and all his career choices would be concerned first with the public interest.

As Hal dressed, Bonnie talked to him thoughtfully. "You know, I do think this ship is a little much."

"Well, it's pretty amazing," said Hal. "As a testament to your powers, it certainly attests that you have a lot of powers. But as magical as it all is, it's no substitute for humanity."

"That's exactly right. When I landed on Earth with my mom, she told me I had to hide my powers. She wanted us to both to live as humans, more or less completely. She was afraid I'd become a tyrant if I was let loose. That hurt me like anything. But the ship has always been my outlet. It's where I can just come and do whatever I damn well please. I used to think of all this as practice for things I could do to benefit humanity one day, as if the day would somehow come when I don't have to stop myself. I don't know if you could understand.

"It's ridiculous! This whole thing is a dead zone. It's an empty city. And the worst part of it is, if I did try to do this out on Earth, if I tried to impose this on humanity, it would be even worse."

"I don't follow…"

"Humanity doesn't need someone like me who can

make big futuristic things like this, stuff that's just the big heroic ideas of one person. It has nothing to do with the real needs on Earth. This is the world I came from. Trust me, I know. If this is what I bring to Earth, then it's better off without me. It's everything Misery said about me. My mother was right all along."

"Interesting," said Hal, "But please don't beat yourself up. I mean, I think this mission does prove that humanity needs you."

"Yes, Hal," said Bonnie, "but not just me."

"Really?"

She smiled. "Hal, you think very differently from me. You're less competitive, more cooperative. You're less confrontational, more conciliatory. You seem to worry less too. That meant everything. It's what it took to help me solve the impasse. I may not always appreciate it, but I need you in this. You should speak up if I steamroll you. You don't deserve it."

"Thanks…"

"I feel like there is something bothering you."

"This is the thing. I appreciate that you thought of putting me to sleep through the hyperspace stage. Just please ask me next time."

Bonnie was open mouthed with embarrassment. "Oh Hal, I'm sorry! Oh no. This is exactly the kind of thing my mother warned me about. You're right. Hal, I'm sorry. I really should have thought of that."

"It's alright," said Hal, now looking more relaxed.

Bonnie spoke gingerly. "There is one thing I've been thinking too. Hal, I need you in my life. I love you. But you were nearly killed a couple of times on this mission. I'm thinking that it's probably not a good idea to take you on any more dangerous missions like this. There are plenty of other things you can do to help, to 'share the burden', as you would say. I want you to be safe so you can."

Hal took a deep breath and smiled. "Yeah. I think you're right."

"Hal, I want to ask you something else. Tell me if you like this idea. I have this dream of taking you on a trip around the world. Would you like that?"

"Would I like it? I'd love it!"

"So, you should think about where you'd like to go. For what it's worth, I do like London. It just has a character to it that charms me. But of course, I'm going to love a place with great phone booths."

"Really?" said Hal. "Don't you bring your cellphone?"

"Hal," laughed Bonnie, "it's not about that. Remember who I am?"

"Oh, right."

As they approached Earth, Bonnie handed Hal his uniform from The Big Box. "Here," she said, "you'll need this. You're going right back to work."

"How is that? We were gone so long that I'm wondering if we even still have jobs there."

"Your break will be ending soon after we get back. As you may recall, you were on split shifts. So, your three-hour break should be about up when we get back. I told you I took care of work."

"What? Are you saying we were gone only three hours?"

"Actually, if I time this right, I'm hoping you'll have a

few minutes left when we get back."

"How did you do that?"

"Well, I don't think I could totally explain it to you, but remember when I said was experimenting with a time manipulation? Well, think of this as putting something bigger into something smaller, but with time instead of space. That isn't something one can usually do, but with a lot of careful consideration and multidimensional movements, well, it's just possible. I also would never consider doing it if we weren't in deep space. Otherwise, it would be way too dangerous, with far too many variables to consider."

"Wait. So, you're saying you can time travel?"

"Oh no! I can't go back into time, or into the future or anything. I move through time just like you. I just squeezed a bunch of time into a cramped period of three hours or so, but just for us on Starship Infinity. It's kind of like stuffing a big mattress into a small closet. Unfortunately, I hadn't considered all the consequences. This is why you thought I was gone so long when I went to the space station. For you, it must have seemed like days or weeks. I was gone for less than an hour."

"Wow! You do have some amazing powers!"

"And you have a killer smile!"

"Well, thank you," he replied as he put on his uniform. Then feeling in his pocket with his hand, he said, "Hmmmm...."

"What is it?" asked Bonnie.

"Look," he said, pulling out a candy bar. "It looks like I found your chocolate fix. I forgot I had this. Want to share it?"

"How did you have that all this time and not remember it?"

"Hey, it's lucky I found it now."

"Yeah, lucky to have me around. You are one spacy cashier!"

It was just before 6 PM on the roof of the Big Box garage. The sun was setting behind the Manhattan skyline, and all was quiet. None could see Ms. Infinity swooping down to drop off Hal Holstein on the roof, then flying away, or Bonnie Boring walking up a few seconds later.

"Feels amazing to be on solid ground again!" said Hal.

"Funny," said Bonnie, "I know I've heard that before. Do you have everything? I can still fly you back to the ship if necessary."

"No need. It's not like I brought much of anything with me. I pretty much left on the spot."

"Okay, so here goes," Bonnie concentrated a moment, then said, "I just sent a command, and returned the ship to its place on the dark side of the Moon."

"Strange," said Hal, "I feel like I spent a lifetime on there."

"So, Hal, you have about five minutes left on your break."

"Okay. I spent two hours and fifty-five minutes on there, give or take a lifetime."

"Either way, I wanted to make our next date. So, Wednesday is your 'Saturday', right?"

"Yup. I'm off Wednesday and Thursday."

"It's my 'Sunday'. I'm off Tuesday and Wednesday. So, what do you say we spend the day together? Lunch, movie, and dinner? Who knows what else?"

"Awesome! I love how you think. It's a date!"

"Kiss goodbye?"

Bonnie and Hal kissed and held each other close. "Let me say this," said Bonnie, "I never expected this, but I would never trade it for anything. I am so glad you walked in on me, Hal!"

"Me too," said Hal.

Bonnie pulled back. "Alright Hal. See you tomorrow. Gotta fly."

Hal half expected Bonnie to transform once again, or maybe to fly away or disappear, but she simply walked away, heading for the stairs like anyone else. Maybe she'd had enough of her powers for the day.

Hal stood on the roof, feeling as if the whole adventure had been a long and strange dream. He looked at the world around him: the Queens landscape, Northern Boulevard with its large stores and car dealerships, and beyond that, the Manhattan skyline. Somehow, it all looked different from how he remembered it. Nonetheless, home had never looked so great before.

He had five minutes before work. There was one thing he had to do. He took out his cellphone. Amazingly it was charged again, nearly to the point where it had been before the adventure had begun. And so, he made the call he both dreaded and desperately needed.

"Hi Mom," he said. "It's Hal... Yeah. I know you recognized me... I love you... I'm sorry it's been so long... Listen, Mom, I have to go back to work in a minute, but do you think I could stay over tonight? Oh, thank you! Thank you! Yeah, I knew you would, but thank you... I missed you too... I love you. I'll see you later."

After hanging up, Hal wiped the tears from his eyes,

and returned to work.

Bonnie quietly arrived at home, feeling exhausted. She entered her house, and made for the steps, hoping to get reacquainted with her room and her TV for a nice long spell. But when she got to the top of the steps, there was her mother, looking at her with an expression so severe, it seemed to signify the end of the world, or at least her corner of it.

26. Between Family

"So let me get this straight," said Bonnie. "I'd hate to misrepresent you, but I'm pretty sure I got this right."

Bonnie and Betty Boring were standing next to each other in the hallway at the top of the stairs. Each was barely able to look at the other in the eye. Betty felt a mixture of anger at Bonnie's brash moves, and embarrassment at her own foolish decisions. Bonnie was just angry.

"This is what I'm getting," said Bonnie. "I just risked everything to save the world from Misery. Do you get what I put up with out there? And now you're saying I'm not responsible enough?"

"Bonnie," said Betty, "I understand and appreciate all that you've done. But can you really tell me I'm wrong? You never did come up with a plan, did you? You just went into it blindly and randomly. And you brought a human up there with you. Do you know how much danger you put him in? It's sure as hell no way to start a relationship."

"You know what? I'm really, really sick of the criticism. You can talk all you want about how lousy a job I'm doing but go ahead and try to do it yourself. I dare you! Go out there yourself and face a giant asteroid. Go and get shot at sometime!"

Betty did not answer, but her face conveyed more worry than anger. Yet Bonnie seemed not to notice.

"I mean, sure. You have your little side job, playing secret guardian angel. Nice and simple when you're invisible, and nobody can criticize you. But do you know what I've been through? I mean, I had to go halfway across the galaxy, and nearly got killed.

"Come on, Mom! Do you have any idea what it's like to face strange people with guns, or to have to fly off at a minute's notice?"

"Bonnie, I'm not sure you understand everything. I think you'd better–"

"Any idea, really? Friggin' nightmare out there! You think this is easy? I don't even know my own powers sometimes. The whole time, I was missing something I needed. I mean, I've been used to getting double strength in an emergency. For some reason, it was nowhere to be found this time. Like this wasn't a big enough emergency. I don't even know what...makes..."

Betty's face was even graver than before. Bonnie stopped and looked her mother in the eye.

"Mom? What are you looking at me like that for?"

Betty continued to gaze at Bonnie. After a few more moments, Bonnie's eyes widened, and her mouth opened wide with shock.

"Oh, no! No! You didn't! Mom, no!"

"Yes, dear. That's what I'm trying to say."

"Oh my God! How could you?"

"How could I? I'm your mother, that's how! How could I not protect my daughter?"

"This is not happening! I mean, I knew you were a helicopter mom on steroids, but I thought even you had your limits. Just how much of my life is a lie, anyway?"

"Now, Bonnie–"

"And how much are you watching me? Are you over my bed when I'm sleeping? Do you have spies at my job? Do I even get to pee without a goddamn audience?"

"Bonnie dear, I only want to protect you–"

"Mom, I'm not a child anymore. I'm twenty-six years old. You can treat me like an adult."

"Oh, really?"

"Yeah, really! I think the least I've earned is the right to be out in the world without my mother looking over my shoulder every single second."

"I don't know," said Betty gravely. "I wish I could be sure of that. But you just swept up a man, and took him up into space. You needlessly risked the life of someone weaker than you. And you took a mission with life-and-death importance and treated it like the whole thing was just a date, just a thrill ride. This is not what I taught you. It terrifies me to think of what was going through your head."

"Excuse me? Why exactly am I taking relationship advice from you, anyway? You're not exactly the great example yourself. You picked one hell of a husband!"

"Bonnie!" said Betty, her reaction showing utter shock.

"Yeah, and good work shopping for the future father of your kid. He wanted me dead! Nice!"

Betty was silent. The subject of Bonnie's father had always been a deep and nearly impenetrable taboo. Indeed, since the day they'd landed on Earth, it was extraordinarily rare for them to even mention him. And hard though Bonnie's memories of her father were, the suffering that the general had caused Betty was perhaps greater still. The hard and unbreakable silence between mother and daughter covered memories too dark to speak of and regrets deeper than Bonnie dared imagine. After a minute of stunned silence, Betty turned and entered her room, and closed the door.

Bonnie stood there for another minute, still angry, still trying to hold on to a posture of defiance. But soon, anger turned to guilt. She knocked on the door. "Mom," she called, "I'm sorry. Let me in."

There was no answer, but it was clear from the sounds emanating from inside that her mother was crying. "Mom, please! You know I love you. I'm sorry."

Another minute passed without further action. "Look, Mom. I've been very upset. I didn't tell you a lot of details, but I did come in contact with him. Well, at least I heard him. Well, not 'heard' him, you know. I was in the presence of his communication? I don't know. However you can say it in human talk. Anyway, it wasn't pretty. Can you please understand if I've been down? I didn't mean to take it out on you."

The door finally opened. Betty was behind it, looking very sad. She did nothing but walk back to her bed and sit down. Bonnie sat next to her and began to cry. "I'm sorry, Mommy!"

Betty embraced her daughter. Her own face conveyed a grief too deep to speak of, but she answered, "I'm sorry about your father. I wish I could make it all better. But I'm always here for you, I promise. Maybe I'm here for you too much. I don't know. But understand dear, you're all I have. We're all that's left of our old life. We're the only people like us on Earth. Nobody else can understand. I need you too, honey. I hope you understand that."

"I do, Mom. I really do. I need you too, but obviously you knew that. And I love you."

"And I love you. Always."

"You know what, though? We still have an awful lot to talk about. We do have ice cream, right?"

They talked far into the night. At times they even reverted to their Centerian communication. They discussed many things, including their native world, their past, and their heritage. Still, their main concern remained their lives on Earth, their friends, and their future.

"I can't say too much about your father," said Betty. "I hope you won't make me. But please understand that I was not much older than Misery when... Well, honey, I'm sorry. Do you understand? But then, I can't regret it completely if it meant that you came into my life.

"There is something else that bothers me deeply, but please dear, do not take it as criticism. What you did to save the Earth was necessary, and absolutely right."

"What are you speaking of?"

"The army you fought. I am quite sure I know who they were. General Imperial told you that you had never known them because we had not conquered them, and that we had not conquered them because they had no natural resources. Both of those statements are bitter lies."

Betty paused a moment. Her face looked even sadder than before, but she continued stoically. "Their name, or at least the name I knew them by, translated to 'slave'. It troubles me to no end that I know no other name. There has to be another name that they call themselves by. Their world was once one of the richest and most diverse environments in the solar system that Center belongs to. Unfortunately, when the junta occurred, well, it began shortly after a large-scale invasion of their planet; one that devastated their entire civilization. That invasion ended with the entire people being exiled to a small moon. That was where you heard that they belonged."

"I don't understand why this is so important. I mean, it is a sad story, but..."

"Please let me finish. This is hard enough. The junta

would not have been possible without this invasion. It brought the military both the economic strength and the political credibility to overthrow the civilian government..."

"Mom..."

"Bonnie, please! This is hard enough. Just please..."

Betty paused for a few more seconds, tears welling in her eyes. "My dear Bonnie," she said. "Your father had me believing a lot of things. He also knew of my abilities, at least to a point. I thought I was helping to overthrow a repressive regime that was harming our people. Honey, I'm sorry. I helped a monster to do many, many horrible things..."

Betty could hold back no longer. She lapsed into tears once again. "My whole family! He killed every single one of them! My mother. My brother and sister! My father! Honey, thank heavens I was able to save you. I live every single day of my life knowing I helped a horrible monster."

"Mommy," said Bonnie, holding her tight, "I know it's not your fault. It's his. He's horrible!"

"It's horrible too that those people had to pay again for his sins. At least you managed to fulfill your mission without killing any more of them. I seriously doubt though that it ended that easily for them. But then, that is not your fault either."

As the night continued, they spoke more and more about their present life. Betty tried to persuade Bonnie to be more appreciative and trusting of Lisa. They also spoke of Bonnie's budding relationship.

"Please dear," said Betty, "don't take anything I say as an attack on Hal. I am glad you have a relationship with him. Everything I know about him suggests that he's great for you. You have wisely gravitated towards a man who is just about the opposite of your father. Please bring Hal over when you're ready, and he will be welcome here."

"Thank you," said Bonnie. "He and I have agreed that he's not going on any more missions like that. He wants to contribute, and I will find a way that he can, but I don't want him needlessly risking his life."

"Alright, as long as you know that. Also, I dare not guess what your time manipulation was, but the very idea of it is terrifying. The very first thing my mother taught me is caution. You know, just because you can..."

"Alright. I get it."

"I'm serious. You are very powerful, and well, you might as well know, so am I. And that is potentially very dangerous. Watch what you do with your power. You should never be reckless like that, certainly not just for the sake of convenience."

"You're right. I'm sorry."

"Okay. You also seemed to be showing off to him an awful lot. I get it. And sure, I can't help but like that a man is looking at you this way. Still, that's the thing with the whole superhero idea. It's a little bit of an ego trip."

"It is, but it's who I am."

"I'll say!" said Betty with a smile," If anything, you were holding back, showing off for only one person."

"I'll suffer your jokes, mainly because you're right, but understand something. There's a place for ego. You might not appreciate it, but people need a personality. I know how you say there's something silly about celebrity, and you're right. I mean, it's ridiculous to have so much interest in a complete stranger. But I eat it up. I can read my gossip magazines all night. And it is stupid stuff about who cheated on whom, and the best and worst beach bodies. But then, if I'm a celebrity, why not use it for something good? The influence is a power too, that I believe can be turned to good purposes."

"Just be careful, dear. It's very easy to say or do the wrong thing, and then there can be far-reaching consequences."

Bonnie thought a moment. "Yeah. I think about these things too, you know. When the news reports one of my rescues, and all they can talk about is what my hair looked like, it gives me pause. And yeah. The interviews are dangerous. I mean, even when you say the *right* thing, they can mess with it to make it seem wrong if it suits them. When I saw Misery mess with the video we took of the battle, I saw how easy it is to take things out of context.

"But you know, fighting battles is dangerous too, and consequences can be unexpected. There are risks that come with being a public figure. As with anything, I have to be brave, and face the consequences of what I do and say."

"My dear, you really have grown."

"Thank you. And maybe there are also things I need to think about doing in my personal life. I need some direction. I'm not exactly burning up the career paths right now."

"I'm glad you brought that up for a change."

"I just don't know. If it makes you feel better, I have been giving it serious thought. Look, there's another thing that's been a burning question on my mind. You always have something to say about my superhero stuff, and I'm always mad about the criticism. But instead of getting into an argument, maybe you could suggest what you might do differently if you were me."

"You're asking me for advice on how to be a superhero?"

"There had to be a first time, right?"

Betty smiled. "Well, I could complain about the flashiness, but I see your point about the need for a 'personality'. Still, I hope you understand how important it is to listen as much as you talk. You should consider carefully how others feel, and what people really need, before you make a big scene. And the best thing you can do is to help others to help themselves. You can't be the only hero. Your ultimate job is to see the hero in each person, and to help them to find it in themselves.

"You need to be on the scene for many emergencies, and I get that. But corruption is usually much more subtle than a super villain hurling an asteroid.

"And it can be people with good intentions trying to find an expedient solution and breaking laws and stepping on other people's feet in the process. Or it can be people who feel they have been wronged and are convinced that they have the right to do whatever it takes to even the score. Or sometimes it is someone with a poor conscience who is simply very good at hiding things.

"But it can also be hiding right under your nose. And you need to not only listen, but also keep your eyes open. If you can see across galaxies, then you can also look across the room and see something as small as a receipt. But then, you don't have to take it from me. You know how clumsy I can be!"

Bonnie looked at her mother sidelong and laughed, "You are still confusing to talk to, but I appreciate what you're saying. I'll try to take whatever suggestions I understand."

"Don't worry, Bonnie. You'll get it all soon enough."

"Okay, Mom. I'd better get to sleep. You know what? I'm going to take another suggestion and put my pajamas on one leg at a time. I'm even going to climb the stairs instead of flying. How's that for progress?"

"Always proud, dear. I can now say it. It only took you until twenty-six before you started dressing yourself."

The next morning, Bonnie walked to work by her usual route. She was using the time to think about a lot of things: her mother, her budding relationship, and her possible future career. She was almost at The Big Box when suddenly she stopped and spoke to herself quietly.

"Wait a minute! Mom only found out I was gone when her student told her about her phone ringing. Then she never caught up to me. That's what she said, right? So then, how did she know I took Hal with me?"

27. Between Friends

As soon as Bonnie entered The Big Box, she was called into Yvonne's office. *This can't be good,* she thought. *One does not get called into the store manager's office for a chat about recipes. Not that anybody would chat with me about recipes, unless they wanted to talk to themselves.*

Yvonne let Bonnie into her office but made her wait while she talked on the phone. There was tension in her voice, and she was being interrupted numerous times.

"No, I promise you, he's gone. I... I know. I agree. The numbers from last quarter are unacceptable, and I promise you won't see anything like it again. I have the complaints, and I'm going through them as fast as I can. So, listen, I have an employee here...Okay. I know. I agree. Yes. I promise you, he is off the floor, and we will find a new one as soon as possible. Right. No, obviously not her. Yeah. Of course, you know I won't let them organize...Listen, can I call you back? Thank you. No, of course. I promise, I will call you back immediately. Bye."

Yvonne hung up and took a deep breath. "Hi Bonnie. I'm sorry to keep you waiting. There has been a lot of commotion here lately. So, I have a few things to discuss with you. I'll start with the easiest. Yesterday you used Lisa to check out. As you recall, you can't check out family or close friends. I'm not making a big deal about it, but if it keeps happening, I might have to. Do you understand?"

"Oh, okay. I'm sorry."

"Here's the second thing. Last week you were written up for an incident with some handbags that somehow ended up in the parking garage. Now I have chosen to review this. Apparently, Denny ordered you to take them to the storeroom in the basement.

"I asked Lisa about this, and she told me that there were some extenuating circumstances. She wouldn't specify, but I'll take her word for it, since that was the moment when we were being held up. I'm more concerned that you were down there in the first place. You're Customer Service. Storing merchandise is not your job. If your supervisor asks you to do something like that again, you can come to me, and I'll correct the matter. Anyway, you're no longer written up for the incident. You have a clean slate again.

"Here is the most important thing: the matter of sexual harassment. We are going to have a workshop by the end of next week. Everyone is required to attend. In the meantime, I have to stress this: if at any time a supervisor, or any other employee says or does anything that makes you feel uncomfortable, you absolutely do not have to stand for it. You should come to me immediately and I will take care of it. If there's anything you want to tell me now, please do so. And you might as well know that Denny has been suspended and is in the process of termination. You don't have to be afraid of any consequences from him, not that you should be afraid anyway."

"Wow," said Bonnie. "You must have had quite a day."

When Bonnie returned to the customer service desk, she saw Hal arriving with a young girl. "Hi Bonnie," he called. Then Bonnie and Hal kissed, to the surprise of the coworkers watching.

"It's great to see you, Bon," said Hal. "You've met my little sister, Stacy."

"It's very nice to see you, Stacy," said Bonnie warmly.

"Hi," said Stacy, "I told my mom that you're really

nice, and pretty."

Just then a woman ran in calling, "Stacy, get over here! How can you be outside without a jacket?"

"A jacket?" shouted Stacy. "Forget it! It would ruin the outfit. Talk about a mother's fashion sense!"

"Put this on now, and don't talk to your mother that way!"

"Bonnie," said Hal, "this is my mother. Mom, I'd love you to meet Bonnie."

"Hi Bonnie," said Hal's mother, shaking her hand. "My name is Sarah Holstein."

"Hi, Mrs. Holstein. My name is Bonnie Boring. I'm very pleased to meet you."

Sarah looked at Bonnie carefully. "Pleased to meet you too. 'Boring?' You don't look like a Boring."

"Yeah. My name was changed…"

"I thought so! My maiden name was Blank. It was shortened from Blankowski. I know. It happened with all of us."

"Oh…"

"I'm sorry to come in shouting. It is a pleasure to meet you. I can see that Hal is very excited about you."

"You didn't have to shout," said Stacy.

"And you don't have to give me attitude," admonished Sarah.

"No," said Stacy, "I guess I don't technically *have* to."

Bonnie smiled ear to ear, but Sarah rolled her eyes. "Stacy, you can at least show your brother's girlfriend some manners. Say goodbye."

"Bye," said Stacy, "I'll see you again soon."

"Bye, Stacy," said Bonnie sweetly. "It was wonderful to meet you, Mrs. Holstein. I look forward to meeting you again."

Sarah smiled warmly. "We will have you over soon." Then turning to Hal, she said, "When you're off, call me and we'll discuss when you're moving back home."

"Can we talk about that?" said Hal.

"We can talk, but you're moving home. This is no life for you. You will call me later. Have a good day."

As they left, Bonnie smiled. "Hal, I really, really like your family."

"Thank you," said Hal, "I know they can be noisy."

"Noisy is fine, Hal. Noisy is great. There's absolutely nothing wrong with noisy. Just be glad that you have them, and that you can rely on them. Your family is important."

"I do know that," said Hal. "I think I know that now more than ever."

"So, I just heard Denny's out," said Bonnie.

"He is," said Hal. "There was a lot of commotion here yesterday when I got back from my break." He raised an eyebrow, and Bonnie smiled.

Hal continued, "There was a lot of talk. Denny had been dragged away by the security guards. Bobbi too. Apparently, he had been using the register to override prices. She was buying lots of expensive items, and he would discount them by something like ninety percent. I guess that was his way of shutting her up. They had been having an affair, or maybe he was trying to have an affair with her. I don't know. I'm hearing conflicting stories. They might never have noticed it, but a security guard just happened to look at the receipt and see the discrepancies. It wouldn't have happened, but Bobbi had just fallen down after a woman bumped into her, and the guard came to help her up."

Bonnie looked away from Hal and thought for a moment but said nothing.

"Excuse me," interrupted Lisa as she walked up, "there's something both of you space cadets don't know. Before that even happened, he was as good as fired. I know because I had just had a long talk with Yvonne about him. Maria and Nadine were in there with me too. So was Teddy. She was just about to call him into her office. While you kids were gone, we had an eventful time. Isn't that right, Julia?"

"Lisa schooled him!" said Julia excitedly. "You should have seen it! He tried to scare her to make her leave for something, and then she just yelled at him. Then he told her to punch out, and she left. Then she came back and got Teddy to film her secretly. Then Denny made an offer to bribe her too. He made an ass of himself, and everyone saw it. It got on the monitors."

"There's really more to the story than that," said Lisa. "I overheard a discussion he was having with Security. I found out he was having the cameras turned off so he could get away with stealing for Bobbi. By the way, those cameras were off when this place got robbed. Hal can thank Denny for that. Anyway, then I saw what he was doing with Bobbi. I told him I knew what was going on. I refused to let him take over Customer Service. Then he sent me home with a write-up. But then I came back, and I set that thing up with Teddy. Then Yvonne called me into her office. Maria and Nadine came with me, and we told her everything."

Bonnie was open mouthed with excitement. "Lisa!" she shouted. "That is amazing!"

"Well, I don't know…"

"Lisa! You are my hero! You are the queen!"

"Thanks, Bonnie," said Lisa, blushing.

"C'mon, Lisa, give us a celebratory burp!"

"Is she going to need to chug some soda first?" asked Julia. But before Julia even finished asking that question, Lisa let out a belch so loud and resonant, it seemed one could hear it from the other side of the store.

"I told you she's my hero," said Bonnie.

Some distance away, Maria and Nadine were watching the conversation. "Yeah," said Nadine, "Lisa's a nice girl."

"Definitely the best of that group of kids," said Maria.

"Does she realize we saved her butt?"

"Nah. I doubt it. After that stunt, she was just going to get herself fired. Denny would probably have gotten away with everything too. You know, it worked because we stuck together. You get that, right? That's what we need here."

"I know, Maria! I know! I get it, okay? Look, now that it's over, I'm glad Denny's gone, but I still have big problems here. Same ol', same ol'."

Maria looked at Nadine sidelong. "Who says it's over?"

Bonnie and Hal's new relationship was quick gossip for their friends and acquaintances throughout the store. Soon, neither one of them could go long without being asked about it. Hal got a particularly hard reception from Teddy.

"What the hell?" he sneered. "Bonnie? I mean, she's gonna bust you left and right! You can't be for real."

"Of course I'm 'for real', Teddy, and I really like her."

"I see how she bosses you around. If you're not careful, that's gonna be for life. C'mon, let's go out cruising after work, and we'll find some real babes."

"You know what? I'm alright. Can you please leave this alone?"

"Alright Hal; your funeral." With that, he walked away.

"Don't worry, man," said Ahmed. "That guy doesn't know what he's talking about. Bonnie's a nice girl. I see it. She's the kind who will look out for you. That Teddy is just immature. One day, maybe he'll find the right girl, and then he'll get it."

Hal then noticed a ring on Ahmed's finger. "Wait, Ahmed, are you married?"

"Sixteen years, with three kids. I wouldn't trade this for anything."

"Wow. You're often here late."

"I wish I didn't have to be. I'm a teacher. It's not exactly paying all the bills. Three kids means a lot of expenses, you know. But that's what makes this life matter. When you have people who depend on you, whether you're working a job, or you're with the kids, or you're doing the housework, then you know that you mean something. That's what life's about." Then noticing a customer at his register, Ahmed waved and returned to work.

Hal smiled. In no way was he feeling 'weighed down'. He was just back from adventures that no other human being could claim.

Thanks to Bonnie, he had been to places in outer space far outside human experience. He had also made the video of a lifetime, a unique and exciting piece of work depicting a superhuman battle in space. He had experienced dimensional planes that other humans had never guessed existed, and even figured out how to operate a spaceship with this knowledge. The mission had nearly demanded the ultimate sacrifice, and he could truly say that he had been ready to give it. He had also contributed to solving a major intergalactic crisis. Hal Holstein was no minor part of the effort to save the Earth. And if hardly anyone knew any of these things, he was fine with that.

And even if they did know, could they really understand? Maybe the likes of Teddy would object to his being behind a female leader, but so what? It was plain to him that he was better off for it in countless ways. He knew a universe that was bigger, stranger, and far more complex than he had ever imagined. He felt braver, wiser, stronger, and altogether greater than he ever had in his life. The possibilities for the future had never seemed more endless. And he was just getting started!

Lisa was particularly welcoming of Bonnie's new relationship. "Congratulations," she said to Bonnie. "You two are awesome together. It's about time you finally did something besides giving him attitude."

"Funny."

"Actually, I thought that was a pretty weak joke."

"No, Lisa. That's not what I mean. It's my mom. She's still on full-out helicopter mode. Somehow, she managed to figure out where I was and what I was doing with him. Whatever she could be doing now to spy on me, I can't even imagine."

"Yeah," answered Lisa, "I wonder..."

Lisa tried desperately to keep her face from showing her guilt. She had not meant to be a 'spy'. In her own mind, she was helping Bonnie's mother watch out for her. But now that she thought of it, spying was exactly what it was.

Meanwhile, Lisa could not help but feel slighted by something else. It was not hard to put two and two together and see that Bonnie had now told Hal her secret identity. That made sense, sure. But she had only known him for about two years, and their relationship was just beginning. Lisa had been friends with Bonnie for well over a decade. How could she not trust her best friend?

Lisa had been Bonnie's first friend on Earth. When they first met, Bonnie said her name, and then burped, just as if it was part of the sentence. Lisa loved that, and soon taught Bonnie how to 'burp talk'. Since neither had siblings, Bonnie and Lisa were effectively the sisters that each didn't have.

Over thirteen years and many ups and downs, there was plenty of time for Lisa to discover that her friend was different.

For one thing, from the beginning, something was not adding up about her. Lisa was told that she had come from an obscure country called *Merkaz*. (Years later, Hal would notice that the word was Hebrew for 'Center'.) But Bonnie and Betty spoke like native New Yorkers.

Also, Bonnie was surprised about very basic things about the culture. A particularly strange and beautiful moment came when she was over at Bonnie's house and the subject of religion came up. Bonnie was completely shocked by the simple fact that there was more than one of them on Earth, and that there was freedom to choose between them, or to choose none at all. At first Lisa thought she was joking, but slowly it became clear that this was very real. As the realization sank in, it was clear that Bonnie was not only fascinated but also deeply moved. Lisa could not help but be strongly affected in turn.

For her part, Lisa was always tolerant and understanding, and Bonnie was more trusting as a result. While Bonnie never exactly told her anything, she did trust her enough to confide her feelings. Nonetheless, it became more and more clear over time that she was holding a lot of things back.

Bonnie also had a horrible time fitting in. She was highly intelligent, and obviously good-hearted. Yet somehow, she could not translate it into finding her place among the crowd. She was just too strange, too offbeat, and always seemed to miss the crucial social cues. And yet, this was fine with Lisa, since she was something of an outcast herself. Bonnie was equally understanding of Lisa's quirks, and her many awkward moments. So effectively the two became a self-contained 'crowd' of their own.

After some time, Lisa began to notice subtle signs of Bonnie's powers. She clearly saw and heard things that other people didn't and performed feats of strength easily that were very difficult for everyone else; indeed, she was clearly holding back. In Gym class, Lisa would often notice her struggling to keep her feats from superhuman levels. It was clear that this was torture for her, so Lisa did all she could to cover for her friend.

There were also a couple of times when she could tell that Bonnie and Betty were speaking to each other when they weren't even talking. She assumed at this point that they were able to communicate psychically. Together, these things made her wonder about Bonnie's obsessive comic book habit.

Yet if any one thing made Bonnie stand out, it was the rare instances when she *couldn't* do something better than everyone else. Bonnie took these things very hard. She would become extremely upset and even angry. Lisa would have to isolate her from everyone else to talk her down.

Besides singing, music in general was an area Bonnie had no particular proficiency in. Her dancing wasn't spectacular either. Her dance with Hal aboard the ship had seemed impressive due to her flying; her powers had effectively served as a cover-up. There was also cooking, though that seemed to be not so much incapability as complete disinterest on Bonnie's part. But above all, schoolwork was her bane.

Numerous times, Bonnie was on the verge of dropping out. Yet Lisa had a remarkable way of both listening and talking to her. She was patient and understanding, but also brutally honest. Even if Bonnie was having a terrible time, Lisa would remind her that her problems were not worse than others'. She would also remind her that she was obviously very intelligent, so she had no excuse. And not finishing high school would be fatal to her future. It was times like these that showed Betty that Lisa could be trusted. It frustrated her that Bonnie didn't trust her more.

Things took a particularly strange turn soon after they began working together at The Big Box. One day, Bonnie came home from Comic Con beaming like someone who had just won the lottery. She had clearly had the time of her life, but her expression seemed to convey more than could be explained by that alone. She seemed a little like someone who had fallen in love, but Lisa figured it wasn't that; Bonnie would have told her of that anyway. It was almost like she had just found religion, or otherwise found a new direction, yet Bonnie could not explain how. She was also wearing a ridiculous costume, but significantly, she was completely comfortable; she almost seemed to wear it like a second skin. At the time, Lisa more or less took it as another of Bonnie's quirks. But then, just days later, a certain superhero appeared on the scene.

Lisa actually got the same introduction to Ms. Infinity

as Hal had; she saw her on the news the day that she rescued the school bus. To all obvious appearances, she was a different person, with a different face and body and a more assertive persona. Yet when she watched closely, there was something distinctly familiar about her. When she spoke for any length of time, her mannerisms were the same as Bonnie's, unmistakably so. After a few such appearances, she was sure of it. Bonnie was Ms. Infinity.

For a time, Lisa felt some anger at this discovery. She had known something of Bonnie's powers, but nothing like this. She could not help but feel hurt. Her best friend was a full-out magical superhuman but had never shared this with her. When she thought about it, the thing that got to her the most was the shape shifting. Lisa hated how she looked, and wished she could change herself as easily as that. Yet before long, these feelings subsided. She also understood that Bonnie faced some unique struggles.

Besides her troubles fitting in, there was also the matter of Bonnie's past. Neither Bonnie nor Betty told much of anything directly, but there were things that both Boring women would say that would unwittingly tell the story. Conversations with them could turn to such dark topics as military juntas, families lost to cruel military officers, imprisonment, dangerous refuges, and most darkly of all, tales of children who have had to escape their own fathers. These might not have been proof of anything, however the constant repetition of these themes made for compelling evidence.

The stories also made for a convincing explanation for Bonnie's missing father, and seemed consistent with other evidence. After all, Bonnie was terrified of domineering men. Denny was hardly the first case she had seen. There had been teachers, school administrators, and others who could easily reduce Bonnie to tears.

In the nearly two years since the appearance of Bonnie's alter ego, Lisa had tried and tried to get her friend to come out to her, using subtle and not-so-subtle hints. Bonnie seemed to have a mental block about it. However, "Mrs. B." soon caught on. One day, she took Lisa aside, and told her the truth: their powers, their extraterrestrial origin, and Bonnie's alter ego. "I'm glad you figured it out," she said. "She needs someone to keep an eye on her and keep her from getting a swelled head."

For her part, Betty was extremely grateful for Lisa's help. For many long years, she alone had been faced with the task of looking out for her daughter. For the first time, here was a trustworthy person who cared about Bonnie as much as she did. And so together, they would effectively become Ms. Infinity's 'Rear Guard'.

Typically, Lisa would alert Betty (usually by text) when Bonnie ran off to transform, and then cover for her disappearances at work or elsewhere. Betty would then appear invisibly on the scene, providing extra strength or other incidental help. In some cases, one or both of them saved her secret identity from her own carelessness.

Lisa was also a willing ear for the rare moments when Betty opened up about her past. She wouldn't tell anything personal, but she did love to discuss the world they came from. At times, she went into some detail about their heritage, including their religion, language, and philosophy. Lisa was fascinated with tales of a culture on a far distant planet. Meanwhile Betty had someone on Earth who listened with an open mind to the things that her daughter refused to hear.

Yet that communication with "Mrs. B." was now proving to be one secret too many. Lisa had decided that she'd had enough. It was time to come clean.

That night, Lisa stayed over at Bonnie's house. After ordering in for dinner, they watched movies in Bonnie's room. Lisa laughed at Bonnie for some of her choices, a few of which were surprisingly old.

"Really?" laughed Lisa. "This is almost as old as we are!"

"I like it," said Bonnie. "I've caught my mom watching it. C'mon, give it a chance."

"Alright, Bonnie. Maybe for a little while."

"Thank you. Lisa, there's something I've been dying to tell you. It's been building up for a long time. I'm finally going to say it out loud."

Lisa's ears perked up. "Really?"

"Lisa," said Bonnie, "I'm finally going to do it. I'm going back to school!"

"Oh." Lisa looked down in disappointment.

"You're the very first person I've told. Hal doesn't know. Not even my mom knows, unless she read my mind or something. I'm looking at applications for a few different schools. I've decided to go for my Bachelor's in Social Work. Then, maybe even my Masters. Who knows?"

"Thank you for telling me, Bonnie. That does mean a lot. I think social work is right up your alley. In fact, I'm pretty sure that you of all people could attack any of the world's problems."

"Oh, I don't know about that."

Lisa was silent. This wasn't the time yet.

"What do you see in this old thing?" snickered Lisa. "I don't even know why you would sympathize with the lead?"

"Maybe not," said Bonnie, "but it's fun watching her screw up. You know, she's a regular girl like me."

As ironic as that line might have sounded, Lisa understood it. It wasn't an effort at disguise. Bonnie really thought of herself that way, and Lisa figured that she had as much right as anyone to such thoughts. Still, it was always time for both friends to pick on each other. "You mean a crazy weird girl like you!" said Lisa.

"Beats a smelly butt like yours!" said Bonnie.

"Maybe, but you have B.O.!"

"Yeah, you win," conceded Bonnie, "I got that one locked up."

"Wait a minute," said Lisa, "I know why you like this movie. It's the scene where that lady tries to sing karaoke. This is probably the only movie where someone sings worse than you."

Bonnie's face suddenly went sullen. She sat down and put her face in her hands. "Thanks a lot, Lisa."

"Come on!" said Lisa. "This can't still be getting to you. So what? I'm just trying to ride you. You can pick on me for a hundred other things."

"This isn't funny to me."

"Unbelievable! If I got this upset every time I couldn't do something, I'd never survive the day."

"Whatever."

"Bonnie, can I just get on your computer? I want to show you something."

"Fine."

"Here, Bonnie," said Lisa as she fiddled with Bonnie's computer. "I wanted to show you this woman's YouTube page. She does this little cooking show online. Now she's not the world's greatest chef, and she's never claimed to be. Some of the things she cooks are kind of hard. Some aren't even that. But she's lots and lots of fun. She loves to crack jokes, especially at her own expense. I absolutely love her show. I've seen every single episode."

"So that's what you wanted to show me?"

"Yes, Bonnie. I have a point. This is about you. You don't have to be perfect at everything to be special to me.

"Everyone we know thinks you're a goofball. That's your persona. But I know you better. There's much, much more to you than that. You are a perfectionist, even a control freak. And I get it too. You would be. You can do things that nobody else can: amazing things, impossible things. It frustrates you to no end that you can't be yourself around people. But inside, you have a need to do something else that you can't do around others. There's a huge vitality inside you that is dying to get out.

"That's you, and I love you for that. But even you can't do everything. Even you have weak spots. And I love you for that too. It's all you. All you have to do is be my friend. We can talk about guys, movies, farting, whatever! No matter what, you are my best friend. That's whether you succeed or fail."

Bonnie's eyes and mouth were wide open in an expression of complete shock. For a few seconds, there was a deafening and unbreakable silence.

Then they heard the news break in on the TV from Betty's room. There was a fire in an 80 story building in midtown. An unknown number of people were trapped on the top floor. Ms. Infinity was obviously about to go into action. Shaking her head, Lisa felt there was little choice but to make an excuse for Bonnie.

"Damnit, Bonnie!" shouted Lisa, in a voice that could hardly contain her disappointment. "Go to the bathroom already! I can't take it when you just let them out like that..."

"Stop," said Bonnie. She got up, and motioned for Lisa to get up, then she hugged her warmly. "Thank you, Lisa."

Pulling away, Bonnie started to transform. "I'm sorry if I've closed myself off to you. You've been on to me for a long time."

It was a strange thing to behold. Bonnie's body and clothes were morphing before Lisa's eyes — even her voice was changing, but she continued talking as casually as if she were changing clothes in the locker room.

"I guess this thing is just a lot of baggage for me," continued Bonnie. "I like to forget about it when I'm with you, but I guess that isn't fair to you."

"I'm your best friend," said Lisa. "I'll help you share the burden."

Bonnie was now fully transformed into Ms. Infinity. "I would love that. I have to go. Could you please stay here? I should be back in a little while. We have a lot to talk about."

"Of course I will."

Ms. Infinity stepped into her closet, where she had an escape hatch built in. "You know Lisa," she said, "I meant it when I said that you're my hero."

"That's sweet, but really–"

"No. You really are. You've done something I only wish I could have done."

"And what's that?"

"Lisa, you have overthrown a tyrant! You have no idea how much that means to me. Look, I have to go, but we'll talk when I get back."

Ms. Infinity flew into the sky. She felt a tremendous sense of relief, and hope for the future. Now she had not only her mother, but also a boyfriend, and her best friend fully in the loop. For the first time in her life, she felt that she really had people she could trust. And within her small circle, there was at last a place where she truly belonged, and it felt wonderful.

"Wow," said Lisa to herself, "those boots are awesome! She has to hook me up."

"I heard," said Betty as she approached from the stairs.

"Of course you did. You hear, like, everything."

"I know, Lisa. I'm sorry too. I used you to spy, and that was wrong. There is nothing worse than an abuse of power."

"Well, it's nothing worse than my own parents would have done. By the way, don't think I don't know when you're active, Guerrilla Public Servant. I know that was you getting Denny arrested. I can only wonder what part you might have played this last week or so. I mean, I can guess at what I was around for…"

"Lisa! What fun is it being an invisible hand when you're exposed?"

"Well, at least spill on the Denny thing. What was it this time? Super senses? Shape shifting?"

"Dear Lisa, I do not give away my trade secrets. I've been at this far longer than you know."

"Yeah Mrs. B., so long you can't stop. I didn't even need you. I had this one."

"Forgive me for overstepping. My daughter was out of town, and I needed a hero to shadow."

"Wow! When you put it that way..."

"Here, Lisa. I'll put on the news. Let's watch Ms. Infinity's latest adventure."

"And you're not joining her?"

"You know it's killing me, right?"

"Aw, Mrs. B., you know she can handle this."

On the TV, they watched their girl in action. She did not disappoint. She flew into the building faster than the cameras could catch her. She had everyone saved almost instantly. It was a dizzying scene. One by one, each person appeared on the sidewalk by the emergency crew, with Ms. Infinity showing up briefly each time as a blur. It was perhaps thirty seconds before all of the nearly two hundred people were rescued. Then the fire was put out seconds later. It was hard to tell how, but it seemed like she might have sucked up the air from the building with her super breath.

As the crowd looked on, there was confusion, but much gratitude. Before long, there was thunderous applause. Yet Ms. Infinity did not stay for an interview. She had a more important engagement. But before she flew away, she faced a line of cameras. With a smile and a wave, she called her tag line: "*Never forget the power you have inside you!*"

Character Art

Ms. Infinity

Bonnie Boring

Lisa Lin

Hal Holstein

Professor Betty Boring

Misery

If you enjoyed this book, please leave an honest review on Amazon and Goodreads.

Reviews are very important to independent authors. Not only do they give readers an idea of the book and what to expect, but they also give the author valuable feedback.

I look forward to reading your thoughts. Most of all, thank you for reading my story.

About the Author

Andrew Kirschner published the superhero novel Ms. Infinity: Earth's Greatest Hero in 2015. A lifelong New Yorker, he holds two master's Degrees, in Secondary Education and Urban Planning, and has worked in many different fields, including advertising, government, manufacturing, and education.

Made in United States
North Haven, CT
07 June 2023

37490082R00214